He had almost lost her today and something deep in his chest had broken lose at the thought of losing her, and he just needed to feel her close to him. He would be damned straight to hell itself before he walked away from her right now.

So he kissed her, he wrapped his arms around her slippery body molding her against him under the pounding hot spray of water. Slanting her full lips over his, pressing them open he sank his tongue into her mouth to tangle with hers. She moaned into his mouth and wrapped her arms around his neck, making it easier to sink further into the kiss.

Victor lost himself in the kiss. The feel of the woman in her arms, full breasts pressed against him. And he grew light headed with desire; he broke the kiss to drag air into his starved lungs.

She tasted like warm sunshine, and the second he could breathe, he dipped his lips back to hers. Elle moaned into his mouth and Victor was lost, he thrust his tongue deep into her mouth, rubbing against her and drawing her tongue into his mouth he sucked on it. Drawing her unique taste and flavor into his mouth. Memorizing her, gods he couldn't get her taste deep enough into him. She made the most amazing sounds as he drifted from her mouth to the side of her neck. Elle burrowed into him resting her head against his chest, he thanked the gods he had left his boxer briefs on. As he tried to control the urge to press her against the shower wall and take her.

"Elle." Her name came out more as a moan.

Reaper Mine

By: Christie Palmer

Jinx Fantasy Fiction LLC
Salt Lake City, UT

Cover Design by: Jaycee De Lorenzo of Sweet N' Spicy Designs
Ebook formatting by: www.ebooklaunch.com
ISBN: paperback: 978-0-9885557-6-1
Manufactured in the United States of America
First Edition August 2015

<u>Dedication</u>

This book is dedicated to a friend who was taken way too soon. Brother of my heart. Gone but never forgotten.

David Kendal
11/1964 ~12/2013

Other Books by: Christie Palmer

Shadow Play (A Tracker Novel)
Lost In Time (A Fallen Novel)
Reaper Mine (A Reaper Novel)

Reaper Down (A Reaper Novel)
Coming Soon

Table of Contents

Chapter 1

"We are being laughed at. Dante sits protected in his fortress in the Infernos mocking us with his repugnant creations," Castor spat as he slammed his hand against the solid marble conference table.

Asplin smiled from where she sat sheltered, hidden in the shadows; she had waited countless years for her chance and it took everything she had not to jump up and scream with joy. All her hard work would now pay off, all the waiting, the years of groveling, of saying what needed to be said. Of putting these sniveling, benign, worthless, idiots and their ignorant needs before her own, all the blood oaths, and giving and giving until she had nothing left. Asplin dipped her head down knowing her abhorrence for these creatures burned bright in her eyes, even in the shadows, she continued to listen as Caster blustered on.

"Dante has gone too far this time. His crimes are so atrocious I cannot begin to even fathom why he still garners a seat on this very council much less we even allow him to live," Castor shouted the last words with such fervor Asplin was surprised he didn't stroke out right there in his seat. "I demand he be thrown from this Tribunal and be held accountable for his latest crimes."

"What exactly would you have us do, Castor?" Felix asked. Asplin barely held back her snarl the ever calm Master Fae was the one Tribunal member she had never been able to buy off. She never knew where she stood with Felix. His all too calm attitude drove her to distraction, she held the sway of the other eight members, so he should have been of no import. But because she could never move him, never buy him off he was a thorn in her side and it made her want to draw his blood. Asplin had set about driving the Fae from the Tribunal a hundred or so years ago and she knew she was close. So close she could almost touch it. She held her breath in anticipation that this would be the straw that broke the preverbal camel's back.

"We have no way of holding him accountable." Felix reminded the group at large.

Castor slammed his hand against the table top again. "That is the problem," Castor shouted.

"We must make a statement." Jens took up the argument from across the room. "It is time to show Dante, and the rest of the Other community that the Tribunal is not to be taken lightly. The Tribunal holds the power on the mortal plane. Not Dante or his Reapers or those they deem worthy."

Several members nodded in agreement. "We have become weak in the face of the Others, impotent!" Castor said with barely controlled rage. "We must make a statement. Force the Others to choose."

Jens stood; leaning forward, he placed his hands flat against the cool marble, stopping for affect, he took the time to look each member of the Tribunal in the eye. Asplin began to shake with excitement. This was it; everything was starting to finally come together. All her hard work, hundreds of years of effort.

"It's time to gather our allies and even more important identify who our enemies are," Jens said his voice dropping just enough so the members had to lean in to hear him.

"And how do you suggest we do this?" Felix questioned. Asplin could see the worry written clearly on the Fae's face but she knew it was too late. The other members of the Tribunal were past the point of reason. They would be pushed to do something drastic and Felix's calm attitude was falling on deaf ears.

Castor smiled at the group, showing them all straight white teeth. "I'm glad you asked, Felix. We have been long in coming to this point and it has been needed for the last millennia at the very least."

Felix shook his head, but Castor continued speaking over any arguments the Fae may have had. "I believe we would all agree it is past time we had a registration of all Others on the mortal plane."

"I second the motion," Jens announced. Sitting back, he crossed his arms over his chest and gave Asplin a sideways look. Asplin didn't look up but kept her gaze locked on the silver lines shot through the black marble of the centuries-old conference table. She heard several others express their agreement as Felix argued against the inevitable. Ancient power surged in the room making the hair on Aspin's arms stand on end. She let it lick over her skin like a mini-lightning storm along her dermal plane, before sucking it into the base of her neck and feeding it down her spine, pulling it into the reserves of her body.

A smile she barely concealed tugged at her lips. It was almost time to show not only the Others, but everyone, everything on the mortal plane, who was in control. Who the powerful really were and who controlled all that power.

"This is only going to make them hate us all the more," Felix argued.

"Let them hate us," Castor argued. His rage caused spittle to spring from his mouth. "I want the heads of the Reapers. Dante has pushed us too far this time. And it is time he pays for thumbing his nose at us."

A sudden silence descended over the room. Asplin couldn't believe what she had just heard. As the head of the Tribunal, Castor could demand the extinction of a Race but he needed cause and he needed the rest of the Tribunal to vote unanimously with him. "I will pay for the heads of each Reaper brought to the Tribunal."

No, not the extinction just the brutal murder of the Reapers; this was declaring all-out war on the Reapers. This was better than she could have hoped for, and her hands fisted at her side to keep herself from jumping up and down with glee.

Felix jumped up from his seat. "Have you lost your mind? You are declaring war on the Reapers; and Dante. He will not sit back while you hunt down his sons."

Castor glared at the Fae. "You dare to question the word of the Tribunal, Felix?" he shouted.

Felix looked around at the other Tribunal members. "I can't believe you all feel the same? Who can possibly second this absurd motion?"

Jens stood without hesitation. "I second the motion."

Another member stood to follow suit, until ever member but Felix stood in favor.

"And what of the souls of the dead?" Felix demanded.

"Dante will submit to the Tribunal and replace his Reapers with Tribunal approved Reapers." Castor announced.

Asplin felt numb with excitement. This was more then she could have expected or hoped for to rule this plane and the next.

Felix shook his head. "The Fae will not stand and fight against you and the Reapers, this action will undoubtedly cause a ripple effect hurting the natural order. Something the Fae cannot abide by." He turned and shimmered away.

Castor laughed. "The Fae have no heart for war. We are better off without them. Get me a messenger; I want the notifications to go out today. Anyone known to work with the Reapers is subject to questioning. All Others are to be cataloged, and their loyalty to the Tribunal noted. If they don't stand with us..." he paused for effect and Asplin felt a rush to her head and she finally let a smile spread across her face. "Then we don't need them."

****

Dante watched his old friend study the statues in his stone garden. "It has been years, my friend. To what do I owe this unexpected visit?"

Felix turned to Dante. "When are you going to release these souls Dante?"

Dante looked at the Fae, Felix indicated. It was a pair of lovers whom had mistakenly crossed Dante and in doing so had forfeited their lives as well as their souls.

Dante shrugged. "Their souls belong to me, Felix. How many times are we going to have this conversation?"

"The Fae are leaving the mortal plane, we can no longer care to live under the current set of rules the Tribunal have set forth for their followers. We chose to move into the Ether. I ask for my brethren." There was more to the situation, and Dante would have the full story. Before he made any decision.

"Why the sudden turn from the Tribunal? You have maintained your seat for several thousand years." Dante maintained. "What conspiracy or war are they weaving themselves into now?"

Felix shook his head and turned sad eyes on Dante, "Weaved to tightly. We chose to remove ourselves all together other than chose sides in an unwinnable war."

"Tell me what is going on," Dante said holding his hands behind his back.

"The Tribunal is starting a war with you and your sons. And the Fae will not choose sides you know we are ever the diplomats." Felix said honestly.

Dante threw his head back and laughed. "This is a war the Tribunal cannot hope to win."

"Yes well they believe differently. Otherwise they wouldn't wage such a war would they?" Felix explained.

"And you came to warn me?" Dante asked, amused Felix would do something so sentimental, typically the Fae didn't bother.

Felix shook his head. "No, Dante doing so would be choosing sides. And as I mentioned the Fae do not choose sides." But the corners of his mouth turned up slightly. "I came to plead for the souls of my brethren." His eyes turned to the two lovers again.

Dante walked to the statues. "Who are they, to mean so much to you?"

Felix looked upon the two. "She is my brother's daughter. He believes her to be dead," he said honestly. "Lost two hundred years ago. When I came and saw her here I could not admit to him she was being punished by you. But to bring her home when we leave the mortal plane would comfort him greatly."

Dante looked at them with interest; Felix had never said anything about them being related before.

He had asked for their release but never showed any real interest.

"What else is the Tribunal up to?" Dante asked not looking from the lovers.

"They are demanding all Others register. They want to know where allegiances lay. They are scrambling," Felix admitted. "They are flexing their muscles and being led by a force which doesn't even sit on the Tribunal," he said with disgust.

"Tell me who it is," Dante demanded.

Felix shook his head. "I'm not sure. Even my spies could not discern who is pulling the strings the web is so tightly wound. But I tell you this my friend. The minute I tug on the right string it is severed, and not in a small way. All links to the string are severed." Dante was shocked to see his friend shiver.

"So you have chosen to leave?" Dante asked.

"We cannot win an all-out war against the Reapers regardless of what the Tribunal thinks," Felix admitted. "They may have an inflated sense of who and what they are but this is a not a fight the Tribunal can win. The Fae do not go into a fight when they are sure to lose. It is fool hearty, and the Tribunal is doing it because they cannot see beyond whoever is holding their strings."

Dante had to hand it to the Fae, at least they weren't going to lose the unnecessary lives on a war they couldn't win.

"I hope you don't think the Fae weak," Felix said looking at Dante seriously.

Dante held his tongue for a long moment. "I believe you and your brethren stronger for understanding your strengths and weaknesses. The Tribunal is starting unnecessary fights and wars just to flex their muscle. Unnecessary lives will be lost."

Felix nodded. "What are you going to do?"

"I should storm the Tribunal and take them all out, prove to them I am not just an Other, or an Immortal. A God in my own right. I am descended from more than mere Gods!" Dante thundered letting his anger display briefly. Felix stumbled back a step before Dante pulled his power back. Dante breathed deeply for several moments letting his anger flow from him before he spoke again. "But they have a hand they have not shown yet, and I will wait to see who is behind this, they have been headed toward a reckoning for some time."

Felix nodded again. "I agree, something is waiting in the wings. They have bred darkness in many different forms. It is time that darkness be exterminated."

Dante agreed, and he could do nothing about it if he went in and exterminated the Tribunal like his temper demanded. He would need to let the pieces fall as they may. He wasn't, however, willing to lose anymore sons. He was still working on rebuilding the losses he had sustained from Calliope. However, that wasn't something he felt compelled to share with Felix.

Dante extended a hand to Felix "I will miss you my friend." Felix took Dante's hand.

Dante turned back to the lovers and touched the statue. "Have your niece and her lover their debt has been paid. Take them back to the Ether with you."

Felix bowed to Dante as the stone started to dissolve. "The mortal plane will be a lesser place without the Fae." Dante stepped back and turned to walk away not bothering to turn back.

The mortal plane was quickly becoming a very unsafe place. Dante wondered if the Tribunal truly understood what they were doing declaring war on him and the Reapers. If they wanted a war, they would have one. They weren't picking a fight with just a mere god. Something they had obviously forgotten. Excitement flowed through his veins, something he hadn't felt in years. He didn't walk away from an outright challenge, or a fight.

He stormed into his fortress and bellowed for an Abda, the skeletal servant came running. "Bring me my sons, along with Celeste and Marcus."

They had plans and decisions to make. It wasn't going to be easy, but Dante would be twice damned if he would allow anything to happen to those he cared for.

****

Ring Ring Ring

Elle rolled over and looked at the clock on her bedside table. Two a.m. "Are you freaking kidding me?" But her phone didn't stop ringing. Picking it up she glared at the caller I.D.

Helena. This wasn't a good sign. Her sister never called unless something was truly wrong. "What's wrong?"

"Olympus." No 'hello', no 'hey, sis, how you doing'. Yeah, this was bad.

Elle sat up straight in her bed a nervous laugh burst from her lips. "You're kidding right?" After Gods knew how long her sister was using the safe word? What in the name of all that is holy was going on?

"Get your shit together and get moving," Helena spat.

"Yeah, not until you tell me what the hell is going on." Elle shook her head trying to wake herself up.

"The Tribunal has lost its god damn mind. That is what is happening. Do you have your bag packed?"

Elle climbed from her bed grumbling under her breath about being pulled from her warm bed, something Helena didn't seem to appreciate. "Are you kidding me right now?" Helena shouted. "I used the safe word, for the first time in..." she seemed to have lost her ability to speak for a moment. Elle knew it wouldn't last long. "Forever!" she shrieked. "And you're upset about being woken up? Don't forget who the weak link in the chain is little sister."

Elle felt tears flood up the back of her throat, choking her. She swallowed past them. An apology on the tip of her tongue. It would just piss Helena off though, so she swallowed it. "Where are we meeting?"

"The Atlanta safe house," Helena barked. "You have seventy-two hours."

Elle quickly calculated it out in her head, realizing they must have decided on the Atlanta house because it was closest to her. Another concession just for her.

"You'll make it?" Helena asked.

"Yes," Elle agreed. Even if she had to drive without stopping for the next two days.

"The Tribunal is sending some type of creatures after the higher orders," Helena explained. Her voice only slightly softer.

"What does that even mean?" Elle asked not really liking the sound of this conversation. She cradled the phone on her shoulder and threw open her closet and pulled out the duffel bag she kept packed just in case something like this happened.

"Just try to stay off the main roads; you have a safe path mapped out? Holy ground mapped out right?" Gods on a spit. Elle climbed into her closet letting the familiar clothes fold around her she let her head fall against the back of the small space. What was happening? This was like some movie, not her life. Not her safe little life. Where she hid out in her little mountain home. Safe from the world, and all the evils that could find her. She felt safe here, she had a safe room. Supplies, she could hide here. Elle momentarily contemplated disobeying Helena and just hiding out in her safe room below her cabin. She could hide down there for a couple of months.

"Elle!" Helena barked. "Did you hear me?"

"Yes, Helena," she answered trying to sound confident. Knowing that she didn't have the balls to disobey Helena. Building the safe room was one thing, but when it came down to outright defiance? She was a lamb, being lead where she was told. "Yes, Helena I heard you. I'm on my way." She tried for confidence but she knew it didn't sound as confident as she would have liked. In fact she was so terrified of what was going on, so terrified she thought she might actually throw up.

"Bet you wish you'd remained with the family," Helena said, her sarcasm not lost on Elle. Helena's sarcastic little barb didn't require an answer. She had to admit, through everything she never regretted leaving the fold.

"I'll see you in a couple of days," Elle answered instead.

"Seventy-two hours, Elle," Helena reminded her.

"I know, Helena."

"Elle."

Elle stopped, hoping her sister would offer some shred of hope, or grain of inspiration, she really should have known better.

"You have the emergency number right?"

Dread pulled in the pit of Elle's stomach making her want to throw up. "Yes," she croaked. Helena hadn't brought up the emergency number in over a thousand years, things were really bad if she brought it up now.

"If you have to use it, do it. Do you understand me?"

"Yes." Elle's voice cracked, she didn't wait to see what else Helena had to say on the issue and clicked the end button. She was ready to go in fifteen minutes; the water and power to her small cabin were turned off, the propane tank valve turned off. She closed her front door and jogged to her old truck tossing her duffel bag into the bed.

Helena wouldn't have been impressed; she would have wanted Elle on the road immediately. Elle pushed those thoughts out of her head and started the truck. Thinking like this wouldn't do anything but pull her mood down. She wasn't sure how much time she would have to spend with her siblings and spending time with them always depressed her. She popped in a Katy Perry CD and turned up the volume and started to sing along. Ignoring the way she had to grip the steering wheel extra hard to keep her hands from shaking.

After an hour and a half she was half way down her mountain and still deep in the woods. She was singing at the top of her lungs when the lights appeared in her rear view mirror.

Elle checked the clock and her GPS; she was basically in the middle of nowhere. She sighed, and glared as the lights gained on her. "Well shit, that's a bad sign"

Chapter 2

Elle stumbled and fell to the dirt, stones digging into her knees and the palms of her hands. Crying out in fear she pushed herself to her feet and stumbled forward. She made the mistake of looking behind her. A shadow moved between the trees stalking forward barely discernable in the inky darkness of the night. It was playing with her, fear enveloped her making her stomach turn and bile rose to choke her.

When Elle finally saw the glow of the hallowed ground she had been looking for, tears she hadn't realized she had been holding back burst from her eyes. Elle pushed herself harder. "Almost there." She told herself. Unearthly screams howled behind her making her stagger in fear. Elle lost her footing.

"No, no, no," she cried as her arms wind-milled around her. She fell hard on her left arm as she went down, the pain zinging up her arm.

It caught up to her as she tried to regain her footing. She screamed with pain as it sunk its claws into her ankle. It took everything she had to not give into the ghastly pain and let the thing just have her. Clambering in the dirt, her adrenaline kicking into overdrive, her free leg kicked out and connected with bone. Rolling onto her stomach she clawed at the ground dragging herself forward through the dilapidated arched gates.

The peace and calm of hallowed ground hummed along her skin. The monster behind her screamed as his claws ripped through the sock and shoe of her left foot.

Elle screamed again and kicked with everything she had left, finally jerking free. She pulled herself the rest of the way into the cemetery. The beast rose and the dark smoke he had used as camouflage rolled off of him like water.

"You can't hide in there forever," The freaky thing growled his voice deep, giving Elle the chills. He snapped his jaws causing Elle's blood to run cold in her veins. He was huge, and Elle just stared for a moment unsure exactly what she was looking at.

He was easily six and a half feet tall. And green, like pea soup green. And muscle. All muscle. Pointy yellow/white teeth which currently dripped blood. Her blood, she thought with a shiver. He was a Freak if there ever was one. Gasping for air, Elle scrambled back on her elbows.

"What the hell are you?" she gasped. Pain radiating up her leg, she looked down at the bite mark, blood poured from the gaping wound. She wouldn't last long against this huge Freak. Helena would have an aneurism when she didn't show up at the safe house on time.

The thing lunged at her but came up against the invisible barrier, and Elle smiled. "Hallowed ground, you soulless piece of freaky shit."

He rolled his head on his large neck and then smiled, showing slathering pointed teeth. "But I can outwait you, little god."

Elle flipped him off and pulled herself behind one of the crumbling headstones she ripped part of her t-shirt off and tied it around her ankle staunching the bleeding for now. She had left everything including her phone back in her truck, in her clamber to get away. After being run off the road by the Freak, she had taken a chance he wouldn't be able to enter hallowed ground, it was pure luck she had been able to sense the darkness sucking at the Freak was the lack of a soul. She leaned back and stared up into cloudless night sky And wondered just what the hell she was supposed to do now?

"You know you can't hide in there forever." the thing snapped irritation dripping off of every syllable.

"You know you're not actually supposed to exist right?" Elle threw back. "I certainly don't make it a common practice to have conversations with creatures who shouldn't exist."

It laughed. A humorless sound she never wanted to hear again. However the sound battled with the ringing in her ears, when had her ears started to ring? Elle had to admit her condition actually couldn't get much worse.

"Give up Elle, and you won't be hurt anymore." He laughed as he said it, making her seriously doubt his words.

"How do you know my name?" she asked as lights started to pop on the edges of her vision. Elle shook her head and took several deep breaths until her vision cleared.

"I've been sent specifically to claim you. My master demanded I know exactly who and what I was retrieving," The Freak expounded.

"You answer to the Tribunal?" she asked peeking around the headstone.

"My master will rule the Tribunal." It laughed again.

"Um okay. Your master seems delusional," she snapped. "Why don't you go get your master and then I'll talk to him or her. I don't think it's safe for me to leave my current position, until I can verify the sanity of this master." Sounded like a sane idea to her. Even though the world was starting to spin.

Her demand met with another guttural laugh. "Why don't you come out and I will take you to my master?"

She laid her head down deciding any further conversation would be a bad idea, she had no phone, had been run off the road, and trapped in an ancient graveyard in the middle of the woods.. Helena had no way of finding her. She had lost a significant amount of blood. And had no way out.

"You have the emergency number right?" Helena's question haunted her.

Elle would have laughed if she had the energy but as she had looked down at her ankle she knew she had very few options. Bleeding out looked like the death option for the day. Regardless she didn't actually want to die.

She cleared off one of the headstones. Dipping her fingers into the blood pooling at her foot, Elle drew the symbols she had memorized over millennia ago.

When had Helena started calling them an emergency number? Helena thought it was hysterical. Elle thought it morbid. Elle had no idea what type of creature she would be summoning. In all her existence she had never truly seen a Reaper. Didn't really want to see one now. But drastic measures and all. She glanced over her shoulder before turning back to the symbols on the stone she had drawn. She drew the last symbol, she merely had to press her palm against the center and wait. Elle leaned over so she could look out at the thing waiting for her. It squatted down drawing something in the dirt. Elle recognized in her heart of hearts whatever happened it spelled disaster for her.

Bleed out in the cemetery or call a Reaper?

"The devil you know or the devil you don't?" She asked and looked again at the thing waiting to take her to the Tribunal or his master? Gods only knew what type of fate awaited her. "Against the devil you don't know?" Elle pressed her palm into the center of the symbols; truly not in the mood to die tonight. It hurt too damn much.

She closed her eyes expecting something cataclysmic to take place. A flash of lightning. A clap of thunder.

Something...

Anything...

Nothing happened. Elle peeked one eye open and looked around. Then peeked the other eye open everything looked the same. She would have laughed if she could but the blackness was starting to swamp her.

"You're going to lose," she muttered over her shoulder. Making the Freak look up from whatever it was he was doing.

"And why is that?" he asked.

"Because I'm going to bleed out long before you come up with an answer," she murmured.

He said something, but the ringing in her ears drowned him out. She wanted to cry, damn Helena and her emergency number. Elle slapped the stone. "Why aren't you working?" She felt tears prick her eyes, and slapped it again. She was going to have to try again. But later, because the ringing in her ears was getting worse and her eyes were too heavy.

****

Victor sensed the tug of the summons from deep in his consciousness and rolled from the bed, he could only ignore Dante for so long. Climbing naked from the bed he ignored the three women as he dressed and Flashed to Dante's Fortress in the Infernos, Dante sat on his throne waiting.

"You thought to ignore my summons?" He questioned.

Victor knelt on one knee. "Of course not, father."

"I summoned you three times, Victor." Dante's voice was deceptively quiet. Enough to make the hair on the back of Victor's neck stand on end.

"I apologize, Father." Victor kept his eyes on the floor knowing he had displeased Dante.

"The Tribunal is demanding all Others register or stand trial for dissention," Dante said shocking Victor. Victor's shocked expression fell onto the marble thankfully as he remained kneeling; head down at his father's feet. "This of course includes your brothers and I."

"My spies are saying they're building an army and demanding Others on the mortal plane pledge themselves to the Tribunal and everything the Tribunal stands for," Dante continued to explain, Victor heard his father move from the dais and walk away. Prompting Victor to move to his feet, he turned to find his father staring out the window. "They are making a move."

"What would you have me do?" Victor asked.

"Someone has summoned a Reaper." Dante changed the subject as he turned to Victor. "You will answer this summons."

"What?" Victor asked shocked. "Who would dare to make a demand on a Reaper?"

"I have no idea. All I know is someone has summoned us. And with the Tribunal acting the way they are, we will not turn our back on possible allies." Dante turned his back on Victor, dismissing him.

Victor wanted to argue, but one certainly didn't argue with Dante. And he had gotten off easy actually.

He had been given a punishment as well as a mission. He moved silently out of Dante's throne room in search of an Abda and the information he needed to find this idiot mortal who had the balls to call a Reaper. It wouldn't be a mistake they made twice.

****

He followed the summons and appeared on a shabby unkempt road. He looked around, but only saw a truck and an SUV. The truck looked like it had been run off the road by the black SUV, there were no signs of life. Well nothing here that could have summoned him.

Victor walked over and put his hand on the hood of the truck: cold. Looking around he let his Reaper sense's expand to encompass the small piece of road around him. There it was; terror and pain. Followed by something horrible and violent.

Ah this made Victor smile. Violence is what he did. Following the trail of violent energy he walked into the woods, for the first time since Dante had summoned him he experienced a thrill flow up his spine.

The stronger the energy became the more excited Victor grew. It swept through him like an evil wind. He pulled his scythe from the holster strapped to his back under his shirt, rolling his shoulders. He stopped and listened, letting the sounds of the quiet night surround him. Victor listened and inhaled, taking it all in.

Then he sensed it, shrouded within the eaves of a large tree; breathing heavily. Blood caked the cracked and dead earth leading to whatever was hiding there, and whatever it was, was sick and twisted. Victor squatted down and touched the drops of blood. It gave him just a glimpse. Like a movie, the scene played out for Victor: a woman kicking and screaming a freakish monster attacking her. They were so fast he couldn't tell if the woman had been killed or not. But the heavy breathing lumberjack several yards in front of him wouldn't just be hanging out if the woman were dead. He was pretty sure the thing hiding within the shadow of the tree wasn't what had summoned him. So it was the dying female, and he needed to get past it to get to her.

Victor let the shadows fold around him making him invisible to anything but another Reaper. And moved silently until he stood in front of a gate, the old iron rusted beyond repair and hanging loose. Victor expanded his senses, and then he heard it. The flutter, barely there, just a whisper of a beat. Whoever it was didn't have long, Victor shook his head. He hoped they hadn't suffered much. At least he could avenge them, it wasn't much but it was all he had left.

Victor stood and shook off the shadows letting them role into mist. He turned toward the violent darkness standing under the cover of a large tree.

"Come out, you piece of shit," Victor demanded. "And answer for the violence you have committed. " The heavy breathing grew stronger and Victor glared into the shadows.

"I don't answer to you," it exhaled.

Victor twirled the scythe between his fingers letting the blade catch the light of the half moon. "Eventually every creature answers to a Reaper what makes you so different."

"Not me." The shadows parted and a creature unlike anything he had ever seen before moved forward with a speed Victor wouldn't have believed possible of something so large. He saw olive green colored skin, and red rimmed eyes before it bent down and plowed a huge shoulder into Victor's stomach. It picked Victor up spinning him around and plowing Victor into the dirt. Victor would have sworn he heard a guttural laugh as he did it.

A couple of Victor's ribs cracked and he lost his breath for a moment. Victor drove an elbow into the side of the thing's neck; it grunted and jumped back to its feet unphased. It grabbed a fallen log the size of Victor's leg and swung it down. Victor rolled out of the way before it bashed the log into the exact spot Victors head had been, shattering the log into bits.

Victor hooked the creature around its huge trunk like knee, satisfied when the thing tittered and then crashed to the ground. Making the very earth tremble. Victor rolled to his feet.

"What the fuck are you?" Victor snarled just staring at the thing in front of him.

The thing laughed again and launched to his feet. "Ah, a Reaper at a loss for words my master would be so pleased."

"You won't be seeing your master any time soon. Unless your master is currently residing in the Infernos." Victor snarled and moving with blinding speed, swept his weapon out in an arch. The beast moved, but not fast enough. Victor's blade sliced through his opponents arm splattering Victor in a dark red blood.

It hissed but otherwise showed no other signs of slowing down. Turning on a dime, it back-handed Victor, picking him off his feet. Victor hit the ground several feet away with such force stars exploded in his vision. The ground shook as his opponent pounded toward him. Victor rolled out of the way. Making it laugh, an irritating sound grating on Victor's every nerve.

"I am really getting tired of hearing your laughter," Victor snapped. Throwing a punch he connected solidly with its face as it bent down to pick Victor up. Victor rolled to his feet as the thing stumbled back a few feet.

"The poor creatures and mortals I have been sent to collect are no match for me," It rumbled, head snapping forward. Wiping the oily red/black blood from its chin, it opened its mouth showing bloody, pointed teeth. Victor's stomach turned at what he could only assume it was a smile. "But you? Ah, it will be a joy to make you scream."

Victor snorted. "Not even on your best day," Victor said crouching down into an attack stance he waited. He didn't have to wait long for the creature to attack. Victor stepped away at the last second, his scythe leaving another gaping wound. This one across the Freaks ribs, cutting straight through to bone.

Victor racked his brain for what type of creature this could be, pasty green skin with demon like features but obviously with a clear mind. Victor slammed a fist into its face, grunting in pain as it landed a few punches of its own. He stumbled back, nearly dropping his scythe again. After this fight, he might have to consider carrying a gun. But he loved his scythe, even though his brothers teased him for using such an antiquated weapon. He swung out, slashing at the beasts other arm. Warm blood splattered out, coating him in it. Twirling the scythe he slammed the butt end of the handle into the Freaks eye socket. It stumbled back howling in pain, causing it to swing out blindly and catching Victor in the thigh making him stumble back several steps.

It advanced. Another smile on its face as it head-butted Victor, stars exploding in his vision.

Meaty hands wrapped around his throat, nearly causing Victor to lose his weapon again. He managed to bury it deep into the Freak's stomach, driving it upward until his fingers dug into the warm, wet wound.

The creature's eyes rounded, as he squeezed Victor's throat tighter. Black spots appeared in his vision, before the creature dropped him and stumbled back, clutching at its stomach. He wheeled backwards until he slipped and fell into the old cemetery gate. Smoke sizzled off the beast as the hallowed gate burned the Freak; it screamed trying to roll free.

Victor spat out blood and walked over to the thing planting a foot on its chest he pressed him into the gate and the hallowed/ blessed earth, letting it finish off what Victor had started. Within minutes the thing burst into flame and after several minutes the screams stopped.

Victor stumbled back and onto his ass, he lay for several minutes staring up at the night sky. The noxious smell of charred skin choked him. He had noticed there had been no soul connected to the mass of horror.

Victor stared up at the constellations and swore to himself, as he let his body heal. Someone thought they were God, and everyone knew how well that always turned out. Dante was not going to be happy about this. Hell Victor wasn't happy about this, why couldn't shit just be easy? And the Tribunal wanted Dante to answer for his crimes? The irony of the situation didn't amuse Victor. This shit just kept getting better and better. Dante was going to have a fit and then some.

"I'm getting too old for this shit!" Victor swore and threw an arm over his eyes, trying to forget all the bullshit he just breathed the cool night air. He tried to imagine himself on a quiet beach his feet buried in warm sand, turquoise water spread out as far as the eye could see. The warm sun shining down on him, no death, no destruction. No damned souls. No wars and people trying to kill him and his brothers.

He didn't know how long he lay there, but when he finally opened his eyes again, he was calm. He climbed to his feet, glared at the soulless piece of shit and shook his head. It was a bad omen if he ever saw one.

"Well, you sure the hell weren't what summoned me." Kicking it away from the gate, he focused on the faint heartbeat he had identified earlier. He ducked through the gate and went looking for an idiot who would summon a Reaper.

****

He followed the Blood Call, and stopped when he found the half-dead female. She lay spread over a headstone. A mangled ankle the obvious source of the blood she had used for her Blood Call. Victor just looked at her, and then looked back at the beast he had just killed. And shook his head. "You certainly didn't have a chance did you?" He was surprised she had made it as far from her vehicle as she did. Long curly hair lay spread out, covered in twigs and dirt. She had high cheek bones and full lips and to top it off she was barely breathing. "Why in the world would you call a Reaper?" he asked the unconscious woman. Not expecting an answer.

He touched her shoulder; she moaned and moved away from him. "Smart woman." He shook his head. Not sure what he should to do with her now. Victor figured he couldn't just leave her in a deserted cemetery. After all, she had used a Blood Call and

Dante had sent him after her. If he followed the Old Laws, he had every right to take her to the Infernos and keep her or give her to Dante.

So really she belonged to him according to the rights of the Blood Call she had used. After all she had used her own blood to make the Blood Call and therefore forfeited her soul to the biding of the Reapers or Dante depending on who answered the call, which meant him. Nobody really used the Blood Call anymore. They used Ink, water, and requested things of the Reapers, but Blood hadn't been used in over a millennia. Who wanted to forfeit their soul to the Reapers?

Of course he had to accept the call either way, and add his blood to it to make it official. If she had used any other medium for her call her soul wouldn't be involved. But she hadn't used another medium. Now this little beauty's soul was vulnerable, Victor smiled. He wouldn't of course take it, but she lay at his mercy. And taking her back to the Infernos for safe keeping wasn't the best idea, but, it was the only one he had. Besides, until she was awake and could explain what the hell was going on, the Infernos was the safest place for her right? It made total sense to him. They could talk about her soul and how fast and lose she was with it later.

Gathering her up in his arms, he tried to Flash. When nothing happened he tried again. The woman in his arms moaned and jerked in pain. "What the f—" he grated, wondering if it had something to do with the graveyard. If the holy ground had been blessed by the right type of holy man it could prohibit him from Flashing. He took the woman and left the graveyard. He tried to Flash again, the woman arched and started to shake to the point he almost dropped her. Blood started to seep out of her nose. Not a very good sign.

He glared at the woman, gently laying her down. "You are becoming a serious problem."

He took several steps away, and Flashed back to the Infernos without a problem. Then Flashed back. "Well, now what?"

They were nowhere near a portal. Swearing, he picked her up and carried her back to the vehicles. Maybe he could just take her to the nearest emergency room and leave her there? After all he had taken care of the Freak that had been after her. And he didn't sense anything Other about her. He looked down at her and wondered who and what she was. He didn't sense anything Other about her. But that Freak was definitely Other, and why had he been after her in the first place, and why did she have a Blood Oath summons, if she wasn't some type of Other? She had a lot of explaining to do, for him to just leave her on the side of the road.

If he couldn't take her back to the Infernos all bets were off. She had just become a liability to him, and one he wanted nothing to do with.

He carried her back to the vehicles and put her in the backseat of the SUV, surprised when he found the keys in the ignition. Still not sure what to do, he climbed behind the wheel. He began punching buttons on the GPS until he had directions to the nearest ER and pulled the car out onto the road. Swearing to himself over the mortal technology and the need to have to use it and not use his Other abilities. He grumbled to himself for the entire ride, when a hand grabbed his shoulder he swerved the car off the side of the road. And nearly ran them into another tree, shouting four letter words the entire time.

****

Bile crawled up the back of Elle's throat as the car rocked her, pain racked her ankle making her want to cry. A man sat behind the wheel. She was weak and it took everything she had to reach forward and touch his shoulder. He looked nothing like the horror stories she had made herself believe, of what Reapers would look like. Which scared her even more, who the hell had picked her up? Had she been taken by the Tribunal? Had her call to the Reapers gone unanswered? Leave it to her to get the emergency number wrong. Helena was going to lose her shit.

She wanted to throw up, and cry all at the same time. She needed a phone, as much as she wanted to avoid it she needed to call Helena.

When she touched his shoulder she wasn't sure who was more surprised by his actions him or her? But, the way he veered the car off the side of the road, she would have to say him. The SUV swerved, throwing her from the seat and landing her in a heap on the floor between the front and the back seats jarring her.

"Mother of all the gods above and below, woman!" The man swore again, and again, using combinations she had never heard before. Until the car screeched to a halt and the door at her head opened. With the early morning light behind him she couldn't ascertain who or what species he might be, just his height.

Elle took a deep breath. "What are you?" she asked trying to mask her fear. Then realized she didn't feel anything. She closed her eyes, and actually reached out. Being bombarded with others' emotions came with being an Empath. But the only ones she was sensing were her own. Those she knew how to handle.

At least, she thought she did. Now, staring at a man she had never met before and feeling nothing but her own emotions, she wasn't sure what to do without her enhanced ability.

Her eyes shot to where his should be, but she couldn't see them. His face was cast in shadow. "Oh my gods, what are you?" Elle shrieked. He crossed his arms over his wide chest, Elle wished she could get a good look at him. Wished she could get any type of reading off of him, but he was a blank slate to her. "You first, sweetheart."

Elle shook her head. This had to be a Reaper, right? Her fear ratcheted up to past anxiety, and right into feeling as if she might just throw up. "Oh Gods, I'm totally going to throw up," she cried.

"Yeah I'm taking you to the nearest ER, I don't do sick." He took a step back.

Elle scrambled forward, as much as the cramped space would allow, trying to grab at him. "No." He must sense the fear in her voice, the horror. "I can't go to a mortal hospital." She practically screamed it at the top of her lungs.

He stopped. "Then you have some questions to answer."

Elle chewed her bottom lip, caught between a rock and a hard place. "Are you with the Tribunal?"

"No."

"Me either," she offered hoping he would say more. When he didn't say anything she sighed. "The Freak?"

"Dead."

She wanted to shake him. "You killed him?"

"Look, lady, you called me. Why don't you tell me what you want?"

And her mouth fell open, she just couldn't help it. She must have looked a sight because he chuckled.

"You. Are. A. Reaper?" She exhaled. Honestly Elle didn't know what she had been expecting when she had used the emergency number. Well she had to be honest with herself she couldn't get a good look at him from her position. But from what she saw, he looked like a regular guy. Well his silhouette looked normal. He didn't have horns, and she peeked down, or hooves. Well he had on boots from what she could see, so his feet could very well be hooves but she was pretty sure you couldn't wear combat boots over hooves. But maybe you could, she didn't know. Maybe they had adapted over centuries to wear regular footwear. How the hell was she supposed to know? Elle clapped a hand over her mouth as a giggle escaped.

"What?" he snapped.

"I just..." Elle stuttered. "I... I...You...feet...boots...a...holy shit," she breathed.

"Are you not well?" he snapped.

Elle laid her head down and took a couple of gasping breaths, her ankle was killing her. She had been run down by some type of Freak of nature. She had almost bled out, and it looked as if she had been rescued by a Reaper. A Reaper for all the Gods Sake! Her life had most assuredly taken an odd turn or two in the last twelve hours.

"I think I might be in shock," she admitted. "And my ankle is killing me. And I just can't believe the damn emergency number worked. So you're really a Reaper?" Elle asked looking up at the man still standing over her. A Reaper, a real Reaper. A creature she had tried to avoid her entire existence for good reason. Well, didn't everyone try to avoid Reapers?

She thought. "A real Reaper?" she couldn't help but ask.

His head dropped just a fraction of an inch. "At your service."

"I can't go to an emergency room," she said with more calm then she actually felt. She tried to make her voice sound self-assured. Talking to a Reaper scared the crap out of her. It shouldn't. After all, she was descended from gods and a demi-god herself, for Hell's sake! A powerless, helpless, worthless demi-god. But, a demi-god, never the less.

"And why is that?" He sounded calm. In control. Maybe even a little bored. She wondered if she asked, if he would teach her to talk like that. Because his voice held this amazing lilting calm she would kill for. People had to take you serious when you spoke like that, because people who spoke like that ruled the world. She didn't know how she knew that she just did. And she would love to be able to talk like that. Helena would have to take her serious if she talked with a calm reassurance that this man, this Reaper, held in his voice.

"I'm not exactly mortal." Her voice cracked and she wanted to crawl under the seat. Her voice wasn't strong or authoritative in fact it cracked just a little. She wouldn't be threatening if she tried.

He leaned in. Strong cheek bones, sandy blond hair and eyes so dark blue, they appeared almost black, came into focus. His eyes were sexy as hell, and with that voice? The combination was undeniably sensual and dammit if it didn't make him beautiful and sinfull. Of course he had to be freaking gorgeous. And with that voice, she wanted to sigh, might have sighed if she wasn't so scared.

"I sense nothing. What are you?" he demanded. The voice had gone hard, it wasn't a tone you said no too.

She pulled as far away as the cramped space would allow. "There is no need to snap at me." She swallowed when his eyes narrowed in irritation. And she spoke before he had a chance. "Well, there isn't! It isn't like I'm trying to hide what I am." Not from him. At the moment anyway.

"Your eyes are gold," he barked and stood up swearing. "Bloody hell," He shouted then leaned close only inches from hers, moving with a speed and grace which made Elle jealous and dizzy at the same time.

"Demi-god," he snarled it like it was a bad word

Air rushed from Elle before she nodded. "Yes, why is that such a bad thing?" she heard herself ask.

"Who do you answer to? Who are you bound to?" He snapped. Elle was surprised her head didn't whip back from the vehemence in his voice.

She shook her head. "No one."

"Bullshit! Who is your god?" He demanded, "Who is the one you answer to?" He spat the words out, like he couldn't get them off his tongue fast enough. This wasn't what she had expected. She had expected a Reaper to come and protect her from the Freak. And to be a gentleman, after. Okay, not really what she had expected, she hadn't known what to expect. But a regular looking guy? Not on her expectation list. It just threw her for a loop. But since a regular guy had shown up, he could at least treat her like a regular person, right? At least make an effort to be nice?

"The Gods of old are gone. Something, I am sure you know." Elle said, waving her hand around dramatically.

"As were their offspring. And their bastards with them!" He barked, making Elle wince.

His words stabbed at her heart. "Not all their offspring," she said defensively. "Some stayed behind, were actually left behind." Since we were of no use, or in her case, too mortal to be useful. She didn't tell him that, since it would only validate what the prickly bastard thought. And she wasn't in the mood for that. "And unlike, mythology states we weren't all mortal." She choked on the last word.

He grabbed her, ignoring her cries of pain as he dragged her from the back of the vehicle. Elle gritted her teeth and forced herself to stand on her good leg. Lights exploded behind her closed eyes from pain, but she forced them open, anyway. She refused to pass out in front of him. She wouldn't satisfy his morbid curiosity. "Why did you call for a Reaper? And let me tell you in doing so you and your soul now belong to me."

Elle blanched, and her stomached dropped into her feet. "That's impossible."

"Nothing is impossible," he growled.

"But Helena... She never said. She wouldn't do that to me." Elle stumbled on her words. "I didn't have a choice."

"I don't give a shit what this Helena did or didn't do. Now tell me what chased you into the cemetery?" His voice was so uncaring it ran chills down her spine. And she felt more alone then she ever had in her entire life. How could Helena have done this to her?

"I have no idea. Some kind of freak."

"Well sweetheart, you don't have a lot of answers. And unless I start getting some damn good ones, I'm not moving another inch." He folded his arms over his chest.

Elle took a couple of reassuring breaths. "The Tribunal sent out a notice that all species of Other, were to register with them. From what I understand, the majority of the Others, basically laughed it off." She took a breath; she had no idea what the Reapers knew of the Tribunal's current actions or why the Tribunal were currently going bat shit crazy. "About six weeks ago they started collecting those who had refused to register with them." She used her fingers as quote marks when she used the word register. "It's a way for the Tribunal to make the Others bow to them."

"Those of us who refused to become pawns for the Tribunal have gone into hiding. My sister called me tonight and said they were going after the higher casts."

"So why you?"

She shrugged, because she honestly didn't know.

"So you stand against the Tribunal?" he asked. His voice had lost some of its fierceness, which she had to be thankful for. Because frankly he scared the shit out of her.

"Yes, what they are doing is inexcusable." Something flashed in his dark blue eyes as she spoke.

"Something happened..." Elle trailed off. "The Tribunal has decided to go after the higher echelon of Other, and that thing...Something isn't right." But she couldn't put her finger on it, and she would be damned straight to hell and back if she would walk away now.

"So you have no idea what came after you?"

Again, she shook her head. "No, but I could tell it didn't have a soul. It's why I recognized I would be safe on hallowed ground."

"You give off no sign of being Other," he accused.

Elle chewed her lip wondering what she could tell him, when he narrowed his eyes she considered lying to him. "I am a demi-god. And I am an Empath, but I am also cursed. I gave away my immortality for mortality's sake." Not a lie, but not the full truth.

The Reaper shook his head and rolled his eyes. "Is that somehow supposed to explain to me your curse?"

"I am cursed to live the life of a mortal." She sighed deeply. "It's probably why you can sense anything Other in me." She offered.

"Still have no idea what you are talking about," he said shaking his head. He looked irritated and for the first time since waking up with him she didn't feel totally overwhelmed by his presence.

Elle sighed. "I killed the wrong mortal a long time ago. A mortal loved by a dark druid. And she cursed me to live the life of a mortal. So I appear to be mortal, but I am not." It wasn't the whole story but he didn't need to know the whole story. It wasn't a story she was proud of, and not one she told anyone if she could help it.

"So what are you then?"

"Something in between... and nothing at all," she said the latter part more to herself then to him.

"I couldn't Flash you out."

She burst forth with a self-deprecating laugh. "No..." She drew the word out. "I'm not able to use any Other powers. I am bound to the mortal plane. You won't be able to Flash me out, while I am cursed."

This time he snorted. "Sounds like it sucks." Then pointed to her ankle. "So are you going to heal?"

She looked down at her mangled ankle. She wiggled her toes and rotated it. Not broken, but it hurt like hell. "Yes, it should be okay in a couple of days. But I will need to get it cleaned and bandaged. I have no real immunities so the sooner the better. I would rather not get an infection."

"Frail. And fragile." He swore and moved past her, climbing into the driver's seat. He turned back to her, "Well?"

She shook her head. He had pulled her from the damn thing! Hopping on her good leg, she climbed into the backseat and lay down. "For the love of the gods, put a seat belt on! The gods only know what can happen to your fragile ass, before I can find someplace safe to stash you." He swore some more as he fiddled with the GPS.

"You're a very grumpy person, do you know that?" She wanted to slap herself the moment the words left her mouth. She had never talked like that to a stranger before. Usually, she was the very epitome of kindness. She was in shock and exhausted. It was the only answer.

"Yeah well, I have other things I would rather be doing then babysitting a fragile and cursed demi-god," he said without turning to look at her. His words hurt more than they should and she couldn't figure out why. And the momentary bout of irritation for being rude flew out the proverbial window.

Elle stuck her tongue out at him.

"I saw that."

She looked up to see him looking at her through the rear view mirror and couldn't help the blush as it worked its way up from her feet. She buckled herself in and laid her head back. Tired, scared and worried. If she could pretty please just have one god smile down on her and help them find a safe place to take care of her ankle, she would be very grateful. She fell asleep chanting to herself: *Safe haven, healing, and then Helena.* But she couldn't help but sneak in a "Please let the Reaper like me just a little." And she definitely tried to forget about the fact that her soul may or may not now belong to that sexy as hell Reaper as well.

Chapter 3

Elle felt like shit, the backlash of her attack and the fury and rage of her attacker was kicking her butt. She snuffled down into the softness of a warm bed letting it fold around her, she knew when to be grateful. But something was different, she let herself relax and then she realized what it was? She didn't feel anything?

Elle couldn't remember the last time she hadn't been aware of everything around her. Or of the barriers she always had to have up when she was away from her cabin, but she was away from her cabin now, and she didn't have her barriers up and she didn't feel anything, no buzzing no low hum, no pressure on her chest no unwanted emotions. And she didn't know if she liked it, the absence of pressure left her bereft.

She pushed herself from the warmth of the bed ignoring the pain in her ankle and sucked in a shocked gasp at the man starring at her from a chair across from the bed. The room was fully lit; and he sat thereblond hair hanging over a strong brow and into dark blue eyes. A scruffy day old beard covered a tough jaw and a tight t-shirt covered a muscled chest.

"Reaper?" Elle wanted to pull the covers over her face when her voice cracked over the single word.

One eyebrow climbed up a smooth brow. "Victor," he provided.

"Ah." Everything from the night before crashed over her and she fell back into the bed. "I'm surprised you're here. I thought you would have left me for dead." Elle pulled the covers up realizing when she did that she didn't have any clothes on and swallowed past the lump forming in her throat.

"Who took my clothes off?" She asked not coming out from beneath the covers terrified of the answer he was about to give her.

"I needed to treat your ankle," he stated his voice an easy rumble showing no emotion she remembered she had envied that voice last night.

"Um, you had to remove all my clothes to treat my ankle?"

He laughed and she sat up letting the blankets fall off her head so she could glare at him she could see the muscles in his shoulders roll under his shirt as he shrugged and she had the strangest urge to fill them with the palm of her hand. The years of living alone in the mountains of Maine stretched liked eons across her memory. Would they feel as smooth as they looked? Elle wanted to throw the blankets over her head and never come back out.

"I took it as my payment."

All thoughts of his muscular shoulders flew out of her mind as her mouth fell open in shock, and then just as quickly she snapped it shut. "I don't think I like you very much." In fact, she very much wanted to slap him in his handsome face.

"It's a good thing I'm not here for you to like then. Is it?" he asked leaning forward he put his elbows on his knees. He nodded toward a bag of food on the bedside table. "I brought you some food. Eat, and get cleaned up. You'll get the rest of the night to rest and heal; we hit the road again in the morning. By the way where the hell are we headed?"

"I need to find my sister Helena," she said stuffing a burger into her mouth. "She was heading to a safe house in Atlanta."

"And you need me for this why?"

Elle's hands dropped to her lap. "There is a war starting. Don't you care? People are dying—mortals; Others. Don't the Reapers care about anything other than the souls they will gain in this war?" They had to care; she was putting everything she had in believing they cared just a little. After last night she wasn't quite sure she would be able to make it to Atlanta without his help.

"The corrupt souls belong to us either way," he said leaning back he crossed his arms over his chest like they were discussing the weather. "What's in it for us, my little demi-god?"

"There has to be some kind of payoff for you to get involved?" The food sitting in her stomach now felt like a ton of bricks.

Victor laughed but it was a bitter sound. "You called us, and Dante does nothing without compensation. And by using the Blood Call, by rights YOU belong to ME. So what bargaining chips do you actually have?"

"Please stop saying that. I didn't have anything else but my blood to use. If I had used wine, or water, or anything else besides my blood would you have come?" Elle asked.

Victor shrugged, "The call wouldn't have been as strong but any Reaper Summons is answered eventually. But you my dear used your blood, a sure fire way to get a Reaper to answer the summons because there is already a payoff: your soul." He finished with a toothy smile.

"I don't think I like you very much?" she said folding her hands in her lap in order to keep herself from throwing something at his head.

"Like I said I don't need you to like me, sweetheart. But from where I sit this entire plan is a waste of time. You have nothing to offer me. So why should I waste my time taking you to your sister? I don't waste my time on mortal issues. And your little issue, although not mortal, is definitely not my issue. So exactly why should I get involved? Basically, sweetheart, the only reason I'm still here, you don't Flash." She was grinding her teeth together as he spoke. And then trying to decide what she might have which she could barter with the Reapers. "As soon as you're healed we hit the road."

"And if I could Flash?" She demanded.

He gave her another toothy grin, "Well then sweetheart you would be incased in the Infernos and most assuredly in my bed by now."

Elle was so stunned she felt her mouth open and close several times.

"Let's not forget your soul belongs to me." He reminded her.

"I don't like you, it's official." Elle glared at him.

"Then give me more of a reason to stick around." Victor said. "To care about your pitiful cause." He said with a roll of his eyes.

He rose slowly stretching from the chair and walked over to the other bed he extended is long body out stacking his hands behind his head he closed his eyes and relaxed. "Why don't you think on the matter for a while, I'm going to get some rest."

"Is this some kind of joke to you?" she spat out. "What the hell are you talking about?"

The corners of his mouth kicked up. "Not my problem."

"People are dying." How could he be acting so callous? Was there anything he cared about? Then she realized she was thinking about a Reaper, he dealt in death. "Is there anything you care about?" The question fell out before she could stop it.

He didn't open his eyes as he shrugged. "You are the one who said a war is brewing, if I am to pick a side it should mean something shouldn't it?"

Elle laid down and pulled the sheet up to her chin, she should clean up. But she wasn't feeling anything, emotions of the world were blocked and even the pain in her ankle wasn't really all that bad, she had to find a reason to make the Reaper stick around and help her, which didn't involve throwing herself at the Reapers feet and begging him for his help.

Which apparently the bastard would enjoy. It was just all too much. Elle pulled the covers over her head and turned away from the Reaper. She couldn't think about everything that was going on. It had been well over twenty-four hours, of the seventy-two that Helena had given her. She needed to come up with something, and she didn't know if any more of those Freaks were coming after her.

Maybe she should think about trying to get away from the Reaper? If he continued to refuse to help her it was her only option. One more day of letting her ankle heal and maybe she could get the keys away from him while he slept. Then she would still be able to get to Atlanta on time.

It was a good plan and with that thought she was finally able to fall asleep.

****

Victor glared at her, a demi-god, what were the odds? Gods, of any kind were trouble, and demi-gods were trouble with a capital 'T'. Trouble the Reapers didn't need at the moment. She had needed immediate medical attention, and he had brought an Abda from the Infernos to treat her. He hadn't felt bad at all about lying to her, if she was afraid of him it was okay. The Abda had used herbs to aid her in her healing. The faster she healed the better.

The faster he found out what was going on, and he got her to her sister the better. He also needed to find out why the Tribunal wanted her. But right now getting them food was at the top of his list. When he was on the mortal plane he ate fast food. It was a huge weakness. It was something he didn't indulge in very often but when he did, he always went overboard.

What the hell was he going to do with this demi-god? Stuffing another cheeseburger into his mouth he glared at the woman who had been sleeping for another twelve hours now. He supposed he should wake her and feed her again. But he was enjoying watching her sleep something he had never indulged in before either, Dante had told him to stay with her. He wasn't really into babysitting, he could think of several things he did want to do with her. However, babysitting her wasn't one of them.

Shaking himself, he threw the wrapper of his burger on the table and went to the window to glare out at the cityscape. He had to admit it was beautiful, after centuries of the oranges, and reds of the Infernos he had a healthy appreciation for the blues, greens, and yellows of the mortal plan.

"Find out what is going on. Find out if they will side with us. But whatever you do, do not let them know about Celeste and Marcus and where we currently stand with the Tribunal. Or that we are still down a Reaper. The last thing we need to do is let them know we are weak. And stay with the demi-god.

You never know when we can use a demi-god." was all Dante had said about the demi-god. Yeah, then he had returned and told her she had to give him something in return for his help. So he was making a great impression on her, leering, lying. Yup this relationship was going great.

Moving to the bed he kicked the mattress. "Time to wake up and eat, sleeping beauty."

She didn't move so he kicked the bed harder. Still no movement, he could hear her breathing so he sat down with another burger and continued to shake the bed with his foot while he ate.

She finally rolled over and took a weak swing at his foot. "Stop."

"Get up." Victor finally left the bed alone. "You need to eat and take a shower."

She made several unlady like grumbles and then squeaked in pain, he turned and she was holding the edge of the bed as she inched around it toward the bathroom. Wrapped in one of the sheets, she looked like a Greek goddess. And he stopped to enjoy the view for a second. But another squeak of pain had him on his feet.

"Gods," Victor muttered and swept her up into his arms. He tried, gods he tried, to ignore how she fit against him. That despite the thin sheet she clutched against her it really didn't cover anything. And damn she was beautiful, her legs were long and toned. Her long honey colored hair hung in tangled waves over his arm. And she stared into his eyes with those golden brown eyes he wanted to drown in.

She flayed for a second. "Calm down." He squeezed her until she quit moving and then walked her into the bathroom, where he deposited her on the edge of the bathtub. "Don't put too much weight on your ankle. I used special herbs which will aid in your healing but not if you do something stupid. Call when you're done."

He kicked the bathroom door closed and had to admit he was getting a strange sort of satisfaction knowing she was helpless without him. Thirty-six hours with her and he was losing his mind. He had never taken care of anything before in his lifetime and it created strange feelings in him, he rubbed at his chest and wondered if he was going soft. "I need to collect a soul," he said more to himself then to anyone else, burying himself in the darkness of the world he was used too.

"What?" Elle called from the bathroom. "Are you talking to me?"

"No," he said back with a smile.

He ate another burger, a helping of fries, and the chocolate milk shake before she finally opened the door and called to him.

"Reaper?"

He pushed himself off the bed and walked to the bathroom. "I have a name."

One delicate eyebrow rose over the pools of golden amber orbs. "Pardon me. Victor?" Something about the way she said his name put him off. He almost preferred she call him Reaper.

"You need to eat more," he muttered to her before dropping her back onto her bed. He handed her a coke and a bag of food.

Victor looked into her eyes as they rounded in shock. "Okay I agree I need to eat more and I am thin but there is no way I can eat all of this."

"You hardly ate anything yesterday and then slept for over twelve hour Elle, eat." Victor settled on the other bed his hands behind his head and closed his eyes, he tried to ignore the way her clean dark brown hair had curled around her round angelic face. He hadn't thought it possible but she was even more beautiful than before. It pissed him off, and he couldn't understand it. "Eat what you can," he said again the words coming out sharp and hard.

"Victor?" she practically whispered, and he peeked open his eyes. "I wasn't kidding yesterday. I have nothing to bargain with. You already said my body and soul belonged to you. Can you explain that in more detail to me?"

He would have laughed at the look on her face, but he wasn't sure if doing so wouldn't just make her cry. So he gave her a pointed look at the food and as she pulled it to her and started to eat he swung his legs off the bed resting his elbows on knees.

"What do you know of a Blood Call, Elle?" he asked.

Elle shrugged. "If I say nothing are you going to be mad?" she asked around a mouth full.

He actually growled at her, and she stopped eating her eyes rounding in surprise. "You used an ancient Blood Call, you put your soul on the line, and you know nothing about it." He wanted to shake her. "The Tribunal is hunting down Others and you throw your soul away?"

"I didn't know what I was doing. I had a slathering Freak trying to tear me limb from limb. When Helena taught me the emergency number she never said it was a Blood Call," Elle cried.

"Yeah well maybe you should have asked her what it might cost you to use this emergency number before you used it," Victor said. "Anyway, the blood has been cast, and you, my dear, now belong to me."

Elle threw her hands in the air. "You are so impossible. Please stop saying that."

Victor pointed to the food. "Eat."

Elle glared at him. "I'm not hungry."

Victor glared back. "I didn't ask if you were hungry. You need to heal and regain your strength. In order to do that you need to eat."

She crossed her arms over her chest obviously ready for a fight. Victor almost smiled because she had no idea what she was up against.

"I need to find my sister." She glared back at him.

He starred at her, and pointed at her food. "Eat."

They starred at each other; but Victor won like he always did. Elle picked up her food and started eating again. When she had eaten enough to satisfy Victor, he took up the conversation again. "Why do you need to find your sister?"

"I need to make sure she is okay? The Tribunal is after us. She warned me they were coming for me. That they may attack me." Elle chewed her bottom lip as she finished.

Victor pulled a phone from his pocket and tossed it at her. "Call her and let her know you're okay. Will that be enough?"

Elle caught the phone and stared at it like she had never seen it before. "Where the hell did you get a phone?"

Victor rolled his eyes. "Just because I'm a Reaper doesn't mean I have my head in the sand."

Victor kicked his shoes off and leaned back on the bed. "Call your sister Elle. And sleep through the night."

"You said last night I had until tonight," she accused.

Victor sighed. "That was until I realized you wouldn't be healed and well. We can't travel with you like this."

"One more night, Elle. And then we are moving. The Tribunal will be moving in on us," Victor couldn't afford to keep them holed up for much longer. It was only a matter of time before who every was looking for her found her.

****

"Where the hell are you?" Helena shouted into the phone. "I've tried your phone fifty times."

"But my seventy-two hours isn't up." Elle started.

"That doesn't mean you wouldn't answer your phone. The Tribunal has been going crazy everywhere." Helena explained. "Now explain why you haven't answered your damn phone."

Elle held the phone away from her ear, and looked over at Victor. He didn't make any move to show he was listening, but she didn't doubt he was listening to her conversation.

"Did you know the emergency number you gave me would sell my soul to the Reapers?" Elle asked.

"What the hell are you talking about?" Helena shouted just as loud as her other questions. "The only damn way it would happen is if you used your own blood to scribe the call. And since I never taught you to use your blood as the medium it wouldn't be a problem."

"Information that would have been helpful a couple of days ago," Elle said more to herself then to Helena.

"Please tell me you did not do what I think you did!" Helena screeched.

"Just stop screaming," Elle said. Pinching the bridge of her nose, she was starting to get a headache. Even through the phone she could feel frustration and anger Helena barely held in check through the phone.

"You should be close, where the fuck are you?" Helena demanded.

"Well obviously I'm not. I was attacked by some Freak who tried to tear my foot off," Elle explained.

"How long before you can get here?" Helena demanded.

Elle felt like she was about to cry just a little sympathy. Could Helena give her a little sympathy? "I don't know. I'm not in control of the situation."

"For the love of the gods Elle, I don't have time for this bullshit. Isn't it enough we have to wait for you?" Helena asked.

"I called a Reaper, and now he is in control," Elle said looking again at Victor.

She could practically see Helena shake her head in frustration. "Then get away from him. He probably has better things to do then babysit a cursed demi-god."

Her words shouldn't hurt, because they were true. But gods did they ever hurt. Like a damn ice pick to the fucking heart they hurt. Elle swallowed past the lump in her throat. "What's the plan?"

"Get to Atlanta, stay in touch dammit." Helena hung up.

Elle starred at the phone for a minute before placing it on the bedside. She curled into her side and pulled the sheets up to her chin. She took several deep gasps and forced herself to relax. Thank the gods her body was still trying to recover and she finally feel into a deep sleep.

****

Victor stuffed a burger into his mouth and glared at the phone as he remembered the words from Elle's phone call the night before the waspish tone of her sister's words still ringing in his mind. Her sister was a piece of work, and she had certainly upset Elle. Why that upset him he didn't know, the only thing he knew was his brothers would never speak to each other that way.

If Elle believed for one second she could run from him she had another thing coming. The assumption was laughable at best. If he ever got the chance he was going to tell this Helena a thing or two about what it meant to be family.

At the moment Elle needed him, and although he hadn't wanted to at first he knew Elle didn't have anyone else in the world, after the conversation he had overheard Helena didn't count. Victor swore and tunneled a hand through his hair. "What have I gotten myself into?"

"Are you talking to me, Reaper?" Elle asked her voice scratchy from sleep.

"Damn, I thought you were going to sleep all damn day." Victor tossed a bag of food toward her.

Elle wrinkled her nose at the food. "Do you eat anything besides hamburgers and fries?"

Victor shrugged. "When on the mortal plan, not really."

She smiled at him. "Well I like to eat more than hamburgers and fries," she said pulling herself from the bed she tested her weight on her leg. "It feels much better today."

"Let me look." Victor sat on her bed and held out his hand. She placed her foot in his hand, and Victor looked at the wound. It was almost healed. The skin was puckered and pink but almost totally healed. "Good, almost totally healed. How are you feeling otherwise?"

Her brow furrowed again in thought and his hand itched to rub the furrows away. "I feel better than I have in a long time. It's weird, typically when I'm in a new place I feel horrible." She shrugged, and he wondered if she recognized she did it and her aura shimmered an almost golden hue trying to break free. She should have shown with it, bright like the sun, being a demi-god she should have shimmered with it. However, it was muted.

When he watched her closely he could have missed it, but watching close enough he saw just a shimmer of her aura. A goldenness so beautiful and lovely it made him want to reach out and touch her, his hands itched to touch her.

"Why is it when I look at you I feel like I've made a deal with the devil?" She exhaled her voice catching.

Victor recognized he needed to put some distance between them even if it was metaphorical. He moved so fast he knew she wouldn't be able to track the movements and he was leaning over her boxing her in a hand on either side of her head he leaned down so they were face to face. She may not like his devastating smile, but she wouldn't be able to resist him when he turned on the charm. He inhaled her scent. She smelled of the motel's cheap soap, but there—something beneath, something only an Other would be able to detect he identified to be uniquely her. Victor drew it into the center of his being, memorizing it for later.

"Not the devil, Elle," he exhaled as she sucked in a shocked breath. "But close."

Elle's eyes crossed as she tried to focus on him and a crease formed between her brows. Then she made a harrumphing noise and stuffed half a burger in her mouth.

Victor pulled back glaring at her, he wasn't sure what he had been expecting but a sudden need to eat hadn't been at the top of his list of reactions. He was about to say something more make another move when a knock at the door startled them both.

"Housekeeping," a heavily accented voice called out.

Victor turned and glared at the door for several long moments.

Elle had a bad feeling. "What?" she whispered, pushing herself to the edge of the bed her food forgotten.

"I don't spend a lot of time on the mortal plane, but since when did housekeeping come to a room at eleven o'clock at night?" he asked in a stage whisper.

Elle looked around for an escape. They were basically trapped. "What are we going to do?" she whispered.

He turned to her and smiled showing her a row of straight white teeth. Victor pulled a weapon from his back and flipped it open with his wrist. An eight inch long scythe extended gleaming in the low light. "We fight."

He moved to stand next to the door. "Not really a good idea." she said as quietly as possible as she rolled to the opposite side of the bed she eased herself onto the floor the only thing she could do was hide and it made her want to scream. She sometimes hated who she was.

"What are you doing?" he asked giving her a look like he had never seen her before.

"I can't fight. So I'm hiding." She looked between the bed and the wall where she had wedged herself.

She would have laughed at the look he gave her but she didn't think it was funny. "What?"

"Empath," she said pointing to herself. "Not a great fighter, more of a..." She let it trail off. Then: "I feel the pain I inflict." She had been known to fight when her emotions were out of control. Take for instance the Freak from the night before. Although she rarely ever fought because the backlash was just too much, the end result was always what had happened the last twenty-four hours; she had to sleep off the horror of the rage and pain.

"Bloody balls of Satan." Victor swore. "Fragile, freaking..." he didn't get to finish as there was another knock on the door followed by a jiggling of the handle.

"Won't you feel stupid if it's really housekeeping?" Elle asked with a nervous laugh she eyeballed the hotel door.

"I'm not the one hiding under the bed," he glared at her, she was about to tell him what she thought about him when the door flew open slamming so hard into the wall behind it embedded partially into the soft wall.

Elle sucked in a gasp, and stared out the doorway into the dark night. She forgot to breathe as she peeked around the end of the bed.

Victor looked at her and she shrugged and leaned forward so she could see out the door. Her breath caught deep in her chest as shadows coalesced, and Elle was pretty sure her eyes were going to bug out of her skull at what she saw.

A burnt orange arm reached through the shadows, a gold cuff encircling the wrist. The hand turned into an arm and a bare chest. A cloven hoof stamped into the room and this time her eyes did bug out. The Freak, stomped and looked around making eye contact with Elle who backed tracked behind the bed.

"What the hell?" she felt the words tumble from her mouth. And she pressed herself into the wall and slid against it she backed as far away from the massive Freak as she could get.

****

"Fuck." Victor looked down at the cloven hooves and the burnt orange legs it was attached to, a loin cloth covered the crotch and besides the gold bands at wrists, and ankles it wore nothing else.

Victor trailed his eyes to the face, and just stared unable to believe what he was seeing, harsh lines and cheek bones. But it took a backseat to the huge horns, the size of his forearms the protruded from the things head.

"What the hell are you supposed to be?" Victor asked in shock.

"Your worst nightmare," It spat between its sharp and pointy teeth. "I want the girl."

The Freak looked over to Elle, its black eyes gleaming unnaturally.

"Why don't you tell me why you want her so bad and we can make a deal," Victor offered.

Elle made a very unlady like noise from behind him.

"No deals, I want the girl. Give her to me."

"Okay then. No deal?" Victor asked. When the thing shook his head, Victor shrugged. "Why don't you try and take her."

The thing threw his head back and laughed. "I am going to tear you limb from limb and enjoy it," it snarled.

Victor wondered what exactly the Tribunal was working at, first the Freak with puck green skin, now this thing. "Let me guess you have no soul."

The thing shook its head and swung one meaty paw at Victor's head. It was surprisingly fast considering it was 300 pounds of muscle. Victor swung his scythe and was gratified when it sliced through the upper arm, black goo oozed from the wound. Victor shook his head.

"What are you?" Victor asked again.

Blood red eyes surrounded in black glared at him just before it barreled at Victor driving a massive shoulder into Victor's stomach. All the air was pushed from his lungs just milliseconds before he was driven into the wall. The flimsy plasterboard gave way and they tumbled out into the parking lot. Victor saw stars as he drove his elbow into the thing's shoulder and neck.

The giant fell to his knees unfortunately he didn't release Victor as he fell. And Victor felt ribs break as he was crushed. Victor raised his arm holding his scythe and drove the blade down making contact with one of the things horns. The beast bellowed in pain making Victor's ears ring, but it also got it to release Victor who took his scythe with it, as he jerked out of Victor's hold. The Freak stood shooting fire at Victor. He obviously hadn't expected this much resistance.

Victor rolled to his feet taking several pained breaths, and motioned for the Freak to come forward. He wasn't about to back down or give him an inch of ground.

The Freak growled low in his throat, reaching up and pulling the scythe free, he tossed it into the shadows of the hotel parking lot. "I am going to make you suffer."

Victor shrugged, ignoring the pain it caused. "It will take more than just you to bring me down. Did you bring along some friends?"

He nailed the beast with a superman punch as it rushed him. Then nailed it with a swift kick to the stomach. It doubled the Freak over and Victor swept his legs out from beneath him. Victor acknowledged he needed to keep the upper hand. Keeping the thing on the ground until he found his scythe was going to be a problem. Victor stomped on one bare orange leg making the Freak roar in pain. The thing rolled trying to get away from Victor's combat boot. It swept one meaty arm out taking Victor off his own feet. Victor hit the ground hard and rolled away. Just as another arm came down trying to smash his head into the ground.

They both rolled free, and back onto their feet. Breathing heavily they glared at each other. Victor very much wanted his scythe so he could bury the damn thing in the Freak's chest. And by the look the Freak was giving him he wanted to break Victor in half.

"Give me the girl, and I don't have to hurt you any further," It snarled spitting out blood.

This time it was Victor who laughed. "Who said I was hurt?" Victor asked, showing the rough Reaper smile they were all known for.

The Freak didn't appreciate it and rushed Victor slamming into him. He drove them both back and into a cement post. Victor felt like his spine might have just been crushed but it didn't stop Victor from fighting. Victor leaned back and drove a fist directly into the ear of his opponent.

The Freak howled, so Victor followed it up with a punch to his Adam's apple. Shutting him up rather quickly as the Freak gasped and gurgled. The thing released Victor and stumbled back holding his throat.

Victor pushed himself to his feet and went in search of his scythe, time to cut the damn things head off. He was done playing with it. And how much longer before the mortals came looking for what was making so much noise?

The Freak slammed into Victor just when he found his damn scythe, knocking the air from his lungs again. "Damn it." Victor tried to breathe, but it came out like a gust of air.

He hated to admit it, but this piece of shit was kicking his ass. It head butted him in the back of the skull and Victor saw stars and hit the ground. He couldn't kill this thing on his own and he wasn't sure what chapped him more about that, but he did know when to call for help.

"Christian, Celeste," he muttered around gasps of air as he tried to push himself to his feet. But the thing was still on his back. He felt more than saw his siblings arrive and then the Freak was off of him, and someone was slipping an arm around him. "Lean on me." Celeste whispered urgently.

"Kill it," he said to Christian.

Christian looked over at the Freak and grimaced. "What is it?"

The beast growled and barreled at Christian, the other Reaper was taken by surprise at how fast the Freak was and didn't move as a shoulder was buried in his stomach and he was pile driven into the gravel parking lot. Victor couldn't help it he got a little pleasure out of it.

"Mother fu...." Victor winced when Christian's words were broken off by a fist to his face.

Victor pushed away from Celeste, motioning for her to help their brother out. "You should probably help him."

Celeste smiled, and leaned Victor against the SUV she turned to the Freak and pulled a short sword from each boot and charged with a smile on her face.

The beast's eyes rounded at her. And was standing there bleeding from several spots before his fight reflexes kicked in. A meaty fist came out and glanced off of Celeste's shoulder. She was fast, and he looked like he might be shadow boxing. "Now you're just pissing me off," Celeste taunted.

Victor steeled himself against the pain he was in and found his scythe with it in hand he moved to fight alongside his sister. She glared at him. "I have this."

But her momentary distraction was all the Freak needed and he clocked her with a back hand taking her right off her feet tossing her back in the air. She skidded to a halt against the ice machine.

"Bad idea, man," Victor said swinging his scythe down he buried it into a meaty thigh, the beast bellowed and swung at Victor who easily sidestepped him. Christian had pulled himself to his feet by then, letting the mace hanging at his side swing on a thick chain wrapped around the Freak's other wrist. Victor and Christian moved in, it was like a dance and the Reapers were the only ones who knew the steps. Weapons flew at a speed mortal eyes would be unable to track. It didn't take long to back the Freak into a corner. He didn't make another noise, Victor stepped in to deliver the killing blow burring his scythe deep in the Freaks chest. Christian added insult to injury by using his mace to lop this things head off. They both stood back breathing heavily as the Freak dropped to the ground dead.

"Now what?" Christian asked.

Celeste stepped forward spitting blood out. "Burn it."

Christian reached forward his brow wrinkled. "Where the fuck is the soul?" He announced.

Celeste's eyes rounded in shock. "Oh this isn't good, at all," Celeste announced. "And the Tribunal thinks Dante is playing at God?"

"Get rid of it," Victor said heading back to the room. He needed to get Elle and get the hell out of there. Their little healing vacation was over; it was time to hit the road.

*****

Elle jumped when the door slammed behind Victor. She jumped to her feet and looked around for a weapon. She shouldn't help because of what it would cost her, but she couldn't allow Victor to be injured protecting her.

"Elle?"

Elle stumbled away from the door in shock. "Chaos?"

"Sister," the demi-god smiled.

"How..."

Chaos looked over his shoulder as though he could see through the door, his golden eyes glowing. "We don't really have time for all this nonsense. They will continue to come for you, so either go with them or let whoever is protecting you die."

"What is going on?" she demanded. "You know what is going on. You've been missing for—"

Chaos grabbed her. "I don't have time to explain." Elle noticed the chain around his neck and blanched.

She tried to pull away from him. "Who has you chained, Chaos?"

"Who has you cursed, Elle?" his golden eyes looked sad. Of all the demi-gods Chaos thrilled in his position as a demi-god and the power he held. He played gods and men against each other at whim. And had been missing for longer than she could remember. The chain at his throat however spoke for where he had been. "I don't have long before I am missed. You cannot fight against what is coming." He looked over his shoulder as if he could see not just what was outside the door but even farther. "The time of the gods has been dead for many millennia."

Elle's mouth dropped open. "So therefore I am to just give up?"

Chaos gave her a sad look. "This is not a battle you can win. They have soldiers we are not prepared to fight against."

Elle glared at Chaos. "Which side of this fight are you on?" Something flashed in the depths of his eyes making Elle cringe with sympathy. "Where have you been Chaos?" she tried again.

He held out his hand. "Come with me, Elle."

"What about, Helena? What about the others?"

"They will follow," Chaos said. But the look in his eyes said he didn't believe it. And how could she just walk away from everything she knew with a sibling she hadn't seen in hundreds of years? Did he even understand what he was asking her to do?

Elle backed against the wall and shook her head. For the first time in her life wishing for her ability to feel something, anything. But since meeting Victor her empath abilities were muted. "I can't. Oh gods... I don't know what I'm supposed to do."

"Still Helena's lackey?" Chaos scoffed. "When will you learn to stand on your own two feet? Haven't you suffered enough?"

Elle pushed herself off the wall. "What are you talking about, Chaos?"

"Cursed and tortured with the emotions of others." He rushed Elle and grabbed her by the shoulders shaking her. "How much more are you to endure?"

Elle tried to pull away. "It was my fault, Chaos." Her worlds trailed off.

"Was it?" he snarled. "Then to be abandoned by your brothers and sisters... How many deaths have you experienced sister?"

Elle shuddered and Chaos released her and she crumpled to the floor. "You don't have to suffer anymore. There is another way, Elle."

She looked up at him through the tears now streaming down her face. He offered her a hand. "Come with me, Elle."

But there was something in his eyes, some glimmer of darkness holding her back. "No." She shook her head.

His golden hue turned dark and as suddenly as he appeared, he was gone. Elle collapsed against the side of the bed, wishing for things she could never hope to have.

She was still there when the hotel door flung open, Victor glared at her. "Still hiding?"

Elle looked up at him, she wasn't sure what she looked like but he rushed in. "What happened?" he looked around the room as he pulled her to her feet. "Are you okay?" Why are you crying?"

"I'm not a fighter," Elle whispered.

Victor's blue eyes softened and he pulled her into a rough hug. "I didn't ask you to fight, Elle," he whispered back. "Isn't that what I'm here for?"

"Why is this happening?" She leaned back to look him in the eye. Something passed in the depths of his dark eyes. But it was gone before she could make sense of it. Elle tried to remind herself why she hated Victor as he carried her out to the SUV and put her in the passenger seat buckling her up he gave her a strange look before slamming the door and collecting there things.

Elle curled into a ball and refused to make eye contact with him as he climbed behind the wheel and pulled out onto the highway.

"Are you going to tell me what happened?" he finally snapped after half an hour.

Elle didn't bother to open her eyes or move. "I don't have any idea what you are talking about."

"When I left you safely," he snarled the last word. "To fight that disgusting thing, you were a sarcastic fighting harpy. Now..." this voice trailed off and she peeked up from the ball of her arms and legs, his nearly black eyes were illuminated in snatches of street lights making him look like the Reaper he was. The lack of light, hollowing out his cheekbones and making his eyes dark and scary. "You look like a strong wind could blow you away, what the hell happened in that damn hotel room?"

Elle brushed a tear from her face, and pulled herself up wrapping her arms around her stomach. "I've spent millennia after millennia hiding. Hiding from mortals, hiding from vengeful gods, hiding from emotions that were not mine. Running to my siblings to save me, running from them because of my weaknesses."

Something deep inside of Elle burst, and the vision of Chaos offering his hand to her, and his taunting words playing in her head snapped something deep in her chest. Her arms unfurled and she slammed them against the dashboard cracking the fiberglass and making Victor swear.

"I'm done running," she exhaled and turned to Victor. He just looked at her his eyes rounded in surprise. "I need to learn to defend myself before I'm killed. Can you teach me to defend myself?"

"Yes?" he looked like he wasn't sure.

She wanted to climb over the console and attack him. "No, Victor I have to learn to protect myself." She wished she hadn't hiccupped in the middle of her request. "I will not be prey for the Tribunal or any other Freak." She grabbed his arm. "You have to promise to help me to defend myself."

Victor glanced at her and nodded. "I promise to help you learn to defend yourself." He promised.

"Thank you." She took a deep breath. After thousands of years she felt like she was taking control of her life. And she leaned her head against the cool glass of the passenger side window. Better late the never.

Chapter 4

""You lied to me."

Asplin wished she had the ability to reach through the phone and tear the idiot to shreds. "I have it under control." He promised.

"If that were the case I would have her, now wouldn't I." Asplin looked around her suite, she had decorated it in the fashion of Renaissance England, and she tried to allow the surroundings to calm her but the bellowing on the phone line was just too much.

"I can't believe you contracted others." The screeching continued.

"And I can't believe you think you were the only one who could get the job done," Asplin snapped, her patience utterly spent. "I believe in covering all my basis. I haven't gotten where I currently am without doing exactly that. And you better hope I don't send someone from the Tribunal after you, your incompetence is evident. She is a cursed demi-god, how hard can it be to grab her?"

"She's no longer traveling alone."

Asplin snorted. "Really and who exactly has she aligned herself with?"

"That's not important, I'll have Elle by the end of the week."

"That remains to be seen." Asplin had her doubts. And she had already hedged her bets. She hit end on her phone and moved to her balcony. The Fae had left the mortal plane, and Asplin now controlled the Tribunal. Everything was coming together, if she could absorb the power the cursed demi-god didn't even realize she possessed Asplin would have it all.

The marble balcony under her hands turned to dust. And she swore under her breath, forcing herself to take several deep breaths. She turned back to her room and rang the bell, her Druid lover appeared in minutes.

"My love?" his ghostly pale skin would make most turn from him. But to Asplin it was beautiful. She rubbed the back of her fingers against his skin marveling at the blue veins that stood in contrast against his pale skin. His eyes rolling up into his skull, his papery white eyelids barely concealing his bulging eyeballs. He had to hide from the Tribunal and those of the household. He would be shunned because of his appearance but Asplin thought him one of the loveliest creatures in the world.

"I hunger," she whispered, the words barely audible.

His eyes snapped open. Showing blood shot orbs which startled even her at times. And then he smiled, pulling thin lips tight against stark white teeth. "I will feed my queen," he promised disappearing into the shadows as quickly as he had appeared.

Asplin smiled feeling at ease for the first time in hours. He would take care of her,

****

Victor cringed as Elle hit the ground again a cloud of dirt dusting her and Celeste. And he wondered again if this wasn't a really, *really* bad idea.

"Celeste is going to kill her," Marcus cringed on Elle's behalf.

"I just asked her to teach her how to defend herself," Victor said as Elle tripped and landed hard on her left knee. Marcus flinched too and turned away.

"She would be better off learning to run in the other direction." They had stopped just after sunrise because Elle hadn't stopped harping about wanting to learn to defend herself. Now Victor didn't think there was that much time in the world.

But Victor had to give her props, Celeste had been knocking her around for the better part of an hour and Elle hadn't complained even once. In fact the first couple of times Celeste had knocked her down Elle had jumped up like a god damned Jake-In-The-Box, now not so much. Now Celeste was actually helping her to her feet and asking her if she wanted to stop.

Victor couldn't stand it anymore and stepped forward. "That's enough."

Celeste turned to him and he had to suppress a laugh because in all his life he had never seen his sister look like this before. But she looked as if she wanted to grab him and hug him.

"I was just catching on," Elle said with her hands on her hips.

Celeste's eyes rounded in shock, and her mouth opened and closed several times. Before she just walked away shaking her head. Which for Celeste was a good thing, several months ago she would have turned and leveled Elle with such sarcasm Elle would have burst into tears and Victor would have had to beat Celeste to within an inch of her life. Which would have of course caused a fight with her unhinged, fallen, dark-angel blood mate. And damn it all to hell Victor just didn't have time for that right now.

Elle's shoulders slumped. "I guess I wasn't catching on like I thought," she said watching Celeste pick up the weapons Celeste had brought but had discarded early on.

All Victor thought was he was going to kill his sister after all. "She was raised with Reapers, Elle. Celeste isn't your normal female."

"I guess we need to keep moving anyway." She moved past him toward the car her shoulders slumped. They had only set aside a couple of hours to train this morning.

Victor nodded to Celeste and Marcus and caught up with Elle. "It's going to take more than one session before you can kick ass, Elle."

She didn't say anything but walked up to the driver's door and held out her hand. "I need to drive."

"Um your ankle is still hurt and you were knocked around pretty bad. Are you sure you should be driving."

Elle turned on him like a woman possessed. "Victor, I have been reduced to hiding in a cabin in the woods for centuries. I was chased into a cemetery after being mauled by gods only knows what. I accidently sold my soul to a Reaper and just had my ass kicked up one side and down the other by a Sex demon. YES I want to drive." She shrieked the last part. Victor handed the keys to her unsure of what she was capable of at the moment and she climbed behind the wheel and slammed the door she gripped the wheel so hard her knuckles were white.

Victor turned back to Celeste. "Find out what the hell is tracking her."

This time Celeste did snort. "You're kidding right? When exactly do you expect me to find this information?"

Victor swore. "How hard is it to find who is creating Freaks? How many Others is creating them?"

"I don't believe those things want her dead," Marcus offered, Victor rolled his eyes at the angel. Marcus was always trying to diffuse the situation. You would think the man would learn it was a waste of time by now. "The question we should be asking her is why they want her."

"Can we go know?" Victor turned and Elle glared at him from the driver's seat she had rolled the window down. Victor waved her off and turned back to Marcus and Celeste.

"Get as much information as you can, I'll be in contact when I can." He turned back to the SUV, and jogged around the hood he climbed into the passenger seat and glared at Elle. "Do you even know where we are going?"

"South," she grated between her teeth.

Victor shrugged it was good enough. They would make it to Atlanta by nightfall if nothing else held them up. And he was more than willing to let her drive if it helped to relieve some of her tension. He sat back and observed her, the tension working out of her body starting with her brow and working down through her body. He enjoyed watching the tension work its way through her. After a couple of hours she truly looked tired.

"Do you want me to take over?"

She looked at him like she was surprised he was there. "Actually I'm hungry."

Victor smiled. "This is something I can get behind."

They stopped at an out of the place diner and Victor watched Elle closely as they ate. Something was different about her and he couldn't put his finger on exactly what had changed about her.

"Why the sudden urge to fight?" he asked once he had finished eating he didn't like to let much get in the way of his food. So he had wolfed down the burger and fries but now he sat back and scrutinized her as she pushed her chicken fried steak and mashed potatoes around her plate. If she didn't start eating it he was going to eat it for her.

Elle pushed her food around for a minute more when her eyes turned back to him they shimmered with tears. "It's not about fighting, it's about defending myself. I've hidden for centuries; I am a liability to my powerful siblings. Why do you think they are calling me to them now?"

"Because you are in danger?" Victor said pulling her plate to him and eating her mashed potatoes.

Elle gave him a sad smile. "Victor I have seen you with your siblings. If one of them was in danger what would you do, would you leave them to find their way to you?"

Victor felt the food in his stomach turn, at the sad look she gave him when his eyes snapped to her at the stupid question. "They are leaving me to find my way to them. Because I am a liability. Helena isn't wasting time to come to me because I am not worth her time. I'm in trouble and Helena knows it, and she is leaving me to fend for myself."

"Elle, they want you to be safe," Victor said but after overhearing the conversation she had with her sister the other night he recognized it wasn't true. And the words felt like the lie they were. And the look Elle gave him said she knew it.

"Of course they do," Elle said taking her plate back she ate the rest of her dinner. "They just are not as concerned with my safety as say your brothers and sister would be for your safety.

Victor didn't think he liked her siblings much, she looked at him. Her eyes dark with emotion. He had the strangest urge to hold her and take away her pain. "What would you do if Celeste's life was in danger?"

Victor wanted to snarl, and barely held back the growl rumbling deep in his chest. "I would eliminate the threat." It really wasn't a question. "Besides, anyone threatening a Reaper/Demon hybrid who is mated to a Dark Angel is taking their life in their own hands wouldn't you say?"

Elle softly laughed. "Yes, well there is that. But that being said, my siblings have hidden me away because I am a burden they would rather not deal with, and deal with me now only because they have no choice. I have been in seclusion for more than a millennia. Moved when there was no other choice. I left the cluster because I made them more susceptible to attack, alone I can hide. But with the group or even with one more demi-god I was like a beacon. I became a weight I caused massive losses to the demi-gods. So I was sequestered away from my siblings and the world in order save them and myself."

"For someone who is sequestered away, you are well acclimated to the world and your surroundings," Victor said leaning back.

"Just because I can't interact with the world doesn't mean I don't have to know what is going on and how it revolves around me." Why did he feel like everything he was saying was hurting her?

"We need to get back on the road, Elle. Don't you want to find your sister?" He pulled himself from the table trying to shake the strange feelings from his shoulders.

He jerked when her cold hand touched him. "Victor I don't want to be a victim anymore."

Victor didn't know what prompted him to do it but he grabbed her and pulled her into a hug, she fit into all the hollows of his body and he soaked her in letting his warmth soak into her. "You don't have to be a victim, Elle," he whispered into her ear. He didn't let her go until she was warm and holding him back.

When he released her the scared look was gone and she didn't look like she was going to break.

"Better?" he asked.

Elle gave him a sad smile, but her eyes weren't so dark anymore. "Better."

"Good, get your ass in the car." She laughed as she moved passed him.

"Have I mentioned I don't like you?" she asked.

"Yeah, but I'm growing on you," Victor said walking past her with a smile on his face.

****

Elle shook herself and jogged to catch up to him.

He grumbled something under his breath and glared at her. "So much for the compassionate Reaper."

The sun had set while they had been in the diner and Elle felt the darkness surround them as she darted a look around at the shadows ready for them to come alive at any minute. If Chaos was part of this there was nowhere she could hide. She should probably tell Victor, Chaos was looking for her, but she just didn't know who Chaos was working for, or if he was working against her or not. She stepped close to Victor, realizing she was putting his life in danger. And it upset her, after all he had done she didn't want to see him hurt.

"You should go back to the Infernos Reaper. I can find my way to Helena from here."

Victor snorted and shook his head. "Did Celeste hit you in the head, or do you have a mental condition?"

Elle stopped and grabbed his arm. "There is no reason to put you in harm's way I'm not worth it. Give me the keys and go back to the Infernos." She held out her hand. "Trust me, my soul is so not worth any of this shit."

His eyes narrowed, the dark depths sparkled eerily making her catch her breath... "You do have a mental condition, don't you?" he asked crossing his arms over his broad chest.

Elle slapped him on the shoulder. "Of course I don't have a mental condition. But there is no reason for you to do any of this."

Victor leaned in so their noses were almost touching. "Listen very carefully, Elle. I am a Reaper, and have been for longer then you have existed. Do you understand?" she nodded her eyes nearly crossing they were so close together. So he continued. "I do absolutely nothing I do not want to. Do you understand?"

Again she nodded. "But it doesn't make sense. I have nothing to offer you, nothing to give you in return."

Victor sighed and Elle admitted it sounded like a combination between growl and the way a large cat purred. And Elle wasn't sure if it turned her on or scared the hell out of her.

"It doesn't have to make sense right now, Elle. All that matters is you used a Blood Call and I answered and where you go I go. If you insist on seeing Helena then this is where we are going. But if you ask me it's a dumb ass idea." Victor did the sigh growl thing and Elle was so surprised by the answer she didn't know what to do. He was sticking with her, and he was going with her because she needed to do this for her. And he had said he would help her learn to protect herself. Even if it meant he could be harmed, none of this made any sense but he was sticking with her. But he shouldn't, and she couldn't live with herself if he was hurt or killed.

Elle threw her arms around him and hugged him. Victor stood stalk still in her arms. But she held him close anyway. "Thank you," she whispered into his ear finally.

"For what?" he snapped.

"For sticking with me," Elle said releasing him and backing away. "But you need to walk away. Because I don't want you to get hurt. Because I realize you could be seriously hurt or killed. This isn't your fight, Victor. Why should your blood be spilt?"

Victor shook his head again, and walked away from her toward the SUV. "Get in the god damn car, Elle. This isn't up for discussion." Each word was like a chip of ice and flung over his should before he climbed behind the wheel of the SUV and slamming the door so hard she was surprised the door didn't fall completely off its hinges.

Elle stomped over to the driver's door and slapped the glass with her palm. "I will not be responsible for you being hurt." She didn't understand why the thought of him being hurt made her stomach ache. She knew what he was doing, and why and she was so grateful but she didn't want him to get hurt.

Victor glared at her. "Get in the car Elle," he shouted through the glass. She shook her head.

Elle glared back and crossed her arms over her chest. She was causing a scene in the parking lot of a diner in the middle of know where. Nevertheless the situation was driving her to do things she had never imagined she would ever do before.

"Don't make me get out and force you into the car Elle," Victor threatened.

"I'm not afraid of you." The words tumbled out and she realized they were true.

Something flashed in the depths of his dark eyes which would have frightened someone else but Victor wouldn't hurt her. She jumped back when the door flew open.

"You have no reason to put your life on the line for me," she said as she danced out of his reach. "And as we both know I can't pay you. And you already own my soul so what are you going to do?" Elle didn't know how she did it as she ducked out of his grasp.

"I'll come up with something. Now this is the last time I'm going to tell you to get in the damn car," Victor growled. Reaching for her as she continued to dance out of his reach. He did his little sigh/growl, and Elle couldn't help it she laughed as she spun on her toes mimicking a move she had seen Celeste do that morning.

"Or what?" She said laughing again. She didn't even see him move, and she was pressed up against the back of the SUV. Elle caught her breath and starred into Victor's dark eyes.

"You learned far more than I thought you did this morning," Victor exhaled against her skin making her tingle and shiver, he shouldn't make her feel these things but oh they felt so nice.

Elle smiled at him, it was a compliment and it warmed her like nothing had in years. "Thank you."

Elle felt him press his entire body against her and everything in her went hot. She didn't know if she should press back or throw her arms around his neck. Or cry from the pure bliss of the erotic feelings suddenly rushing through her body.

His hands roamed down her body stopping at her waist, he gave her a devastating smile that went straight to her heart. Victor stepped back and picked Elle up he threw Elle over his shoulder. Elle squeaked and grabbed handfuls of t-shirt to steady herself. "It didn't have to be this way, Elle," he muttered, and she was pretty sure he swore. He tossed her into the front passenger seat and glared at her. "Do I have to restrain you?"

She glared at him. "Are you talking about tying me up?"

He rose one eye brow and a smile curved the corner of his eyes. "Sweetheart I would love to tie you up, so it's really up to you."

She shoved him with her foot and slammed the door. Scrambling over the seat into the driver's seat, there was a spectacular flash of fire and she was sitting in Victor's lap.

"Is that a yes, on being tied up?"

Elle scrambled away from him. "Can't you understand I'm trying to help save you?"

"Now see, I thought I was the one trying to help save you," Victor said turning the key he started the car and pulled out of the parking lot and onto the highway. "Besides I'm a Reaper remember. Pretty hard to kill me, so stop worrying about saving me."

Elle decided she was going to ignore him, he just didn't understand. These things whatever they were, were not going to stop. And they wanted her dead or alive, Elle shivered. She didn't do dead well.

Victor must have seen her shiver. "Stop worrying Elle, everything is going to be fine."

Fine was relative at the moment, especially since Chaos was somehow playing with the pieces. If only she knew whose side he was on.

How did she explain she believed she was being used as bait by her brothers and sisters? And the

Freaks just wanted to use her for the curse she had. Elle laid her head against the glass letting the cool feeling penetrate into her mind as she tried to figure out a way to get out of the predicament she was in, somehow she had gotten herself wedged in between a rock and a hard place and now she had gotten the Reapers involved.

A panic attack seized her and her heart rate increased, and tightness banded around her chest. Elle tried to take breathes but she didn't seem to be able to get them deep enough. She leaned forward and put her head between her knees.

"Elle?" Victor asked.

She held up a hand. There were just too many moving pieces in this damn chess game. Why were there so many damn pieces? And she didn't even know who the hell all the players were. Or whose side the players were on, all she knew was she was the pawn. Just her, oh wait she had a Reaper on her side she couldn't confide in because if she did she would put him in more danger. Oh and she couldn't confide in him because she didn't even have the right answers.

No answers, and now clues, just Elle the cursed pawn.

Her panic attack got considerable worse.

"Elle?" Victor asked when she didn't move after a few minutes.

She lifted her head and looked at him, tears ran down her face. "Stop the fucking car." She reached over and grabbed the wheel forcing the car to the side of the road.

Victor swore trying to regain control of the vehicle, Elle didn't wait as the SUV slowed before she jumped out.

Stumbling away from the car, her vision tunneled to small pinpoints. She wretched empting her stomach and then started to run. Blackness was closing in around her, and no air was getting in and she clawed at her chest trying to pull at whatever was clinging to her throat and chest prohibiting her from breathing.

Something stopped her, strong arms wrapped around her and Elle blinked trying to focus.

"Hello, little demi-god." Elle looked up and all she saw were black eyes, hands so cold they burned her arms gripping her tighter and tighter. "You belong to me," The black eyes whispered.

Elle opened her mouth to scream in pain but nothing came out. She jerked trying to get out. Get away. "Oh little one, I've waited so long for you."

Elle shook her head, trying to make her voice work. Trying to draw air in. Where the hell had Victor gone?

Then the fathomless eyes turned from her. "I wish I had more time." One cold hand released her, and pain seared through her chest. It was a pain she had felt before. With everything she was worth Elle shoved away from the thing holding her and looked down.

A pearl handled dagger sticking from just below her left breast. "Damn it," she gurgled as blood poured from her chest.

****

Victor watched Elle tumble from the moving vehicle swearing the entire time. What the hell was wrong with her? His heart skipping. He jerked the car to a stop and jumped out trying to figure out where the hell she had gone.

"Christian," he bellowed for his brother as he took off down the road. It only took a moment for Christian to appear next to him.

"Contrary to what you might think I do have a damn life," he muttered.

Victor grabbed his brother by the collar of his shirt and shook him. "She took off."

Christian looked around. "How far could she have gone?"

Victor knew he had to be right but they couldn't see anything. Then he heard a moan and both turned to see a flicker of light, and Elle stumble from dark shadow.

A man stumbled through as well wrapping his arms around Elle.

Victor and Christian both reacted; Victor grabbed Elle as Christian slammed a fist into the large man's face.

Elle stumbled into Victor's arms, her mouth was open in shock and he immediately wrapped his arms around her as he swung her out of the fight. "Don't move." She didn't say anything, and he only hoped she was finally listening to him.

He turned back to the bastard who had thought to take Elle from him, Victor pulled his scythe out and smiled, he could feel the black soul radiating from the bastard. The pits of violence were going to feast on this soul.

"Make sure Elle is okay," Victor told Christian, as he stepped into the fight. Christian nodded and stepped back Victor glared at the guy. "You picked on the wrong demi-god." He swung the scythe, burying it in the man's shoulder he cut the guy deep.

He grunted and stepped back. "She belongs to us now. Go back to the Infernos."

"Yeah, go fuck yourself." Victor swore and lashed out with his scythe again. The guy side stepped just barely missing another slash that would have opened up his stomach.

"Do you honestly think you can continue to run? Continue to fight us?" he laughed. "Hiding is out of the question. We know every step she takes."

Victor snarled and lashed out again, the guy stepped out of reach yet again. Now Victor was just getting pissed off. "When I have your soul I will feed it into the pits of Violence one small piece at a time."

This had him laughing again. "You think you Reapers have all the power. You think you control the market on suffering." He leaned forward, black hair fell across his forehead and over his black fathomless eyes and for just a moment Victor was caught staring into them and he thought he saw an empty black eternity stretched for as far as he could see and it made him cold and empty.

Victor stumbled back shaking his head of the bleakness he had seen, but it was enough and the guy rushed him fists flying. A fist connected solidly with Victors chin knocking him back several steps, it was followed with a kick to the stomach doubling Victor over, he collapsed into the gravel it rubbed the skin of his palms raw as he slid to a halt.

He heard Christian swearing and then the sound of a shot gun action and firing several times. Then silence, Victor lay in the dirt trying to gasp for air which didn't seem to want to enter his lungs. He finally rolled to his hands and knees. "Christian?"

"Damn man, who the hell was that?" Christian asked, helping Victor to his feet.

"Shit if I know, but I bet it would have something to do with those Freaks that have been attacking Elle." Victor pushed his brother's hands away from him he was bruised but didn't think anything was broken. "Where is Elle?"

Christian's face fell and he stepped in front of Victor. "Man..." his voice trailed off. "It was too late." Christian kept talking but blood started rushing in Victor's ears and he couldn't hear him. He looked over Christians shoulder at the huddled form on the side of the road, in the dark it could have been anything. But Victor knew it wasn't anything it was Elle and she had been terrified, so terrified she had run from him.

Ran from him right into the arms of the creature that had killed her.

The pounding in his ears turned into roaring and he launched toward the small form on the ground but Christian stopped him. "There is nothing you can do Victor."

"Let me try," he growled. "Let me at least try."

Christian wrestled with him until they were both on the ground. "Let the Angels come for her." Christian's words finally penetrated Victor's anger. Stopping his rage to fix what had happened to Elle.

"Fuck the Angels," Victor snarled. "They can't have her." Victor tried to push past his brother but Christian held tight.

"Victor think man. She deserves to go." Victor felt such rage he knew he wasn't thinking straight. But Christian wouldn't let him go.

He stopped fighting Christian and looked around. "How long has it been?" he looked around.

"A couple of minutes," Christian said, they were both barely breathing.

"She's not dead," Victor said rushing forward. If she were dead then the Angels would have come for her. She was a pure soul, who could she have hurt, what ails could she have done in her life time to deserve to go to the Infernos? No the Angels would come for her, if not then she wasn't dead.

Victor scrambled on all fours over to her, turning her over as gentle as possible he rolled her over gasping at the knife protruding from her stomach. He pulled it out and tossed it away then he checked her for life signs but found none. "Gods, please," he found himself begging.

He placed his hand over the wound trying to heal it. But nothing happened no warming sensation like he had with his siblings. Knowing, he wouldn't be able to heal her. Cursing he looked at Christian. "What the hell?"

He reached forward, he could feel her soul but it was still in her body. "I feel it, it's still there."

Christian moved, placing his hand over her heart and shrugging. "I don't understand it."

Victor grabbed her and shook her by the shoulders. "Elle." He shook her. "Damn it."

He didn't expect anything to happen, then suddenly her eyes popped open; white orbs starred up into the dark night. She sucked in a deep gasp of air, arching up as she did it. Then collapsed back down into the dirt she took several deep shuddering breaths, desperately deprived then convulsed with bone breaking jerks, she finally rolled to her side, she let out a blood curdling scream. She scratched at the dirt, clawing for perches, for gods only knew what, until one nail came off. Her body continuing to jolt in pain.

Christian scrambled away as she groped at the dirt, her entire body convulsing. She coughed up blood, and vomited, and she screamed in pain, flipping over several times. Her pain so intense it made Victor fill utterly helpless as he tried to stop it, tried to wrap himself around her but touching her only seemed to make it worse, bloody tears ran from her sightless eyes. Blood leaked from her eyes, nose, ears and mouth, her limbs twisted and snapped.

"Blood hell." Victor had never seen anything like this in all his life. He didn't think anyone could live through what she was enduring. And watching it was painful enough, it seemed like hours passed before her body settled down to small twitches. In reality he knew it had been less than fifteen minutes, he felt worn out.

When her eyes opened again, they were the golden brown he was used to, she reached a shaky hand out. "Cold," she whispered hoarsely. He could tell she was starting to shiver.

"What the fuck was that?" Christian practically screamed.

Elle's head didn't move but her eyes rolled so she was looking over at him. "Curse" she whispered. "Live and die like a mortal. Over and over and over again. Not immortal anymore...but not m-m-mortal either." She closed her eyes as her body started to shiver uncontrollably. She wrapped her arms around herself and curled into a ball. "H-h-hurrts."

Victor gathered her into his arms and rushed to the car. "You're driving, get us to a hotel. We need to get her warm."

Victor climbed into the back of the SUV trying to rub some warmth into her, but she moaned in pain wherever he touched her. Her body was so cold. "What can I do?" he asked as Christian took off down the road.

Bloody tears ran down her face. "Everything hurts. I feel every death." Her teeth clacked together as she tried to speak. "Every way I have died. In the past I revisit it when I return," she cried burying her face into his chest she wrapped her arms around his neck. "I can't get close enough," she whispered.

Victor pulled her as close as he could pulling her knees up so he had her on his lap. She burrowed into him her bloody tears soaking his shirt. He rubbed her cold back with one hand and her legs with another hand. "Can't you drive any faster?"

"Shut up Victor," was Christian's reply.

Victor leaned forward and looked at the speedometer Christian was pushing the speed at nearly 100 miles an hour. But it wasn't fast enough because Elle was shivering uncontrollably, and her skin was pale as death.

It felt like forever but finally Christian pulled up to a motel.

"Stay here I'll get you a room." Victor was ready to bust someone's head in by the time Christian came back. He jumped behind the wheel and pulled the SUV to the back of the lot. Elle had stopped crying, but her body was jerking violently. Victor couldn't imagine how someone could live through what she was going through at the moment.

Christian had the door open and Victor rushed into the room, the motel was your standard issue and he went to the bed he laid her down and pulled all the blankets around her bundling her up he wrapped her up tight tucking her in so all he saw was her face. Standing up, he and Christian stood back and watched her continue to shiver.

"What the hell are we supposed to do now?" Victor asked Christian.

Christian rolled his eyes. "Why the hell are you asking me?"

"Should we call Celeste?"

Christian snorted. "No. That would be a bad idea."

"H-h-hot b-b-bathhh," Elle barely muttered from beneath the blankets.

Christian threw up his hands and glared at Victor. "I am so leaving. You've got this right?" he left before Victor could answer."

Victor swore and looked around the room. "Garrett," he called out. His other brother appeared after another moment. He looked at Victor and then and Elle.

"Do I even want to know?"

Victor grabbed him by the shirt and shoved him toward the door. "Guard the door, Christian is a pussy. If anything comes anywhere near the door kill it." Garrett laughed and went through the door.

Victor went into the bathroom, and swore when he realized they only had a shower. What type of place only had a shower?

He turned the shower on and adjusted the knobs until they were hot, but wouldn't burn her then went back into the room. "Elle?"

She peeked her eyes open, she wasn't shivering as violently but she didn't look comfortable either. "Let's go sweetheart."

"Hurts." She squeaked.

"I know, you'll feel better after your shower." She nodded, her eyes were slightly glazed and he wondered if she knew what was going on.

He undressed her and carried her into the bathroom, she was so cold she made him shiver. He stepped under the hard spray letting its spray over him first then turning so it was spraying over her. He used one hand to anchor her to him around the waist,

Elle moaned, her head falling back letting the water run over her head.

Victor used his other hand to wipe her hair back, his entire body reacting to the lush body pressed against him. The water ran down them making them slick and hot, Elle slid her arms around Victor's neck her head rolling from side to side. "So nice." She moaned, her legs weren't touching the floor and they wound around his legs rubbing against his calves, one leg wound up hooking around one of his hips. She pressed into his heat.

"You're so warm." Her head tilted up, and water clung to her lashes as she focused on him. "Death is cold and lonely Victor," she whispered before she leaned forward and pressed her lips against his.

He should have been stronger, hadn't she been through enough? Someone was hunting her down and trying to kill her, had actually killed her for god's sake. But she was naked and in his arms and she had instigated the kiss for all the god's sake he just wanted to taste her.

He had almost lost her today and something deep in his chest had broken lose at the thought of losing her, and he just needed to feel her close to him. He would be damned straight to hell itself before he walked away from her right now.

So he kissed her, he wrapped his arms around her slippery body molding her against him under the pounding hot spray of water. Slanting her full lips over his, pressing them open he sank his tongue into her mouth to tangle with hers. She moaned into his mouth and wrapped her arms around his neck, making it easier to sink further into the kiss.

Victor lost himself in the kiss. The feel of the woman in her arms, full breasts pressed against him.

And he grew light headed with desire; he broke the kiss to drag air into his starved lungs.

She tasted like warm sunshine, and the second he could breathe, he dipped his lips back to hers. Elle moaned into his mouth and Victor was lost, he thrust his tongue deep into her mouth, rubbing against her and drawing her tongue into his mouth he sucked on it. Drawing her unique taste and flavor into his mouth. Memorizing her, gods he couldn't get her taste deep enough into him. She made the most amazing sounds as he drifted from her mouth to the side of her neck. Elle burrowed into him resting her head against his chest, he thanked the gods he had left his boxer briefs on. As he tried to control the urge to press her against the shower wall and take her.

"Elle." Her name came out more as a moan. But she didn't immediately respond. And Victor said her name again, he leaned back and looked down into her eyes they were closed. And he realized with a frustrated sigh how exhausted she was and she was half asleep. Still wrapped around him like an octopus, unfortunately he was hard as a rock and it looked like he was going to remain just like that. The heat of the shower wasn't helping; he needed it to be cold; ice fucking cold. But he stood under the hot spray for several more minutes and ran his hands along Elle's body, torturing himself as she continued to relax until he was sure she was totally warm, and unfortunately for him, totally asleep. Leaving him in acute pain.

Climbing from the shower he dried her off and then wrapped her back up in the bedding and took her out to the bed once she was wrapped up and sound asleep like a baby he headed back to the shower. He glared at the horrible thing, he wanted to burn it to the ground, swearing he climbed in, turning the water on as cold as he could stand it. He climbed back in.

****

Victor threw the door open, startling Garrett. "Get lost."

Garett glared at Victor. "You sure? Cause you look like shit." Garrett checked his watch. "Why don't you get a couple more hours of sleep? I don't mind standing guard."

"I'm not getting any sleep," Victor snapped. He had tossed and turned for the last four hours lying next to Elle after a cold shower had turned into his own personal hell. Sleep wasn't happening.

"Whatever man. Let me know if you need anything." that said Garrett Flashed away.

Victor went back into the room and glared at the woman in the bed, it really wasn't her fault. And he didn't know what he had been thinking when he had kissed her last night. He shoved a hand through his hair, he hadn't been thinking. Her story about being alone had gotten to him. It was the only explanation it pulled at something deep within him. He had always had his brothers and Dante. He had never been without his brothers. A family that cared, a crazy family but still his brothers always had his back no matter what. And when Celeste had showed up five hundred years ago, well the Reapers would pretty much do anything for their sister. And that didn't say anything next to what Dante would do for his daughter.

No, Elle's story had definitely pulled at Victor's heart strings. But he would never let her know how much. Reapers were supposed to be heartless monsters. Victor snorted, god's mortals and others would die laughing if they knew Reapers were such pushovers.

As fucked up as they were, they counted on each other and found comfort in their crazy family no matter what happened in the worlds around them they always had each other's backs.

But Elle had forged the world alone. He wondered how long she had been alone? How long had it been since she had leaned on another person? He would like to find her siblings and ring their collective necks. He knew she felt alone and worthless. Her light and sense of self had been extinguished a long time ago.

And to top it off, this curse she faced. It was six degrees of fucked up. Victor shivered, how many times had she died? He couldn't even fathom it. Just remembering what she went through the night before made him sick to his stomach. He never wanted to see it again. The pain she went through to come back, much less the fact she fucking died! Hell, that's what it was, just plain and simple hell.

Damn he paced the floor tunneling an agitated hand through his hair, he wouldn't wish what she went through last night on his worst enemy and he had seen some crazy shit in his life time. After all he was the Reaper of Violence.

He paced and watched over her, wondering how long she would be out this time. Hours passed and she slept like the dead, he couldn't blame her but he also needed to get back on the road. After six hours he couldn't wait any longer. Bundling her up in the blankets he put her in the back seat of the SUV she didn't stir. He climbed behind the wheel and tried to decide what to do next. She had wanted to find her sister. But he didn't know if it was such a good idea anymore. He couldn't leave her to go back to the Infernos to confer with Dante.

So many damn questions and no damn answers. He slammed his hands a couple of times on the stirring wheel. He just needed a safe place to hide for a couple of days.

Where could he take her where they could be invisible?

When the answer came to him he smiled and felt a shiver of relief.

Chapter 5

"Who?" Falcon bellowed.

Victor smiled. There was something about pissing off the Trackers that made him happy. He wasn't sure why, but it brought him joy. "I'm telling you," Lykar said in a forced calm voice. "Victor is standing at the front door."

"The hell you say," Falcon shouted again. And this time Victor actually laughed, as he heard footsteps stomping through the house. And it wasn't just Lykar and Falcon. Several more and Victor wondered if he wouldn't have to fight his way through the Trackers.

Falcon threw the door open and glared at Victor. "Well damn," Falcon exhaled and crossed his arms over his broad chest. "Not your usual mode of transportation, using the front door."

Victor shrugged. "Sometimes even we Reapers slum it once in a while."

Falcon nodded. "Slum it somewhere else." And slammed the door in Victor's face.

Victor blew out a puff of air and waited, he counted to ten. But the door remained closed. He heard several voices raised in argument.

He turned back to the SUV. Elle was still sleeping. She had slept through the day and a half drive to Illinois and frankly, he was getting worried about her. She had to wake soon. The moment he had driven through the gates of Staten, he had felt the wards that protected this land. And knew they were finally safe.

Now he just needed to get the Trackers to let him stay here until Elle was well enough to travel and he had some answers.

"Are you just going to let him stand out there?" Kyra asked over the voices.

Ah, Victor thought he might have an ally there.

"Don't you dare stand up for that bastard," Ryder snarled.

Well there went all his allies.

"He wouldn't be here if he didn't need our help," Kyra pleaded. "Plus he drove here, he didn't just Flash in. That says something funky is going on."

"Last time we helped the Reapers, they turned one of our brothers into a Dark Angel." Victor was pretty sure that was Skylar. And he didn't think Marcus becoming a Dark Angel was a bad thing. In fact Marcus was pretty happy with the situation.

"Argh, Marcus and Celeste are happy, you idiots. And with Marcus being mated to Celeste doesn't that make Victor sort of related to us?" Again Kyra was the voice of reason. Victor wondered how the woman put up with these Neanderthals. "Besides aren't you even curious as to why he is here?"

"Not even a little," Falcon said. "If he is here, probable means bad news. Especially if he showed up in a car."

"Oh my gods. You are all impossible. I don't even know why I try." Victor smiled at the exasperated sound to Kyra's voice. Even though she sounded irritated, she still loved them all.

"Don't you dare open the door, Kyra," Ryder snarled.

"Fine," she shouted back.

Victor stumbled back as Kyra appeared in front of him. "Damn." He jumped away from her tripping down the front steps, where Kyra appeared Ryder soon followed. He was a large, grumpy Tracker with the ability to kill a person with his bare hands. The last thing Victor needed was to be caught manhandling the woman. Even if accidently.

No sooner had Victor cleared the front steps, then the front door flew open. Ryder stormed out and glared at Victor. His face softened when he turned to Kyra. He was still pissed but she seemed unphased. Kyra leaned forward on her tiptoes and kissed Ryder on his grumpy lips and patted him on his wide shoulders. She turned to Victor. "Victor, what in the world are you doing here?"

"Looking for some place safe to hide," he said honestly.

"Are you kidding me?" Ryder growled. "You, need safe haven? Has the apocalypse, started without our knowledge?"

Victor snorted he just couldn't help himself, before he moved to the SUV and opened the door so they could see the woman he had in the back seat. "Not me, her."

"Oh, my." Kyra rushed over to Elle. "What happened to her?"

Ryder snorted, "Kidnappings against the law dude."

Victor raked a hand through his hair. "It's a long story Kyra. But she needs help like you wouldn't believe."

"Go to The Haven. You're not welcome here." Falcon said, moving to stand in the open doorway.

Victor turned to him. "The Enforcers cannot help me. I need the type of help only the Trackers can provide."

"Of course you need help only we, Trackers can provide. The Enforcers can be such pussiess." Skylar screamed from inside.

"I heard that." Kyra called from the front steps. "Don't make me come in there and kick your ass.

"Ah, hell. Why are you Reapers so much trouble?" Falcon threw his hands in the air. "Is this going to turn into some kind of war?" He asked.

"Because I couldn't imagine you being here otherwise."

Victor ground his teeth together, "I wouldn't say a war. Maybe a fight or two."

Ryder barked out a laugh, "What a load of shit. Sounds like a war to me."

"Shut up." Victor snapped.

Only making Ryder laugh harder.

Falcon started swearing a blue streak from the where he still stood at the front door. "You're fucking trouble. But the woman obviously needs help. Safe haven." He snarled and turned his back and walked back into the house. Dismissing them all.

"Wait. Am I the only one still worried about the fact that a Reaper is bringing a woman here?" Ryder tried again. Everyone was still ignoring him.

****

She felt like her head was stuffed with cotton. Rolling over she wrapped her arms over her head. "Why does dying have to hurt so much?" She wasn't sure who she was asking the question to, but it felt good to ask. Her tongue felt like sand paper.

"Well I don't recommend it," a female voice spoke from Elle's left.

Elle pushed the blankets down and yelped at the site of the women sitting next to her. Then emotions flooded her. Strength, power, possession, scents, everything bouncing together making her head feel like it was going to explode. Elle shook her head, and took a breath trying to construct emotional defenses she hadn't had to have up in days.

"Oh my gods!" Elle cried, as she tried to erect a wall between herself and the emotions around her. So many different things fighting for dominance all at once. Especially with the strong males with even more powerful emotions. Elle scrambled to block them as she was bombarded by things she didn't want to sense. Concern etched the woman's face as she reached for her and Elle scrambled back. "No!" She cried, backpedaling, until she fell off the bed.

"Too much emotion..." Elle was reeling with all the emotions that weren't hers.

"VICTOR!" She screamed his name with everything she had. She was going to kill him! Where had he gone?

Where was she?

The pain from all of the flooding emotions was the only thing that made sense. Had she been prepared, she could have put a wall up to block it all. Instead, she was laid bare. It felt like her brain was bleeding from the intensity of it all reverberating through her mind. She saw the strong frequencies of male emotion, bouncing around her like sound waves. Elle clutched her head.

"Victor!" she screamed again. The woman rushed her as Elle screamed in pain, trying desperately to remember how to protect herself from it. The woman was speaking to her in a calming voice, but nothing was getting through the emotional wave. Confused and wishing for oblivion, she saw her door fly open, and was rushed with another wave of emotions. It was one of the males she had sensed in the house. For the love of the gods, didn't anyone in this house shield their emotions? The woman gave her an apologetic look, right before she clocked her with a left hook under the chin, knocking her out.

Elle would thank her later.

****

"YOU WHAT?" Victor was beside himself. He had never wanted to hit a woman in his life, but Kyra was currently pushing him beyond his limits.

"You might have mentioned she was an empath, before you left," Kyra said by way of an apology.

"Is this supposed to make it okay?" Victor shouted.

"Don't scream at her," Ryder growled.

Victor glared at Ryder. "She slugged a woman who was obviously in pain."

Kyra made a whimpering sound. "I really didn't have a lot of choices. She was screaming and flailing her hands. I couldn't get her to calm down. Honestly I thought she was having some kind of episode or something."

Victor was about to start screaming himself. "So knocking her teeth down her throat was the answer?"

"She has all her teeth!" Kyra shouted back.

Victor felt his eyes round in shock. "Did you check?"

"Of course I did," Kyra said in her defense. "What do you think, I'm some kind of barbarian?"

"She helped me." Everyone in the room stopped when Elle spoke.

Victor rushed over to the bed. "How do you feel?"

Elle gave him a small smile. "Well my lip is swollen." She tongued her bottom lip which was indeed swollen. "And my head is pounding. But other than that, I think I'm fine."

"Wait, why isn't she screaming in pain?" Kyra asked.

"Good question." Victor looked at Elle.

"For some reason, Victor blocks emotions," Elle shrugged. "That's why my shields were down. Otherwise, I'd have had them up."

Ryder snorted, and Victor turned to glare at him asking, "Why, exactly, are you here?"

"So, you don't feel anything when Victor is around?" Kyra asked, sitting on the bed next to Elle.

"No other emotions, no." Elle looked at Victor and gave him a small smile. "As long as Victor is around the emotions of others are blocked."

Kyra looked from Elle to Victor and back. "Interesting."

"Why is that interesting?" Victor asked. He hadn't known he'd been blocking emotions for her. Now that he did, he wouldn't be leaving her alone on the mortal plane. He looked at her and wondered how she had survived this long on her own. The look she gave him let him know she recognized exactly what he was thinking. He winked at her, and she rolled her eyes at him.

"Reapers have taken emotion out of what they do. No offense." Kyra smiled at Victor taking the sting out of what she said.

Victor shrugged. "None taken." It was the truth after all.

"I noticed it the first time I met you. You have a type of shield around you. All the Reapers have them," Kyra explained. "But I never thought it was something they projected." She looked between Victor and Elle again. "Interesting."

"Excuse me," Elle said. Getting everyone's attention. "Who are you?"

****

She didn't think what she said had been funny, but, everyone in the room burst into laughter, lightening the mood. It just irritated her. She pressed her lips together, keeping her thoughts to herself. The woman sitting on her bedside extended her hand. "My name is Kyra and I am an Air Element and an Elemental Enforcer. The big guy by the door is my bonded mate Ryder, he is a Tracker."

Elle rifled through the information she had on the Elemental Enforcers and Trackers and came away with a conclusion she didn't want to believe.

She looked at Victor. "Could you please excuse us for a moment?" she asked Kyra. Trying to give her a smile she knew didn't reach her eyes.

"Of course. You must be starving I will get you something to eat and be back in a moment." Kyra and Ryder left them alone.

Elle took a couple of deep breaths with her eyes closed. Before opening them and looked at Victor who was propped up with his arms crossed over his chest and a hip leaned casually against one of the four posters of the bed.

"I have researched all species and their locations. When I was killed," Victor flinched as she continued. "We were hours away from my sister in Atlanta." She emphasized the last part, watching him closely. Noting the almost imperceptible shift. She wanted to point and scream at him, but instead, continued on calmly. "The Trackers and Elemental Enforcers are located in Illinois."

"Correct," Victor said, his eyes leaving her face to stare at something over her right shoulder.

Elle started to breathe heavy. She was going to hyperventilate. With nothing in her stomach, it pitched and rolled nauseatingly. She couldn't believe this was happening. "Please tell me they came to us. That we're in a hotel or something. Or that I'm dreaming. That we're not where I think we are."

Victor calmly walked over to her and put his hands on her shoulders. "Just breathe, Elle."

Elle shook her head. "You were so close to getting rid of me! So close to being able to walk away! Why would you do this?"

"Who says I want to be rid of you?" he asked sitting down next to her. "Elle, breathe."

Elle sucked in a great big breath, and then let it out. "This is just prolonging the possibility of you getting hurt, of me being killed again," she screeched the last part. "Do you have any idea how much it hurts to die? And it's not just the dying that hurts, the coming back. Victor every time I come back I feel each and every death I have gone through. Each one."

Victor shuddered and gathered her into his arms, as if doing so would take away the pain. But nothing could take the pain away, nothing would fix this. She realized she was crying, she couldn't remember the last time she had cried over the pain she endured during her deaths.

She couldn't remember the last time she had cried in front of another person. She tried to push away from Victor, but he only pulled her closer.

"I'm going to fix this," Victor whispered into her ear. "Just trust me." He kissed her forehead.

She pulled back so she could look into his dark eyes. "How are you going to fix this, Victor? The Druid who cursed me is long dead. I searched for her for years."

Victor kissed her forehead again and smiled. "We will figure it out. We were sitting ducks out there I am not putting your life on the line anymore. You're safe here and that is what matters. Your sister can kiss my ass if she cares for you she will understand I wanted you somewhere safe. She can come for you if she wants you. No more of you running to her." Elle sucked up the last of her tears, the problem was she wasn't sure if Helena cared whether Elle was safe or not. She didn't know how Helena felt about Elle. "I'm tired." She pulled out of Victor's arms and laid back down.

"You need food. How far can I go before you start to feel things?" he asked standing.

Elle shrugged. She really didn't know. "I have no idea. As long as I know what's going on, I can put my barriers up. It's when I'm not prepared, then it's a problem." She waved him off, wanting a few moments alone. Putting up every wall she possessed, she laid back down and put her arm over her eyes.

How the hell had she gotten into this? She had just wanted to do what Helena had told her. Like she always did, wasn't that what she was supposed to do?

Now monsters where chasing her and trying to kill her. A Reaper was trying to save her. And she wasn't sure if her sister was on her side anymore. Chaos was trying to get at her and she didn't know if that was a good or bad thing. And she might be falling for a Reaper. Oh and let's not forget that her soul might belong to him. No she couldn't forget about that. Yes it was official her life was falling apart. Had they really kissed in the shower?

Elle peeked out from under her arm; Victor was looking at his phone but was still perched on the side of the bed. He noticed her peeking and smiled. "Do you need anything?"

Elle blushed. "No." She went back to hiding under her arm. She was pretty sure they had kissed in the shower. And it had been wonderful, and passionate, and the most wonderful kiss she had ever experienced. And hiding under her covers was the best option at the moment.

"Okay. Well, Kyra will be back with your food soon." He squeezed her arm and left. She blushed again.

When had everything gone to shit? What happened to the girl who wanted to learn to protect herself?

Oh, right. She had ended up with a pearl-handled knife in her heart. Now, she was laid up thousands of miles from where she thought she wanted to be. She wasn't sure who the good guys were. Freaks were knocking on her door. Reapers were kissing her in the shower. And she was pretty sure she was being sheltered by Trackers and Elementals. Her life couldn't get much stranger.

****

"So you want to explain now what the hell you're doing here?" Ryder asked.

Victor sat down at the kitchen counter with his head in his hands. "I left for an hour. How did things get so out of hand, in an hour?" He asked. More to himself than to anyone in the room.

"You are acting like a whipped dog," Skylar said joining them in the kitchen. "You mind pulling your head out of your ass?" Skylar laughed slapping Victor on the shoulder, practically shoving him off the stool in the process.

Victor didn't appreciate it and kicked out the legs of the stool Skylar tried to sit in. Skylar toppled to the floor, in a mess of ruined wood, arms and legs.

"Mother Fu..." Skylar rolled clear and shot to his feet. "Reaper I was going to be nice, but now I have to kick your ass."

Victor didn't even raise his head. "Get in line."

Skylar shoved him but Victor didn't react. "Dude if you don't play along it isn't any fun."

Victor heaved a sigh, and dropped his hands. And turned to Skylar. "Like I said get in line. Dante wants his pound of flesh. The Tribunal is out for blood. Freaks are hunting Elle down. You don't rate high on the scare factor for me."

Ryder whistled low. "Never thought I'd see the day. Honestly I have to admit, I'm glad I was here. What did you do? And what does she have to do with it?"

"Man, she summoned the Reapers. But there are more questions than answers. And I don't know shit." Victor swore again. And he couldn't think around the woman. One minute he hated her and the next he wanted to screw her brains out. Just to be stopped so he could hold her and protect her. Damn he wanted to bash his own brains in.

"The Tribunal is up to something. Their stench is all over this shit. But I'll be damned if I can figure it out." Victor admitted. Only to want to kick his ass. Was he really whining to the Trackers for god's sake?

"Have you tried asking the woman upstairs?" Kyra asked. "Demi-gods usually have some answers."

Everyone in the kitchen turned and looked at Kyra, Ryder whistled again. "I knew something smelled off about her."

Victor shook his head. "A cursed demi-god. She doesn't have any answers."

"The hell she doesn't!" Skylar said. Kicking aside the pieces of the stool, he pulled another one over. "I bet she knows exactly what is going on. The Demi-gods always knew, they had their golden little fingers in everything. It was why they were hunted down and enslaved to masters or outright killed."

Victor inwardly flinched at how callously Skylar lumped Elle with her selfish siblings. He had gotten to know Elle and she was nothing like the demi-gods of old. "She's not like that."

"Really? Then why was she cursed?" Sky asked, reaching past him to snag an apple out of a basket on the counter. "Might want to ask her how that happened."

"How do you know about that?" Victor asked, glaring at Kyra and Ryder. Kyra rolled her eyes, "You just said it.

Ryder glared at Victor. "Besides, was it a secret? It's a small house, old man. You can't sneeze without someone knowing your business. Get over it."

"We got a problem," Lykar said coming into the kitchen.

Victor stood ready to fight. "What kind of problem?"

Lykar handed him a tablet. "What the hell is that?" Lykar stabbed a finger at the picture that appeared on the screen.

Victor was staring at another cloven hoofed green Freak, but this time it was attacking the front gates of the Staten. "Well, shit."

****

"Tell me you're kidding." Victor stared at the contraption Ryder had pulled up to the front door.

Ryder climbed from the camouflaged tricked out golf cart. He caressed the hood. "Say hello to my Bad Boy Buggie Ambush iS©" Lykar and Skylar both came from the house and jumped on the back. Victor almost didn't believe what he was looking at.

"It's best if you just don't ask," Skylar said. Lykar sat down next to Skylar nodding at what Sky said.

"They're just jealous," Ryder said still petting the vehicle. "This baby is an off road vehicle, and can pull your fancy SUV out of the mud." He climbed behind the wheel and pushed a button to start it. "And purrs like a kitten. And the best part? It's electric. No nasty gas smell." He smiled so big Victor couldn't help but smile back. Ryder looked like a boy on Christmas morning.

"Where the hell did you get this contraption?" Victor asked.

"Don't call her that," Ryder said, his eyes rounding in shock. "Kyra bought her for me. Because she loves me." Ryder patted the Buggie.

Victor climbed in next to Ryder and looked at the array of munitions strapped to the inside of the thing. "Not sure if you have enough weapons, Ryder," Victor said sarcastically.

"We come prepared," Ryder said with pride. "And my Ambush iS©, is perfect for this fight. You did say there were Freaks at the gate right? Well this baby will make them go away."

They didn't say anything else as they rode the mile and a half to the front gate. The Freak was ramming his shoulder against the huge iron gate. But the wards were holding him off and he was bouncing off of it with shocking sparks of orange and red electricity. With grunts of pain, it would stumble back shake it off and ram itself against the gate again and again.

Victor and the others climbed out of the Buggie, Ryder and the other Trackers loading up with guns and knives. "What do you want?" Ryder asked.

Victor shook his head and pulled his scythes from under his jacket. "I don't need your weapons." He flipped his scythe out letting it catch the light. "I want to spill his blood before I make him tell me who his master is."

"Oh so we aren't just going to waste him?" Lykar asked.

"Damn it," Skylar cursed.

"You ruin all the fun," Ryder swore and put his weapons back in place. "I'm going to wait here."

The Freak at the gates hadn't stopped in its quest to beat down the gate. And Victor moved over to the gate and regarded the ugly thing it was a dead ringer for the first thing he had come across in the graveyard.

"Does that thing have cloven feet?" Skylar asked. "It doesn't smell right." He sniffed the air. "I need to get a closer smell."

Skylar walked to a hidden door. Using a keypad, he unlocked a door, popping it open with a click. The Freak stopped mid-step and snarled at Skylar, who slid through the door. Letting it close silently behind him.

"Bring me Elle," It snarled.

Victor stepped forward. "Go to hell," he snarled, getting the attention of the thing.

"Ah, the Reaper. Do you think you can keep her from my master? She belongs to him." The thing ran at the gate slamming against it. Causing sparks of electricity to fly at Victor where he stood just on the other side.

"You'll have to go through me first," Victor snapped.

This time it didn't back up, but reached through the iron bars toward Victor. His clothing starting to smoke as he tried to get a hold of Victor. "Bring her to me and no one else has to get hurt."

Victor stepped forward and slammed a fist into the thing's face through the bars. It stumbled back into Skylar's arms who put him in a strangle hold.

He watched as the thing started to fight off Skylar, and Skylar's eyes flickered as he processed information. When he released the monster, he stumbled back, his eyes rounded. He grabbed it by its shirt, spinning it. He pulled a gun from the holster at his side and put a bullet in its forehead. It stumbled back several steps then crumpled to the ground.

Victor screamed in outrage. "That kill did not belong to you."

"What the hell, man?" Lykar bellowed.

Ryder burst out laughing. Victor swung around and glared at him. "Don't make me stab you." He waved one of his scythes at him as he stalked over to the hidden door. "Give me the god damn code."

Lykar jogged over to let him out, they both stalked over to Skylar and the thing that now lay twitching in the dirt.

"What part of I wanted to question him was so hard to understand?" Victor snarled.

"That thing isn't actually alive," Skylar said. "And anything that isn't alive doesn't have anything to lose. He didn't have anything to say."

Victor swore and glared at the Freak, then hauled off and kicked it. Which made Ryder laugh even harder. "That's it. I'm going to stab your brother." Victor glared at Ryder, who had his feet propped up on the dash of his Buggie.

"Be my guest. Just remember you have to deal with Kyra." The last thing Victor needed was an emotional female. Besides stabbing Ryder wouldn't solve any of his problems.

They were surprised when three more Freaks appeared with a snapping sound. Making a growling noise, they grouched down into a lung position. Surrounding them, Victor looked at them and shook his head. "What the hell?"

Victor, Skylar and Lykar all took on attack poses.

"Hold." The commanding voice spoke from Victor's left. Victor turned to the man he had fought several days before. The man who had killed Elle. Victor wanted this man on the end of his scythe, he wanted his soul delivered directly to Hell itself.

"You're not long for this world," Victor said pointing his scythe at the man. Black eyes glittered back at him.

The Freaks backed up, and surrounded the man. The man's head tilted to the side as he regarded Victor. "Give me Elle."

Victor advanced swinging his scythe at the first hooved Freak who got in his way, carving a deep groove into the bicep that swung at him. He followed up with a side kick to the things stomach knocking him back on his butt.

"Go fuck yourself," Victor snarled. The other Freaks surged forward, and Victor could feel the two Trackers move in behind him. In short order, they had removed the Freaks standing between them and the man. "He belongs to me," Victor said to Skylar and Lykar.

"Who is Elle to you?" he asked.

Bottomless black eyes stared back at him. Hair hung down over a broad forehead. "More of my pets where they came from," he said of the things laying in heaps at their feet. "And the beautiful Elle has been promised to me. Now bring her to me."

"What is she to you?" Victor demanded. He needed some damn answers. Whatever was going on, this piece of shit had the answers. And Victor needed them, before he took his soul to Lucifer.

"Hiding her behind those pitiful wards is useless." He looked over Victor's shoulder at the gates to The Staten.

Victor snorted. "It seems to be keeping your ass out."

"For now."

"Victor." Lykar spoke close to Victor's ear. Victor shrugged him off.

"Tell Elle, Aldon awaits her." Victor had heard enough. He stepped forward and swung one of his scythes at Aldon. Who moved with a speed Victor hadn't been expecting. One moment he was standing there and in a blur of movement, he shifted away. Victor swung again, but Aldon continued to move with blinding speed.

Victor snarled and moved just as fast, the two shifting around the space neither touching each other. Until the sound of several guns cocking into action stopped Victor. He pulled up short next to Lykar and Skylar.

More than a dozen slavering Freaks stood between them and the gates to Staten.

"As I mentioned, I have many more pets where they come from. How long do you really think you can keep your wards up, while under constant attack." Aldon laughed and with a snapping sound, he disappeared.

"What the fuck is he exactly?" Victor snapped.

"Smells mortal," Lykar said, and added. "But something Other added in there. Not sure what else. Has to be something very ancient."

"And these undead pieces of shit?" Sky asked pointing at the group; cloven-hooved, multi-colored, horned and unhorned, and some hairless, others with hair flowing down their backs. One had dreds, another had a high and tight haircut. All of them looked like they wanted nothing other than to tear the three of them too shreds.

"I'd say kill them but since you say they are already dead." Victor shrugged.

"Well dead is relative. They have all the parts." One rushed at them as Skylar started to explain. Lykar shot at it, he hit it in the shoulder. It was smaller than the rest but the bullet didn't even slow it down as it charged.

"Really?" Sky turned on his brother. "Who taught you how to shoot?" he stepped out of the way as the thing rammed past them. Lykar rolled his eyes and put a bullet into the thing's head as it passed. It crumpled to the ground. "Anyway, they have a beating heart and everything else, but there is nothing going on inside. There is nothing there."

Victor looked on as several more broke from the main pack. "Was there ever anything there? Where they mortals at some point?"

Skylar shook his head. "Naw, man. No lingering mortal there."

They fought a couple which had broken from the main pack and had attacked the gate. Finishing them off quickly. The fact that they hadn't been mortals at some point, relieved Victor slightly. He didn't want to report to Dante that something was turning mortals into hideous freaks. On top of Reaping their souls, to boot!

"Now what?" Sky asked.

"Yo, Ryder?" Lykar screamed over the noise of the Freaks.

"Falcon is going to be so pissed," Ryder screamed back.

"Yeah, but, you're ok?" Lykar asked.

"No. I need a fucking hug because Freaks are attacking you piss ants." Was the sarcastic reply.

Lykar shook his head. "Well at least Ryder is fine."

"We need to get back behind the gates," Victor said.

"Shit." Skylar swore and turned from the gates. "If you thought it was hard to get into the Staten just wait."

****

"Eric, for the love of all the gods! The Staten is under attack! We need to get back in there."

"Go to hell. I'm not allowing a Reaper into the Haven," came the calm reply.

Skylar grabbed the box and shook it, but it didn't move.

"Skylar, I can see you. You dumb ass." All three men looked up at the camera over the gate. Lykar waved, which made Skylar shove him. And flip the camera the bird.

"Eric for the love of all the gods. The Staten is under attack, we need to get back in there." Skylar forced the words out between his teeth. It was all Victor could do to keep quiet. He knew anything he said would only antagonize the leader of the Elemental Enforcers.

Eric didn't like him, and he understood why. If Celeste had been punished like Kyra had for crimes she had committed by the Elemental Enforcers, then Victor would have a beef with Eric. So he was just going to keep his mouth closed for the moment.

But Kyra had been punished by Dante, for foolishly and accidently opening a Pandora's Box. And she carried the scars on her soul to prove it. But this wasn't about Kyra, and damn it he needed to get back to Elle.

There was a buzzing sound and then Eric appeared as the gates swung open. He held a gun to Victor's forehead. "Don't by any means, think this makes us even, Reaper. Or friends. You will follow them to the tunnel you will touch nothing. And you will never return."

Victor just nodded. He didn't care, he just wanted back in. Eric lowered his gun. "Follow me."

They ran the two miles to the Haven, and took an elevator down two floors. "What's with the golf carts?"

Eric just gave him a strange look. "This one will take you the six miles between the Haven and Staten in four minutes."

"That's pretty fast."

They climbed behind the wheel. "Seal the entrance," Sky said.

"Tell Kyra to let me know what the hell is going on," Eric said as he closed the door and Victor could feel the wards come down around the room sealing them in.

Sky smiled. "Let's go home."

The ride back to Staten made him vomit, and Lykar and Skylar laughed so hard he ended up slugging them both in the face. He wasn't sure who ended up the worse for the ride. When the three of them stumbled into the kitchen Sky was holding a bloody lip, Lykar was trying to stop his bloody nose and Victor was trying to keep his stomach under control. He was sure none of them were ever going to speak about it, ever again.

He barely caught Elle as she threw herself into his arms. "Oh, my god, they said you were coming back but until I felt you a minute ago I wasn't sure. Are you hurt?"

"Elle..." Victor tried to pull away from her but she was plastered against him. And part of him was glad she was there and in his arms.

"Don't 'Elle' me," she muttered against him.

"Ryder said there are Freaks attacking the gate. That you guys were trapped outside the gate." She pulled away from him, ringing her hands as she worried her bottom lip with her teeth.

Victor sighed and cupped her cheek, he eased her lip out from between her teeth. "I'm fine, Elle. Have you gotten something to eat? How are you feeling?" He tucked a stray hair behind her ear.

They both realized at the same time how quiet the room was and turned to look. The room was occupied by five different Trackers and Kyra. All of whom, starred at Victor and Elle, as if they had never seen them before.

Victor glared at them "What?" he demanded. Wanting to pull Elle behind him, he wasn't sure what they were staring at. His only instinct was to protect Elle.

Kyra was the first to recover. "Um... nothing. I just finished making her eat something. Didn't I, Elle?"

Elle nodded. "I'm feeling much better. We should leave."

"Are you kidding?" Skylar barked with laughter, making him grin around his spilt lip. "Just how do you plan to get around the dozen or so Freaks at the gate sweetheart?"

Victor shoved him. "Don't call her sweetheart."

"Christ above and below. We literally have Freaks at the gate and you have an issue with me calling her sweetheart?" Sky asked.

"Yes, do it again and I'll split your other lip," Victor said.

"Elle?" Skylar looked at Elle as he spoke.

"Don't do this Skylar." Kyra tried to step between the two men. But Ryder grabbed her around the waist and picked her up to pull her back against him.

Victor growled low, Elle looked confused as she looked at Skylar and back at Victor.

"Yes?" Elle looked at Skylar and back at Victor.

"We haven't been introduced," Skylar said holding out his hand. "I am Skylar."

Elle took it and Skylar shook her hand gently. "Nice to meet you."

"The pleasure is all mine," she said with a tentative smile.

"Do you mind if I call you sweetheart?" Sky asked with a devilish smile not releasing her hand.

Elle caught her breath as Victor pulled her back severing their linked hands; she grabbed Victor before he did something stupid. "Um…Elle is fine thank you."

Skylar laughed. "Then Elle it is."

Elle turned from him and back to Victor. "We need to leave. And you promised I could call Helena as soon as we were safe."

"Um Elle," Skylar emphasized her name and Elle turned back to him. "Did you miss the part where we have slavering monsters at the gate? Cause if so I can show you a picture. Falcon, show the girl a picture." He elbowed a large man standing next to him.

Things were getting out of hand; this wasn't the way this was supposed to go. Helena was probably out of her mind with worry, it had been several days since Elle had checked in. This wasn't how this whole thing was supposed to work out.

Elle's mind was going in several different directions at once, and she looked around the room. They were all in danger now because of her. And to make matters worse, Kyra was a Druid. And although she was as tough as nails and an Elemental Enforcer, she was still not immortal. This was dangerous for them all. Her ever present guilt kicked up several notches.

Even with her shields up, Elle could feel the love between Kyra and Ryder. It was like a beacon. Especially when they were in the same room. When they touched, a blue light shined between them, making Elle catch her breath. It was something she had never seen before, and lovely to view. The Gods would never forgive her if she destroyed something like that.

"I need to call Helena," she said around the lump in her throat. The sooner she was able to contact her sister the better. She couldn't put these people in danger.

Kyra stepped forward and offered her a phone. "Here you can use mine. It can't be tracked."

She thanked her and turned to leave. Victor stopped her by placing a hand on her shoulder. "Don't go far." His words should have irritated her. But they didn't. His worry warmed her. She had never had anyone ever worry about her before. It was a novel experience. But she knew she shouldn't get used to it. She gave him a smile and moved down the hall to make her call.

"Elle?" Helena picked up on the first ring.

Elle let out a gasp. "Helena?" It was good to hear her sister's voice. After everything that had happened over the last couple of days, she was sure concern was there.

"Elle, where are you? You were supposed to be here two days ago!" Helena shouted.

"I told you the last time we talked, things weren't going the way I had planned. I had to use the emergency number and call a Reaper. I was munched on by some horned green Freak and had to hide in a graveyard. I was attacked in a motel, then stabbed in the chest on the side of the road." The words tumbled out of her like a damn had been broken.

"My gods, Elle," Helena exhaled. "Where are you now?"

This is where Elle's tongue froze to the roof of her mouth. She had been hours away, now she was days away. Being hidden by Trackers and Druids, Helena's number one rule for Elle was to stay hidden.

When she didn't immediately answer Helena asked again, "Elle, where are you?"

"I'm still with the Reaper," she said avoiding the question. But Helena had known Elle her entire life. "You remember him don't you, the one I accidently sold my soul too?"

"Elle where are you?"

"I believe I am in Illinois," Elle said holding her breath.

Helena let out an audible sigh. "How long until you get here?"

"To the safe house?" Elle asked.

"Elle, how many times do I have to explain you are in danger? I can't keep you safe if you don't get here." Elle wondered, not for the first time, why Helena hadn't come for her herself. But then Helena never did come for her. She sent others to come for her, always had.

"I know, Helena. The situation is out of my hands at the moment," Elle explained. "Why don't you tell me, what the hell is going on. I feel like there's something you're not telling me." Like usual.

"Why would you say that?" Helena barked.

"Because it is usually the case," Elle barked back then bit her lip. It was unlike her to snap at anyone much less Helena.

"When have I ever steered you wrong Elle? Who has taken care of you for the last millennia?" she asked curtly.

Elle felt a tug of irritation when she knew she should feel bad for snapping at her sister. Helena was right. She had been the only one of her siblings to not turn her back on Elle, after she'd been cursed.

"And you would turn on me now? When so much is going wrong?" Irritation layered each word, and Elle did feel horrible now. "After everything I have done for you, Elle. I can't believe you. You would be a mindless slave if it wasn't for me. It's bad enough you let yourself get cursed but now after I warned you about getting out of the cabin. You turn on me?"

"You told me to leave the cabin. It wasn't a warning," Elle argued. "You told me to leave."

She could hear Helena take an outraged inhalation. "A warning," she argued. "Those things were coming to get you. If I hadn't warned you. You would have been a sitting duck just waiting to be grabbed."

"You're kidding right?" Elle asked. She could have made a stand in her cabin. She had a safe room there, weapons, enough food and ammunition and wards to keep her safe for years. "I was safe there."

Helena huffed. "Don't kid yourself, Elle. I need you here with me. Where are you? How soon can you get here?"

Elle felt the lump in her throat sink into her stomach. Who was this woman she was talking too? Was Chaos right? Who were the bad guys in this war?

"I'm safe where I am," Elle said with more conviction then she had felt in years.

"Elle, don't joke with me. This isn't funny." She could almost hear her sister grind her teeth together. "Tell me where you are."

"I told you somewhere in Illinois."

"Dammit, Elle. There is more at stake than your sorry ass in this war," Helena ground out.

"Explain it to me, Helena," Elle pleaded.

"If I thought for half a second you would understand, Elle, I would." Helena said Elle started to cry. "Why do you do that, Helena?"

"What?" Helena bit out.

Elle cried quietly for a minute listening to her sister breathe. "Treat me like such a child?"

"Because you are a child, Elle." And then Helena hung up. Elle pulled the phone away and stood there for a moment, staring at the phone in her hand. Clutching it to her chest, she leaned against the wall and sank to the floor.

She had known her sister felt that way about her, for a long time now, maybe even her entire life. But to hear her say the words were like a knife to her heart. All of her siblings had abandoned her, one at a time. Some rather quickly, after she'd been cursed. Being the eldest, Helena had stayed with her. Finding her hiding places and identities. She hadn't actually seen Helena in several centuries. So in her way Helena had abandoned her as well. Elle sobbed for the loss because she knew it was real now. Elle truly was alone, had no ties to anything or anyone in the world. And the reality of it made her feel so small and insignificant it was over-whelming in its completeness.

And now, she had dragged all of these innocent people into a fight. They could be hurt or possibly killed for no reason, other than being good people. Well she couldn't allow this to happen. She was done hiding. Done being a victim and done being a child and burden on everyone else. Tired of a game she didn't know the rules to. It was time for this shit to end.

Chapter 6

"I'll need your blood and of any of your brothers if you plan to have them come and go through the extra wards," Kyra explained.

Victor nodded watching the door. Elle still hadn't returned and it had been almost twenty minutes. He was starting to get worried.

"Gods, why don't you just go check on her?" Ryder asked.

"She deserves her privacy," Victor said. Turning back to the group.

"She stopped crying if that is what you are worried about," Skylar offered. As he dug into the steak he'd been making on the inside grill. Oh Gods she had been crying. He had refused to listen to the call she had made with her sister. He wanted her to have her privacy but now he wanted to kick himself.

"Yeah her sister is a total bitch by the way," Sky said around his mouth full of steak.

"You're an ass," Victor said and he pushed himself away from the counter.

"We got a problem," Bowen said over the intercom system.

Everyone stopped, and Falcon shot to his feet. "What's the problem now?"

The screen over the table flickered to life showing a color image of the front gate. The monsters stood motionless, which was eerie in itself. But what stopped Victor in his tracks was the image of the woman slowly walking toward the gate.

"Christ on a cross." Falcon swore.

Victor was already running. He couldn't Flash. He couldn't use a Portal. All of his Reaper abilities were on lockdown, because of the damned wards Kyra had put into effect that morning. He screamed in frustration, hoping Kyra or one of the Trackers had something up their sleeves that they could use inside of the wards. Cause if not, he was going to kill them all! He was half way to the gate when Ryder pulled up next to him in his souped up cart, he didn't even slow down as Victor jumped in next to him. "Marlee took off in wolf form and Kyra was able to Shift."

Victor said nothing. He was thankful the Lycan was there and that Kyra was able to Shift.

They heard the commotion of the Freaks, and the fight a second later. The cart skidded to a halt, spitting out gravel as Ryder slammed on the breaks.

Somehow, two of the Freaks had been able to get through the gate.

"What the fuck?" Ryder scrambled from the cart, pulling a gun as he went. Victor knew he wouldn't get a shot off without risking Kyra or Marlee. Who were both in hand to hand combat with a Freak.

Elle lay in the dirt several feet from the gate. Victor let out a guttural roar and ran toward her. Kyra spared him a sad look and he recognized it before he reached her what he would find.

Sightless eyes stared up into the evening sky. "No, no, no. Gods please." He shook her and pulled her into his arms. She'll come back he told himself. But he didn't know for sure. He didn't know if this was the time she wouldn't come back. "What were you doing?" he shook her again. "Come on, Elle. Time to come back." He willed life back into her limbs rubbing her arms. Nothing was happening. And anger permeated him, so deep he couldn't think straight. Leaning down he kissed her forehead and closed her eyes. "I'll be right back sweetheart." He kissed her cold lips and laid her gently on the ground.

He walked calmly over to the fight. Ryder was fighting off the bigger of the two combatants. "Who killed her?" Victor asked.

Kyra side kicked one Freak making it grunt in pain. "This one," she said slightly out of breath. She stepped forward trying to get into position for another blow but Victor's blood boiled over and he grabbed the thing spinning him around.

"Your Aldon's pet, yes?" Its eyes glimmered in acknowledgment. Victor pulled a scythe from his back and sliced a deep groove down the thing's chest.

It barely winced. So he sliced through a bicep leaving his left arm totally useless. Still no noise left its mouth. Victor could see Ryder and Kyra had moved into help Marlee and heard the sound of a gun and knew the other one had been taken care of.

Victor stepped out of the way as the thing swung his right arm out, he ducked and rolled swinging the scythe as it went cleanly, cutting the back of his knees out. He sunk down to its knees with a moan.

Victor was back up on his feet and standing behind him. His breathing hard, he wrapped an arm around his neck. He bent to whisper in the things ear. "You soulless son of a bitch, I will do this to you and all your brothers. As for your master? I will personally take his soul to Lucifer himself." Then he snapped his head from his shoulders and tossed it over the gates and into the dozens of Freaks on the other side.

"How the hell did they get through?" Ryder asked.

"They grabbed an arm" Kyra said. "Touching her was enough. Once they had her they popped through. One let go and charged Marlee the other broke her neck." Kyra turned to Victor. "I…"

Victor waved off Kyra. "She'll be fine."

Kyra had tears in her eyes, and turned back to Ryder. "He's in shock."

But as she said it, Elle took a shuddering deep breath making Kyra yelp in shock. Marlee on the other hand growled and stepped away from the group.

Ryder grabbed his wife and stepped in front of Marlee at the same time. "Gods."

Victor held up his hands. "She is going to convulse, then we need to get her back to the house."

He watched as she did just that, fifteen minutes of pure hell. And he swore it was worse to watch knowing what she was going through.

"We need to do something," Kyra kept saying.

"There is nothing we can do," Victor explained.

Finally, Ryder took Kyra away and put her in the cart. Marlee took off toward the house. The Freaks stood watching, quietly watching. Victor wished he could make them turn away, knowing they would report back to Aldon everything they were seeing.

Finally she stopped convulsing, her bloodshot eyes peeked open. "Victor?" she whispered. Her hand reached out and Victor scrambled over to her. "I need to go to them." She pointed to the monsters. "End this."

"Over my dead body," he growled. Picking her up, he gathered her close. She was already starting to shiver.

"Not worth this," she whispered, tucking her head into the crook of his neck.

"We'll talk about it when you wake up," he promised.

"No." She wiggled. He knew she was trying to break free. But it was so pitiful it was almost laughable. "Nobody else needs to be put in danger."

"What the hell were you thinking?" Victor growled, pulling her closer.

Her shaking was starting and he had to get her in a hot bath or shower fast, her teeth chattered as she looked at him. "Not worth it." She shivered.

"I'll decide that," Victor said climbing into the Buggie. He nodded to Ryder to get them back to the house.

Victor swore. "Can't this damn thing go any faster?"

Ryder gave him and incredulous look, but Kyra reached forward and put a hand on Ryder's shoulder. "We are moving as fast as we can, Victor."

"V—v-victor?" Elle shivered. Victor looked down. Elle's golden eyes glowed in the low light. And her voice was barely a whisper he leaned down so he could hear her. "Why is this happening? I'm not worth this."

Something tore from deep in his chest. "Yes you are." The words were torn from him. He meant every word as he crushed her to his chest. "You are worth it to me. And the next time you try to give up like you just did, I will kill you myself."

She laughed. "No you won't."

He leaned back so he could look back into her eyes. "You don't think so?"

"No." She shook her head. Her body was wracked with such deep shivers her lips were starting to turn purple. "I don't think you like to see me die."

They pulled up to the front of the house and he was saved from having to answer. He jumped from the cart and bounded up the stairs to the house, the door was thrown open. He didn't stop moving until he was in Elle's bathroom. He balanced her on his knee as he turned her bathtub on.

"So cold." She held onto his neck as he adjusted the water temperature.

Kyra was behind him. "What can I do?"

"She needs to be warmed up. Her body is cold," Victor barked. Elle was trying to take off her clothes but her hands weren't working.

"While I'm dead my body stops working. Ttttakes ttttimes for ittt..." She shivered again, stopping what she was saying.

Victor slapped her hands away. "We get the point."

"Do you want me to do this?" Kyra asked pointedly. Looking at Elle now semi dressed and Victor trying to undress her.

A blush crept up Elle's neck and cheeks, but she kept her mouth closed. "I've got this Kyra. Would you mind getting her something to eat? Maybe check with Fiona about how to break this damn curse?"

Kyra nodded closing the door quietly behind her.

Elle visibly relaxed as Kyra left. "There are so many people here. Even with your block their emotions bleed through a little." Her voice was shaky, and her skin was pale.

"Let's get you in the bath before you freeze." Victor steeled himself for the ordeal ahead. He finished undressing her, ignoring how beautiful her ivory skin was.

He picked her up to slip her into the tub, she hissed in pain. "It hurts." She jerked her toes back.

"I know sweetheart. It's just the blood flow coming back." He continued to lower her into the water. She worried her bottom lip as tears flowed down her face in pain. It felt like forever but he finally had her in the water and her head sagged back against the side. She still shivered but after a few minutes it went away. Victor kneeled down next to the tub and brushed her hair from her face. "Please don't do this to me again."

She gave him a weak smile. "You'll get used to it, if you continue to hang out with me."

"How many times, Elle?" He wasn't sure he wanted to know the answer to the question but he had to ask.

That weak smile faded. "Thousands." And she rolled her head away from him, her eyes drifted close. But, not before tears leaked through, to run down her cheeks.

Victor turned her face back to him. "How many of them alone?" Again a question he didn't know if he wanted the answer too.

"I'm tired Victor." Her shaking had stopped, and the glowing in her eyes had died down. Her eyes were a deep chocolate ringed in gold.

He should press her, but the answers weren't something he wanted to here. He trailed his fingers down the side of her face and over her shoulder watching goose bumps raise on her beautiful skin.

"I'm not going anywhere, Elle. I'm here for you." She didn't move or respond to his words, so Victor settled down beside the tub. And rested his head against the side, he would wait until she was ready.

****

The knock on the door startled Victor who jumped to his feet. "What?" he barked before he realized what he was doing.

Kyra peeked in. "It's been an hour. I was wondering if everything was okay?" she whispered.

Victor rubbed the sleep from his eyes. "Shit." He looked at Elle who was sound asleep. He stuck his hand into the water. It was luke warm. "Damn it." He looked around for a towel.

Kyra handed him a warm towel. "Thank you."

She gave him a smile. "I have to admit I've never seen a Reaper so…" He glared at her.

"What?" he asked once he had taken Elle out of the water and wrapped her in the warm towel. Kyra handed him another then wrapped Elle's hair in a third.

"So… un-Reaper-like." She smiled at him.

"Just don't tell my brothers," he said walking into the other room. Elle's bed was turned down, Fiona stood next to the bed. Victor nodded at the older woman.

"How about Celeste?" Kyra asked with a smile.

"Oh, gods. Especially not Celeste," Victor said. Gently laying Elle down in the bed, he turned to Fiona. "What can you do for her?"

"She is weak," Fiona said looking at Elle carefully. "Years of solitude have weakened her further. We need to build her demi-god strength." She reached for a small vial on the table side. "We need to wake her up and get her to drink this. We can mix it with water."

Victor took it from Fiona and smelled it, it smelled horrible. "What is it?"

Fiona nodded. "It will awaken her dormant side." She reassured him. But he was anything but reassured.

"Will it hurt her?" The last thing he wanted was to cause her pain.

"From what Kyra has said, she has been cursed," Fiona said softly. "I cannot remove the curse. However, she seems to have let her demi-god senses go latent. Something she probably didn't even realize she was doing."

Fiona placed a hand on Elle's cheek, her eyes drifted closed for a moment. "Her demi-god abilities are what bring her back. Then they go latent again. If she is to heal completely then we need to strengthen her further."

"She slept for three days the last time she was killed and came back," Victor explained.

Fiona nodded, and shook her head. "She is weak, do you think she could survive doing it so close to the last time?"

Frankly Victor didn't know. "What do we do?"

"Let's wake her up." Fiona started to mix several drops of the liquid in a glass of water and Victor looked at Kyra who motioned to Elle.

She smiled. "Be my guest."

Victor wasn't sure how he was supposed to do this, he leaned down and gently shook Elle. "Elle, wake up."

She didn't even budge. Didn't make a sound. He shook her harder. "Elle. You need to wake up."

Still nothing.

He looked over to Kyra. "Try harder."

Victor sighed. "God's help me." He sat on the edge of the bed and took a hold of Elle by each of her shoulders and shook her. "Elle."

She moaned and her eyes peeked open. "Tired," she muttered.

"You need to wake up." Victor shook her some more.

"No." she swatted at him. "I'm tired, Victor."

"I need you to drink this." He reached for the glass Fiona was holding.

"No." She tried to pull away from him. But he wrapped an arm around her to keep her from lying down. Instead she curled into him, he leaned away from her. "Elle stay awake."

"No. So tired." She yawned.

"Elle I will let you go back to sleep after you drink this." He leaned away from her. Trying to get her to sit up. He looked over at Kyra. "Can you please help me?" he asked.

Kyra was hiding a smile behind her hand. "Yes," she said stepping forward. "Elle?"

Kyra sat down facing Victor and pulled Elle back away from Victor. She was asleep again, and Victor was forced to shake her again. "Elle, wake up."

Her eyes cracked open. "Leave me alone," she snapped.

"Elle, if you drink this I will leave you alone."

She shook her head, dislodging the towel wrapped around her head. Sending her wet hair cascading around her. Kyra gathered it and pulled it aside. Victor had to admit she looked like a fallen angel and he caught his breath as her eyes dropped again. He shook her again. "Elle, you need to stay awake."

"No."

He was getting sick of that word. Dipping his fingers in the water he splashed the cold liquid into her face. Kyra opened her mouth in shock, and Elle's eyes snapped open. "What…"

"Don't make me throw the cup in your face," he threatened.

"You wouldn't dare."

Victor held up the cup. "You just have to drink this and I won't have to throw it in your face."

Elle sighed and held out her hand. Her hand shook slightly and he felt bad for threatening her but wasn't going to fight with her over it.

Kyra steadied Elle's hand as she pressed the glass to her lips. She tipped the glass up and finished it off.

Then tossed the glass back at Victor. It hit him in the chest. "Happy?"

Victor handed the glass back to Fiona, who nodded. "Yes."

"Now can I sleep?" she glowered at Victor who nodded back. But Elle had already pulled out of Kyra's arms and rolled over into the bed and was asleep before her head hit the pillow.

Victor snorted. "I thought you said she would be stronger?"

"We need to get her to drink this at least every hour until she is strong enough to stay awake."

Victor felt like shit. And they needed to do this again? Kyra patted him on the shoulder. "Get some sleep, I'll wake you in an hour."

She turned off the lights as they left. Victor wasn't sure if he should thank her or not. He should go to the Infernos and let Dante know what was going on. He needed to gather his brothers to fight off those Freaks. He should be finding out who the hell Aldon was and why he wanted Elle.

Instead he laid down next to Elle and pulled her into his arms. He feel asleep about as fast as she did.

****

Elle was pretty sure the next time she saw Victor she was going to cause him some serious physical harm. When someone knocked on her bedroom door, she grabbed the shoe she was putting on and threw it at the door.

It cracked open and Kyra peered around. "Was that a come in?" she asked with a smile.

Elle felt horrible. "Sorry, just irritable." Kyra bent down and grabbed Elle's shoe and tossed it back to her.

"I understand. Being woken up every hour and forced to drink that foul liquid would put anyone in a horrible mood." Kyra leaned against the door.

Elle couldn't agree more, but she had to confide she felt better then she had in years. "What is going on this morning?"

"Well figuring out what to do about with those Freaks is at the top of the list," Kyra said.

"I still think we should look at the option of handing me over to them. I mean they might kill me but I'll come back." The thought caused her shivers.

Kyra shook her head. "You can't want to be taken by those things. And we don't have any idea what Aldon wants with you."

"Who is Aldon?"

"The man controlling the Freaks. The master mind behind all the voodoo," Kyra said with a smile.

"Was anyone going to tell me?"

Kyra gave her a strange look. "Actually, I'm surprised Victor hasn't told you already. But those Reapers the Gods themselves don't know what they are thinking."

Elle had to agree with her on that. "Let's go down and get some breakfast. I'm not allowed to cook anymore but I'm sure one of the boys has thrown something together."

"Why aren't you allowed to cook?" Elle asked following Kyra out of her room and down the hall.

"Because she poisoned us one to many times." one of the Trackers she didn't know said, coming through a door, as they passed.

Kyra introduced them. "Elle, this is Bowen. He runs all the electronics and gadgets."

Elle nodded at him, and then looked back at Kyra. "Poisoned?"

"It was an accident," Kyra said in her defense.

Bowen's laughter followed behind them, Kyra glared at him over her shoulder. "It really was."

"The first two times we sure thought it was," Bowen said.

"The first two times?" Elle asked.

"That is why she isn't allowed to cook," Bowen said as he pushed passed them. "Kyra would kill us all with her cooking."

Ryder was the one standing in front of the stove cooking when they came into the kitchen. When he turned and saw Kyra he smiled at the woman and turned back to the stove. Victor immediately stood up from the table.

Elle walked over to him "Who is Aldon?"

"What are you talking about?" He looked past her to Kyra, giving the Elemental a dirty look.

Elle stepped in front of Victor so he had to look at her. "I asked you who Aldon was."

"I have no idea."

Elle felt like punching him in the face, instead she turned on her heels. If he wasn't going to give her the answers she wanted she would get them herself.

"Where the hell are you going?" he demanded.

"To find out what is going on?" she said over her shoulder.

"And where do you think you will get your answers?"

She stopped and turned on him. "I'm pretty sure those things at the gate will be more than happy to answer my questions."

"Did you just growl at me?" she was so stunned she was frozen in her tracks. Victor grabbed her arm and forced her over to the table and into a seat.

"You are not going back out there. You are going to sit here and eat breakfast." She pushed him away.

"Don't you dare start treating me like a child." Elle slapped at his hands and tried to rise from the table.

"Then don't act like one," Victor snapped. "You need to build your strength. Or you won't be able to fight off those things and find out what the hell Aldon is."

Elle stopped pushing at him. "You don't know what Aldon is?"

Victor rolled his eyes and sighed. "No, now will you eat?"

"Well why didn't you just say so in the first place? Why do you always have to make everything so damn difficult?" she reached past him to the plate of eggs Ryder had just put down on the table. She smiled at the Tracker and dished some onto her plate.

"I'm difficult?" Victor looked at her and then to Ryder.

"Of course you are," Elle said taking a bite out of a piece of toast Bowen had handed her. She smiled at him, as well. Skylar loaded some bacon onto her plate, while a different tracker she didn't know, loaded her plate with potatoes. Kyra handed her a glass of orange juice. "You never give me all the details. Why don't you start with those?"

"Yes, why don't you?" Skylar asked.

"Shut it," Victor snarled at the Tracker.

"Be nice." Elle waved her fork at Victor as she ate. She smiled at Skylar. "What is the plan?"

"First on the list is find out how those damn things are tracking you. And then find out who Aldon is," Victor snarled.

"Don't forget I need your blood," Kyra said.

"Why do you need his blood?" Elle thought it a morbid request over breakfast.

"The wards won't allow him in or out. If he is going to be able to Flash in and out of the wards, or any of his kin, I will need their blood as well." Elle nodded. It made sense, but she didn't know if she liked the thought of Victor leaving her, and it must have showed in her eyes because Victor immediately sat down next to her. The irritation he had been showing her all morning instantly gone.

"I have to return to the Infernos to report to Dante what is going on. As well as bring some of my brothers back to help fight. I promise not to be gone long." He reached under the table to squeeze her clenched fists.

"I have some questions." A large Tracker said, striding into the kitchen. He was easily the largest of them all. Long dark hair brushed his shoulders, and dark green eyes pierced her with cold intent. She couldn't help the shiver running down her spine.

Victor squeezed her hands again. "Don't let Falcon intimidate you. He thrives on scaring people."

"We are running out of time." Falcon shoved Victor out of the way, and sat down across from Elle at the table. "You may continue eating. How are they tracking you?" he demanded.

Elle felt her mouth sag open. Victor reached over and closed it with the press of his index finger on her chin. She pulled away from him. Then shook her head. "I don't know."

She shoved more eggs into her mouth as Falcon glared at her.

"You have to know, you just don't know you know." He tapped a pen on a pad of paper. "Where have you lived lately?"

She told Falcon about living up and down the east coast, for the last couple of hundred years. Of settling in Maine, the last sixty years or so. About her secluded little cabin in the mountains there. How she didn't have neighbors for miles. She didn't mention she could let down her walls. Her wards kept her safe from mortals and Others.

"Doesn't make sense," Falcon said gruffly. "There is nothing about you that would interest anyone."

"Thanks," Elle said, pushing the rest of her breakfast away.

Falcon huffed. "No offense, but you just aren't a person of interest."

"I wouldn't say that," Kyra said. "She is a demi-god after all. They as a race are very interesting."

"A cursed demi-god," Falcon offered just as disgusted as before.

"Again thank you," Elle said.

Falcon shook his head. "Look sweetheart, if you are going to spend any time with us, you are going to have to get a little thicker skin. I call it like it is. You are neither interesting nor have anything worth taking. I'm not sure I would cross the street to sniff your skirts."

"Um..." had he just insulted her?

Victor confirmed her thought by leaning back and crossing his arms over his chest. "What's your point Falcon?"

"There is more to this than meets the eye. We don't have all the pieces and I don't like playing the game without all the rules." With that he stood and walked out of the room. "I'm going to kill something," he said over his shoulder. The rest of the Trackers followed him, obviously liking the idea.

Victor snorted. "This is my queue to go to the Infernos." He turned to Elle. "You stay out of trouble."

Elle stood with him. "And exactly what am I supposed to do?"

"Actually." Kyra drew the word out. "Fiona would like to speak with you."

"Fiona?" Elle wasn't sure she wanted to know who that was.

"Fiona is a Druid High Priestess. She is who made the tonic that helped you heal, and she would dearly love to have the opportunity to speak with you about the curse you received." Kyra explained.

"Received?" Elle asked. "You say it like it was a gift."

Kyra nodded. "It's all the way you look it at it, Elle. How you decide to perceive it. How you choose to live your life, now that you have it."

Elle felt hot anger rise from deep in her stomach. "Do you know what it feels like to die, Kyra? What the hand of death feels like?"

"Yes," Kyra said without blinking, taking Elle by surprise. Taken aback, Elle just stood there for a moment.

"May I?" Victor looked at Kyra who nodded. "Kyra accidently opened a Pandora's Box and for a time was touched by Dante."

Kyra waved off Victor's words, but it didn't make Elle feel any better. "It's over and done with, but don't expect Ryder to ever forgive Dante. Anyway, I could never hope to understand what you go through, Elle. And what the horrible Druid did to you was unthinkable and I'm sorry for it. But let us see what we can do to help you."

Elle doubted very much they could do anything, but they had made her feel better so talking to them wouldn't hurt. "Fine."

"Wonderful. First I need Victor's blood. Then Fiona," Kyra said. The darkness Elle saw in her eyes faded as quickly as it had come.

"I'll bring her out in a minute," Victor said to Kyra.

As soon as they were alone Elle couldn't help herself. "Do you really trust these people?"

"They are not my family. But they will do," Victor admitted.

"What the hell does that mean?" Elle asked.

He cupped her face so he could look into her eyes and she felt so small. "It means, that I can't stand the thought of leaving you alone. But, if I don't go back to the Infernos and check in, Dante may rip me from this plane without my consent. And trust me that is a very unpleasant experience."

"What's it like in the Infernos?" she couldn't help but ask.

"Home," he whispered.

"That doesn't answer my question."

"It's a feeling." He released her and placed a hand just below her collar bone. "Just here, a warmth that seeps into your soul. Warms you from the inside out. Makes you heavy and light all at the same time because you know it is where you truly belong. Then the colors burst before you like an artist's palette exploding, oranges, reds, yellows, purples and blues and black flowing through each other to the point it's almost painful to watch but you can't look away. Because you know if you look away you'll miss the most amazing thing you'll ever see."

"The Infernos are a contradiction, Elle." His voice caressed the skin of her cheek. "It is the most beautiful and horrible thing you will ever see in all your existence."

She turned into him, so his lips brushed against her jaw. And they both caught their breath. "Why?"

"One moment you will see colors race across the sky that will take your breath away." He ran his thumb along her collarbone and Elle leaned toward him farther until his lips connected with hers. Victor moaned, and pressed closer capturing her lips with his. Elle didn't think she had ever been kissed like this before. Colors cascaded through her brain as Victor deepened the kiss.

As his lips pressed hers opened, reds, oranges, pinks and purples flooded her brain as his tongue swept into her mouth. He tasted of exotic forbidden fruit. And she soaked it deep into her bones. Elle wrapped her arms around Victor sinking into him, anchoring herself to him. She felt safe this close to him and didn't want to let go. How had she come to trust him, this Reaper, in so short a time?

Elle pressed herself closer to Victor wanting the kiss to go on forever. Wishing it would erase all the darkness surrounding them. She wanted nothing more than to drown in those colors Victor painted of the Infernos, wanted to drown in Victor. But she knew this was fleeting, he was a Reaper and her life was limited to snatches of life and death. One moment here, and then those horrible bone-breaking and soul-stealing moments of returning.

Elle forced herself to break the contact and step back, the images he created turning to shadows and she choked them down barely holding back the urge to cry out.

"You make the Infernos seem like a beautiful place, when it is filled with the souls of the damned," she accused.

Victor's eyes turned cold, and his hands fisted at his sides as he released her. "Deserving of their fates, Elle, never forget, we don't just grab people from the mortal plane willey nilly."

She needed to put distance between them even if it hurt. She snorted. "You've never taken a soul by accident?"

"Never," he said without hesitation. "I rule over Violence, Elle. The souls there are black and tortured and more than deserving of their fates. If anything they should be sent to the pits of Hell."

Elle shivered at the thought. "And who does your collection while you babysit me?"

"My Abda. They are bonded servants to the Reapers, they help in the collection. After all, we cannot be everywhere at once. There are also the Death Ringers." That really had Elle shivering. She had encountered one of those before. Small little creatures flittered in and out touching mortals here and there marking them for death. They moved with the speed of light and if you saw them it was a miracle or a seriously bad omen.

"You've seen a Ringer before?" Victor asked.

"Only once," she admitted.

"For you?"

Elle shook her head. "No. It was during one of the plagues, I was dying. Or I might have been coming back. I don't remember. But it was between." She shuddered. Victor reached for her but she stepped away from him. The thing had been small, but human looking with long white hair. Long flowing robes, it had jumped from person to person not actually touching everyone but the people it did touch, Elle could see started to breathe differently and she had known without being told they were dying.

A dark figured had stood in the shadows. Elle had refused to look deeply into the shadows at that one figure. She hadn't wanted to look, because she had been terrified to. Afraid if she looked into the eyes of a Reaper and she died if her soul was taken she would never find her body again and therefore never be reborn again. Or whatever it was that happened to her that brought her back to life when she died and came back. But the figure in the shadows hadn't moved when people had died. And light didn't shine for them either.

Elle had prayed for them hoping they had gotten where they had been meant to go.

"All souls end up where they are meant to be Elle," Victor reassured her.

"Can you read my mind?" she accused him.

Victor snorted. "Of course not."

She wasn't sure she believed him. He often said or answered questions she had before she even knew she was asking them. "Don't you have somewhere you should be?"

"Yes, in point of fact, I do. Do you have your walls up?" He asked. Even though he shouldn't care, he did.

She rolled her eyes. "Yes."

"Humor me," he growled. "I don't know how long I will be gone."

"Just go already." She brushed past him. "I'm sure I will survive while you are gone. Believe it or not, I was able to keep myself alive, long before you came along."

"Really because the last couple of days were such a stellar example of your ability to take care of yourself," he shot at her.

She continued walking down the hall, she was not going to let him goad her into an argument.

"And if I recall, it was you that asked for my help. You called me remember? You essentially, begged me for my help," he reminded her. "And, if it wasn't for me, you'd be fodder for Aldon, and his pets. And he would be doing gods only knows what to you! I mean, each time they've gotten their meaty paws on you, they have killed you!" he ended. Bellowing the last words.

She saw red and turned on him; he was so close to her, she ran into him. She pushed him away. "You are an overbearing asshole. You realize that, don't you? If I recall I begged, pleaded for you to leave. I ran away from you, twice. This isn't your fight," she screamed back.

"You made it my fight when you summoned me," Victor shouted back.

"I unsummon you." Elle dusted her hands off. "Problem solved. Go back to the Infernos, back to your life. I don't want you here anymore. "

His eyes turned nearly black and he walked away from her. Elle just stood there unable to believe he had walked away from her without saying a word. The moment he left, she felt the crushing wave of emotions settle around her. Thank the gods her internal wards were strong enough to hold them back.

"He didn't even say goodbye," she whispered to herself, and tears rose up to choke her. She swallowed past the lump and the tightness in her chest. She suddenly felt alone and looked around not sure exactly what she was supposed to do or where she was supposed to go. She didn't know these people. Didn't know what they expected from her? She was a burden on them, and she had put them all in danger.

It wasn't just the emotions crushing down on her; it was the weight of the lives here as well. And, she could blame it all on Victor. When next she saw him she was going to kick his ass. If he came back. She wasn't sure he would after the way she had just treated him.

Elle lowered herself to the floor, and rested her chin on her knees. It was a horrible position she was in and she had no idea what she was going to do. And right then, she didn't even know who she could trust. It was all she could do to hold back the tears.

That was exactly where Kyra found her, like a child, sitting on the floor trying not to cry.

"Hi." She said it quietly as if speaking too loudly would frighten Elle.

Elle looked up at her, noticing how strong Kyra looked. As a Druid, and an Elemental Enforcer Kyra must have her shit together. It only made Elle feel that much more insignificant. "Hi."

"I know things look pretty bleak, but I'm sure we will come up with a solution," she offered.

Elle couldn't stop the hysterical burst of laughter that came tumbling out. "Are you being serious?" she asked.

Kyra lifted her shoulders in a casual shrug. "I've seen worse. Been in worse circumstances." Kyra offered Elle a hand. "Let's see what Fiona has to say."

Elle really didn't have any options open to her so she took Kyra's hand and followed her down the hallway, and down a flight of stairs. When they came to a large doorway made of iron Elle stopped in her tracks. "Um, so not going to happen."

She wasn't about to willingly go into a room of iron, she could be trapped in there.

Kyra opened the door and showed her the room; it was well lit lined with rows and rows of bookshelves as far as the eye could see. The actual size of the room was undetermined because it was so large and packed with so much stuff Elle couldn't see where it ended. Tables cluttered with items, pots, and books and so many different items she couldn't begin to put names to them.

It looked like a treasure trove of old and new things. But she still wasn't setting foot in there. An old woman, with salt and pepper hair hanging to her waist, walked around a corner. A book in one hand and a smoking pot of incense in the other.

Elle felt a little dizzy looking at her. She tried not to prejudge the Druid, but couldn't help it. The last powerful Druid she had had contact with, cursed her. Elle could feel the power practically radiating off this woman. She took a few steps back. "Ah there she is," Kyra said stepping into the room. "Fiona I have brought Elle to meet you."

Fiona looked up with soft brown eyes. She smiled at Elle. It reminded her of a warm fire and comforted her immediately. Which Elle thought was odd. Then it struck her. She had a spell of some kind to make her feel comfortable. It irritated her and put her on edge. Which was at odds with how comforted she felt at the same time.

"Please come in, come in. I am so happy to see you up and moving around. I was very worried about you," Fiona said putting down the book and pot she was holding.

Elle moved to the doorway but still didn't cross the threshold. "I'm not sure I want to."

Fiona laughed quietly. "Oh I totally understand. It being iron and all, but I can assure you the wards on this room are against darkness only and it bars it from entering." She smiled and beckoned Elle in.

"Uh… You do realize a dark Druid cursed me right?" she asked. "Are you sure the wards against the darkness won't attack me on that level? I mean what is it supposed to do against darkness?"

"Render it lifeless of course." Fiona said it as if she was giving her an update on the weather.

"Yeah I've already died twice this week. Can we go upstairs?" Elle asked stepping away from the door.

Fiona nodded. "You do have a point," Fiona said moving toward the door. "However, I would love to try it out."

Elle shook her head. "Maybe another day."

Fiona took her arm as she moved through the door. "Of course. Let's go upstairs and have a cup of tea."

Kyra followed behind her. "Don't let her kindness fool you. She's a shark."

Elle stumbled at Kyra's words, but Fiona patted her arm. "Don't let Kyra worry you. I'm a lamb, she just thinks that because I helped to train her."

Kyra laughed. "That and she has threatened to turn me into a frog."

Elle couldn't stop herself from laughing. Druids were many things but workers for magic like that they were not. "That I would like to see."

"I'm sure I could find something in a book somewhere," Fiona said as they made their way into a large living room.

"I'll go get the tea," Kyra offered.

Fiona sat in an overstuffed chair and motioned for Elle to take another chair close to her. Elle looked at the window. "Shouldn't we be out fighting those things?"

Fiona shook her head. "No. The brothers are probably having the time of their lives out there, killing the beasts at the gates. They may bluster and complain but they live for this type of thing."

"There will just be more were they came from," Elle said sadly. It broke her heart. The last thing she wanted, was to think more and more monsters would appear and one of them might get hurt.

Her feelings must have been written on her face. "Don't worry about them. They fight like a well-oiled machine when they are together. Why don't you tell me how you got cursed?"

Elle chewed her bottom lip, she hadn't talked about it for so long. Had kept everything about her curse locked down so tight she was almost afraid to talk about it.

"Is talking about it hard?" Fiona asked.

Elle laughed a little. "I have forced myself to not talk about it so long it feels weird to do so."

Fiona nodded and leaned back looking like she had all the time in the world.

Elle sorted through her memories. "It was so long ago," she started. "Back when the world was such a different place, when the Gods had rule over a landscape, fought for their lands and their people."

"When I was brought into being during the great reign of the Gods, when Atlantis was still new and the Gods played at being Gods, I was one of many demi-gods; hundreds tossed among the mortals as play things. When demi gods were both mortal and immortal." She shivered. "I was able to control emotions, I banded with Helena who was deified by the gods and mortals because of her beauty, and Tiffany for her golden hair. And Others, so many Others. We thought ourselves above the laws of man of man because of all the demi gods we were immortal, we held sway of even the demi gods. Not even some of the children of the gods were immortal." Elle stopped to wipe tears from her face, she didn't realize she still held so much emotion over the situation, she hadn't thought of Tiffany and the others for so long.

"We were cursed originally by the Gods because we felt we were not as strong as the gods themselves and cursed to roam the mortal plane. When the mortals realized the Gods had abandoned us, and realized they could harness our gifts for their own means we became a plague to ourselves. The Gods hunted use. Destroying us, before we became a weapon against them. The mortals and Others hunted us to use against the Gods." She shivered. "I was caught in a war, when a Dark Druid found me and cursed me."

This was the part she dreaded, and she thanked the Gods when Kyra interrupted by bringing in a tray of tea. She poured it for the three of them. Elle went to pick up her tea, but her hands shook so much she nearly spilled the tea all over herself. She put the tea down and smiled at the two women, taking several deep breaths.

Fiona asked her to continue her story. Elle looked at her, dreading what was to come. "Please understand I am not proud of who I was then. The demi-gods then and some now are selfish and horrible creatures. This is not who I am now, I have learned so much since then." She would pay for the rest of her existence for what had transpired then. And it made her sick to think of what happened.

Fiona gently patted her hand. "We understand things might have been done different then.

Elle shook her head. "No. You don't understand," she said. "I was cursed for a reason. When it came down to a push and shove situation, I sacrificed mortals, to save myself." Kyra jumped up. Elle wouldn't blame her if she threw her out of her house. Fiona gave Kyra a pointed look.

"Let her explain. "Fiona said.

"How many?" Kyra asked.

Elle was breathing heavy, and her hands were fisted in her lap. And lights were flashing in her vision. "It was a contingent of soldiers. About eighty men. They had been sent by a lord who thought to imprison me and my brothers and sisters. They were simple soldiers hired by a petty lord who just wanted to control the demi-gods."

"And what of your brothers and sisters?" Kyra asked roughly. "Why did none of them dirty their hands?"

Elle looked at Kyra. "Chaos…" Elle started. "He… usually helped me. Only he had already been caught years before. The others abilities had lain in other directions. But, in using ones emotions, I had the ability to turn them against each other. So, it was up to me to keep the group safe. So when they moved in to attack…I turned them against one another."

It had been an ambush. Absolutely no warning. Taken completely by surprise, Elle hadn't thought, she had just reacted. Before she knew it, the men had turned on themselves and killed one other. She had just stood there, in the early morning light, while her brothers and sisters had stood watching the fighting. Cheering them on, until no one remained. It had made her sick. She had stumbled into the bushes and thrown up.

Helena had pulled her out of the bushes and hugged her telling her how wonderful she was. But Elle hadn't felt wonderful, and all the power she had over the mortals felt like a burden for the first time in her life. And she understood why the gods had abandoned them from the heavens. However, none of them expected the flurry from the dark druid, who swept through their camp as dusk.

"We should have left, but we were cocky demi-gods," Elle said shaking her head. "We won the battle. We thought we had at least a couple of day's grace. She showed up that night as soon as the sun set, right at twilight."

"Did she give you her name?" Fiona asked in a whisper.

"No," Elle whispered back. "One moment, I was sitting before the fire. The next, the fire was banked and I was floating above it. My brothers and sisters scattered, like leaves in the wind. I have never seen a power like hers before or since."

Fiona sucked in a ragged breath. "I was stripped of my clothes, as the woman threw back her cloak. I only knew she was a druid by the markings on her exposed skin. Her eyes were black as pitch and her hair was white and hung nearly to the dirt. She pulled a dirk from her waist and sliced at both my wrists, and my ankles. Then she collected my blood and used it to painted symbols on my skin. The entire time she chanted in an old language even the gods did not understand. Then she took a burning stick from the fire and drew symbols in the dirt. The entire time my body was suspended over the fire. My siblings fought against an inviable wall she had constructed around the fire and the two of us. When she was done she looked at me, her eyes black. And spoke, "Today you killed without remorse without thought. You used your infinite power to kill innocence. You cared not who you erased from this plane. Mortals that had families, not in league with the filthy lords you are at war with. Only simple men, soldiers for hire. You killed without thinking." She screeched. "Now you will live the life of a mortal, the mortals you take for granted. And die as a mortal will. I turn your emotions back on you. Feel that which you have forced on others without remorse. Die the death of the mortal loop."

Fiona visibly shivered. "You really pissed someone off."

"Yes." Elle wrapped her arms around herself and swallowed past the lump in her throat and shivered. And wondered how many more times she would die and hear those words echoing in her head?

She had crashed to the ground then. The crazed druid then grabbed her by the head, still smiling and slashed her throat. Elle had bled out and died for the first time. Each and every time she died, it was the last one she experienced before she came back. So when she did come back, it was the freshest in her mind. Those black eyes, held so much hatred and knowledge she would never in any amount of life times be able to correct that wrong. Those lives she had taken that night. She would never be able to redeem for the souls lost on that night.

It was what had separated her brothers and sisters, what had been the downfall of them all. Why they had ultimately been scattered to the four winds. Why she was now alone in the world. And now she was being hunted by gods only knew what?

"I had hoped by hearing what had happened there might be a way to turn this curse around but it was imprinted in blood and fire," Fiona said shaking her head.

"Meaning nearly unbreakable," Kyra said shaking her head.

"At least you said nearly," Elle said with a sad laugh.

Fiona gave her a sad smile. "Yes, she could have frozen it into you after it was done. And then it would be unbreakable."

"No I haven't had anything frozen into me before," Elle said.

"Well then let's worry about the other problem," Fiona said standing.

"Getting your strength back." Fiona said, giving her a gentle smile.

Elle grimaced. "You aren't going to make me drink more of that horrible tonic are you?"

Fiona chuckled, "No of course not. But I will tell you that drinking it will help heal. When you die, the only thing bringing you back is your demi-god heritage. And it goes into over-drive to bring you back. The tonic I gave you should help you recover faster. But you really should get more in touch with your demi-god side."

Elle had no idea what Fiona was a talking about, and it must have showed on her face, because, Fiona shook her head. "Don't you remember what it felt like to be a demi-god Elle?"

Elle shook her head. "No, it's been so long. And the thought of being a demi-god again makes my stomach hurt."

Fiona reached forward and patted her hand, "Well, you need to get in touch with your demi-god side again it's dormant but the stronger it is the healthier you will become."

"I'm pretty sure the dark druid killed the demi-god in me." Elle said.

Fiona shook her head, "You will always be a demi-god Elle. Nothing can take that away from you. No spell can change that, it's still inside of you. It's what brings you back each time you die. So it's there."

Elle wasn't so sure.

"It's something to think about." Fiona said with utter assurance. "But why don't we think about something else."

Elle snorted. "And that would be?"

"Why, the Freaks at the gate of course."

Elle moaned, and flung herself back in her chair covering her face with her hands. Fiona and Kyra both laughed.

"Isn't there any good news?" she muttered.

"Afraid not." Kyra laughed.

Chapter 7

"There doesn't seem to be any new information," Dante said, steepeling his fingers under his chin.

Victor shrugged. "More questions than answers."

"Christian." Dante motioned to Victor's brother who was standing back, Christian now stepped forward. "I want to study them, bring me several and put them in the catacombs. Take whoever you need."

Christian smiled and nodded at Victor before disappearing. "Do you think bringing those things here is a good idea?"

"Who is behind the attempts on the demi-god?" Dante asked ignoring Victor's question.

"He calls himself Aldon," was the only thing Victor had to offer.

"What species is he?" Dante demanded.

"Unknown." And driving Victor batshit.

"Do you have any information that is helpful?" Dante asked. Victor could see a vein throb in Dante's temple and knew his father was far more irritated then he let on. Victor would be better off treading very carefully.

"I apologize, father. However, there is no information at the moment. I am working with the Trackers to get answers."

Dante flew from his chair sending the large heavy throne soaring back into the recesses of the room. "The Trackers? Those would be the Species that hate us correct?" he bellowed.

Victor held his ground. "Yes, however, they hate us less than a significant number of other creatures. I trust them to keep Elle safe."

"Elle, is it?" Dante asked his voice dropping to a deceptively quiet tone.

This time Victor's ire was pricked. "What would you have me call her, Dante?"

"I care very little for her safety, what I care about is what the Tribunal is doing," Dante said obviously irritated with Victor. "Don't get overly involved with the female. There is a war brewing and I need you to be prepared to fight. Will she be a problem?"

A cold chill wrapped around Victor's spine. "No."

Dante watched him closely. "She is not our problem, Victor. Nor is she one of use. Do not forget, were your loyalties lie. She may have used the Blood Call, but you didn't Blood Rite it. No matter what you tell her."

Victor swallowed past the argument he wanted to scream at Dante. He needed to go back to the cemetery and add his blood to hers. It was the only way he could tie Elle to him permanently. Turn her call from just a 'call' into the soul claiming he claimed had already happened. The moment Dante released him he was going to do just that. He couldn't afford to lose her now.

Victor nodded to Dante's words but held his tongue not sure if he was able to speak at the moment. Elle was his responsibility no matter what Dante said. Dante had made her his responsibility when he had sent him to her and Victor wasn't about to walk away from her.

"Find out who Aldon is, and who is controlling him. I am sure it is the Tribunal. As soon as you have the information we can destroy him," Dante said without feeling.

"What about Elle?" Victor asked.

Dante looked at Victor. "Does it matter?"

"Yes." The word slipped out before Victor could stop it.

"Why?"

"She is alone, Dante." Victor couldn't help tell him.

"She is a cursed demi-god. She will remain a cursed demi-god, and not our problem. Don't let her get to you." Dante moved down his dais, and toward Victor. "In all your life, I have never seen this type of weakness in you before."

Victor fisted his hands. "And what weakness is that Dante?"

"Your angel side," Dante said quietly. "Don't force my hand Victor. Don't make her the problem, she is a means to an end. Find out why the Tribunal is using her, who and what Aldon is. And then walk away."

"She is more than just a means to an end, Dante," Victor argued.

Dante backhanded him, sending Victor skidding across the floor and slamming against the solid stone wall. Dante was there to grab him by the shirt front. He pulled him up and slammed him against the wall, rattling Victor from head to toe.

"Don't be an idiot." He slammed him against the wall again, making Victor see stars. "She is a female, and not one of us. There is a war starting and you are thinking with your cock? We are still down a Reaper, and you are worried about a cursed demi-god?" he asked his voice dropping to a near whisper. "They were hunted down, and sent into hiding or wiped off the mortal plane for a reason."

He dropped Victor, who spat out blood and wiped it away with the back of his hand. "Get out of my sight!" Dante spat. Victor pulled himself up and rolled his shoulders. "Pull your head out of your ass, Victor." Dante said, as Victor walked away.

****

Victor Flashed to the cemetery, it was dark and he let the darkness surround him. He breathed deeply of the cool night air. The Infernos were his home. But after spending the last several days on the mortal plane, he had grown accustomed to the heavy feeling of being here.

He accustomed it to being with Elle, and new he would be with her soon. Walking through the iron gates of the old cemetery he felt the small kick of the hallowed prayers protecting the cemetery. He bent to the headstones where he had found Elle the first night.

And swore; it was missing. The dirt was dark and disturbed, and Victor knew only one person who would have taken it. He wanted to go directly back to the Infernos and confront his father. But he couldn't do so without showing Dante how much he cared for Elle and doing so would put Elle in danger, and she was already in danger. Putting her in the crosshairs of the ruler of the Infernos was just cruel. He would deal with Dante later.

Swearing, Victor stood and left the cemetery. This issue was far from over. At least Elle still believed her soul belonged to him. As long as she believed it, it was all that mattered. Victor wanted to kill something as he Flashed back into the Staten's kitchen. Ryder, Lykar and Skylar were in the kitchen laughing.

"Something funny?" He asked, looking at the clock and noting it was 3am.

"Besides the fact that you look like shit?" Skylar asked.

"Fuck you," Victor snapped at him.

Ryder snorted and pushed a plate toward Victor. It was loaded down with steak and potatoes. "You look like you could use this more than I could."

Victor looked from the plate and back to the Tracker. "Thanks."

Ryder just nodded. "Well?" Victor asked as he dug into the food.

"We just came in from our watch," Ryder explained. Telling Victor about what they had been up to since Victor had left. They had burned all the bodies and no other monsters had appeared which they thought was really weird, now they were taking turns in two and threes to watch the front gate and do perimeter walks.

"Christian showed up this afternoon to take some of those things back with him," Lykar said.

Victor finished off the food and pushed the plate away. "Was there anything left?"

"Just one," Sky said with pride. "He was lucky to get his hands on it. Had to fight off Falcon for it too. Falcon was pissed as all hell about it too. Christian owes him a kill."

"You Trackers are blood thirsty bastards you know that?" Victor said, standing he put his plate in the sink. All he wanted was to check on Elle, the brothers laughed behind him like what he said had been a compliment. "Anything else?"

"Nope, we had too much fun killing them then waited to hear back from you," Ryder said joining him as he left the kitchen. "Now I'm tired I just want my woman, get some sleep, and we can start again in the morning."

They were at the bottom of the stairs when Victor felt Christian call him. "My brothers are calling me." He reached into his pocket and pulled out several vials of blood and handed them to Ryder. "Can you give these to Kyra, so my brothers can Flash in? I'm going to check on Elle."

Ryder nodded. Victor jogged up the stairs to just look in on her. What he wouldn't give to just climb in the bed with her and grab a couple hours of sleep. But when he felt his brother, Christian Flash in, he knew that wasn't going to happen.

"We have a problem." Christian announced as Victor came back down the stairs.

"Do you want to get the brothers together?" Victor said to Ryder.

"Did I say this was information for the Trackers?" Christian asked Victor.

Victor rolled his eyes when Ryder growled low. "We are staying here, and any information you have for me, I am sharing with them."

Christian snorted. "That's stupid. We can leave," he offered.

"Elle is safe here," Victor told him when Ryder walked away to gather the other Trackers.

"I don't give a shit about the demi-god," Christian added. "And Dante isn't happy about your present interest in her either."

Victor turned on his brother. "And where is it that you stand, brother?"

Christian gave Victor a long look his head tilting to the side just slightly. "The reason war is threatening is because we have strayed from the old ways. If we had stayed within the Infernos, do you honestly think we would be at war with the Tribunal?"

Victor wanted to slam a fist into Christians face; he couldn't believe his brother was saying these things. He would have bet his brothers would have stood with him.

"However, I stand with you." Victor felt himself go lax with shock. "You are my brother and I will stand with you till the end no matter what. Whoever it is, be it the Tribunal, or someone else. They will regret picking a fight with the Reapers," Christian finished extending his hand and arm to Victor.

Victor grabbed Christian by the forearm and pulled Christian close. "We could not stay in the Infernos forever Christian. Whether it was ruling there or hiding, it is time to come out of the shadows. Time to take a stand among the Others."

Christian nodded. "So you want to start with this demi-god? A cursed little demi-god who can't keep herself alive? You couldn't go for a demi-god with a little more power? Someone maybe Dante would approve of?"

"Elle. Her name is Elle," Victor told him. It didn't matter what Dante said. He was going to keep her safe. He would deal with Dante, and the consequences be damned.

"Whatever," Christian said shaking his head. "You realize you are playing with fire don't you? And pissing Dante off in the process?"

Victor nodded and followed Ryder and the other Trackers back down the hall and into the dining room where there was a large dining table that had seen better days. And had been glued and nailed back together.

There were six trackers in residence, Falcon, Bowen, Ryder, Skylar, Lykar, and Kean then Christian, and Victor.

"Well?" Victor asked.

"Dante took the specimen of the dead Freak. It has a mix of Mortal, and Other DNA," Christian said.

"Duh," Skylar said. "Tell us something we don't know."

"Is it possible for you to shut up for five minutes?" Christian asked turning to Skylar.

"No," Skylar said leaning back in his chair he crossed his arms over his chest.

Christian pushed himself up and Victor had to stop Christian from leaping from his seat and attacking the Tracker. "Just continue."

Christian leaned forward and looked at Skylar. "You and me?" Christian said his voice quieting. "We are going to have a serious disagreement."

Skylar gave him a two-finger salute. Victor just let it go, knowing at this point it was between the two of them.

"The Other DNA is from a dead race," Christian said to the group.

"Not so dead if they were just outside of our gates," Falcon said leaning forward he folded his hands on the table.

"Well don't keep us in suspense. What dead race?" Ryder asked.

Christian turned to Victor. "The Sons of Adam."

Victor laughed, he couldn't help it. "The Sons of Adam?" he asked.

Christian nodded. "It is of course been mutilated into something horrible. I would assume this Aldon would be a pure specimen."

"The Sons of Adam?" Falcon asked from his seat. Causing Victor and Christian to both turn and look at him. "How is that even possible?"

"Okay," Bowen said putting his hands on the table he got everyone's attention. "What exactly do we know of the Sons of Adam?" he asked.

Victor snorted again. "They claim to be the fathers of mortal man. They are capable of Magik and very hard to kill. Very ritualistic, they go through a horrible ritual of having a rib removed when they come of age to prove they are worthy. Prime goal in life is procreation; with the life span of a mortal, which is something that irritates them to no end. And until five minutes ago, they were said to have died out."

"They mated with the Daughters of Eve to keep their line pure for the royal house," Falcon mentioned. "So if the Sons of Adam are still around I would assume the Daughters of Eve are as well."

"Okay so now we know what we are dealing with, now what?" Bowen asked the group.

"Why?" Falcon asked. "Why would the Sons of Adam want Elle? Why after being in hiding for Gods only know how long, would they risk their necks to come out now?"

The questions left everyone at the table silent. The answer hit Victor like a punch to the gut. "Mother of the Gods." He felt the air sucked from him lungs. "Tell me this is impossible." Victor looked around the room desperate for someone to give him another answer then the one he had come up with.

"He wants to mate with her?" Bowen said

Victor growled, startling everyone in the room including himself. "Over my dead body."

Bowen stood and looked at the group. "Umm…So now would be my opportunity to throw a wrench into the mix."

Victor just wanted to kill something and he growled letting the group know exactly how he felt.

Bowen gave him a smile. "So now we know why Aldon wants her, would you like to know why the Tribunal has a hard on for you girlfriend?"

Victor snarled something unpleasant. "I'm not really in the mood right now Bowen, would you just mind telling us what you found?"

Bowen laughed, what was with these Trackers and their sick sense of humor. "I found an extra protein base in Elle's blood work. In fact she had such a high protein base I sent it over to X to have him confirm it for me."

Victor shook his head and looked over to Christian. "It's like he is almost speaking English."

Christian snorted, but didn't say anything else.

Bowen slapped the table. "Yo, Reaper man. She has an enzyme in her blood. That curse she has, that brings her back to life? Well it has mutated her."

That got Victor's attention. "And…"

"Well, it's mutated her blood on a very cellular way. When she dies her demi-god voodoo whatever…" Bowen waved his arms around. "Kicks in and brings her back. When that happens, poof!" He threw his arms in the air making Lykar who was sitting next to him jump back. "But the curse is still in control of her physical form. So her physical body has mutated," Bowen practically screamed.

"Your girlfriend's a mutant," Skylar barked with laughter. Ryder slammed a fist into his jaw sending Sky flying out of his chair.

Victor nodded his thanks to Ryder, who only lifted a chin.

Sky picked himself up. "Sorry dude came out before I could stop it," Sky said as a way of an apology.

"Can I continue?" Bowen asked. Victor nodded. "Okay so Elle's cells have mutated. She isn't a mutant you dumbass," he said to Skylar shaking his head. "Her cells have created a protein that heal her body. The demigod in her brings her back, I took some samples of those Freaks and dropped some of Elle's proteins in with the dead tissue. It regenerated the dead tissue."

Everyone at the table fell silent.

Victor was the one to finally break the silence. "Shit."

Bowen jumped up from his seat. "So you see? You understand? The Sons of Adam will want her, because she could carry a new immortal Son of Adam. Be their answer. Pull them out of the shadows where they've been hiding for gods only now how long. And the Tribunal will want her, because she could be the God they have been waiting for, like for, forever. Isn't this awesome?"

****

"Wake up, Elle." The words were whispered into her ear and Elle reached toward Victor.

"Aren't I mad at you?" she asked, her voice gruff. Elle tilted her head to the side, thrilling in the feel of Victor's gruff beard against her cheek and neck.

His laughter rumbled against her. "Hmm" he pressed a kiss below her ear. "But I forgive you."

"That's very kind of you," she breathed, forgetting for a moment exactly who was mad at who.

Elle speared her fingers through his soft blond hair. "I'm glad you're back." She heard the words tumble from her mouth and pressed her lips together before something else came out before she could stop it.

"I hate leaving you." Something warmed deep in her chest at his words. Elle pulled back so she could look into Victor's eyes. "I'm going to keep you safe, Elle," he promised. The way he said it, the promise in his voice, gave her chills. The way he seemed almost desperate. Made her catch her breath, frantic for more.

She closed her eyes and buried her face into the crook of his neck, and let him wrap his arms around her. For this moment it was just the two of them and it was all that mattered.

Elle shouldn't do it, but she also knew something had changed she could feel it in the stiffness of Victor's shoulders. She had been alone for so long, and then Victor had swept into her life and made her feel important. And she wanted to hold onto it for just a little while longer.

Elle pressed a kiss to the underside of Victor's chin. "Yes, I know you will keep me safe," she whispered. She followed the kiss up with another at the corner of his mouth.

"Elle?" Victor pulled away slightly.

She looked into his dark eyes knowing what he was asking and knowing the answer. Elle gave him smile. "Are you sure? This is going to change things between us."

Elle shook her head. "Don't say that."

Victor tried to pull away from her, but Elle wouldn't let him go. "Victor please." She pressed herself against him and kissed him. She didn't want anything to change between them. But neither did she want him to leave her.

The thought of him leaving her made her physically want to scream. "Don't leave. Kiss me."

And then he was kissing her, and it was so hot and passionate and it felt so amazing her brain stopped working. His taste was so strong, it went to her head. Like a drug, making her lightheaded. Elle's body felt heavy but light at the same time, thankfully Victor anchored her to the bed.

His lips moved over hers, across her face. Elle relaxed back into the bed, drowning in the feelings and sensations, Victor created with his lips. Then his hands started to move over her body. She jumped when they moved to her hips, gliding up her sides, and she felt him smile against her throat. But he said nothing, her head falling to the side. She was losing her mind to this man. And she didn't care, his hands glided up her sides stopping just under her breasts making Elle catch her breath. She pressed herself into the bed so she wouldn't arch into his hands.

One hand crawled up between her breasts, to tickle her collar bone, while he licked and kissed her throat.

Elle was panting by this time, she needed to feel skin. She was pretty sure if she didn't she might scream. She clawed at his t-shirt. "You really need to lose the shirt right. Now."

Victor laughed. The sounded rumbled deeply in his chest, vibrating against her. She couldn't help it as she moaned and arched against him... getting him to do it again. "Damn you're so fucking hot."

Elle tried uncrossing her eyes to look at him. "Skin, now." Were the only words she could get out.

He leaned back and winked at her making her insides go a little haywire, reaching back he pulled his shirt off. And gods above and below he was awesome. Golden and beautiful, six pack abs any god would be proud of.

Elle wanted to touch and taste every inch of him. Victor moaned. "Shit Elle, you look at me like that and

I'm gonna make a fool out of myself before the party even starts."

Elle's eyes shot to him. "What?"

"Like you're going to eat me alive." Victor's words were said between gritted teeth.

And Elle smiled. "Not eat, but lick, kiss, suck," Victor moaned and swooped down pressing his lips against hers in an almost violent way. But Elle didn't care she needed this; she hadn't been with a man in so many years she didn't even want to think about it. Especially not a man as amazing as Victor. And gods, was he amazing! All she felt was how wonderful he made her feel. No backlash of his emotions or lack thereof.

When he pulled back, it was to pull her small cami over her head, and toss it the gods only knew where. "Fuck, Elle." Victor swore as he looked down on her now. He was gasping for air. "So beautiful."

"Ahh. Victor," she cried out, as Victor latched onto one nipple. All thought flew out the window.

Victor was sure this was a piece of heaven; he couldn't remember ever being with a woman this responsive and it feeling so incredible. He wanted this to last forever; Elle was pure ecstasy beneath him. He suckled one nipple thrilling in the satisfying little cries of pleasure she made as he flicked the hard nub with his tongue or sucked her deep into his mouth. She had large breasts and he knew he could feast on them for hours.

But she grew restless and he knew why. "Shh, Elle, I'll take care of you sweetheart." He blew over a nipple making her jump.

"Please, Victor," she moaned, he looked up at her. Her golden eyes stared down at him and her honey colored hair was spread over the pillows, and he couldn't remember ever seeing anything as beautiful in his life.

He moved up her body, placing gently, wet, kisses along the way. "Didn't I promise to take care of you?" he asked

She nodded, a smile playing at the corners of her full and kiss swollen lips. "Yes but if you don't do something soon I might have to take control of the situation."

Victor laughed, and Elle moaned pressing into him. "Oh Victor I really like it when you do that." Her eyes had closed, and she looked ready to come. So Victor leaned down and hummed deep making his chest vibrate against her, and Elle nearly came off the bed as her entire body arched into him. "Holy shit." She could barely draw air into her lungs to say the words.

"Wait until I do that with my cock buried to the hilt inside of you," Victor promised.

Elle's eyes snapped open and she gasped and shook her head. "You can't. It will kill me, I swear to the gods, it will."

Victor laughed again, making her thrash from side to side. Her bottom lip sucked between her teeth, she bit down until he was afraid she was going to draw blood. So, he bent down and sucked it into his mouth, soothing it with his own tongue. After a moment, he leaned back, "I'm going to climb off the bed and take my pants off. You will climb out of those shorts."

She nodded, chewing her bottom lip again. They were both breathing erratically. Victor lifted himself off of Elle and stripped out of his fatigues in record time. As he turned back to the bed, Elle was kicking off the boy shorts she had on. She stopped mid-kick, her mouth going slack.

"Holy holy cow." Then she grabbed a pillow and pulled it over her face and screamed.

Victor looked down at himself wondering if something horrible had happened. Nothing horrible disfiguring had happened beside the fact he was painfully and might he say impressively erect.

He pulled a corner of the pillow away, so he could see Elle's eyes. "I know I've only known you for a week. But, I feel like I've come to know you rather well in that time. These little freak outs are rather cute. Right now though… a little weird." Elle's eyes just rounded on him, and then words he couldn't make out muffled through the pillow.

"Yeah, sorry sweetheart. I don't speak pillow," Victor said giving her a smile.

Elle pulled the pillow down and climbed up the bed using the pillow to cover herself. Which Victor wasn't happy about, he had actually been enjoying the view. "I like that you don't have cloven feet." Of everything he had been expecting her to say that hadn't been it.

"Um thank you."

She gave him a smile. "You're welcome."

"That is why you screamed?" he asked.

"Oh no. I screamed because you have a very very large penis," she said. "And…it's been um…a significant amount of time for me. It was a knee jerk reaction. I apologize for that. It just kinda happened. Then I screamed more because I was screaming. And then I hid, because I was screaming. Now, I would like to just die, thank you. Do you think anyone else heard?"

Victor was positive everyone in the house heard, but he wasn't going to let her know that, and if anyone else brought it up he would kill them. "Of course not," he lied without even blinking.

Victor climbed on the bed and pulled Elle down half under him surprised when she went willingly. "I didn't mean to act like some virgin or anything. I'm not. I was just shocked for a second. Then I was shocked at how I reacted. Can we start over?"

Victor shook his head. "No, starting over would likely kill me. But we can start from here."

"Let's pretend you didn't just scream because I have the largest cock you've ever seen," Victor said placing kisses along her shoulders.

Elle laughed this time. "Um, that's not really what I said."

"Really?" Victor asked, kissing the shell of her ear. "Hmmm, that's strange. Because that's what I heard."

She started to relax and he rolled her over him. "How about you show me some of that, licking and kissing you told me about earlier. Then you won't be so intimidated." And hopefully she would relax again, before he died. She gave him a shy smile that made it worth it, and he lay back with his hands stacked behind his head and vowed he would do whatever it took to make her comfortable. But gods it was going to be difficult.

Elle looked over Victor, she had never had a man at her disposal before. Being an empath she had sensed so much backlash. She felt it had mixed with what she had wanted during sex, but with Victor, it was about what she wanted.

She loomed above him. He was watching her with his dark hooded eyes. She couldn't feel anything from him. She should ask him what he wanted but it was about what she wanted, passion and need crashed through her making her feel almost out of control for this man.

She started by running her hands up his glorious chest, then dragging her fingernails back down over his chest and his abs. Then she bent down and kissed his stomach, she ran her tongue along the ridges of his muscles. She found the sacred V and worshiped that with her mouth, leaving wet trails. Elle massaged his chest and collarbone. She kissed him on the mouth, tangled her tongue with his.

Elle turned him over and explored his back and dipped her tongue into the dimples just above his ass. When she was done with his legs she turned him over again and sucked on the insteps of his feet giggling again about thinking he might have had cloven feet.

When she was totally done with his entire body she was so hot, she could barely breathe and was seriously thinking about humping his leg. The only place she hadn't touched was his large cock, and it stood out, proud waiting its turn. She looked at it now. Then looked up at Victor, his eyes burned with passion.

His breathing had grown hard and fast, and she knew what he was waiting for she couldn't put him off any longer. She kneeled before him now and reached forward. Victor's entire body jerked, as she took his cock into her hand

"Elle, I'm on a short leash sweetheart. I need you bad." His words were uttered in such a hoarse whisper it made her wet, and she didn't think she could get any wetter.

She needed to let him know she was just as hot for him, so without breaking eye contact with him she reached down and with one finger she swirled it deep in her wet folds. Victor hissed. "Fuck, Elle."

She drew the finger out and took the finger and swirled her juices around Victor's hard cock. Victor let his head fall back and he moaned as she wrapped her fist around his base and squeezed. "Gods Elle, I need you so bad," His hips jerked up. And she pressed him down.

"Calm," she whispered squeezing him tight.

Victor's eyes snapped open, for a second he looked like he was about to lose control. Then he was taking deep breaths. "I need you, Elle."

She rolled onto him and fused her lips with his. "I'm right here Victor."

He rolled her over as he kissed her, and Elle let the kiss sweep her away. He took one leg, holding her open to him. He moved down, so he could see her. "You are so beautiful."

Elle turned her head embarrassed, but Victor turned her so she was looking at him. "You are beautiful and don't let anyone tell you different." He held himself so close to her all thought was gone.

Elle nodded and then she wasn't thinking anymore because Victor was pressing into her. And he was so big, it was uncomfortable and it was so amazing. Victor was sweating trying to hold back from slamming into her, she was so tight.

Victor couldn't believe how amazing she felt, it felt like a million tongues licking at him at once. And he wasn't even in all the way. "Elle?" he asked.

She was so tense under him he had to stop. "Baby, just let me in." He was a god damned Reaper, and she had brought him to his knees. Brought to his knees begging to be let into her body. And he would continue to beg, because she was worth it.

She relaxed and Victor could feel himself slide in just another inch. "That's it baby." He dropped kisses along her jaw. Against her hairline, he whispered words of praise into her ear, begged her to let him in. Said whatever it would take, as their sweaty bodies' glided and slide together.

Gods, he didn't know how long it took, but he finally slide the last little bit. And he was in. Elle smiled up at him. And he kissed her long and hard, she was his. Dante may have the stone that prohibited him from claiming her soul but she was his and he was never going to let her go.

"Do you trust me?" Victor asked.

Elle nodded, and Victor wanted to shout to the gods, that she now belonged to him. To the Freaks, there was no way they would ever touch her again. He leaned down and kissed her gently. Then he started to move, gliding out until just the tip of his throbbing cock balanced at her hot wet entrance. Elle clenched trying to keep him inside of her body rejecting his retreat.

Victor flexed his hips driving himself deeply back into her, making Elle gasp. He pulled back out and flexed forward and backed out. Until Elle was wild. When she was gasping, Victor pulled all the way out, and he bent down pushing two fingers into her, flicking her with his tongue. Elle came undone, calling out his name.

Elle came undone calling out Victor's name, as she came down Victor straightened and smiled. "That was beautiful." He buried himself into her and laughed pressing himself against her.

She shrieked into his mouth making him laugh all the more and she shuddered around his cock. He pounded into her, his mind and body coming unhinged. He wasn't thinking anymore. It was all about feeling now. Elle shattered around him, and he lost control pounding into her. Finally finding his own release, unable to hold anything back, he buried himself inside Elle. He called her name and wrapped her in his arms so tight, he wasn't sure where she started and he ended.

****

They stayed wrapped around each other for a long time neither moving, but she knew they couldn't stay like this forever, life would eventually come knocking.

"Something's happened?" she asked not pulling away from the safety of his arms.

"Yes," he whispered. But didn't say more for a long time and she let him hold her until he was ready to explain. "Aldon is a Son of Adam."

Elle pulled away from Victor. "Excuse me?"

"Aldon is a Son of Adam," he said again. Elle processed the information and she opened and closed her mouth several times before she pushed away from him and scrambled from the bed. She needed to get out of there, she needed to hide. If the Sons of Adam were able to get ahold of her, they could bind her to them. And unlike any other Other being, a demi-god didn't fall under the same laws as the Others. And being cursed they could kill her, this Aldon could force her to mate with him and then the Sons of Adam would be invincible and they would be immortal like they always wanted.

"Elle!" Victor shouted.

"What?"

Victor grabbed her as she passed and held her by putting a hand on each of her shoulders. "You are running in circles, ringing your hands. I told you I was going to keep you safe."

She laughed, she couldn't help it. "Really? How?" She was bordering on hysteria but this was insane. Elle couldn't fight an entire race of men.

"Haven't I kept you from him so far?" Victor's dark eyes were hard and he looked so sure. Elle had to admit as she looked at him she felt calmer.

"This is absurd, why is this happening?" Elle asked folding herself into Victor's arms. She wrapped her arms around his stomach and held onto him. How had he become so important to her so fast?

"Do you really want the answer, Elle?" Victor asked.

Elle cringed at the way he asked the question. She pushed away from him and moved to the window she hugged herself. "I'm the weakest," she said more to herself then to him. It was something she had heard numerous times. It was why she hid, why Helena did everything she could to keep her hidden. Why she was so isolated, and why Victor had become so important to her so fast because he showed her attention and Elle just soaked it up because she was starved of it. And who wouldn't want to soak it up like a little sponge.

"I'm pathetic," she said turning to Victor, tears she desperately wanted to hold back sprung to her eyes. Her hands fisted as they dropped to her sides. "I'm a cursed and pathetic demi-god."

Victor started to interrupt her and she stopped him. "Don't," she shouted at him. "Don't you dare start to make excuses. You have no idea who I am, what I am. Do you think because we had mind blowing sex, you understand who I am? That you somehow know me? You don't. You don't know me, or know what I have done to survive. Why I am cursed. I was deserving of my curse, Victor. Don't you wonder why no Reaper or Angel ever comes for my soul? Because I am damned, not just cursed but damned as well," she shouted her voice cracking with the tears now running down her face unchecked.

Her words didn't stop Victor from moving towards her and she slapped him on the chest when he tried to gather her close. "I am the most pathetic creature on the mortal plane." She pushed him away. "I think my sister is working with the Tribunal, now the Sons of Adam want to mate with me and that bastard has an endless number of Freaks at his disposal fighting for him. And to top it off I summoned a Reaper to be my champion." Elle threw her hands in the air and collapsed down on the floor. Elle pulled her knees up. She hid her head in her arms and cried. "I should have never answered my phone. I should have climbed into my cave and pushed my panic button and come out in ten years."

"Are you done?" Victor asked from above her.

Elle didn't look up. "No," she answered.

Victor snorted his laughter, and then picked her up. She squeaked as he threw her over his shoulder, realizing she was naked as the day she had been created. "As much as I would like to let you have your moment of pity, we really don't have time. Get over it." He carried her into the bathroom and she hung limply over his shoulder as he turned the shower on.

"Victor what are you doing?" she asked warily.

She gasped as she was swung upright and she had to grab him while the room spun for a moment.

"Take a shower and get ready we have plans to make." He kissed her on the cheek. "Everything is going to be okay, Elle. Aldon and the Sons of Adam can go to hell, and I will personally take him there." He winked at her.

"But..." Victor put a finger on her lips stopping her from saying anything more. "Elle you can stand here and worry yourself sick or you can get in the shower and then we can make plans to kick their ass. Which would you rather do?"

She growled at him. Which only made him laugh at her. But he turned and walked out of the bathroom leaving her to shower in peace. Elle just wanted to have her pity party, but she knew it wasn't worth it.

Victor was right, she needed to suck it up and get to work. Crying about it wasn't going to get anything done. But she wasn't going to let him know he was right.

****

"There's another two dozen Freaks at the gate," Bowen announced as Victor and Elle came into the kitchen.

Victor nodded, and pulled on Elle who hesitated at Bowen's words. Christian and Garrett were standing in the corner glaring at the Trackers at the table. "I thought we were going to try and get along?" Victor asked at the obvious hostility in the room.

"Yes, that was until that one thought it would be funny to pick a fight with Garrett." Victor looked at Garrett and noticed he had a black eye and fat lip. "You want me to fix that?" he asked.

Garrett shook his head but his eyes never left Skylar who was eating a bowl of cereal. Victor turned to Skylar. "What did you do?"

"Asked him who the fuck he was?" Skylar shrugged, shoveling his cereal into his mouth. Taking Elle by the elbow, he pulled her into the seat next to him. Making Victor want to skin him alive. "You want some cereal, love?"

He was going to kill the Tracker, that was all there was to it. Both Garrett and Christian took menacing steps toward Skylar and Victor had to step between them, making Skylar smile around another spoonful of cereal.

Elle glared at the Reapers. "Yes please, Skylar, and the name is Elle. We've had this conversation before haven't we?"

Skylar reached for a bowl and the cereal and milk. "Have we?" he said fixing her a bowl.

She pushed at him with her shoulder. "Yes and stop trying to piss them off."

"But it's so much fun." Skylar laughed.

"Yes I can see that. But it's a little early, why don't you save something for later in the day," Elle offered eating her breakfast. Skylar grunted and went back to his cereal.

Victor shook his head. "You want something real for breakfast?" Ryder asked from the grill. Where he was grilling steak and eggs for breakfast. Victor nodded and grabbed the plate Ryder offered, pulling a chair over to sit next to Elle.

After several minutes of silence Skylar threw his spoon into his now empty bowl and glared at Christian and Garrett. "Are they just going to stand there and glower?"

"No," Victor said.

"Then what are they waiting for?" Skylar asked Victor.

"They are waiting for you to finish your breakfast," Victor said not looking up from his own breakfast.

"Well I'm done," Skylar said.

Victor nodded and pulled on Elle's chair so she was flush with Victor. Ryder muttered something from his position at the grill, Bowen said something. Skylar looked at the group like they had all lost their minds.

But before he could say anything more the Reapers moved in. Garrett caught Skylar with a solid punch throwing him back from the table.

Elle made a squeaking noise. "You done?" Victor asked.

Elle looked from her breakfast, to Victor to the fight and back, Victor reached over with an index finger and held her chin. "Ignore them."

"Kinda hard," she said when a wild kick connected with her chair making her jump.

"Watch it," Victor snapped over her shoulder at the fighting duo. Victor finally turned to Christian. "What exactly did Skylar say?"

"Why is it always me?" Skylar muttered from the fight on the floor.

Bowen and Ryder both snorted.

"Called Garrett a pussy for once being a Guardian," Christian answered making Victor shake his head.

Victor had to grab Elle as she leaned over and grabbed Skylar by his t-shirt. "You stop fighting right now." She pulled the two of them apart, climbing onto the back of her chair. Victor was now holding her around the waist keeping her from tipping over the back of the chair.

"You are both acting like children." She slapped Skylar upside the head. "How dare you call Garrett names? Are you ten?" Skylar just stared at her for moment. And then shook his head.

"Did you just hit me woman?" he glared.

So she hit him again. "Being a Guardian is a noble thing, you idiot. What is it with you calling people names? You need help. And Garrett, grow a pair, so what if he called you a name. I'm sure you've been called worse. And if not…" She hesitated and looked around the room. Nearly toppling off her chair, Victor had to tighten his hold on her. ""You will be, if you hang out with this crowd for too long. So, you'll need to get used to it. Not everything can be solved with fists. Don't make me hit you too."

She turned back around and ignoring the stunned looks on the men's faces she continued to eat her cereal. Not realizing she had threatened to hit a Reaper, and had actually hit a Tracker, not once but twice. Or the fact she had stepped into a fight between the two. Something you just didn't do.

Now the Trackers and Reapers in the room weren't sure if the woman was crazy or not. One thing was for sure. She had just earned their respect. And possibly the love of every single one of them.

****

"We need to draw Aldon out," Falcon said again. Making Victor grind his teeth together.

"How many times do I need to say no?" Victor said.

"He is the key." Falcon slapped the table making it wobble on its repaired legs.

"If we draw him out, and bring him through the wards, we could be leaving ourselves open for attack," Kyra explained.

"We should leave," Elle offered.

"Oh you want to leave now?" Sky asked sarcastically.

"Your being a complete ass, you realize that don't you?" Elle asked him. "Would you like to explain that?"

"Because," Sky said petulantly.

"Well at least you're acting like an adult," Elle said crossing her arms over her chest she glared at him.

"Can I just go out and kill something?" Sky asked standing, he glared at the group.

"No." Falcon glared back at him.

"Can we circle back to us leaving?" Elle addressed Victor.

Victor rolled his eyes and turned to Falcon. "I don't want to bring Aldon into the wards if it will weaken them."

Falcon thought for a moment. "I agree. We need to find some common ground that will be safe."

"We try to leave and that horde of Freaks will be on us." Victor swore.

"Not if you go out through the tunnels," Falcon offered. "We can get you out the tunnels when we are engaging the Freaks. Create enough of a diversion. We could give you a day, maybe more. Then meet up with you. But where?"

"Hallowed ground," Elle offered.

Victor turned to her. "What?"

"The Freaks. They're soulless. They can't go onto hallowed ground. But the Sons of Adam can. You would be able to fight Aldon one on one." Elle smiled.

"Yeah, but Aldon isn't just going to show up for a fair fight. He's smarter than that. Plus I'm pretty sure he knows who we have on our side." Victor looked at the six Trackers and three Reapers, an Elemental Enforcer, Elle. "All of us against him?"

"Yeah that's why it will be just you and Elle against him," Falcon said with a smile. "Until it's too late. Then the rest of us will show up and we will kill the bastard."

Victor wasn't sure about this, but he didn't really have another plan. "Okay but where is this going to take place?"

Falcon gave him another smile. "Oh I have the perfect spot. And the perfect hiding spot for the rest of us. The bastard Aldon will never see us coming."

Chapter 8

Elle clutched the gun Victor had given her as she hid behind the large tombstone. She could feel Victor somewhere in the recesses of the huge cemetery but with the moonless night she could barely see her hand in front of her face.

"This is such a bad idea," she whispered.

"We're supposed to be silent," Victor whispered back. They had on some high tech equipment Bowen had given them before they had left Staten. They all had them but the Trackers and the other Reapers wouldn't be activated until they showed up. And she wasn't even sure it would happen.

"Yes, because radio silence going into this plan is such a good idea," she muttered.

She could hear Victor chuckle but she didn't mention it. They had escaped the Freaks, and fled to Louisiana where the Trackers had several properties and where there were more graveyards and hallowed ground. In fact Elle was pretty sure you couldn't throw a rock without hitting hallowed ground. Not that mortals would understand, but Louisiana wasn't just a hot bed of supernatural but historically had the most hallowed ground per square feet in the United States, besides Utah and New Mexico. So they were here because they could hide. Elle shivered, tucked behind a huge stone angel wondering if this was where it was all going to end. And she couldn't help but think this was one of their stupider ideas. She had stayed alive for the last several millennia by running and hiding and it really appealed to her. Elle was about to make another appeal for that argument. What could it hurt? Just sitting there, awaiting a madman who wanted to mate with her, was making her want to cry. She was pretty sure her night was going to get pretty shitty. Either way, at least she would be heard.

"Hello, Elle."

She shrieked, just like every girl in every scary movie ever had. Then she scrambled out from the shadows of the huge angel watching over her.

He reached for her but she slapped his hand away. "Don't you dare touch me."

Aldon held his hands up in supplication. "I only wanted to ensure your safety," he said quietly. "I would hate for you to trip and fall. Without even the moon to lighten your way."

"I'm coming Elle," Victor whispered in her ear.

Aldon looked around with a smile. "It took me some time to locate you, but from your surroundings I assume you know what I am?"

Elle shrugged. "What makes you think that?" she took a step back putting some distance between them. Remembering the last time they had been together he had put a knife in her chest. She wasn't keen on a repeat performance.

Aldon gave her a smile, showing her straight white teeth beneath the gray pallor of his skin. She had to say although he looked slightly sickly he was a nice looking man. If he had a little sun he would actually be good looking. With broad shoulders, sandy blond hair he flipped out of his amber brown eyes.

Wait, hadn't his eyes been fathomless black? "Your eyes? And your hair is different."

He smiled at her. "You prefer this don't you?"

Elle shook her head. "I prefer the truth." She shook her head again and blinked several times and re-focused on him. When she did his eyes were black again as was his hair.

He sighed. "It is hard to hide the truth from you, Elle." He shrugged. "But I guess if you are to be my mate I would prefer to have little between us."

"Yeah about that, I'm not really interested in being your mate." Elle took another couple of steps back." She searched for the slab of granite she knew was back there. "If it's all the same to you."

Aldon took a step toward her. "Now see, that isn't going to work for me. There is so much more at stake than whether or not you want to be my mate. And well…" he took another step toward her. "It's really not up to you."

Elle glared at him, "No you see, that really isn't going to work for me." She threw his words back at him. "Not sure how you found out about me, or what you might have heard but I'm not really in the market for a man."

Aldon chuckled, but it was a dry and humorless sound. "I'm sorry to hear that, Elle. However, I must insist that you reevaluate your decision. I will not take no for an answer. The fate of the immortal world lies before you."

"Yeah, I could give two shits about the fate of the immortal world." Elle said.

Something hard flashed in his dark eyes, "Elle that can't possibly be true. Everyone cares about their own Fate. Don't you have a legacy you wish to pass on?"

Elle thought for a moment, "I suppose. But it isn't something I want to pass on with a stranger."

"That's all I ask." He jumped at her. Making Elle jump back. "Just a chance to get to know you. To plead my case."

Elle barked out a harsh laugh, "Kidnapping is against the law in both the mortal and Other worlds."

"I am offering you the chance to be someone." He pleaded. He was so earnest; it almost tugged at her heart strings. If he hadn't sent savage Freaks after her she might have listened to him.

"I'm already someone, Aldon." She said quietly and she actually believed it.

Aldon growled something low that she didn't catch right before he sprung at her. He moved so fast Elle almost missed it, if Fiona hadn't been helping her regain some of her demi-god abilities she wouldn't have been able to see it. But she had regained some of those abilities and she saw him move just in time.

Elle ducked as he moved in to grab her, and rolled like Victor told her to. And thank the gods she was in the exact spot she needed to be, she rolled under the granite alter. Victor snarled as he arrived, Aldon laughed.

"Do you actually think you can fight me?" Aldon growled from where Elle had been just seconds before.

Elle scrambled to her feet on the opposite side of the alter. Victor stood facing Aldon, his scythe in his hands. "I plan on trying."

Aldon threw his head back and laughed. "I answer to a god more powerful than you."

Chills raced up and down Elle's body, she was truly freaked out. Aldon was either truly insane or he knew something they didn't.

Victor said nothing as he swung his scythe at Aldon who moved out of the way as if he was swatting a fly. Throwing a punch that connected with Victor's chin sending the Reaper back several steps. Elle was so shocked she just stood there, Victor recovered only to have Aldon attacking again and again. Victor swung and attacked but Aldon side stepped each swing and countered Victor's attacks like Victor was a toy. Soon Victor was bloody and beaten.

"Elle, now!" Victor bellowed.

Elle shook herself and scrambled for her backpack she dumped out the contents they had gone over the plan so many times, but now it was happening she felt like they hadn't gone over it enough.

"Please, please, please," she begged, not sure who she was talking to.

"Elle, now would be good," Victor called.

Elle looked up. "I'm working on it."

It was a modified Pandora's Box, Tracker/Elemental style, it hid whoever was inside. Without trapping the soul or torturing them. Falcon, Kyra, and Bowen had been working on it. Elle put it down and flipped open the lid. Whispering the words that Kyra said would activate it. Praying it worked.

Six Trackers and Kyra popped out like genies from a bottle. And as they did there were Flashes of light. The box activating was the sign for Christian and Garrett.

Aldon stopped pummeling on Victor to stare in shock as the Trackers attacked. "How the hell?"

"It's about damn time," Garrett snapped at Elle. "Thought you were going to leaves us out of the fight."

Christian grabbed Victor and pulled him to safety, Elle rushed to him.

"Victor?" Elle crouched down. He looked so terrible Elle wasn't sure he was even breathing at the moment.

"That bad?" Victor muttered.

Elle didn't even want to touch him. Sure anything she did for him, would surly hurt him. "Yes."

When everything went quiet, Elle looked up.

Aldon held Garret by the throat with a wicked looking dagger. "Give me Elle."

"Fuck you." Garrett swore.

Aldon laughed. "You first."

Elle was climbing to her feet, she had to get to Garrett first. Everything was happening so fast. People were moving, Victor, and Christian were bellowing.

But none of them got there. A blur moved in, pulling the dagger away. Garrett was cute and blood splattered everywhere. He was also pushed away as Aldon's face was smashed in with an elbow. His arm was wrenched and the bone snapped. The noise so loud, it seemed to echo in the night. Aldon's scream split through the dark night. He doubled over, and the blur solidified into the form of a darkly cloaked figure holding a limp arm. A leg coming up to slam into Aldon's stomach, so hard Aldon came off the ground a good foot.

But Aldon wasn't cowed. He growled and tried to stab at the figure holding him. The figure released him to spin free of Aldon. It was enough for Aldon who winked away, one moment he was there and the next he was gone.

The cloaked figure swore, and then swore again. And to the surprise of the group, turned to the group and threw back the hood.

"Of course it's a girl." Skylar shook his head.

"Get me to Garrett," Victor wheezed. As he clawed at the dirt.

Garrett was gasping and clutching at the cut on his throat. Elle and Christian dragged Victor over to Garrett who was bleeding out. Victor lay on top of his brother,

"What the hell?" Christian asked Victor.

"Blood Rite Dagger," Victor said just before he passed out.

"Oh shit." Christian swore and grabbing Garrett, he Flashed out.

"We got huge problems," Falcon said to the group. "Get Kyra," he said to Ryder.

Elle just looked at the group. "What now?"

"We regroup," Falcon announced.

"Just who the fuck are you?" Skylar barked at the woman, still staring.

She ignored them all and walked up to Elle and held out a hand. "I am Tabitha. Please understand the very last thing I want is for you to mate with the Sons of Adam. I am here to protect you."

Elle took her hand. "Umm...okay then."

"You will come with me?" Tabitha asked.

"Uh, I'm kinda with them." Elle looked around.

"These males are a hindrance," Tabitha explained.

"Well, fuck you too, bitch," Skylar said.

Tabitha turned to Skylar. "A very loud and obnoxious hindrance," she said turning back to Elle. "I don't work well with others. I am here to protect you and you alone."

Elle bit her lip to keep from laughing. "I understand. But these men are with me."

Tabitha stepped forward and whispered words Elle couldn't understand, and the world around her slowed to a stop. She looked around shocked at the frozen men around her.

"Um what the hell?" she asked Tabitha.

Tabitha gave her a small smile. "I can't hold this spell long. You need to trust me Elle, I am here for you. What can I do to make you understand?"

"Why should I trust you? You just pop in and try to kill Aldon, and you think that makes you trust worthy?" Elle asked. "Plus you froze everyone? They aren't going to like this."

"I promise, I'm here to help you," Tabitha insisted. "They aren't even going to notice. Their simple minds, cannot possible comprehend my abilities."

"That's just not enough," Elle said. She had been burned just too many times. Abandoned by those who she cared for. "And for the love of the gods, don't tell them how 'simple' their minds are."

"I will give my life to protect you," Tabitha pleaded.

Elle stood over Victor's body while everyone else stood frozen, as tears ran down her face. "How do I know that?"

Tabitha slashed her hand, making Elle stumble back in shock as the tall amazon advanced on her. But Elle tripped over the uneven ground, and Tabitha was faster than she was, anyway. Taking her by her hand, she grabbed her hand and sliced Elle's hand. Pressing them together. Elle protested but it was happening so fast. Images started swimming through her mind at a break-necking speed and she couldn't pinpoint any of them.

Then Tabitha was speaking, "I swear a blood oath to you; I am here to protect you. By my blood I swear you are a sister of my heart and I will do everything within my power to protect you." Elle was swimming in memories as Tabitha shared with her small tidbits of her life before she released her hand.

Elle looked up into her green eyes and tried to shake her head. "Why would you share a blood oath with someone you don't even know?"

Tabitha shared a sad smile. "Because it is my destiny." She released Elle and pulled a cloth from a backpack she cleaned the wounds on their hands with a salve. "This will aide in the healing." Tabitha cleaned off the blood and Elle was surprised to see that the wounds were already closing up.

"Now what?" Elle asked looking at Victor and the others who were still frozen.

"I will un-freeze them. And we will continue with our mission. It is taking a great deal of my Magik to sustain this spell," Tabitha admitted.

"They aren't going to like this," Elle said again.

"Yeah, the male race typically doesn't like anything they cannot control." Tabitha agreed. Slipping her back-pack back on.

"I can't tell them about this, can I?" Elle asked.

Tabitha laughed. "Oh please do. I'm sure they'll love it."

Elle groaned knowing just how wonderful Victor was going to respond to the blood oath Tabitha had sworn to Elle. Yep. It was going to go over like gang busters.

Tabitha regarded her for a moment. "Fine. I will keep you safe. If you insist on traveling with them I will not argue for now."

Elle rolled her eyes, things just kept getting better. How many more people were they going to add to this merry group? Tabitha unfroze the group.

"How gracious of you." Skylar snorted as they were unfrozen.

"Shut it." Falcon slapped Sky in the back of the head.

Elle suddenly felt exhausted. "Where are we headed?"

"Safe house." Falcon nodded.

Elle nodded, this was plan B. Skylar and Ryder picked up Victor and they headed out. Tabitha stopped Elle. "It is very important you know I am here for your safety, Elle. When we reach the 'safe house, you and I need to speak privately."

Elle nodded, she felt like she had fallen down the rabbit hole. Tabitha nodded and before she let Elle go she checked the path forward several times and then walked beside her and a step or two behind her but she could feel Tabitha was aware of absolutely everything going on around her.

Tabitha never left her side, and Elle never went far from where Victor was.

"This place isn't safe," Tabitha informed her when they got to the house.

Elle looked around. "It's warded," Elle explained. "And it's kept us safe so far." She followed Ryder up the stairs, as he carried Victor up to a room. He put Victor on a bed. "He should wake up soon. His wounds are already healing."

Tabitha was checking the room like she expected something to jump out from the closest or from under the bed.

Elle stood to the side, all she really wanted was to climb into the bed and sleep. "Okay want to tell me who you are now?"

Tabitha looked from Elle back to Victor. "You want to have this conversation in front of a Reaper?"

Elle laughed. "Not sure he is going to have anything to say about it."

"You trust him?" she asked surprised.

Elle didn't even hesitate. "With my life."

"Considering the situation, you have no other choice," Tabitha said crossing her arms over her chest.

"Who are you?" Elle asked shaking her head.

"I am a Daughter of Eve. I am a Warrior class and in this case judge and jury. We were informed that a Son of Adam was attempting to mate with a demi-god. We didn't know who it was or why, I was sent out to find out what was going on. And if necessary protect the demi-god from the Son of Adam. And where possible reap justice on the wayward Son of Adam. My spies led me to the Freaks and you, and then to Aldon. What he is trying to do is against our laws. He has broken the Compact, and his life is now forfeit." Elle sighed, looked around and found a chair, and then sat down heavily as Tabitha finished. "You have become a pawn and it is paramount Aldon does not succeed in mating with you. I have sent a message to the Daughters of Eve as well as the Sons of Adam on the Judgment."

"So neither fraction knows what he is doing?

Elle had a hard time believing that. "Who is funding his little science project then?"

Tabitha shrugged, "Aldon is breaking many of our first laws. I have a hard time believing he is in good standing with the Sons of Adam." She admitted. "Like I said, I was sent out to find out if the rumors were true. And if they were I was to take care of the issue. The Sons and Daughters have long been thought gone, and we are not part of the Tribunal. We do not fall beneath there rules. Unless otherwise stated from my council Aldon is a dead man walking. And I will protect you from him till my dying breath."

Elle rubbed at her temples, "Sorry but none of this makes sense to me."

Tabitha nodded, "You're exhausted, and you need to get some rest. And will be no good to anyone if you collapse from exhaustion. Get some rest. I will stand guard." Tabatha motioned to the bed.

Elle agreed completely and climbed into the bed next to Victor, Tabitha turned the light out. Elle watched as she moved to stand by the window. The sun was just rising, Elle placed her hand over Victor's heart.

The night had been so busy and fraught with so much excitement and fights and information she couldn't begin to wrap her brain around it all.

She should stop and think it all through but she was just too damn tired. Tomorrow would be soon enough.

****

"Who the fuck are you?" Victor growled. Bringing Elle fully awake, she rolled to her feet and looked around the room.

Victor had Tabitha by the throat; Tabitha had a gun to Victor's temple. "Release me," Tabitha growled back.

"Let her go." Elle stumbled toward them.

"What?" Victor snarled. "What the hell is she? And why is she in our bedroom?"

"I'm here to protect her, you imbecile?" Tabitha said. With a calm Elle wouldn't have believed possible, with a Reaper holding you by the throat. "Now let me go, or you'll be recovering from a bullet wound instead of an ass kicking."

Victor snarled and released her, then turned to Elle. "We have to talk," he grabbed Elle and walked to the door. He made it to the door but was stopped when Tabitha grabbed Elle by the other arm.

Elle groaned because she just knew this wasn't going to go well. "She doesn't go anywhere without me, Reaper."

Victor turned slowly, and Elle rubbed at her forehead. "Excuse me?"

"Sorry Tabitha, we just need a minute." Elle reached around Victor and opened the door. She motioned for Tabitha. Tabitha glared but nodded and went through the door.

"I'll be right outside." Tabitha said, pointedly. Elle nodded and then closed the door.

"How long was I out?" Victor asked pushing his hand through his hair. "And who the hell is that?"

"You were only out the day. And she is Tabitha, a Daughter of Eve," she explained where Tabitha had come from.

Victor growled and started to pace. "How many more players are going to join this game?"

Elle shook her head and sat down on the edge of the bed. "Victor what the hell is going on? How has everything gotten so out of control? And what the hell is the Blood Rite Dagger? And why does the sound of it scare the hell out of me?"

Victor kneeled down in front of her, and took her hands. "We are going to get through this, Elle."

Elle pulled her hands away from him. "You keep saying that, and then we go out and come back with our asses handed to us." She stood and pushed past him. "I'm kinda starting to care about you and these horrible Trackers and I don't want to see anyone of you hurt. And every time we go out there we get hurt."

"Don't worry about the Trackers." Victor swore. "We have more to worry about."

Elle turned on him. "How can I not worry about them? We brought them into this fight!" She all but shouted.

"I didn't mean not to worry about them, just that they can take care of themselves." Victor sighed heavily. "You are all fighting because of me. Fighting to keep me safe. To keep me from being a brood mare for Aldon! How am I supposed to not worry?"

"What in the hell are you talking about?" Victor demanded.

"I should never have called for you. This isn't your fight, Victor. This isn't the Trackers' fight." Elle pushed past him again and threw the door open. Tabitha came in with a smile on her face. Elle just knew the woman had been listening at the door. "This is a fight for me and Tabitha."

"The fuck it is," Victor said pushing Tabitha out of the room.

Tabitha pushed him back, Elle tried to get between them.

"Don't push me Reaper," Tabitha snapped.

"Don't get between me and Elle, bitch." Victor got right in Tabitha's face.

"She is not your problem. I am here to kill Aldon and stop him from his attempts." Tabitha grabbed at Elle and pulled her behind her. Elle shook her head and tried to step out of the way, she wasn't about to get in between these two.

Victor growled. "Don't get between us."

Tabitha laughed at him. Making Elle flinch. "And just who is going to stop me, Reaper?"

"Uh, Tabitha…" Elle started.

But Victor moved fast, pulling Elle close he spun around so Elle was now behind him. "Are we truly going to go through this shit?" he snapped.

Elle felt like she was still asleep and just wanted everything to go away. "Victor I don't want everyone's life to be put in jeopardy."

"Have you thought, maybe just for one second that I have started to care for you? These people are willing to fight with you, have started to care for you?" He looked like he was ready to strangle her.

Elle shook her head. "No, because they don't know who I am. They just met me. You don't know me."

Victor grabbed her and she was sure he was going to shake her. But Tabitha grabbed him breaking his hold on her.

"Don't touch her." Elle was shocked into immobility when Tabitha back handed him. "It sounds like she wants you to leave."

Victor shook off the blow and glared at Tabitha. "Touch me again woman and I will retaliate."

Elle felt her mouth drop open, Tabitha stepped forward. Her nose almost touching Victor's. "If you think I am afraid of you, Reaper, you would be mistaken."

Elle couldn't help the snort of laughter that escaped. She was just stunned. "You're insane woman."

Tabitha and Victor both turned to Elle. "Am I supposed to cow to him because he is a Reaper or because he is male?"

"Both," Victor snarled.

"Well…" Elle drew the word out at the same time.

Victor glared at Tabitha. Elle gave him a weak smile. "Whose side are you on?" Elle snapped.

Victor leaned close making Elle catch her breath. "Elle, I am always on your side," he inhaled her scent. She wanted nothing more than to wrap her arms around him and draw him close. And the look in his dark eyes said he knew it.

"I'm not leaving you, Elle," Victor told her.

"I can't stand the thought of you or the Trackers being hurt," she whispered.

"Nobody needs to be hurt," Tabitha said from behind Victor. But Elle ignored her now.

Victor tipped her head up so she was looking at him. "I can't promise what is going to happen Elle, all I can tell you is I will stand and fight for you." She wanted to bury herself into him.

"We can do this without him," Tabitha said again.

Elle smiled at Victor who couldn't keep the irritation from his eyes. "Why do you care?"

"I'm a sucker for golden eyes." He trailed a finger down her cheek.

Elle heard Tabitha snarl something and then the door slam behind her. "I didn't think she was ever going to leave." And then he was kissing her. Burying his tongue in her mouth, he pulled her close to him. Tunneling his fingers in her hair, he held her close. Elle knew this was the last thing she should be doing but she was losing her footing on reality, and when Victor touched her like this she couldn't think.

"This is a bad idea." Elle moaned when Victor released her mouth. She felt him smile as he tipped her head to the side his fingers delving into her hair. She tried to push him away so she could think straight again but he wouldn't allow much distance between them. And the more his taste flooded her the more she lost hold of reality and fell into the grasp of the sexual reality he wove around her.

"This feels to damn good, to be bad." He whispered, as he placed kisses against her mouth. Deepening his kiss until she couldn't think, couldn't feel anything but his lips, his tongue exploring her mouth. She was lost to him, and she didn't care.

Victor wouldn't allow her to push him away. Her damn siblings had convinced her it was her place to be a martyr. But Victor wasn't going to allow it to happen any longer. Not now, not ever again

Caring for her had been the last thing he had wanted but now he had her in his arms he knew he wasn't about to push her away. He had never met anyone who needed him as much as Elle did. And he enjoyed the feeling of being needed. And the greatest part was she desperately didn't want him hurt.

How many times had he been used, for who and what he was? Elle would walk into the belly of the beast, if it meant others would not be hurt? Even others she had never met before. Victor had never met anyone so selfless before. He felt awed to just be in her presences, how could anyone want to hurt her?

Even the thought of Aldon possessing her made him want to drag the bastard straight to hell.

Victor picked Elle up cradling her until she straddled him. He pressed her against the wall she moaned low making him a little crazy with need. Victor finally carried her to the bed. She had tried to get rid of him this morning and he was going to prove to her he wasn't going anywhere. She was his, he was going to fight for her, and she needed him as much as he needed her.

He laid her down on the bed. He stared down at her golden eyes. Eyes that stared up at him. "You can't ever get rid of me, Elle."

He dragged his fingers through her hair combing the thick strands across the sheets. "I'm not going anywhere, Elle." She shook her head, and he knew she wanted to argue.

"You're not alone anymore," he whispered against her throat as he pressed his tongue along and down her chest. He needed her naked like he needed his next breath. He pulled on the helm of the t-shirt and she allowed him to pull it over her head. His breath caught at the site of her full breasts, incased in her lace bra.

"Gods Elle, you're so fucking beautiful." He felt his brain scatter as he focused on the woman. He couldn't remember wanting anyone the way he wanted her. He shook with his need, his hands settled beneath her breasts and felt her shudder beneath him.

"Victor." She moaned his name. Making his cock kick and strain against his jeans, begging for release "Please."

He smiled, as she arched into his kiss. "Tell me what you want, Elle."

"Gods Victor, I don't know." She squirmed and simultaneously pulled and pushed him away. "But don't stop."

Victor had no plans of stopping any time soon. His hands circling her, and flipping the clasps to her bra. He peeled the lace away baring her beautiful breasts to him. He smiled and held her eyes as he lowered his mouth to one hard peak. He chuckled softly when her eyes practically crossed as he tugged the peak into his mouth flicking the nipple with his tongue.

"Gods, Victor, don't ever stop," Elle cried out again, making Victor feel like a god.

He was about to move to the other breast when Dante called, sending a sharp stab straight through the base of his skull. He growled low, burying his face in Elle's throat. He tried to ignore it but within seconds the call came again. Dante wasn't going to be ignored and Victor shook his head trying to dislodge the sudden and searing pain that warred with sexual frustration coursing through his veins. "I need you so bad, Elle." The words groaned out between his teeth.

"I'm right here." She spiked her fingers through his hair. Holding him close and making his body ache to the point of pain.

Dante's call came again and Victor stumbled away from the bed clutching at his head. He felt something trickle from his nose and he wiped it with the back of his hand; it came away bloody.

"Dante is demanding an audience," he snarled through his teeth. "Elle…" he took a step toward the bed. He needed to explain.

But when he looked at her the passion shinning in her eyes made him falter. "Ah sweetheart don't look at me like that." He was gasping for air and she looked so freaking hot and ready to be fucked. Her lips were puffy and kiss swollen, breasts full and nipples hard. His body was at war with itself. His head was pounding, nose bleeding, demanding he answer Dante. But gods damn, the rest of him demanded he satisfy his woman.

She bit her bottom lip, confusion written all over her face. And when he stumbled back as Dante called again, she gave him a look like he was betraying her.

"I can't ignore Dante." He took a step away from her before he fell on her; he felt something snap in his head and damn him he stumbled and was that him crying out in pain? Fuck he had turned into a pussy. He was fighting the call and it was showing. "I have to go, Elle. I'm so sorry babe."

She looked alarmed and recognition showed and she nodded, just as another call came and whether he liked it or not he was going.

Victor felt himself being ripped apart as he was pulled through time and space. It felt like he was being stabbed by a million burning needles. Another agonizing scream of pain was ripped from deep in his belly as his body was pulled apart atom by atom and then jammed back together just as roughly and then he was on his hands and knees gasping for air covered in his own blood. He was naked, and bleeding from several places but was in too much pain to find out exactly where. Taking inventor would have to wait. He felt Dante standing over him. Victor concentrated on breathing and waiting for Dante to speak.

"You try to deny me?" Dante asked softly.

"No, Father," Victor answered just as softly. It hurt to speak. It felt like he had gargled with glass. Probably from all the screaming he had just done.

"The method by which you appeared would speak otherwise," Dante said.

"I apologize, father," Victor whispered.

"You have grown too close to this demi-god." Dante's voice was growing angry and Victor was in too much pain to even rise to meet his anger. "And now the Blood Rite Dagger almost claimed one of my sons."

"I was able to save Garrett," Victor reminded him.

"Do not contradict me." Dante swore, making Victor flinch.

"Why did we not know the Sons of Adam had the Blood Rite Dagger?" Dante roared. Making the marble floor beneath Victor tremble.

Victor could not continue to stay in this subjugated position, and he forced himself to stand. He wobbled on shaky legs, but was able to meet his father's eyes. All his brothers stood around them, including Celeste and Marcus. And they all looked just as upset as Victor felt. So this was a dressing down for them all, not just Victor. Somehow it didn't make him feel any better.

"It was a surprise," Victor admitted.

Dante's eyes were furious. "Is that supposed to make me feel better?" He roared.

"Of course not." Victor nodded.

"Have you figured out how the Tribunal is involved?" Dante demanded. "Or have you spent your time bedding the demi-god whore?"

"Not yet," Victor admitted grinding his teeth and swallowing past the insult he had leveled over Elle's character.

Dante slammed his hand against the arm rest of his throne causing it to crumble beneath his attack.

"Because of the female," he spat.

Victor kept his mouth closed. "What exactly is she to you?" he demanded. Victor continued to keep his mouth closed. "Obviously a distraction. Do I need to have her killed?"

"She can't be killed," Christian offered.

"You are banned from the mortal plane," Dante dictated.

Victor blanched. "No." He stepped forward, making a stand. For the first time, he held his father's gaze.

Dante glared at him. A collective gasp rose from his siblings.

"I will not walk away from her." Victor spoke the words, unsure what he was doing or how Dante would react to outright mutiny. Dante could destroy Victor if he wanted. Send him to Hell, or place him in a Pandora's Box for all of eternity. But Victor wouldn't walk away from Elle. He would fight for her. Do whatever it took to keep her. Even stand up to Dante.

"I have made my decision, she is a distraction. One apparently you cannot handle. One of your brothers will handle the situation. You are banned from entering the mortal plane," Dante said again. Victor felt the subtle shiver pass through him that would make it impossible for him to move out of the Infernos. Fury like nothing he had ever felt, replaced everything. All the pain and fear in him.

He had feared Dante his entire existence. But this fear? This fear of losing Elle? Of being taken away from her? This fury? It eclipsed all of that. He would fight his father for the right to protect her, to be with her.

Victor took a step up the dais. "I will not allow you to keep me from her. I have made a promise to keep her safe and I plan to follow through on the promise," Victor repeated.

Dante stood and walked toward Victor, his bare feet making no sounds on the plush carpet. He was a slight figure when it came to the muscular builds of the Reapers. But, what Dante lacked in build, he made up for in different ways. And you never under estimated the ruler of the Infernos. If you did, it was usually the last thing you did.

Dante stood nose to nose with Victor. For several minutes, neither one spoke. Then Dante's head tilted to the side, as if in thought. "How many millennia have you ruled in Violence, Victor?" he asked so quietly Victor would have missed it had Dante not been so close.

Victor considered the question. "I've lost count," he said honestly.

"Yes..." Dante said thoughtfully. "I have as well," he said backing up and moving back to his chair. "So long, I had forgotten the flaw," he said with disgust. "That you and your brothers were spawned from the Angels." He emphasized the last word with disgust.

Victor flinched at his father's revulsion. "Is she worth it?" Dante asked.

Victor closed his eyes wanting to scream in anger and pound his father in the face. Had it been so long, Dante had forgotten once he had been an angel? That he had stepped from that lofty perch, to rule the Infernos? He had searched the levels of Infernos, for an Angel who would spawn the Reapers. An Angel, he had once loved and coveted beyond all others. In the end, even she had turned on him. Like those early Reapers. Like so many others in the Infernos. He would do everything in his significant power, to keep his sons from living through the kind of pain, love ultimately caused.

Victor opened his eyes, glaring at his father. "Yes. She is worth it."

"She will turn on you eventually." Dante explained.

Victor flinched. "No, she won't."

"You are prepared to pay the price?" Dante demanded.

Victor didn't even hesitate. "Yes."

"A pound of flesh then," Dante said motioning to Victor's brothers who stood behind him.

Victor nodded and moved to the pillars where he would be chained for the punishment. Christian held up the chains, and Victor allowed his brother to slip them on his wrists.

"Are you sure about this?" Christian asked.

Victor only nodded.

Christian shook his head. "No woman, much less a demi-goddess is worth this," he swore. Before moving to the other side.

Celeste moved over to him, tears glistened in her eyes. Marcus stood at her side. "Please go to Elle and stay with her until I can make it back there. A Daughter of Eve, Tabitha, is there with her. Do not let this woman move to action, before I am well enough to come back. And whatever you do, do not tell Elle about what happened here."

Marcus nodded and tried to drag Celeste away but not before Celeste threw her arms around her brother. "You heal everyone else. Who is going to heal you?"

Victor said nothing but nodded to Marcus who pried his sister away from him. They Flashed away, and Victor was glad they were gone before the punishment started.

His other brothers circled around him, and he stood proud as they nodded to him. They would stand with him in this. They didn't agree with what Dante was doing. By standing so they could make eye contact with him, instead of on Dante's side they were showing whose side they were on. That alone brought a tear to his eye.

"Is that the way of it then?" Dante snarled from behind him.

Christian nodded, taking the lead for the brothers.

"It makes me proud, to see you stand together," Dante said, laughing. "I ask again, Victor. Is she really worth a pound of flesh?"

"Yes," Victor said again without hesitation. He stared at his brothers but his mind was back in that room kissing Elle, the taste of her on his tongue. The smell of her skin surrounded him.

"She better be," Dante said just as the sound of the whip cracking tore through the air.

Chapter 9

Elle groaned she could hear the arguing from where she was hiding in the library. The very last thing she wanted to deal with was another fight between... She listened carefully; Tabitha and Celeste. Those two really were a matched pair when it came to a fight. And they knew it, so when they were bored, irritated, frustrated...basically when they were awake. They looked for each other to pick a fight.

So here Elle was, hiding in the one place, Celeste and Tabitha wouldn't come looking for her. Marcus or Falcon might come looking for her here but Celeste and Tabitha wouldn't. So here she hid from the two.

Elle laid her head against the door trying to pull up a picture of Victor hoping it would calm her. And hating him for leaving her. But she couldn't get the look Victor had given her right before he had disappeared. His look of pure pain, she knew he hadn't wanted to go. And she kept telling herself he hadn't wanted to go. It was the only thing that bolstered her enough to open the door and go break up another fight between Tabitha and Celeste.

"We can't stay here," Tabitha said for what seemed like the millionth time.

"We aren't going anywhere. So shut up or I'll shut you up." Celeste got right into Tabitha's face. Their noses almost touched. The two had come to blows several times in the last week. And Elle was tired of pulling them apart. Let them kick each other's asses again; they truly seemed to enjoy it.

For the moment, Elle was tired of sitting and waiting. Tabitha had a good plan. And frankly, she was tired of the Daughter of Eve keeping her up at night with her insistent plan which she would go over and over with, Elle. Besides, it was actually a good plan. And as much as she wanted to be with Victor, they couldn't continue to sit here waiting. It was bad enough the Freaks were trying to kill them, they didn't need the infighting.

"I agree with Tabitha. Victor will find us. The attacks are getting out of control. We need to leave as soon as possible," Elle said. Leaving the group, she headed to her room to get her things ready. She didn't fully understand why Victor had left and not returned she only knew he had to leave. And Celeste had refused to tell her anything about what had happened with Victor after he had left. Christian and Garrett had shown up two days ago both grim and refusing to say a damn thing either. Damn them, and their closed mouthed ways.

She heard fighting start up behind her, as she stomped down the hallway, but she didn't care. Victor had left and she was barely holding onto what little sanity she had left. Emotions were pulling at her, slowing driving her mad. If she could get a few minutes of quiet she could think in peace. But, she wasn't going to get that, without Victor. And her mind was constantly working on blocking out everyone's emotions. Elle was exhausted and wished for the umpteenth time for Victor to return. Then wondered when had she become so dependent on him? Then damned him straight back to the Infernos for making her want and need him so madly.

"Are you sure about this?" Falcon asked, jogging to catch up to her. Of everyone in the house, he was the most meticulous, and his emotions rarely bled over. For that reason, Elle enjoyed his company the most. She admitted, she had been terrified of the man at first. But, once a person got past the rough exterior, Falcon was a nice guy who controlled his emotions remarkable well. It left Elle wondering what had happened to the Tracker to leave him so in control all the time. When all this was over, she wanted to sit down and find out what had happened to him.

Elle slowed her steps and turned to Falcon. "The Freaks are getting past the wards, and that is too close, we can't maintain our position. Someone is going to get hurt, if not killed. If we leave today we can separate into groups. Maybe confuse them, sitting here and fighting them by playing a defensive fight isn't getting us anywhere."

"What about Victor?" Celeste asked coming down the hall.

Elle turned to the woman. "Are you going to tell me where he is? Are you going to tell me if he is going to come back?" Celeste just gave her one of her blank stares. Making Elle want to scream and cry and pound Celeste into the ground.

"What about him?" Elle demanded. "He isn't here. I'm sure he'll catch up where ever we end up. I'm not going to sit on my thumbs waiting for him. We are sitting ducks here. We need to move." She was glad her voice didn't crack when she spoke. Because it took everything she had to make sure it didn't.

"About damn time." Tabitha said, pushing through the small group and took a defensive position next to Elle. "Let's get the hell out of here."

Elle felt the hostility and irritation roll off Tabitha. She tried to block the emotions. But they were so strong. They bled through her defenses as if they didn't exist. She gritted her teeth trying not to let them become her own, but it was impossible.

"Let's get this fucking plan on the move, I'm feeling the need to kill something." Elle snapped at the group making everyone stop and look at her as if she had sprouted horns. She rolled her head on her shoulders listening to it pop and crack, she just needed to relieve some of her tension.

"Can we just do something, already? All this inactivity is killing me." She muttered, not caring if they thought she had lost her mind. It was time to get moving. She turned and walked away from the group. None of them understood her. They didn't know the frustration that plagued her. The emotions that clawed at her, how they were affecting her. And that was just from the individuals in the house.

If she went anywhere near the Freaks, she could feel the soullessness sucking at her; like a black hole trying to suck her down. More than that was the rage the Freaks felt that boiled just below the surface. It took everything she had to not let it consume her. She had given in to it once and the backlash had been horrible, she wasn't interested in giving into it again.

Everyone was getting to her, and all she wanted was Victor. To drown in the calmness he offered so she could think with a clear mind for a few minutes. She was going to kick his ass when she saw him again. The bastard. He had promised to never leave her. The very morning, he had disappeared, he had whispered those words against her skin.

Now he was in the Infernos and gods only knew when he would come back to her. How many times had she been abandoned like that? The pain lanced through her like a knife. What she wouldn't give to have an ounce of her demi-god powers so she could look into the Infernos just to see if he was okay. His infallible siblings wouldn't even tell her if he was okay or not. She didn't know if he was harmed, and the only thing she had to go on was the scream of pain and the way he had left.

"Please come back." She whispered.

She shivered remembering how Victor had left her. Then he had stumbled away from her and Flashed away. She knew from his broken words it hadn't been his choice, that Dante had demanded an audience, he had cried out in pain the seconds before he had left.

"Damn you, Victor." She kicked her bedroom door for good measure. "When are you coming back?" she asked the door. Tears choked her, tears she refused to let fall. Elle balled her fist and pressed them into her eyes, she was not going to cry.

Maybe if she repeated it over and over it would be true.

Tabitha burst into her room, hitting Elle with the door. "Why are you standing so close to the door?" Tabitha demanded.

"Why don't you knock?" Elle demanded.

Tabitha glowered at her. "Why are you so grumpy? It's not like you."

"You don't even know me! So how can you even make that assumption?" Elle asked. Turning from Tabitha and grabbing her duffel bag, she started throwing in her things. Anything to keep herself from bursting into tears.

"He's coming back Elle," Tabitha said, almost being kind. Stopping Elle in her tracks.

"Why do you suddenly care?" Elle snapped.

"I'm not heartless. It obviously means something to you..." she hesitated. "He...I mean the Reap... Victor means something to you." She tried to smile but it looked more like a grimace.

Elle slumped down on the bed. "Tabitha why is it so hard for you to show any emotion other than hostility?"

Tabitha took a step back as if she had been slapped. "I have other emotions."

Elle shook her head. "No you really don't. I'm an Empath. I would be able to feel them. Your primary emotion is hostility. Even when you're trying to be nice, hostility is the emotion you're emanating. What happened to you...?"

Tabitha looked like she wanted to kill something. "Nothing happened to me, Elle. I am a trained killer. Hostility is what I do."

"Tabitha, you are not a killer. You might have killed, but a stone-cold-blooded killer?" Elle regarded Tabitha. "I don't think so. You chose to be hostile or not. Take Marcus for example. He has a darkness in him, simmering just below his surface. He could bring an apocalyptic-like death upon the mortal plane. A palpable darkness and hostility that he controls, and only the gods know, how he does it. But he chooses calm, not hostility."

Tabitha snorted. "Marcus is a Fallen Angel, and a love sick fool."

Elle smiled, feeling a slight lift in the antagonism bearing down on her. "Yes, but it is so wonderful. He chose's to not be hostile; you can chose to not be hostile."

Tabitha snorted again adding an eye roll. "I am neither in love nor a fool, Elle. I apologize if my hostility affects you because of your frail emotional state. However, this is who I am. Who I have trained to become, and I am not going to change, not in the thirteenth hour. Are you ready?" she asked motioning to the duffel bag.

Elle was not going to let Tabitha's brutal honesty hurt her, but she had to admit her words did. Elle sighed and finished cramming what little she had left of her own into a duffel bag. She was going to get Tabitha to relax if it was the last thing she did, damn it. Celeste was waiting for them in the hall. "So where we headed?"

Elle knew better than to argue with her, and she looked over her shoulder at Tabitha. "What do you think?"

"Safe house in Houston," Tabitha said glowering at Celeste and back to Elle who glared back. She wasn't going to argue with Tabitha about it either. Celeste and Marcus were coming with them, if Tabitha had a problem with it them Tabitha would just have to suck it up. They all had to work together.

"What about everyone else?" Elle asked walking down the stairs.

"Skylar is coming with us," Celeste said making Tabitha swear under her breath. The Tracker and Tabitha rubbed each other the wrong way. But at least they spoke to each other. It wasn't pleasant words, and most of them were four letters. But they were words. Tabitha had completely ostracized all the other Trackers by day four.

"If you didn't make the other Trackers hate you we wouldn't have to bring Skylar with us," Elle told her dropping her bag by the front door.

"Hate is a strong word." Marcus said, he was ever the diplomat.

"We don't have to bring any of the Trackers with us," Tabitha snapped.

Elle just rolled her eyes. "It's not up for debate, Tabitha. We are all in this together. What about the other Reapers."

"Garrett and Christian are with the Trackers. Nathaniel and Hunter are here as well," Celeste explained.

"More Reapers?" Elle asked surprised.

"Yes, would you like to meet them?" Celeste asked. "I know they would like to meet you. They don't get out much. So you might have to excuse their bad manners," Celeste said laughing. Making her expressive violet eyes shine.

Elle allowed Celeste to lead her into the large great room where everyone was gathered. The sun was just rising, the Trackers were sprawled on the furniture. Ryder held Kyra who was curled up asleep.

The Reapers stood in one corner, and like every other time they took her breath away. They were just so good looking. But this time there were four of them and damn if Celeste hadn't been holding her arm she would have stopped dead in her tracks and just stared at them. All tall and broad shouldered they were a mix between GQ, old Hollywood and the best in bodybuilding. Dressed in jeans and tight t-shirts there was so much hard masculinity and dark hotness it was male beauty personified.

They all turned to her and Celeste, and Elle actually caught her breath. They shared the dark eyes of Victor. The hard, chiseled bone structure. How did they keep woman from throwing themselves at their feet?

"Nathaniel, Hunter, this is Elle." Celeste introduced her. The two Elle didn't recognize, stepped forward. One with sandy blond hair brushing his shoulders bowed his head, but didn't extend his hand.

"I am Nathaniel, I rule over Lust." His voice just barely above a whisper.

"He doesn't touch. It's a Lust thing," Celeste said. Elle nodded back and gave him a smile.

The other Reaper stepped forward; he had dark hair cut close to his head. When he smiled at her it didn't quit reach his eyes and she noticed a scar running the length of his face from his left eye along his hair line to below his jaw and disappeared into the collar of his black t-shirt.

"I am Hunter, I rule over Treachery." He extended his hand. And Elle took it, the moment his fingers touched her she felt something kick her in the chest. Bands of steel wrapped around her chest and started to squeeze making it impossible for her to breathe and she stumbled back gasping.

The moment Hunter released her, the feeling went away. "What the hell?" she gasped. "What was that?"

"Interesting," Hunter said calmly. Like they had been discussing the weather.

Tabitha pulled a knife from a boot and held it to the Reapers throat. "What the fuck was that, what did you do to her?"

"I did nothing to her," Hunter said. "I apologize, Elle. I had no idea my touch would affect you so."

Elle shook her head and grabbed Tabitha. "It felt..." She tried to put it into words.

"Like lies, betrayal, treachery perhaps?" Hunter asked leaning forward just a little. His eyes if possible turned a shade darker than before. Elle saw shades of black shift in his eyes, like clouds passing over the moon. It was breathtaking and Elle wasn't sure if she should be terrified or mesmerized.

Elle caught her breath and looked up at him. "Yes," she gasped.

"Again I apologize. Some of us…" He motioned to his brothers and sighed. "…are a little closer to our work than the others. We are more Reaper than man, mortal or beast. Or at least that is the case with Nathaniel and me."

Both Reapers stepped back and shadows seemed to blur their edges making them seem more ethereal then real. And Elle had to shake her head to bring them back into focus. Hunter stepped forward again and smiled. "However, these Freaks and the uniqueness of the situation, Elle…"

The way he said her name sent chills down her spine, and she would have stepped back, should have stepped back but dammit she couldn't have moved if her life depended on it.

He quirked one eyebrow at her and smiled. "…require our intervention."

Elle gave him her full wattage smile. "Well thank you very much. I'm very grateful for both of your unique gifts. And if you see Victor would you mind telling him to get his ass back here?"

Nathaniel and Hunter both burst out laughing, and Elle finally felt like the rope which had held her in place snapped and she stepped back and looked at Celeste who was shaking her head at Elle.

Celeste took ahold of Elle. "Told you they don't get out much. But they wanted to help."

"Why?" Elle asked never taking her eyes off the two Reapers. Her feelings immediately went to Victor. "Is

Victor okay? Where is he?" she demanded for the hundredth time.

"He will be here when he can," Celeste said but the way she said it gave Elle the chills. It was more the way she said it. And Elle recognized Victor couldn't come to her. What had happened to him?

She jerked her arm free and glared at the smaller woman. "You are going to tell me right now where the hell Victor is."

"He is in the Infernos," Celeste told her without blinking.

"Dammit." Elle wanted to shake her. "But why can't he be here."

Marcus stepped around his mate and gave Elle a reassuring smile. "Elle please don't ask any more questions. We are all walking a very tight line. Victor would be here if he could. In his absence, he has sent his brothers and sister to protect you. Those he trust beyond any other. He will explain and has asked that we say nothing because he wants to be the one to explain. That is all we can tell you."

It was more information than anyone had given her in the last week. They still weren't the answers she was looking for, "It's not enough Marcus."

He gave her a reassuring smile, before continuing. "We have all agreed moving out of Louisiana is the best course of action. Let's concentrate on doing that right now."

"I want some answers," Elle snapped.

"And you will have them as soon as you are safe," Marcus said taking her by the elbow he led her toward the front door. Celeste at his side, Tabitha on her other.

Elle wanted to fight him, but everyone had a sudden sense of urgency she hadn't sensed before.

"Gods something is going on," she said as the front door was thrown open.

"One of my vampire spies said there is a movement of Freaks down by the river an hour ago," Marcus said quietly, pushing her through the door. "Something has them moving and all riled up."

"But they have never attacked during the day," Elle said swinging her pack over her shoulder.

"Never say never," Celeste said, scanning the open space between the door and the cars lined up on the dirt path about twenty five yards from the house. "I never liked this house. It's just too out in the open."

"That's what makes it great, no neighbors for five miles," Skylar said jogging toward the SUV.

"He means no witnesses." Marcus tried for a smile but nobody laughed. They had wards up and it had kept the Freaks out but they weren't holding and a couple had gotten through last night. It had kept them all on edge and nobody had slept.

They climbed into the SUV with Marcus behind the wheel. "It's about a four hour drive. I don't want to get pulled over so get comfortable. We all love the speed limit."

"It would be faster if we could just use portals," Sky grumbled.

"Don't be a dumbass," Celeste said rolling her eyes she slapped him upside the head.

Sky rubbed his head and mumbled an apology to Elle who just shrugged. "You didn't have to come with us."

Sky laughed. "You would miss me horrible, if I didn't come with you, sweetheart. I couldn't hurt you like that. Having you cry yourself to sleep every night pining for me just wouldn't be right."

"Do you ever get tired of hearing your own voice?" Tabatha asked.

Sky gave her a blinding smile. "Nope." He folded his arms over his chest and settled back in his seat he looked ready to argue with Tabitha the entire ride to Houston.

"Don't make me pull this car over children," Marcus warned from the driver's seat.

Elle narrowed her eyes at Skylar who winked at her. She just knew the Tracker wouldn't be able to keep his smart mouth closed.

"She started it," Skylar said with the best pouting voice.

"Just shut up," Tabitha snapped at Skylar.

"Sweetheart, it's going to take you and an army of Daughters of Eve to do it." He shrugged dragging his eyes over Tabitha. "But you can try."

Tabitha launched herself over a row of seats to attack him. "I'm truly going to kill you this time," she snarled. Elle climbed into the cargo area as Marcus maneuvered the SUV to the side of the road. The two fought on, never noticing as Celeste and Marcus attempted to pull them apart.

They hadn't even made it an hour into the trip. It was pitiful really. Soon Celeste was swinging at Skylar and Tabitha, swearing like a sailor at them both.

"Really?" Marcus shouted at the trio. Which Elle was pretty sure none of them heard. The fight spilled out onto the road. Since they were just using their fists, Elle was sure they were more blowing off steam and frustration then actually trying to hurt each other. As she watched, she had to admit, it was almost entertaining.

Well except for Tabitha she might in reality want to hurt Skylar. But most people wanted to hurt Skylar. But since she hadn't pulled out a knife or a gun, Elle was pretty sure the Tracker was safe for the moment.

Marcus stuck his head into the car. "You okay?"

Elle smiled. "Yeah."

He laughed his green eyes sparkling; when he looked like this she could see the Angel in him. "I'm going to pull Celeste out of this and then we'll be on our way."

Elle laughed. "What about the other two?"

"Oh they'll have to find their own way back to us," he said also laughing. He pulled out of the SUV and slammed the door. Elle climbed into one of the seats and watched as Marcus wrapped his arms around the waist of his small mate physically extracting her from the fight.

He turned so her flailing arms and legs were swinging at air. She immediately stopped and her head dropped back to rest on Marcus's shoulder and her eyes closed. She said something which made Marcus smile and kiss her cheek.

Elle felt something close to her heart tense, what would it be like to have a love match like that? They had a love that wrapped around them and was so intense it was visible with the naked eye. Well it was visible to her anyway.

"Touching, isn't it?" Elle squeaked and whipped around.

Aldon sat in the driver's seat, but was turned and looking at the scene. She still didn't feel him. "How..." she gurgled in shock.

"Ah..." he leaned over and dragged a finger over Elle's cheek sending shock waves of revulsion through Elle. "You can thank Chaos for this." He whipped around and started the SUV slamming on the gas.

Elle reached for the door, but the locks clicked into place. At the same time, Freaks popped into place outside surrounded the group. Elle let out a blood curdling scream, she didn't think anyone heard, as Aldon left her companions in a spray of gravel as he speed away.

Elle sat in shock for three minutes and just stared at the back of Aldon's head.

"This isn't happening," she finally said, looking around for a weapon. She didn't even have a gun on her.

Aldon smiled in the rearview mirror. "Oh it's happening alright. And it was frighteningly easy." He smiled. "I'll have you bedded by nightfall."

"The hell you will," Elle said. "I would rather die."

Aldon laughed. "We both know that could be arranged and when you wake then I will bed you. I expect you to die many times in my handling that is why it can only be you, Elle. So it doesn't matter now does it?"

She blanched. "What?"

He was insane, it was the only answer. And if he was insane she didn't have any options, she would rather kill them both. At least she would come back. Throwing caution to the wind she jumped forward and covered his eyes with her hands. Then wondered what the hell she was going to do next?

The SUV immediately started to swerve when his hands left the steering wheel. She slapped at his hands and tried for the locks. A book sat on the console and she grabbed it slamming it into the side of his head he grunted in pain and she was able to get the doors unlocked. Luckily the SUV had slowed down leaning back in her chair she took both legs and kicked the chair with everything she had.

The chair slammed into the steering wheel his face and head making contact with the windshield blood splattering and making a horrible crunching noise. He grunted, and his hands went limp. His head was tilted at an odd angle, an angle totally wrong to support life.

When she released her legs Aldon crumpled over the console in a heap as the car slowed and rolled to a halt at the side of the road.

"Oh shit," Elle breathed. She had done it, she had killed the bastard. She scrambled for the door throwing it open and stumbling out she fell to her knees and vomited. Was it over? Could it possibly be done? She couldn't wait to tell Victor.

She pushed herself to her feet and let the SUV support her as she started to walk then run back to where they had left her friends. Elle wasn't sure how far she had gone when Tabitha appeared.

Elle fell into the Tabitha's arms. "Oh Gods Elle, I thought for sure he had taken you. But you had an energy trail," the woman screamed at her and then shook her. "When I found the SUV, there was blood everywhere. I thought for sure…" Then she shook her a second time. "Don't ever do that to me again…"

"What? Kick Aldon's ass and kill him?" Elle said pushing away from Tabitha.

"What?" Tabitha barked. "What are you talking about? Do you have a head injury?" Tabitha started to run her hands over Elle's head.

"Where is everyone else?" Elle asked.

"I have no idea. As soon as I could, I came after you," Tabitha admitted.

Elle wanted to slap her. "You left them to fight the Freaks?" Elle turned and continued down the road.

Tabitha grabbed her. "It would be faster to go back to the SUV and then drive to them."

Elle shuddered "What about the body?"

"What body?" Tabitha asked.

Elle went cold. "Aldon's body," she whispered.

"Elle" Tabitha said just as quietly and looked around. "I created a portal to you and the SUV the moment I could get away from those Freaks. It led me to the SUV, when I got there the SUV was running, there was a great deal of blood but no body."

Elle grabbed Tabitha. "I thought I killed him."

"How?" Tabitha asked.

Elle explained what had happened. "But you didn't check the body?"

"He was slumped over, not moving. His neck was broken, it had to be broken. The way it looked I assumed… I didn't think I needed to…" Elle said ringing her hands.

Tabitha looked at her like she wanted to ring her neck. Then grabbed her by the arm and started to drag her back toward where she had left the SUV. "Always check the body, Elle. And if possible burn the fucker."

****

"Is that my t-shirt?" Sky asked when he opened the door.

"I had to clean up the blood," Tabitha said with a shrug.

"And the only thing you could find was my t-shirt?" Skylar asked.

"Yep." Tabitha said with a smile.

"I see," Skylar said. Reaching in, he grabbed the garment and threw it into the dirt. Sky climbed into the farthest back seat, and he stretched out, using his duffel bag as a pillow. He curled up as much as a man over six feet tall could and closed his eyes.

"What happened?" Marcus asked as he and Celeste climbed in.

Tabitha let him know.

"I see," he said. Marcus pulled out his cell phone, and made a call. "Time for plan 'B'." Was the first thing he said. She ignored everything else he said. Elle just sat in the passenger seat trying to look as small as possible. When Marcus hung up the phone he asked Tabitha to change direction.

"Why?" She demanded.

"Because the others were attacked too. We can't stay out on the roads. We're going to fly."

****

They flew for over two weeks. Handing Elle and Tabitha off to different people she didn't remain on the ground for more than an hour. And the flights ranged from two hours to fourteen hours. She hadn't been on a plane in years, before then, and she had loved the chance to take the different planes. From luxury private planes to cargo planes and jets, and a couple commercial flights.

She saw glimpses of the Eiffel Tower, The Great Wall of China from the air of course the expansive desserts of Africa, the ice caps over the North Pole. The Aura Borealis, the great plains of Australia, the expansive Pacific Ocean. One pilot had skimmed down so she could see pods of wales in the Baring Sea. A helicopter pilot took her and Tabitha through the Grand Canyon on her way down through the coast of Mexico, she saw dolphins playing in the ocean. She had been in a boat plane that landed in an amazing cove in Iceland. She slept in a beautiful king size bed on an amazing jet, and had also barely slept in the cargo bay of an army plane. She flew over the time exchange so many times she didn't know where she was or what time it was.

But after a week of it, the shine had worn off, for her and Tabitha. After the sixth day Tabitha had stopped talking to her, now she was a silent and extremely grumpy partner.

But everyone recognized keeping Elle on the ground meant exposing everyone to unnecessary fights with Freaks and exposure they couldn't handle. Nobody knew what to do, or how to fight them off. And Aldon had appeared several times just as she had taken off, she was exposed anywhere she landed and so were the people she was with.

She didn't know what everyone was waiting for. Was it Victor? Was it information? Nobody said anything to her or Tabitha. It rankled Tabitha so much, she was sure Tabitha was about to start killing people. And she didn't blame her. But when Tabitha had stopped talking to her, Elle had grown worried. She wasn't sure if Tabitha was planning something or if the woman was slipping into a depression. She prayed Tabitha was planning something, because Elle was so tired from all the plane hopping and time zone jumping she was too exhausted to figure out a way to escape their current hell.

So when she woke to a hand covering her mouth, Elle opened her eyes to Tabitha with mixed feelings. "Don't say a word," Tabitha whispered.

Elle nodded, happy Tabitha had finally figured a way to get out of their current predicament, and happy she was finally speaking to her. "We need to move now. Do you understand me?" Elle nodded again. Tabitha handed Elle her duffel bag.

Slinging her bag over her shoulder Elle swung her legs over her side of the bunk she was sleeping in. Today they were in a make shift jumbo jet which had been outfitted for soldiers, it sounded like it was about to land. It was dark and the entire jet was shaking. Elle had to grip the metal posts to keep from falling over and landing flat on her face.

"What about Bowen and Garrett?" Elle whispered to Tabitha. They were sleeping in bunks closer to the cockpit.

Tabitha put one finger to her lips her green eyes telling her to keep quiet. Elle wasn't sure this was a good idea. For the moment, she was going to follow Tabitha. At least, for now. Because it was a better option than getting on another flight bound for gods only knew where. Anything was better than the last two weeks of running.

Tabitha dropped to her hands and knees, and Elle followed, as someone on watch passed by. The jet bumped as it descended. They remained on all fours, until Elle felt the jet slid unto the tarmac. At which point, Tabitha looked over her shoulder and signaled her to follow.

Elle moved to a crouch and wondered again if this was a good idea, she was pretty sure Tabitha was making a run for it and not really forcing Elle to come with her but… This was the point Elle had to make the choice.

Tabitha, or the Reapers and Victor? Victor, who she had known less than a week. Elle looked back to Bowen and Garrett, Elle felt something close to her heart pull and she knew her heart was breaking. She loved that stupid Reaper. But he had been gone for almost a month. He had promised to never leave her but then he had. Just like her siblings, she had come to count on him. Then he had left. She needed him so bad, it was painful. Where was he? Tears welled up in her chest. And she whispered his name.

"Ready?" Tabitha whispered. Asking so much more then Elle was ready to admit. But she nodded and followed Tabitha as she quietly knocked the one guard on watch out and they exited the jet without making a sound.

A small car was waiting for them, and a helicopter was waiting for them a mile away. They were flying away before the jumbo jet had come to a complete halt. Before the other occupants had even awoken.

Elle felt more broken then she ever had, when she had left her siblings before. And she curled in a ball on the helicopter as it flew them away. Tabitha patted her on the shoulder, as she sobbed. For once, not saying anything. Not caring that she was crying like a baby in front of Tabitha.

"It's going to be okay," Tabitha whispered to Elle.

Elle just shook her head and continued to sob. She cried until she had nothing left, she cried until her body gave out and she fell into a dark dreamless sleep.

****

"What do you mean she's gone?" Victor shouted.

"Gone. Like poof! Into the wind," Bowen said, making weird movements with his hands. Victor couldn't even begin to interpreter.

"You're a fucking Tracker. So track her." Victor was pretty sure he was going to strangle the Tracker, Garett pushed the Tracker away.

"What do you think we've been doing?" Garrett said. "She took another flight, it's the only explanation. Her trail goes cold about a mile from the plane."

"Didn't you tell her I would be here? She wouldn't have left if she had known I was going to be here." This wasn't happening. This was the only thing that had kept him from giving into the bleakness of his punishment. Knowing she would be back in his arms. And she wasn't here.

"No, we thought after the last couple of weeks it would be a nice surprise. She was pretty worn out," Garrett said with a grimace.

"What the fuck?" Victor threw his hands in the air. "I need to kill something."

Both Garrett and Bowen took a step away from him. His back was killing him, it was nearly healed but he wasn't about to stay in the Infernos while Elle was running for her life on the mortal plane. And damn it, the time difference had meant he had been gone for almost three damn weeks! She probable felt like he had abandoned her. Like everyone else in her life. He felt so helpless right then he wasn't sure if killing something would be enough. Victor spiked a hand through his hair, how in the name of all the gods was he going to find her? And damn that Daughter of Eve straight to Hell and back. Victor looked around and for a moment he wasn't sure what to do, but then forced himself to be calm.

"Bowen?"

"Ah, shit man. I'm not immortal. Kill your brother. He comes back," Bowen whined.

"No. I need you to find someone else," Victor snapped.

Bowen smiled. "Ah, that I can do. Who, what, where and when?"

"Atlanta, I think. She's a demi-god. And if she sold out her sister, I'm going to rake her over the coals of Hell its self."

Chapter 10

"Doesn't look like the abode of a demi-goddess," Bowen said, from where he stood, leaning against a tree. He chewed on a toothpick his arms folded over his chest. They were both trying to blend in but it was impossible.

Victor had to agree. This wasn't the worst part of town but he could have picked a hundred other places a demi-goddess would chose for a hiding place. "You sure this is the place?" He wasn't sure the place was going to remain standing for long.

Drug dealers hung out on the corners. He heard police sirens blaring in the distance. The place was a beehive of activity there was no way they would be able to go unnoticed here. They had already been solicited by a prostitute in the ten minutes they had been standing there.

"Of course not. But the only way you'll know is to go inside and find out," Bowen said. "Garrett is round back. Shout if you need backup."

"I'll need a fucking tetanus shot," Victor said heading across the street glaring at the looks he was getting by the street rabble. He didn't want to get into it with them. He wasn't about to back down, either. It had taken Bowen four days to get this far. He was about to start killing people if they got in his way. Tabitha and Elle had disappeared into the night and Victor was beyond pissed. He would kill for a word about where the hell that halfcocked Daughter of Eve had taken Elle. All he knew was when he got his hands around Tabitha's neck he was going to strangle her.

He pounded his fist against the front door. It was mid-afternoon and he heard a television blaring from inside. If this was the demi-god's idea of a safe house, she had a strange idea of safe. He thought looking at the broken down porch. When nobody answered he pounded again. Gods only knew what could be happening to Elle, and if this was a wild goose chase he was going to murder whoever was at the end of it.

"Dude, you got a problem?"

Victor turned toward a kid leaning against the fence. Pants barely on, shirt so big it could have held three of him, baseball cap turned sideways. Tattoos covering his arms and crawling up his neck.

Victor shook his head. "No." He turned back to the door. The kid had no idea what he was messing with and Victor was a lot of things but he wasn't about to murder a child.

"Seems to me you do," the kid said again before Victor could knock again. "The way you pound'n the door."

Victor turned back to the kid. "This doesn't concern you." The kid had moved to the end of the stairs. "I'm thinking if Hell wanted to come to the door she'd a come out by now."

"Hell?" Victor asked. "See I don't give a shit if Hell don't want to see me," Victor said adopting the silly vernacular; he was quickly losing his temper. And this kid didn't really know what he was up against. "I'm not going away." Victor said this loudly enough so anyone in the house could hear it. And he was rewarded when the curtains twitched.

The kid laughed, and Victor stared at him for a moment. "Wrong answer," the kid said with a smile pulling a gun from his baggy pants.

Victor sighed as he noted several of the other kids on the street had moved into strategic positions boxing Victor and the kid in. So not just standing around, but guarding the place, interesting. Helena had them all working for her, Victor had to rethink this spot as a place to hide.

He knocked again. "Hell come out now and nobody has to get hurt," Victor said.

The kid laughed again. "Now see that's what I'm supposed to say." He turned his gun sideways. "Get off the fucking porch, pretty boy."

Victor heard Bowen snort all the way from across the street. And Victor's patience started to unravel.

Victor crossed his arms over his chest. "And if I don't?"

He saw it, the fear. It flickered for just a moment in the depths of the kid's eyes. And Victor actually took pity on the kid. He had thought he was going to need to kill the kid and the other kids on the street but they were innocents.

Victor leaned over and hit the door one more time. "Helena," he screamed. "Open the fucking door before I call a Ringer. We have a mutual interest here. And I don't want these souls."

The door immediately opened and he was grabbed by the shoulder, he smiled at the kid as he was yanked into the house. The door was slammed behind him. He was thrown up against it, an arm was pressed against his throat. The most intense blue eyes glared at him.

"Who are you and what do you want?" she breathed.

Victor just stood there staring at the most beautiful woman he had ever seen. Golden curls surrounded a rounded face with sea blue eyes. Eyes that looked ready to kill him, but still beautiful. She had perfect pink lips, and high color to her cheeks.

"Holy shit you're gorgeous. What the hell?" Victor tried to shake his head but her arm tightened on his throat making it almost impossible to breathe.

"I asked you who the hell you were?" Her perfect eyebrows drew together in anger and Victor had a hard time thinking.

Lights were going off in his line of vision and then he let the darkness swallow him. And the next thing he knew she was screaming and slapping him.

Victor pushed her away. "Fuck."

"Who are you?"

"Victor." He pushed her away again and he blinked rapidly trying to right himself and a world turned upside down. He glared at the woman. But the mesmerizing beauty that had floored him moments ago was now gone. "What the hell?"

She opened her mouth, but Victor held up his hand. "Is it a curse?"

Helena laughed, but it was more of a sad sound really than anything else. "I wish," she sighed. "I'm more beautiful than can be explained. And at first glance men would kill for me. But trust me it lessons after time."

"Not for everyone," Victor said more to himself if he remembered history correctly.

Helena gave him a sharp look. "No, not for everyone." She stood. "Sorry for the choke out but it's the fastest way to get you to think straight. If you are Victor, and you are here, then where the fuck is my sister?"

"I'm hoping you can tell me." Helena turned back to him with fire flashing back into those beautiful blue eyes.

"Tell me you're kidding. How in the world did you lose her?" she glowered. "Can't anyone keep track of her?"

"It's a long story." Victor picked his ass up off the floor. "And does it look like I'm kidding?"

"I gave her the spell that would call a Reaper because you guys were a last resort in keeping her safe," she screamed making Victor wince and take a step back. Her voice had a pitch to it that made his skin crawl. "Because you were the only ones. The only ones that could keep her safe."

"She thinks you sold her out." Helena blanched at Victor's words. "Trust me I wouldn't be here if I had a choice. I can't find her. You're my only chance at getting her back Helena. Tell me you can help me find her."

"I know she thinks we sold her out. We are all being watched." Tears clouded her eyes and Victor took another step back. "But it isn't safe here. Aldon is having this place watched. Damn Chaos and his lying thieving ways. Plus the Tribunal is up to something."

"Wait, who the hell is Chaos?" Victor demanded.

Helena rolled her eyes. "Chaos is one of our brothers. He was taken by the Brotherhood..." she waved her hands... "Millennia...several millennia ago. He is more of a Son of Adam, an acolyte now to their ways, then a demi-god now. He is why the Brotherhood knows about Elle. He is how they track her."

"Shit." Victor swore then swore again. "Does Elle know this?"

Helena looked at him. "I don't know, maybe... probable... I don't know." She shrugged.

"Shit." Victor needed to find Elle. Needed to protect her, if she was on the mortal plane then Chaos could lead Aldon to her. She was in danger and he couldn't get to her. He itched to just hold her, know she was safe. "Can you lead me to her?"

"No, I don't have the powers the Sons of Adam have. Or even the powers Chaos has to track her down. That is why I had her call on the Reapers," she shouted again. "Mind telling me how the hell you lost her?" Her voice had taken on the screeching tone again.

This was the last thing Victor needed. He grabbed Helena and barely stopped himself from shaking her. Instead he placed a hand over her mouth shutting her up. "I got it, Hell. I failed her. No need to remind me." He said, using the nickname the hoodlums outside had used. "No need to raise your voice or go over it again. Trust me nobody understands this more than I do. But that isn't why I am here," he ground out between his teeth. "Now are we going to use an inside voice?"

She nodded and he released her. "What happened?"

Victor told her. "Oh my gods, she is with the Daughters of Eve? Holy shit, this is so much worse."

Helena ran from the room and Victor had no choice but to follow her into a room where she was throwing things into a large duffel bag. "You need to take me to the last place you saw her."

"Okay how is that going to help?" Victor asked.

"The Daughters of Eve? Are you kidding me?" Helena explained. "From the frying pan into the fire. That girl just goes from one problem to the next, it's why she has been kept secreted away. Can't keep her out of trouble. I mean she got herself cursed didn't she? Now she gets herself captured by the Daughters of Eve?"

Victor ground his teeth together, "Shut up Helena."

"What, you disagree?" Helena asked. "Do you have any idea what the Daughters of Eve are going to do with her?"

Victor only glared at Helena until the woman continued, "The Daughters of Eve are going to try and recruit her, they are just as bad as the Sons of Adam."

"What?" Victor asked. He knew he couldn't trust Tabitha.

"The Sons of Adam, would try and impregnate her. The Daughters of Eve would try and recruit her to breed from them." Helena said, looking at him like he had just fallen off the turnip truck.

"I don't think so. They sent one of their warriors to kill Aldon. They don't want him to breed with her," Victor explained.

Helena stopped and glared at him. "Are you really that naïve? If so then you and Elle belong together" Helena spat.

Victor glared at her. "Tabitha is a lot of things Helena but she is not a recruiter for the Daughters of Eve."

"The Tribunal, and Sons of Adam are not going to stop, until they have her, Reaper. The Daughters of Eve may think they can stave off the tide for now with their holier than though beliefs but when it comes down to brass tacks, do you think Elle will be able to say no?" Helena asked folding her arms over her chest.

Victor thought about it for a moment. Elle was one of the kindest and gentlest and most caring individuals Victor knew. It was what drew him to her. Why he cared for her.

"She will be beholden to these woman for saving her life," Helena said with one elegantly arched eyebrow.

"Shit." Victor swore again. "Does any of this have to do with the Tribunal?" he asked.

Helena stopped and looked at him like he had sprouted a second head. "Of course it does. Everything comes back to the Tribunal and their new screwy ass dictates."

"Do you mind explaining it to me?" Victor asked.

"Really? You want me to explain it to you now?" Helena asked.

"Yes please," Victor asked sitting down in the only chair in the room. He felt like his head was spinning. Everything was turning to shit, and the information he was getting was turning everything upside down and sideways, Dante wasn't going to be happy about any of it.

"Gods don't you have any spies?" Helena swore as she stuffed clothes into her bag.

"Of course I have spies," Victor said in his defense.

"Then your spies suck," she said. "Because as soon as I found out what the Tribunal had cooking is when I tried to pull Elle from her little compound up north."

"Are you going to tell me what the hell is going on?"

"The Tribunal offered any Other who currently didn't have a seat on the council a seat if they could prove they had a way to kill a Reaper." She kept loading up her bag as she spoke. She looked Victor up and down like he was a piece of meat, "You and your brothers' heads are worth quiet a pretty penny by the way."

But Victor had jumped to his feet as she spoke. He wasn't worried about getting killed he and his brothers could take care of themselves, in fact bring it on. They always did enjoy a good fight. But a seat on the Tribunal? "You have to be immortal to be on the Tribunal."

"Exactly." She was back to shouting. "And now the Sons of Adam, and Daughters of Eve have that ability with Elle."

"Gods above and below." This was bad, worse than anything he and Dante could have ever imagined. And with the extra protein in Elle's blood, she was not just any demi-god anymore. She was a God in the making; she could bring down the world as they all knew it. And he had no idea where she was. Victor felt like he was going to be sick. He lowered himself back into the chair and took several deep breaths. So this was what real panic felt like. He did not like it.

"Yeah ya think?" Helena asked.

"You really make me want to slap you," he said honestly. "I need to go back to the Infernos, I have my brother Garrett and a Tracker here. They will take you to the airport where they last had Elle. Do you have a glamour so you can leave the house?"

She glared at him. "Of course I do." She went into her bathroom. Victor headed out and to the back of the house. He threw the door open and called to Garrett. Who appeared immediately. "We got a problem."

Garrett smiled. "When don't we?"

"I have to go back to the Infernos. Take Helena to the airport in California. I'll be back as soon as I can." Victor motioned Garrett to follow him into the house.

Helena was standing on the front porch talking to one of the kids, but they stopped talking the moment Victor and Garrett showed up. "When did pretty guy two show up?"

"Who is he?" Garrett asked at the same time.

But Victor wasn't paying attention to him he was staring at Helena, her glamour had changed her from a blond bombshell to a mouse brown haired short woman with brown eyes. "Your glamour is full of shit," Victor said laughing.

"Go to hell." Helena emphasized her words by flipping him off. She finished talking to the kid and grabbed her bags, she waited for Garrett and Victor to exit her house and she locked up.

"How do you plan on finding Elle?" he asked Helena.

Helena rolled her eyes, "How long ago did she get away from you?"

"Four days." Garrett offered.

"Her energy will still be there." Helena said. "I should be able to follow it from there."

Bowen jogged across the street. "Where we headed?"

Victor slapped Garrett on the back and Flashed out.

****

He was surprised to find Dante in the stone garden. Dante rarely ventured into this part of the Infernos, in fact Victor couldn't remember the last time he had seen his father here. He stood back in the shadows knowing it wasn't the right time to interrupt Dante.

"That was the first time since your creation I have had to discipline any of you," Dante finally said. But Victor heard him even standing across the courtyard, Victor moved out of the shadows and walked toward his father. "You understand I could not back down, I had to punish you."

Victor did understand, Dante had to punish him, but he hadn't thought for one moment Dante felt any type of remorse for it. Dante turned to him and remorse shown in his eyes he extended his hand and Victor took it. "Don't make me do it again."

Victor nodded. "She is worth it Dante, and I can't wait for you to meet her."

Dante raised one eyebrow. "I will of course hold my opinion until I am graced with her presence."

Victor laughed. "I have information."

Dante nodded and Victor explained everything he had learned as they walked up to the fortress. "Find out which member of the Tribunal put a price on our heads," Dante said. "I want the name and I want the individual."

"Of course." Victor turned to leave.

"And Victor."

Victor stopped and turned back.

"Good luck getting Elle back safe and sound."

Victor almost tripped he was so stunned at Dante's words.

Dante smiled. "It's the Angel in you, and I can't deny that Celeste is happier with Marcus. I could not deny you that same type of happiness."

"Thank you, father." Victor left the great hall in a daze. He had just had the strangest conversation of his existence with Dante. Now he just had to go get Elle back. And kill Aldon, and find out who had put a bounty on the Reapers.

****

"It's an enzyme, a protein. A new kind of protein only you could create." Doc was talking so fast Elle was having a hard time following her. Tabitha sat next to Elle with the same look of confusion Elle was sure she had on her face.

Elle nodded as Doc continued talking, they had ran a plethora of tests on Elle when she had arrived. From blood tests, to full body MRI's, CT scans X-rays and others she didn't know the names of. Shamans had looked at her. She had gone into prayer circles and sat for twelve hours in a sweat lodge.

Now she was sitting across from a woman who went by Doc for the simple reason she was the doctor for the Daughters of Eve, going over the results. And Doc was so excited about what she had found, the tiny woman could barely sit still. She kept shifting in her seat, had actually come out of it several times, in her excitement.

"So you see? You are literally a God in the making," she finally said, this Elle did understand. And the information sat like a heavy rock in the pit of her stomach.

"Excuse me?" Elle asked leaning forward. "Can you please repeat that part?"

Doc jumped out of her chair. "Have you been listening to me?"

Tabitha gave Elle a strange look and shook her head. "Of course we have but you have to admit this is a little hard to believe. Why don't you try explaining it to us again Doc?" Tabitha asked.

Doc slapped her hands against her desk. "This is why those things have been going nuts! Those Freaks, why Aldon wants you so desperately. Why the Tribunal can't wait to get their greedy hands on you." She said enthusiastically. "I mean, if I had heard about you, I would want to test you myself. Not like, in a test-tube baby kind of way, of course. You are an amazing find. You are going to change the world, Elle."

Now she really did have Elle's attention. The last thing she wanted was to change the world. "What have you found?" Elle asked shaking her head.

"Your test results of course." Doc said with a satisfied smile. And then nodded, "It sure explains those things continued bombardment. Thank you for the sample by the way." She said the last part to Tabitha.

Elle glared at Tabitha, "What things?" she really didn't want to know the answer because she was 99% sure she knew the answer to her question.

Tabitha stood and glared at Doc, turning to Elle. "Don't worry about it, Elle."

Elle turned to Tabitha. "What is she talking about?"

"You didn't tell her about the Freak attacks?" Doc asked, surprised.

Elle felt her stomach bottom out. "There have been Freak attacks? Here?"

Tabitha rolled her eyes and turned so she was facing Elle. "It's nothing we haven't been able to handle. If it had been a problem I would have told you." She said, with the same damn placating tone that Victor had used with her.

Elle wanted to smack the woman. "Why wasn't I told either way? I thought you said we would be safe here. You said Aldon and his Freaks wouldn't be able to touch me here."

Tabitha shrugged like it wasn't a problem. "Because, it isn't anything we can't handle," Tabitha said again. "We haven't even sustained any injuries. This entire compound, gods Aldon's Freaks can't come within fifteen miles of our compound the place has been blessed by our priestesses. As for Aldon if he desecrates the Daughters of Eve, we will kill him on the spot. The only reason we haven't killed him on the spot is because the Sons of Adam pulled the kill order."

Elle came out of her own seat on that, "WHAT?"

Tabitha swore, "Don't worry I expect it to be put back in place any day now."

"What happened?" Elle demanded.

"They didn't know about the Freaks." Tabitha explained. "If the Freaks are somehow Sons, and we are killing them, then we are breaking one of their laws. One of their highest laws."

"You're kidding me right?" Elle asked.

"The Sons, never kid when it comes to their offspring." Tabitha said seriously,

"The Freaks are soulless beasts." Elle said.

"Yes well they wanted to see for themselves. They have sent an emissary to work with Doc. Luckily they showed up when the Freaks were attacking." Tabitha explained.

Elle laid her head on the conference table, "Tell me this is a bad dream I didn't come here to bring danger to the Daughters of Eve," Elle said trying not to panic.

"This isn't something we can't handle." Tabitha reassured her. "And he and Doc got the samples they needed from a Freak."

Elle peaked up from where she was hiding in her arms.

"Yes, they are fascinating creatures. Soulless as all get out, and beastly. I wouldn't want to go up against them in a fight I'll tell you that much. Aldon is a mad scientist to have created them, spliced together several species DNA its quiet fascinating really. They have thought and everything they need to be fighters, but soulless..." Elle was sure Doc would have continued. And Elle was feeling sick to her stomach. But Tabitha cut Doc off.

"I think that's enough Doc." Tabitha glared at Doc, and then pushed Elle back into her chair. "So this emissary took everything back to the Sons, and we should hear back any time now. Until then we have it under control.

"And Aldon's requests can be ignored then." Doc said happily.

"Excuse me?" Elle asked.

Tabitha turned to Doc and sighed then turned back to Elle.

"Aldon has requested we release you into his custody, Diane has rejected his request." She said between her teeth. "Doc is full of information today."

Doc had the sense to look everywhere but at the other two people in the room.

Elle felt sick and put her head back on the table, Tabitha patted her on the shoulder. "Aldon thinks he can circumvent the rules."

"What are you talking about?" Elle muttered not bothering to raise her head. She didn't know if she could take any more information at the moment.

"You are here with the Daughters, now," Doc said it like it should explain everything.

"And?" Elle asked when no further information was offered. She peaked up from her arms.

"Well as long as you are with us, you fall under our jurisdiction." Doc smiled. "But that isn't the problem we came here to discuss." She said shaking her head. "Let's get back to the real issue here." Elle didn't really want to discuss the real issue. She had way too much on her mind now. "What we need to discuss, is the fact you have this awesome new protein. This new enzyme is being created from your curse. Frankly, it's amazing. It's turned your curse into a god send. What is happening inside you, is absolutely amazing."

"A god send? Really?" Elle asked, she was honestly too tired to be as excited as Doc. "Okay I'll bite what are you talking about?"

"You have an extra protein! This new, amazing type of enzyme in your blood. I couldn't believe it; I had to run the tests like six different times." Doc was back to bouncing in her chair like a kid.

"And what exactly does it mean?" Elle asked, sitting back in her chair.

Doc finally couldn't control herself, she jumped out of her chair. "That is the thing!" She shouted, making Elle shrink back.

"We know why Aldon wants you! Any child you bare, would be a demi-god. Who has given birth to demi-gods? Nobody. Not just a normal child but a DEMI-GOD!?" She emphasized. "Who can do that? Who can do that? You! That's who! If you mated with that nut-job, Aldon, your child would be both a Son of Adam and a demi-god. A demi-god would mean the Sons of Adam would finally, after eons, have the one thing they have always wanted. Immortality." She danced taking breaths and wringing her hands. "But this enzyme…" she stuttered. "It's basically made you a God in your own right!" Doc stopped and starred at Elle, apparently waiting for her amazing proclamation to garner some type of reaction.

Elle just stared at Doc unable to believe what she had just heard. "What?" was all she was able to say when she finally found her voice. She felt bands wrap around her chest and the breath in her chest slowly seep from her lungs. The pit of her stomach grew heavy and she wasn't sure she wouldn't just throw up right there on the glossy conference table.

Doc sat heavily in a chair next to Elle. "You seem really less excited then I thought you might be over this type of news."

Elle nodded. "I'm not sure I understand what is going on."

Doc nodded and patted Elle's hand. "I don't know all the specifics. But, I think this is how it works. You die, the demi-god kicks in, however, your body from the curse is human so to counter that and still bring you back, over and over and over…" Elle held her hand up. Doc smiled. "And repair your body, but still make your body go through all the same deaths again this protein regenerates the dead tissue. Your body has done something amazing." she shouted. "This protein and enzyme, it's a medical breakthrough. Not only in the Others medical world and we have some amazing medicine. But in the mortal world of medicine? This is life changing. I gave it to a lab mouse that had cancer and it healed it. You would be able to re-grow limbs. Regenerate, regrow, reanimate, you are practically a God. If you could get past the dying thing you would be a god."

"That's why the Tribunal wants me," Elle said putting her head down on the table. She felt the world descended onto her shoulders.

"Didn't Victor tell you this?" Tabitha asked.

Elle peeked up. "What?"

"Victor and his little band of merry men had to know about this. Didn't he tell you?" Tabitha asked.

Elle shook her head. "No, he would have said something if he had." Why was she bringing this up now? "It doesn't matter now anyway," she said waving her off.

"This doesn't change anything," Tabitha said pushing herself away from the conference table. "Aldon is going to continue to try and take you. He is the current threat."

Elle shrugged, she didn't know what she was going to worry about right then. "Okay."

Doc gave her a huge and a smile. "I thought you should know everything." And patted her on the arm before gathering the files she had spread out over the large table.

Elle felt compelled to thank the woman. "Thank you, Doc."

Doc smiled. "You are very welcome. When this is all done I hope to have the chance to work with you some more. There are many illnesses you will be helpful in curing, Elle."

Elle wondered if that were really true or if she would be the catalyst to something more horrible. After all, isn't that why the Tribunal wanted her?

****

Elle traced patterns in the dirt, her body completely tense, her head resting on her knee. She was still trying to absorb everything Doc had told her that morning. Elle wondered if the Druid had known what she was creating so long ago if she would have cursed Elle in the first place. Would the years of pain, out weight the ultimate gift/punishment on the current society?

Ultimately the dark druid, who had cursed Elle, had done so because she had been in pain. Someone who she had loved had been killed by Elle that horrible day. Either way Elle would have been cursed. And who would have thought Elle would have survived this long anyway? Regardless of her curse, something bigger and stronger should have come along by now and taken her out. It was a miracle she was still here. Helena told her so whenever she was with her.

Elle felt a stab of pain. Her life was so messed up, cursed and kept getting worse.

"What are you doing?" Tabitha asked, coming to sit down next to her

Elle looked down at what she had drawn, it was the Reaper Call. All she needed to do was add her blood, or wine, or water. Would he come? Her heart twisted at the thought.

Elle looked at the twisted etchings in the dirt and turned away. "Nothing."

"We're almost ready," Tabitha said, as she sat down next to her. She motioned to the women still training. Elle sat in the shade of a tree next to the training yard, where Tabitha was training with fifteen of her best warriors.

They were training for when the call came that Aldon's death sentence was back on.

"You keep drawing that, what is it?" Tabitha asked pointing to the drawings in the dirt.

Elle shrugged. "It's nothing."

"If it was nothing then you wouldn't keep drawing it," Tabitha said shoving her with her shoulder.

"It's the emergency number Helena gave me," Elle told her.

Tabitha gave her a strange look. "What does that mean?"

Elle shrugged again. "It's a spell. To call the Reapers. But it back fired, I didn't know by using it I would bind my soul to Victor's. Helena didn't explain that part to me."

Tabitha burst out laughing. "Your soul doesn't belong to that bastard," she finally said.

Elle shook her head. "Oh it does. I used the Blood Call and now my soul is his."

Tabitha rolled her eyes. "You really need to get out more. Do you think if your soul belonged to him, I would have been able to take you from him? He would be able to find you anywhere you went if your soul belonged to him."

Elle felt like someone had kicked her in the stomach. "What?"

"Show me the spell again," Tabitha demanded.

And Elle drew out the Blood Call again in the dirt. Making sure to include all the pieces.

Tabitha nodded. "Yes. I see it now. Victor would have had to add his blood to it, to make it complete. Did he?" She asked.

Elle thought back to the night and realized, she didn't know. She had woken up later. She didn't know if he had added his blood to the stone or not.

"Look Elle, I can tell you right now, if he owned your soul he would be able to find you anywhere on any plane of existence if he wanted. You wouldn't be able to hide from him." Her words cut her like a knife. Victor didn't own her soul, and she wasn't sure if he even cared for her anymore. And that thought hurt so much she could barely breathe, she loved him. And she didn't know what to do now. "And if he does own your soul he doesn't give a shit."

She could have cold cocked her with less affect. And Tabitha knew it the moment the words came out. "Shit Elle, I'm sorry that came out wrong." Tabitha said.

"It's not like you gave him a chance." Elle made the excuse.

Tabitha shook her head. "Well it's neither here nor there. Aldon is the problem not the Reaper. Have you thought some more about what you are going to do when this is all over?" Tabitha asked, brushing dirt from the long tunic she wore. And changing the subject.

Elle sighed and looked up through the tree at the light sifting through the branches. "Do you mean will I become a breeder for the Daughters of Eve?"

Tabitha blanched. "Gods no! Why would you even think that?"

"I overheard some woman talking about it," Elle admitted. Not many of the Daughters talked to Elle. In fact, most of the woman avoided her like she was the plague. Being an outsider and all, they didn't trust her. She understood that. The warriors only spoke to her when they had to train with her. Doc loved to talk to her, because of what she possible could bring to the world of medicine. Otherwise, the other woman just pretended like she wasn't there. Diana, the leader, spoke to her once in a while. Although, Elle had to admit, only when Elle cornered her. The conversation she had overheard was in the mess hall, between several of the other 'breeders'. The thought had made Elle's stomach turn. "I was wondering if that is what is being expected of me."

Tabitha shook her head. "Of course not. We are trying to stop that from happening. We left the guilds, we left all that behind us. We don't want immortality, Elle."

Elle wasn't sure if she believed her, and she felt another heavy weight descend on her. She turned to look at Tabitha. "All Others want immortality; even mortals want to find a way to live forever to leave their mark. Why wouldn't the Daughters of Eve be looking for the same thing?"

Tabitha gave her a smile that radiated from deep inside her. It was a genuine smile and it took Elle by surprise. Tabitha never smiled and to do so with such radiance, was both surprising and beautiful. "I am a Daughter of Eve" she said with such calm it was contagious and wrapped around Elle making the heavy feeling wash away. This was something Tabitha felt from deep within her soul. "From the very beginning we have made our mark. Mankind suckles at our breast, look at the world, Elle. We are everywhere. That is our mark, our legacy. I don't need immortality, I am already immortal. If I die tomorrow? I will have done what I was meant to do I will go to the bosom of mother and be still."

"We." She paused and looked around at her sister's still training in the field nearby. "We pass our customs on from generation to generation. Knowing we can leave this earth anytime. That is how we stave off mortality. I shall pass my knowledge on, what was passed to me, and what I have learned in this life to others. My missions in this life, my fate with you, I will pass this on and in doing so I will immortalize the Daughters of Eve."

"And what about the Brothers?" Elle asked.

Tabitha shook her head. "They strayed, as men often do. They view power and strength as something to possess." She shrugged. "They must grasp it and hold it tightly." She made a fist. "It kills it, if held to tightly. Like anything else living, once you hold it too tightly, grasping it to you never to let it go, to grow and live. It dies. That is what some of the Sons of Adam have become. Not all, some hold to the old ways as the majority of the Daughters have," she sighed. "But most have turned and believe a seat on the Tribunal will give them the power they so desperately desire. Give them the immortality they think they rightly deserve."

"So that is what they ultimately want? A seat on the Tribunal?" Elle asked.

Tabitha nodded. "Yes and it is being dangled in front of them like a shiny lure they cannot resist. But the price is too high."

She was almost afraid to ask. "What is the price?"

A commotion and alarm caused Tabitha to jump to her feet. She grabbed Elle and pulled her to her feet as well. "Go back to your quarters and lock the door."

"Why?" Elle yelled over the sound of the alarms blaring.

"Because we are being invaded." Tabitha shouted over the alarms before she started running, dragging Elle by the hand. Emotions Elle wasn't prepared for bombarded her. Fear and rage made her stumble as she threw up more walls. Tabitha stopped. "Elle what's wrong?"

Elle shook her hands. "I'm fine! Go! Go!" she stumbled along.

She was half way to her room, when she felt it. The calm, the lack of emotion settle around her like a blanket around her soul. Elle stopped dead in her tracks. She hesitated for just a moment as the familiar sensations wrapped around her.

"Victor." The name whispered from her lips. Elle tried to remind herself he didn't love her like she loved him. He had lied to her, about her soul. And if he had lied to her about that what else could he have lied to her about? But in the end her heart won out and she turned and ran toward the feeling letting it encompass her, gods she had missed him so much. All her walls fell, all her worries collapsed. She didn't notice the men and women fighting. Or the fact it was Trackers and Reapers, or that they stopped and followed her. Or that they called to her, she was totally focused on getting to Victor.

When she got to the clearing where Victor was, Tabitha had him on his knees his blond head forward and a sword and his throat. Elle let out a scream as she threw her body into the fight.

Victor looked up just in time to catch Elle as she threw herself at him. But it was also the same time the crazy bitch Tabitha was trying to bash his damn fool head in. Luckily Tabitha didn't want to hurt Elle and she changed the direction of her swing, and he grunted as he swerved out of the way of the butt of her sword trying to put a dent in his skull at the same time as he cushioned the impact of Elle plowing into him.

Elle knocked the air out of him. Stunned, he lay in the dirt for several seconds, incapable of stopping her from crawling away.

"Have you lost your mind Tabitha? You could have killed him!" Elle bellowed at the bitch who had definitely tried to put him to sleep for a while. Making Victor smile. It wouldn't have killed him, but it definitely would have fucking hurt.

"He's immortal!" Tabitha bellowed back.

"I don't give a damn. What where you trying to do? Bash his brains in?" Elle stomped her foot sending dirt over Victor and making him cough

Tabitha moved with lightning speed. A speed Victor, who was still recovering, couldn't match. She was standing over him when she kicked him in the stomach and he curled in on himself cursing her. "Why are you here? How are you here?" She kicked him again. "Call off the Neanderthal's you brought with you, NOW!" she bellowed over him. Victor flipped her off. It was all he was capable of, as she continued to attack him.

"Stop kicking him," Elle said putting herself between him and Tabitha. "Oh my gods! Get up and defend yourself," Elle said, pleading with Victor.

Victor blinked through his pain. "I'm trying," he said through his teeth. He was bleeding from a cut on his neck. And he was pretty sure he had a concussion, from being cold-cocked by the bitch as he had come to call Tabitha. She had already slammed the butt of the sword into his skull once. He had broken ribs, an arrow wound to the left shoulder getting into the place. And a plethora of other wounds, plus the wounds to his back were still healing. Elle had slammed into him so hard he wasn't breathing right.

Yeah, he was a mess and Tabitha looked like she wanted to put a bullet in him. Or that sword in him, or try and cut his head off. Then he looked up into Elle's golden brown eyes and his wounds were forgotten. Damn he was glad to see her.

He rolled to his feet and grabbed her pulling her into his arms. "Don't ever, do you hear me, ever run from me again," he whisper-growled into her ear.

She tried to pull away from him but he wouldn't let her go. "I wasn't the one who left, remember?" She said in her defense but he wasn't going to argue with her about it.

"I've got her," he said quietly knowing his brothers would hear him and stop their fighting and come to him from wherever they were. "And I didn't want to leave, dammit." He muttered.

"We see that," Garrett said coming to stand next to Victor. Soon the clearing held several Reapers, and Trackers, Celeste, and Marcus.

"Helena?" Elle tried to pull out of Victor's arms but he wouldn't release her. He wasn't sure he was ever going to let her go again.

"Just give me another minute. I missed you," he whispered. He couldn't bring himself to release her just yet and held her close breathing in her scent. Elle melted into him at his words she had missed him too. And she had to admit the feeling of being in his arms felt right. But part of her still hurt, if maybe just a little.

"You left me," she said again quietly so only he could hear. But he grunted. And Elle closed her eyes and burrowed into his chest.

"We'll discuss it later, right now I just need to feel you close to me." Victor said squeezing her.

Tabitha was screaming at someone, probably Skylar. "They are going to kill each other soon."

"I don't care," Victor said. But after another minute of holding her close he pulled away and they faced the group.

Skylar was indeed in Tabitha's face. "What in the name of all the gods made you think taking Elle was good idea?"

"I don't recall asking for your approval," she barked getting right into the Trackers face. "And don't expect me to ever ask for your approval."

"We had everything under control." Sky looked ready to tear her apart.

"Really?" Tabitha laughed, but the sound was bitter and hard. "Because from the information you were giving Elle and me you had nothing under control. In fact, you had less than nothing under control. You were shipping her around like a sack of potatoes, and telling her even less."

Elle needed to defuse the situation and stepped forward, but Victor stopped her. "We're leaving."

"What?" She tried to pull away but he wouldn't let her. "No wait, we have a plan," she told Victor.

"Who is we?" Victor demanded. "We as in the crazy bitch who wants to use you like Aldon? Who took you from me?"

"What?" Elle asked at the same time Tabitha did.

"I didn't take her from you," Tabitha snarled. "She didn't have to go with me. I gave her a choice. Something none of you males did. Tell them, Elle."

Victor turned to her and Elle swallowed. "I went with her willingly. I wasn't being told anything. I have been safe here. And I am not going anywhere until the situation is resolved."

Victor wasn't listening. He grabbed Elle and steered her toward the way they had come in. "I don't give a shit, we are leaving. I don't trust the bitch." He threw over his shoulder.

Elle tried to yank her arm free but he had her back in his arms and he would be damned if he was going to let her go.

Elle dug in her heels. "Victor, stop! You don't know what you are talking about."

"We can talk once you are safe," Victor told her.

She gave him a look that told him she thought he was nuts. "I have been safe here for the last week. They have been able to handle the attacks. Aldon is following the rules of the Daughters of Eve."

Victor looked like had seen a ghost. "He has attacked?" he shouted.

Elle regretted saying anything.

"We are leaving," he said pulling her in close again.

"She is safe here," Tabitha said just as loud. "Or did you miss the part, where she said Aldon's attacks have been ineffective? This is hallowed ground, the Freaks can't get in here. And Aldon wouldn't dare desecrate this land."

Victor wasn't even going to answer those stupid questions. Elle was in danger, as long as Aldon was after her she was in danger and he needed to keep her safe.

"You should ask him about your soul. And that special enzyme," Tabitha said.

Elle sighed heavily wishing Tabitha would just stop talking. Couldn't she just give Elle a moment to gather her thoughts?

Elle turned to Victor but the look he gave her made her pause. "Which is it?" she advanced on him. When Victor took a step away from her she felt like she was going to throw up.

"I was going to explain about the enzyme to you. I didn't want to upset you. You have enough on your plate," Victor said.

"And my soul?" Elle asked trying to keep from crying. She was not going to cry, she promised herself.

Victor grabbed her. "That is something we will discuss when we are alone. Tabitha should mind her damn business, when it comes to your soul. And especially, mine. She needs to back the hell off." Actually about the souls Elle couldn't agree more, so she nodded.

Victor glared at the group. "How many attacks have there been?" he demanded from Tabitha.

Tabitha snorted. "I don't have to tell you anything."

"Oh, for the love of the gods." Elle threw her hands in the air. "Just explain it to him."

"He has demanded we hand Elle over to him three different times, and each time we have rejected his requests. And after the rejections he has sent in a group of four to six Freaks. But they cannot cross into our land," Tabitha explained.

"Why?" Victor asked.

Tabitha sighed and rolled her eyes, obviously hating having to answer any questions Victor asked. "Because this is hallowed ground and if he desecrates it his life will be forfeited as will his Freaks."

"Really?" Victor couldn't believe what he was hearing. "The same way he should be killed for what he is trying to do to Elle? Or the way you said you were going to kill him originally?"

Tabitha growled at him. "Don't you dare throw our laws at me. You don't know anything about our laws. And until you do, Reaper, you should keep your opinions and your mouth shut. Before I shut if for you."

Victor dropped Elle's hand and advanced on the bitch, Christian grabbed him before he did something stupid.

"Don't stop him." Tabitha laughed just out of arm's reach. "Do you think I'm afraid of him?"

"Tabitha, you realize he could reach inside of you and take your soul don't you?" Christian asked. "Without a Ringer you would live but you wouldn't enjoy it."

Victor took little joy in seeing fear flit through those green eyes. All he wanted was to get Elle out of here. Then he wanted to sleep. Reapers didn't need to sleep often, but gods, he was tired. The thought of pulling Elle into his arms and just relaxing and sleeping, sounded like a slice of heaving to him.

Helena had come over. "Elle what the hell are you doing with the Daughters of Eve?"

Elle glared at her sister which made Victor smile. "Why the hell do you care?"

Helena glared right back. "Because I do that's why. The last time we talked, you were with the Reapers. You were fighting."

"What the hell do you think she is doing with us?" Tabitha interrupted.

"You are going to use her to get into the Tribunal," Helena snapped.

Tabitha turned on Helena. "And who the hell are you?"

For all the irritation between Helena and Elle, Helena was still Elle's sister and Elle grabbed Helena and pushed the woman behind her standing up to Tabitha. "Don't talk to her like that, she's my sister. Helena."

Tabitha actually took a step back. "Sorry Elle," Tabitha looked around Elle's shoulder and nodded at Helena. "Pleasure to meet you." It was the nicest Tabitha had ever been to someone, outside of the Daughters, that Victor had ever seen.

Helena flipped her off, which Victor had come to realize was a favorite form a communication with the woman. "Get away from my sister."

"Mother of the gods. Why does everyone think I have it out for Elle?" Tabitha asked the group in general.

"Maybe, because you kidnapped her from the group keeping her safe." Skylar threw out for the group.

"Keeping her safe?" Tabitha laughed. "And by the way, nobody is talking to you Tracker."

Elle threw her hands in the air. "Are we back to this again?"

"No, because we don't need to revisit anything. We are leaving." Victor tried to grab Elle, but she avoided him.

"Victor, the Daughters of Eve are not trying to control me. They have a good plan to destroy Aldon." Elle pleaded with him. "And if anyone is asking, I'm safe. Hello? Isn't that what's important?"

"We do not work with men," Tabitha snarled between her teeth.

The look Elle gave her nearly made Victor snort. "Seriously?" Elle barked.

"Well that answers that," Victor said, happy Tabitha had said what she said, and now they could all move on.

He grabbed Elle's hand and pulled her to him. "Let's get out of here."

She came quietly into his arms. "I can't go Victor."

"Elle." he growled.

"Their plan is a solid one," she admitted to him with a sigh. Then turned to Tabitha. "They are here to help. Surely, the more the merrier? The less the risk to the sisters, right?"

Victor snarled low when Elle said that and Tabitha nodded. The last thing he wanted was to put his life on the line for this bitch. For Elle he would do it without a qualm, but for Tabitha? He wasn't sure he would walk across the street to put her out if she were on fire.

Nope.

He wouldn't.

Especially, when she agreed to his help, if it only meant less risk for her and her precious sisters.

"Who said we were willing to work with them?" he said to Elle. Because he damn well hadn't.

Elle turned to him, her beautiful golden eyes beseeching. "I'm tired Victor." And he could see it in her eyes and she had him and they both new it. "I'm tired of holding my walls up. Of fighting off Freaks and watching over my shoulder. We need to end this. Do you have a plan?"

"Damn it, Elle. We would if we didn't have to run all over the mortal plane to try and find you." He pushed a hand through his hair.

"You didn't have a plan before then. We were running scared before that. Admit it." He damn well wouldn't admit to anything, she must have read it in his eyes.

"Why do you make it harder than it needs to be?" he demanded instead.

"Me?" she asked. "I am not making it harder. You are being impossible. Not me."

"Do you have any idea what we have gone through to find you?" he asked, right back. "If you could have just done as you were told."

Ryder snorted. "Ah now you've gone and done it you dumb ass."

Victor noticed several women who were standing behind Tabitha shake their heads and take several steps back.

Elle sucked in a breath. Her mouth opened and closed several times, not actually able say anything for a moment.

It should have been a sign for him to keep his big mouth shut but he didn't.

Celeste stepped forward and put a hand on his forearm "Victor maybe you should take a moment." Victor shook it off.

"Do you have any idea how worried I was? What could have happened to you? I told you, I was coming back! Why do you always have to push the envelope? Why can you never just do as you're told? None of this would have been necessary." Victor threw his hands up; he wanted to throw her over his shoulder and take her to the Infernos and lock her up where she would be safe. But he couldn't even do that; he was trapped here on the mortal plane where she was forever in danger. He was so upset he didn't see the danger right in front of him.

"Excuse me?" Elle asked her voice had dropped to a near whisper. "Done as I was told? Like a good little girl?" She pushed him. But Victor refused to give an inch. And stood his ground, she could push him all she liked. Everything he was doing was to keep her safe, didn't she see that?

"Yes dammit. Is it that hard?" he leaned down so they were nose to nose.

"Yes!" she practically shrieked. Making everyone step back but Victor. "I have spent the last, gods only know how many years, doing exactly what I was told to do. And do you know what that has done for me?" she asked. She didn't wait for him to answer. "It made me a sitting duck, for that bastard, Aldon! And weak. So weak, the only thing capable of protecting me, was you." Her voice dropped, to a near whisper "And even you left me, when I needed you most."

The words cut so deep he stumbled back like a physical blow straight to the solar plexus. Christian caught him.

She advanced with her amber/golden eyes flashing fire on him. She stabbed him in the chest with her index finger. "So, don't you think for one second, that I don't have the ability to make a decision! Now, I'm not asking you, I'm telling you. You can go along with it or not. The Daughters of Eve have a sound plan. One I am going along with, because from what I understand, you-" She glared at the general group."- don't have one. So, I would love, and I truly mean that, if you would all stay and work with us. If you don't want to, then you all know the way out." She shoved him for good measure and walked away.

Leaving Victor shocked and in awe, of his woman. Somewhere along the way she had found her voice. And it was fucking sexy as hell, even though his feelings were hurt over it. He pushed away from his brother. But she was already walking away with Tabitha. The Bitch had a satisfied smile on her face. He wasn't sure what he wanted to do more. Kiss Elle or wipe that self-satisfied look off the Bitch's face.

Victor went to go after Elle, knowing he was about to eat some crow, but a wall of women separated them; a tall woman with dark robes put her hand up. "I am Diana, the head of The Daughters of Eve. I recognize your claim here, Reaper. We are not using Elle for the nefarious means you claim." She glared at Helena as she said the last part. "I am requesting you and those in your party, remove yourselves to the clearing where your vehicles are. We will discuss the possibility of an alliance there. We have been waiting for a notice from the Sons of Adam, and our higher order. Lucky for you, we received it this morning. The kill order for Aldon is back in place. Let's hope we can learn to work together."

Victor ground his teeth together. "I'm not leaving, Elle."

Diana looked over her shoulder where Elle and Tabitha were having a heated conversation. "We do not allow men here. You must leave. If Elle wishes to go with you, she can. As she mentioned, they have a well thought out plan of action against Aldon. It would be beneficial for all of us to work together." With that said, Diana walked away, taking her contingent of women with her.

"No men at all?" Christian looked around at the bevy of beautiful woman. "What a pity."

The other Reapers, and Trackers started to back off, Victor held his ground. He wasn't moving until he spoke to Elle again.

Tabitha glared at him where she and Elle spoke, Helena stood at his side. "What are you going to do?"

"I'm going to get Elle out of here." Victor held his ground with his arms crossed over his chest.

"She doesn't look like she wants to talk to you or leave," Helena said.

"I don't care what she wants, Helena." Victor swore.

Helena swore too and grabbed him, turning him until he was forced to turn and look at her. "You may have to listen to her. Why are you being such an ass? Can't you maybe admit you were wrong?"

Victor had no problem admitting he was wrong. But, he needed to get Elle in front of him to do it. And she was with the Bitch. The gods only knew what Tabitha was spewing at her. Helena looked fit to be tied about the entire situation. "Regardless of whether I'm going to admit if I am wrong or not, speaking to her again face to face would be paramount don't you agree?" he asked pointing to where Elle still stood with the Bitch.

"I agree, but standing here being a disagreeable ass is going to get you absolutely nowhere." Helena added. "How about you agree to listen to what the Daughters of Eve have to offer."

Victor wanted to swear and scream but if it would get him alone with Elle then he would agree to anything. "Fine, I will listen to what they have to offer."

Someone snorted behind him, and he turned to Tabitha. "It would be more like what you have to offer my team, because from where I stand you have nothing we want nor need and my sisters and I can do this without you. And as for the Sons of Adam? They can have their seat on the Tribunal, it's not something the Daughters of Eve are concerned with."

Victor wanted to throttle the woman. "Remove Aldon, but still offer the Reapers up to them on a silver platter?"

Tabitha shrugged. "I think you and yours can take care of yourselves. It's not my concern."

"What?" Elle asked. "What are you talking about?"

Victor smiled as Tabitha's smug smile slipped from her face. "Ah so you didn't tell her your part did you? You gave up all my secrets but failed to give her this one?"

Elle glared at Tabitha "What is he talking about Tabitha? Why is everyone keeping things from me?"

"It's nothing, it isn't an issue since the Daughters of Eve aren't pursuing a seat on the Tribunal." She said with that smug smile back in place.

"But she isn't a Daughter of Eve, Tabitha," Victor pointed out.

"Not yet, anyway," Helena said. "Or not until this is all said and done. Then you really won't have a reason not to be."

Elle sighed. "I'm not going to become a Daughter of Eve, Helena."

"What's stopping you, Elle?" Helena shouted. "These woman have been so kind to you, took you in, and sheltered you. Now they are taking care of the pesky Aldon issue. You will be beholden to them." Helena glared at Tabitha, and the other Daughters of Eve.

Victor had to give it to the woman, if anyone hated Tabitha more than him, it was Helena.

Elle just shook her head. "I'm not going to join the Daughters of Eve, Helena."

Helena glared at Tabitha and the other Daughters. "We'll talk later," she said.

"Let's get back to what we were talking about, Reapers on a silver platter? Tabitha?" Elle turned to the bitch and Victor almost wanted to clap his hands together. Tabitha crossed her arms over her chest.

"What about them?" she demanded.

"Yes, but the Sons of Adam and Aldon," Elle said, and turned to Victor. "Tell me exactly what is going on."

Victor would be more than happy to. "Aldon and the members of the Sons of Adam are attempting to gain a seat on the Tribunal." Elle nodded. "The Tribunal has offered a seat to any Other who isn't already a card carrying member if they can kill a Reaper."

Elle sucked in a breath. "But you have to be immortal to have a seat on the Tribunal."

She turned and glared at Tabitha. "Is this the price you mentioned earlier?"

Tabitha nodded. "You don't have the means to kill a Reaper?" Elle asked.

"No one has the means to kill a Reaper," Tabitha explained.

Victor shook his head. "Don't speak too soon. Your buddy, Aldon, has a dagger we have been looking for. It's called the Black Dagger. Created by one of the first Reapers named Calliope, and who was recently destroyed by Marcus. Aldon has the Dagger. It can kill a Reaper. If he gets his greasy paws on Elle, he'll have the means to create immortal heirs for the Sons of Adam. To make those Freaks immortal. And the Tribunal? If they get their hands on Elle, the gods only know what they plan on doing with her. They could make Gods from the Immortals they have on the Tribunal! Or build an army of un-killable demi-gods." Really, the sky was the limit, if you thought about it. Victor looked at Elle, realizing who and what she was. She was a God unto herself, and didn't even realize it. It was part of why he loved her so much.

Tabitha and Elle both looked at him with their mouths hanging open in shock, Elle recovered first. "You need to go back to the Infernos and stay there." She rushed over to him and pushed him in the chest, her eyes swimming with tears. "Victor, he can kill you, please go back to the Infernos now."

Victor couldn't believe what he was hearing. "Have you lost your mind, woman?" He had just been thinking how amazing she was. And now she was trying to get rid of him? What the hell?

"It was bad enough when I thought he could hurt you, but now I know he can actually kill you. Wipe you out of existence, I feel like I've been kicked in the chest and I can't breathe." And she was indeed taking short little gasps.

Victor wrapped his arms around her. "Elle he isn't going to hurt me, nor is he going to get his hands on you. I am going to kill the bastard for terrorizing you, and I'm going to take the Dagger and destroy the bloody thing."

Elle looked at him like he was crazy again. "And just how the hell do you plan on doing that? If I remember correctly the last several times you have gone up against the bastard we have lost. And not lost like ha-ha he got the better of us but holy shit, he killed me twice and I barely got away with my life the last time." Victor pulled her head down onto his shoulder. "Elle, trust me I won't let him hurt you again."

Tabitha snorted. "Really? You and what army?"

Victor glared at her. "Look, I want to kick your ass. But I'm going to refrain. Can we please work together? We apparently want the same damn thing."

"I don't think so," Tabitha said without even thinking about it.

He was going to kill her, that was all there was to it. "We could do good things together, Tabitha. We could stop this from getting out of control."

"See you see it that way. What I see is being left out of the plans and shipped around the planet like a sack of potatoes," Tabitha spat out obviously still upset about her and Elle's treatment from a couple of weeks ago.

Elle pulled away from Victor and looked at her friend. "Tabitha, stop being such a bitch. I know you like this power trip and all but pull your head out of your ass. You can use the man power and you know it."

Tabitha just glared at Elle. Victor wanted to laugh, but he steeled his features. He wouldn't laugh, no matter how hard he wanted to. At least, until he was alone with Elle. Then he was going to laugh his ass off.

"I need to sleep on it." Tabitha started to stalk off, but stopped at the edge of the clearing. "Are you coming back with me?" she turned and asked Elle.

Elle looked from Helena to Victor, and back to Tabitha who threw her hands into the air. "There are guest quarters that are warded, just be careful." And the woman stalked off.

Finally Helena took her sister into her arms and hugged her. But just as quickly Helena pushed her away. "I'm still mad at you."

Helena slapped her on the shoulder. "I did what I had to do to make you strong enough to survive."

Elle had tears in her eyes. "Really? Because from where I was, it felt like you fed me to the wolves. And turned on me."

Helena had a sad look in her eyes. "Elle, I'm sorry but I couldn't help you. I had to pull back. I was being watched. I didn't want to give away any information about where you might be or who was with you."

"I know that now, but it still hurt." She hadn't moved from Victor's side and Victor could see the hurt in Helena's eyes. It was going to take time. Years and years of feeling abandoned. It wasn't going to go away with one conversation.

"Let's get back to the others. And figure out what's going on." Victor took Elle's hand and headed back to where they had left the vehicles. Just glad for the moment Elle was giving him the chance.

****

It was much later when Elle and Victor finally found a room. Elle had wondered if she should find a room of her own. But Victor hadn't let her so much as leave his side all evening. And when everyone had gone to find a bed he had pulled her along to a room in the large dormitory.

The room was large but still only had one small dresser. One night stand, and a twin bed. Victor groaned when he saw the bed.

"They don't have very many men your size come to visit." Elle giggled burrowing her head into his shoulder

"We'll make it work," Victor whispered. His voice had dropped to that deep growly whisper she dreamed about. As he dragged his mouth across her cheek. Not exactly kissing her, just tasting her. Until he reached her ear, she felt his moist tongue dart into her ear. "Gods I've missed your taste. Do you know how much I've missed you?"

She wanted to answer, she really did. But her mouth had forgotten how to work. His hands were tickling up and down her sides and she just wanted him to surround her. She wanted him to be everywhere at once. And when she finally found her voice the only word that came out was his name, and it was moaned, broken and hard.

Victor chuckled against her throat. "I feel exactly the same way."

He pulled away and Elle nearly shrieked. He was pulling her shirt over her head and came back just as quickly, his heat enveloping her. Elle bunched up his shirt and he pulled it over his head, at some point he had disposed of her bra and when they came chest to chest she nearly orgasmed from the sheer pleasure of the heavenly contact.

Elle's head fell back as she rubbed her chest against his, anchoring her hands on his broad shoulders. "Victor, it feels so good."

"Yes, Elle," he moaned dragging opened mouthed kisses along her throat and collar bone.

Then he was cupping one breast, his mouth closing around the nipple. She felt weak, and was panting for breath. "Don't stop," she begged. His rough tongue abraded the nipple until she wanted to scream with pleasure only to move onto the other one. He gave the second nipple the same treatment. Elle clutched at his shoulders her legs totally useless.

Victor swept her into his arms and carried her to the bed. He lay her down and kneeled on the floor he placed opened mouthed kisses between her breasts. "You're so beautiful."

Elle leveled herself up on shaky elbows and smiled at him.

Over the last couple of weeks she worried she would never see him again. "What happened to you, Victor?" She had to know. Had she done something wrong? Needed to have this closure before they could move forward.

Something flashed in his dark eyes and he moved so he was pressing his forehead against hers. "I'm sorry I had to leave and I couldn't come back immediately." He kissed her nose. "Please know it was nothing you did that kept me away."

"Then why?" His non answers weren't good enough.

"Dante was not satisfied with the job I was doing. And thought I had become too close to you," he said honestly, and the look he gave her broke her heart. "I was punished."

Elle couldn't breathe for a moment. "You were punished?" She felt like the words were torn from her.

"Yes," Victor said honestly.

"You were punished for being too close to me?"

"Yes."

Elle wanted to curl into a ball and cry. "How were you punished?" Gods please don't answer that question.

"I was whipped, it is the standard punishment." Victor didn't even flinch.

If he hadn't been laying on top of her she would have toppled over with shock. "Your father whipped you because you care for me?"

"Elle."

She pushed at him but he didn't move. "Get off of me, Victor."

He still didn't move. "Elle, I would take that punishment and more," he whispered. She fought him but he didn't budge. Her breathing grew ragged as she desperately tried to move out from beneath him. Victor fought against her, whispering gently to her the entire time. Nonsense words, which eventually comforted her. And she stopped fighting him, she lay there as tears welled up, Victor holding her close.

Elle felt the tears well up and start to fall, but still Victor didn't move. He lay there his forehead pressed against her as she cried. Cried for the pain he had to have gone through because he cared for her. She wiped at her tears but he didn't move and she couldn't actually get out from beneath him.

When she was done crying he kissed her, and kissed her. And she kissed him back. Because she had been in love with him before and now she couldn't deny it. She held him to her and her hands caressed him in a new and gentle way. What he had endured, to just be with her? She couldn't fathom, the type of pain he had gone through. Her heart filled to bursting, and she hugged him close.

"I'm so sorry." She whispered brokenly.

"I'm not." Victor whispered back.

"Are you still in pain?" she couldn't help asking.

"No." she didn't know if he was lying or not but it didn't matter. The fact he had gone through it was what mattered. She leaned back and cupped his face staring into his dark eyes. They shown with passion and love and she let it suck her in. Elle knew she would never feel this type of passion and love for anyone else, ever. Leaning up she kissed him, pouring everything she felt into this one kiss. Hoping to obliterate any remaining pain from his horrible punishment. Let him know it really was worth it, their love was worth it. She kissed him. Opening herself up to this hard Reaper, who new Violence intimately. She wanted all of that erased, in this single kiss.

Victor couldn't get close enough to her. He wanted to mentally and physically climb inside of her and never leave. He had never felt this way with a woman before and it should scare the hell out of him. But, with Elle, if felt right. So damn right. It was almost wrong not to feel this way with her.

Her taste, her smell, the feel of her skin against him, it all felt right. When she had cried for what he had gone through just so he could be with her. It was all right because he knew he would do anything to just be by her side. Even put up with that crazy bitch Tabitha.

Gods how he loved this woman. So much it was overwhelming, it filled him so completely it terrified him but at the same time made him so happy he wanted to scream with joy. He leaned back and looked down at her. Her lips were plump from their kiss, and her eyes were drowsy and filled with passion. He did that to her, filled her with passion. And in return is filled him with such passion he almost couldn't control himself.

He wanted to fall on her and ravish her like a crazy person. She was his, and he wanted to stamp it on her damn forehead for everyone to see. "Promise me you won't ever run from me again," he demanded as he ran kisses down the center of her body his hands cupping her beautiful breasts, thumbs strumming her pert nipples. Her breath caught, and she nodded. Her breath starting to shallow out. As her desire started to take her over.

"Say the words Elle," he growled as he flipped the clasp of her jeans with his teeth. Her eyes watched from under heavy lids. "I need to hear the words." He tongued the zipper and dragged it down with his teeth. His hands skimming down her ribcage. He tugged on her jeans, easing them over her hips and down her legs. Leaving her in just her lace panties. Her entire body started to shake with need.

Victor stopped to place open mouthed kisses along her hip and upper thighs, Elle's hands had wound in his hair and she tugged and pulled. Moans and grunts of ecstasy were the only sounds she was making as she writhed beneath him. He had never seen anything as beautiful, as the woman he loved, caught up in need.

But he was going to get the promise from her before he allowed her, her passion. His fingers trailed along the lace of her panties, and her eyes opened as she chewed her bottom lip. "Elle, are going to run from me again?"

"Victor please," she begged.

He smiled. "Oh I love the begging sweetheart. But not what I'm looking for."

Elle took one leg and wrapped it around Victor's shoulder putting the apex of her sex directly in his face and for a moment he forgot everything. And he buried his face against her, Elle came off the bed. Her low moan burned through them both. As she ground herself against him.

Victor lost himself in her for the moment, the smell and feel of her. "Gods your smell, Elle. I've missed you so damn much." He dug his hands into her ass holding so he could push his face against her.

Even through her panties he could tell she was wet for him, and his world spun out of control. As his tongue sought out her clit, when he found it. Elle shot off the bet as he pressed it with his tongue.

"Victor." She moaned his name, her fingers digging into his shoulders.

He needed to stop before things got out of control. After all he was waiting for a promise from her. Victor pulled back and bit the inside of her thigh, not hard but Elle yelped. "Bad, Elle." Victor moaned.

Elle pulled away, and Victor sucked the spot where he had bitten her, kissing and caressing it with his tongue.

"Now where were we? Ah yes, Elle, are you going to run from me again?" This time he backed up as he pulled her panties down and in doing so forced her legs together. They were just above her knees and left them there.

Elle glared at him. "Why is this so important?"

"Because it kills me when you run from me," Victor said honestly. "And I don't know if I can live through it again."

Victor stood and removed his pants. He was so hard, he was pretty sure he could cut glass at this point. If she didn't agree soon, he was going to embarrass himself. At this point in the game, he was making a stand. Elle sat up, and with her panties still around her knees, she clutched his cock at the base. And licked the pre-come off the tip, making Victor sway on unsteady legs. His eyes crossed as his hand covered hers at the base of his cock, and his head feel back. He enjoyed the feel of her stroking him. But it was too much, and he tried to get her to let him go but she shook her head. Gods was she trying to kill him?

"And what about you?" She looked up at him. "Do you promise to never leave me like you did?"

She emphasized by circling the head of his engorged member with her tongue. Then sucking him all they in, past her soft palette, Victor nearly blew as she continued to suckle him.

"Gods, Elle." He pushed her away before he went off.

She gave him a smile and one eyebrow came up. He was gasping for air and griping his cock trying to regain control. "I don't have control." He said "when Dante calls" he admitted. "He pulls me to the Infernos whether I want to go or not. But I swear by the Gods, if I have control, I vow I will never, ever leave you."

The look she gave him was so shocked he didn't believe it for a moment. "You didn't think I would give you the oath?"

"No," she whispered. Victor fell on her. He kissed her gently. "I give it freely not just because of the sex. I give it because I mean it, Elle. And I ask it from you for the same reason."

Elle cupped his face. "I swear to never run from you Victor," she whispered.

Victor just looked into her eyes, the amber, a dark intense color. Then he was kissing her again. He wasn't sure how he got her panties off, and he didn't care. Her legs were around his waist. Her hot, wet core surrounding his cock, as he slid into her.

Elle's head bobbed back on the bed and Victor let out a moan as he slid home.

Victor filled her so totally, she wasn't sure where he started and she began. When he was fully imbedded, he stopped and Elle wasn't sure she could breathe. Then slowly he started to move.

Their entire bodies were touching as he moved in and out of her. Sliding out, until just the tip of him lay at her entrance. Sliding ever so slowly all the way back in. They moved together both gliding and sliding together, their breathing, and bodies in total sync.

The friction turned, and started a deep burn, their bodies becoming slick with sweat. Victor placed an open mouthed kiss against Elle's ear and leaned up on his elbows. He increased the speed, he took one of Elle's leg and put it over his shoulder kissing her ankle he reached down and flicked her clit with his thumb.

"I want to watch you fall apart, Elle," he moaned, as he continued to thrust into her. His thumb flicking her clit. He didn't have to wait long. "Open your eyes, Elle."

Golden amber eyes opened just as the orgasm struck, her body bowed up. Her inner walls grasping his cock tightly, her mouth opened on a silent scream. And those beautiful golden eyes screamed pleasure.

It was just what Victor needed, he slammed into her. Once. Twice. Still watching the tremors flood through her, he let his own release surge through him.

He held her, rocking against her slowly, as small tremors spiked through them. He didn't know what he had done to deserve her, and gods help anyone who tried to take her from him. He held her close as they came down from the sexual high.

Victor pulled her into the circle of his arms as he waited until he was sure Elle was asleep, before he snuck out of the bed, and went in search of a shower. When he made it back to the room, she was curled up in the small bed. He climbed in, pulling her close, knowing she was all he would ever need. He kissed the top of her head. Now, he just needed to kill the bastards that wanted to take her away from him. Then everything would be find.

Chapter 11

Victor sat back after Tabitha finished explaining the Daughters plan. He should tell her what a good plan they had. He should but he wasn't going to. The last thing the woman needed was for him to inflate her ego.

"What do you think?" Elle asked.

Victor shrugged. "I think it will work. My only concern is making sure we get the Dagger back."

Tabitha nodded. "We didn't know anything about the Dagger until yesterday. We might have to play that by ear.

"Hunter," Christian said and Victor nodded. Christian stood from the table they were all sitting around and left.

"Hunter is the Reaper of Treachery. He will be able to ferret out the Dagger during the fight." He pushed away from the table. "Where do you think Aldon is holed up at?"

"I had him followed last time he came here," Tabitha said but Victor stopped cold and glared at her.

"When?" He scowled at Elle.

"Couple of days before you arrived," Tabitha said it like she was imparting news about the weather.

"Are you joking?" Victor snapped.

"He came in peace," Tabitha snapped back. "And the Sons of Adam have every right to come here, in peace. More so, then you and the Trackers, I might add."

"And you just let him leave?" Victor finally shouted.

Tabitha rolled her eyes. "Didn't I say I had him followed? Geez, calm down."

"Do you honestly think he was just going to let one of your sisters follow him?" Victor wanted to shake the woman. And he was beginning to think she really needed to have some sense knocked into her.

"How stupid do you think I am?" Tabitha asked with her hands on her hips.

Skylar went to say something but Falcon slapped him on the back of the head before he could toss his two cents into the heated conversation.

"I put a tracking device into the sole of his shoe, like a tack. When he left Diana's sitting room he stepped on it. And my little tracking device went with him." She gave him the smug smile he hated so much.

Bowen perked up. "What kind of tracking device?"

"If I told you I'd have to kill you," she said casually. But Victor had known the Tracker long enough to know the tech junkie was going to get the information out of the woman. Even if it meant hacking into whatever system the Daughters had. At lease now, Bowen knew they had some system to hack into.

Tabitha pulled her phone out of her pocket. "With an app on my phone I can find out exactly where he is."

"Doesn't do us any good if we don't know what we are walking into," Victor said turning to Bowen and Skylar. "Get me everything we need."

Bowen rubbed his hands together and Skylar smiled. "Finally something to do."

Bowen held out his hand. "Gimme the phone." He had a smile on his face nobody could resist.

Tabitha narrowed her eyes, but then handed the phone to Bowen. Victor should have felt guilty but he didn't even feel a twinge of guilt Tabitha had just handed over the key to every bit of technology the Daughters of Eve had to the techy Tracker.

"How long?" Victor asked.

Bowen smiled as he scanned the contents of the phone and said something to Skylar who nodded.

"I don't like the look on your face," Tabitha snapped at Skylar. Who blew the woman a kiss.

"Twenty-four hours," Bowen said.

"Can you be ready?" Victor asked Tabitha.

Tabitha was still glaring at Skylar, but muttered, "Yes."

****

Elle fell into the twin bed, she was exhausted and her body hurt all over. She would have curled into a ball but it would have required energy she just didn't have. So she lay there not moving.

"Oh sister you look so tired. This fight is so futile," Chaos crooned.

Elle scrambled from the bed, her weak legs nearly giving out on her as she scrambled away from Chaos. She backed away pressing her back against the far wall. "How the fuck did you get in here?" And where the hell was Victor?

Chaos smiled, his nearly black eyes held no emotion at all. Chills danced up her spine making Elle shiver. "What do you want Chaos?"

"Do you really want this war, Elle?" he asked his head tilting as he watched her.

Elle took several breaths trying to calm herself. "This isn't a war, Chaos. This is madness! Aldon is insane. He wants me because I won't die, caring his science project."

Chaos walked toward her and Elle pressed herself against the cold brick wall. "That's where you are wrong Elle, and why you are so unique. Aldon needs you to give souls to his Freaks, and immortality to his off-spring. It can only be you. He will pay any price to get his hands on you. Sacrifice anything."

Elle swallowed the bile rising in her throat. "What kind of monster is he?"

Chaos shrugged. "He has become what he must, to survive. Do you want to see those you have come to care for, die? You will, of course, survive, Elle. But, what of these Trackers? The Daughters? The Reapers? All their lives…Forfeit. Do you want all their blood on your hands?"

She rushed at him pushing at Chaos, her anger getting the better of her. "What happened to you?" He stumbled back a step. "What happened to the brother I knew? The brother that made me laugh? That played the harp? That joked with me?"

Chaos grabbed her with a power she had never seen him use before. He flung her across the room. Elle slammed into the opposite wall, stars exploded behind her eyes as her face made contact with the cold cement, as she slumped to the floor.

"He died, hundreds of thousands of years ago. Crumpled in a cold cell forgotten by the light and by anyone who cared for him," Chaos snarled, his voice grew louder as he moved across the room toward her again. "Choose, Elle. This stupid little rag-tag team, who is going to die one by one? Or the power of Aldon and the Tribunal?"

Elle tried to push to her feet but the lights were blinking in and out. "I'm sorry we forgot about you Chaos."

He laughed at her. "Keep your pity for someone who needs it sister. I no longer do."

She tried to move away from his voice but he was faster than she was, and he grabbed her by her hair. Elle screamed as he pulled her into a standing position. "Time to leave sister, Aldon won't desecrate these grounds but I have no compunction about doing just that."

Elle grabbed at the hand holding her hair. "I'm not going anywhere with you."

"Okay you can walk out on your own two feet or I kill you and carry you out dead." He pulled out a knife and pressed it to her chest. "Aldon doesn't care how he gets you, in fact he has to repay you for how you left him the last time you separated. So you might as well show up dead. I don't really care."

Elle swallowed, this was bad. And where the hell was Victor? She thought about screaming, but Chaos only shook his head. "Dead is dead, Elle. But recovering from a slit throat is probably a real bitch."

"How did you get past the Daughter's wards?" Elle asked instead of thinking about recovering from a slit throat.

"I'm your brother, the sisters aren't warding against me." He shrugged. "Now let's get moving."

Elle didn't see a way out of it but what would Victor do when he came back to the room and saw she was gone? Would he think she had run off again? How was she going to get out of this one?

She was about to all out panic, when the door flew open and Helena came rushing in. Elle sighed. "Thank the gods. Helena, kill him." Elle tried to pull away from Chaos, but he held her firmly.

"You were supposed to meet me ten minutes ago!" Helena snapped. "What the hell? That damn Reaper will be here any minute."

Elle was so shocked she almost crumpled to the floor. "Helena?" Her world was suddenly turning upside down.

Chaos lifted one shoulder. "She wanted to chitchat."

Helena grabbed Elle and pulled her through the door. "We don't have time for chitchat." Elle was so numb she just stumbled along with Helena as she pushed and shoved Elle down the hallway.

"Why?" Elle asked finally finding her voice.

"Because it's about damn time we get our seat on the Tribunal," Helena said shoving Elle through a side door. "And Aldon has promised to put me on the Tribunal with him, for helping out. I'm done playing hide and seek with the world. It's about damn time I get to have a seat and a say." Her words were like venom.

This was about power? Helena wanted power? "What the fuck?" Elle practically shouted. Helena backhanded her knocking her to the ground. But Elle was past angry, this was the final betrayal. When Chaos reached for her, Elle slapped his hands away. She would rather be dead then go with these two. They were supposed to be her family! And they would rather have power, and a seat on the Tribunal then their sister.

"And then you had to come here? Get involved with these stupid ass Daughters of Eve." Helena swore. "I thought using your Blood, for the emergency number was stupid. But you have to go and bring the Daughters of Eve into the mix?"

Elle's mind was reeling. "You bitch."

"Blah, blah, blah." Helena rolled her eyes. "You have been a weight around my neck for the longest time. But finally, finally." Helena called out to the heavens, "you are going to be useful. If I could just get you to Aldon." She said the last to Chaos. "Dead or alive I don't give a shit. Right Chaos? No more, poor pitiful cursed little Elle?"

Chaos only laughed at what Helena had to say.

Elle glared at the two, "You realize the both of you are going to burn in Hell right?" Elle asked.

Helena laughed, and shook her head. "Oh no little cursed sister. You are the one who is going to wish she were in Hell after what Aldon has planned for you. He isn't right in the head. All the time spent hiding you is finally going to pay off."

Elle felt bile rise in her throat at the mere thought of what the sick bastard had planned. No. She would rather be dead than go to the alter of Aldon. Elle wrenched her arm free of her sister in a wild attempt at freedom. If she was going to go down she decided she was going to go down fighting.

Helena swore and went to grab at her, Elle kicked Helena's knee in. Helena hit the dirt like a dropped sack of potatoes screaming in pain. Chaos swore and told Helena to shut up as he slashed at Elle.

Pain seared across Elle's arm as his sharp knife sliced into her. But it wasn't a mortal wound, and she grabbed a hand full of dirt and flung it into Chaos face. The demigod back peddled. It was enough for Elle, she let out a blood curdling scream.

****

Victor heard the scream as he was finishing up the last of the preparations. Thank the gods everyone was still up. Nobody even stopped to think they just all grabbed a weapon and started to run.

Victor had never been so terrified in all his life, the scream had come from the guest quarters. The only people in the guest quarters were Helena and Elle.

"I'll take the back," Garrett said running around the back of the building. Victor headed toward the room he was sharing with Elle. She had gone to bed half an hour ago.

Hunter grabbed him before he turned down the hall. "She won't be there," he said pulling him toward the back of the barracks. Victor felt lightheaded with fear and followed his brother.

Hunter pushed through a side door just as a man plunged a knife into Elle's chest silencing her screams.

Victor let out a horrible bellow as he attacked the man. He pulled him off Elle and pummeled him until he was a bloody mess. He was holding some type of stone around his throat and chanting but his words were choppy around his broken and bloody teeth.

Hunter pulled him free. "See to Elle."

Victor rolled off of him and over to Elle. He pulled the dagger from her chest. Blood gushed from the wound. "Thank you for coming for me," she whispered.

"Don't talk." Victor kissed her as he wrapped her in his arms.

Elle shook her head. "Fiona," she gasped trying to get the words out. Victor shook his head he didn't want her to speak she smiled and when she opened her mouth again blood trickled out. "Tea, in my bag. Healing tea." The words were choppy but he understood and nodded. The tea that helped her heal.

"Quiet now." Victor kissed her and she smiled.

"Knew you would come."

He was choking on tears. "You promised not to leave me," he whispered into her ear.

"I'll be right back," she whispered and then she gasped once, then again. And then her breathing stopped altogether. He had seen her die before but each time it hurt, each time it felt like she took a piece of him with her. Each time he didn't know if this would be the time she wouldn't come back. Would this be the time the Angels would come to claim her perfect soul.

Victor bellowed, crushing her to his chest. He bellowed to the heavens because he hadn't been in time to save her the pain. And she died again.

When he was done he looked down into her lifeless body and prayed to the Gods for her to come back.

And he was left waiting, blocking out the sounds around him. He held his breath and waited.

"Breathe dammit," he whispered.

After another minute. "Breathe dammit." He said a little louder.

"Elle, breathe." He gently laid her out. "Breathe."

He felt rather then saw people surround him and knew his brothers were there. And still she didn't move.

"BREATHE, DAMMIT!" Victor slammed a fist into her chest.

"Victor." One of his brothers put a hand on his shoulder but he shrugged it off.

"Elle" he felt utterly defeated. "Please"

She sucked in a breath, her entire body sucking in the breath bowing her body, she pulled the oxygen into every inch of her body. "I need a blanket," Victor said over his shoulder.

He didn't leave her until she had had her first dose of the tea. But once she was sleeping again he went in search of Hunter. He didn't have to search far.

"Where are they?"

Hunter nodded toward the door he was standing in front of. "They are mine," was all Hunter said before he stepped aside, his hand shot out to stop Victor. "I kept them here for her. She needs the closure. But their treachery goes much deeper than Elle and this incident. It is not a stain, but part of their souls."

Victor nodded and walked into the room. Everything had been removed, Helena and Chaos sat in the center of the room. Chained together with chains brought from the Infernos. They'd never break free of those chains. They would suffer for eternity, but he wanted to look at them first. And their sentence would mean they would suffer internally for what they had done. Not only for what they had done to Elle but for their tainted souls.

Helena's glamor was gone but she wasn't beautiful any longer in fact the beauty was no longer there either. It was like it was overlaid with something black and horrifying, Victor looked at the blond woman and watched as her beauty was marred by something ugly.

Chaos still clutched at whatever hung around his neck, chanting.

Helena laughed. "He thinks his master will still save him."

"Your master can't save you, Chaos," Victor said reaching over Helena he took the necklace from Chaos who screeched and tried to grab it back from Victor.

"Give it back." Chaos clamored for it.

"Do you have any idea what has happened to you?" Victor asked the demi-god.

Chaos glared at him. "My master will come for me he always comes for me," he said raising his chin he glared at Victor.

Victor shook his head. "Your master can't touch you where you are going. Those chains you wear, they are bound for one place, and one place only."

Helena blanched but Chaos smiled. "My master will not allow me to be sent to the Infernos."

"Don't be an idiot, Chaos. It's no longer up to your master." She tried to shake free, but the chains only tightened. "What do you want? Money, drugs? Power? I'll tell you were Aldon is, I'll bring him here for you to kill."

"I know where Aldon is. And anything you touch Helena is tainted. So I want nothing you have." Victor said crossing his arms over his chest. "What I want to know is why you sold your own sister out."

Chaos snorted. "Who hasn't she sold out? Do you see any other demi-gods around?"

Helena jerked on the chains. "Shut up," she snarled.

"Is that so, Helena? Is that what happened to all the demi-gods?" Victor asked.

Chaos raised one eyebrow. "Not all of them, some of them have hidden really, really well." He laughed, but the sound was maniacal and slightly crazed.

"Shut up," Helena snarled again.

"Or what?" Chaos asked. "What can they possible do, Helena? From where I'm sitting, we are totally screwed."

"When they take these chains off I am going to strangle you." Helena swore.

"Yeah, good luck with that," Chaos said. "According to the other one, when they take these chains off, the last thing we will care about is hurting each other." It was the first bit of truth Chaos had uttered.

"All your plans have sucked. If you had just listened to me in the first place, none of this would have happened." Chaos muttered.

"Shut up, Chaos!" Helena jerked, trying to get toward Chaos. The chains tightened making her cringe in pain. Chaos only laughed harder.

Victor snapped his fingers getting their attention. "Let's get back to the matter at hand, why screw over Elle? She wanted nothing but your approval, and love."

Helena gave him what Victor was sure she considered her best smile, and if he didn't see through to how ugly she was he might have fallen for it. "She wasn't usefully anymore. Not that she ever was. And do I look like the approval, and love type?"

Victor wanted to kill her, but he wasn't going to. "Aldon offered me something I wanted more. A seat on the Tribunal. How could I turn that down? Finally, Others would have to bow to me! I would be making the rules, instead of cowering and hiding. And finally, Elle would no longer be a problem. Then she had to go and call you in and she had to do it using blood. Who does that? And then the Daughters had to get involved. I should have let Chaos kill her, and kidnap her, the first night in the hotel!"

Victor stepped forward, and grabbed her wrapping his hands around her throat, it was an unconscious action. The only thing stopping him, was the mad laughter from Chaos.

"If you kill her will her punishment be over?" Chaos asked in a sing-song voice.

Victor swore and released her. She glared at Victor as she was gasping for air, trying to regain her breath. "Look, Victor. I've spent more time then I care to remember, taking care of Elle. It was her turn to take care of me. So she had to breed with Aldon? And his genetically altered science projects? It was probably going to kill her. That's what she gets for being cursed. At least her curse will come in handy. Don't you think it was time it was useful? Frankly we all have a cross to bare."

Victor lost it again and he grabbed Helena picking her up and pushed her against the wall. Unfortunately she was chained to Chaos and both demi-gods slammed into the wall, shaking the bricks. Hunter came rushing into the room.

"Do you have any idea, how much pain she goes through when she comes back after a death? You selfish, heartless harpy?" Victor growled.

Victor let her go and both demi-gods slumped to the floor. He stomped away. "Take them to Treachery, Hunter. And make sure they suffer. If she cares at all, I'll bring Elle there, when this is all done. Maybe they will be more inclined to offer an apology for their lies, deceit and actions toward their sister, after some time spent suffering for their sins."

Helena finally blanched. "He can't just take us there."

Victor turned to her. "Actually, yes he can."

"We deserve a trial! Or at the very least an audience with Dante!" Helena demanded. "You can't just take me to Treachery and leave me there. Do you have any idea who I am?"

Victor laughed and looked at Hunter. "Do you know who she is?" he asked his brother.

Hunter nodded and turned to Helena. "I am Hunter, the ruler of Treachery. What I know, is that I have seen your soul. It is heavy with the treachery, of lies and deceit you have served upon others. You are beyond guilty; your soul reeks of treachery and deceit. That is who you are, and that is all I need to know. There will be no trial, no 'deserved' audience with Dante. You have been bound for Treachery for thousands of years. And that is where you will go. That. Is who you are."

Helena's mouth dropped open. She slumped over knowing, that she had been tried, and found guilty, nothing she said or did would change it now.

Chaos breathed out. "We are so fucked. Aren't you at least going to call a Ringer?"

Hunter smiled. "But that would make it easier on you. Taking you whole," Hunter leaned forward, smile still on his lips. "will increase the torment. Something, we all know you deserve. And I wonder…How many of your victims did you spare comfort for?"

Chaos shook his head. "So fucked." He shuttered.

"Get them out of here." Victor turned.

"You'll lose her in the end," Helena screamed to Victor. Victor ignored her, because she was wrong and he was going to do everything in his power to make sure in the end he kept Elle safe. It was his only mission now. It was all that mattered.

****

Victor woke Elle again to drink her tea, and as before she was grumpy as hell. "I swear I'm going to kill you this time," she grumbled as she slapped his hands away when he tried to help her into a sitting position.

"It's why I removed all the deadly weapons," Victor said holding out the mug.

"And this stuff tastes like shit," she grumbled again taking the mug she pulled up her legs and sipped the hot liquid. She felt more awake than the last time. "What time is it?"

Victor checked his watch. "Almost midnight."

"Have you gotten any sleep at all in the last forty-eight hours?" she hadn't meant for her question to sound so waspish but it did. She promised to work on that, when she wasn't coming back from the dead.

"No, I haven't," Victor said. Sitting down on the side of the bed, he rubbed his face. And she felt sorry for him.

"Why don't you get some rest? I'm feeling a lot better now." And she was, the time of her sleeping for days on end after dying were in her past thanks to this god's awful tea and Fiona.

"Good, to know. We are just waiting for you, and then we are moving out," Victor said.

"We can't be attacking Aldon. You're exhausted." Finishing her tea, she placed the mug on the side table and wrapped her arms around Victor. "Just rest for an hour?"

Victor shrugged her off. "Stop. You want to prolong this bullshit?" he snapped. "Dammit Elle, your life is on the fucking line and you want me to sleep? I'm not tired." He got off the bed. And since the first time she had met him he was that cold Reaper again. "I'm sick of having your life on the line. I'm sick of showing up to see you dying."

"Excuse me?" Elle climbed out of the bed, not caring she only wore only a bra and underwear. "Not like it's a party for me or anything."

Victor looked like he wanted to shake her. "How many more times do you have to fucking die before this shit is over?" he shouted. "Because I can't handle it anymore."

"You?" Elle shouted. "You can't handle it?"

"No!" Victor shouted right back. Grabbing her by the shoulders, he jerked her flush with him. Elle caught her breath, when she saw the tears in his eyes. Tears. In a Reapers eyes…who'd a guessed? Her anger flew out the preverbal window. "Put yourself in my shoes, Elle." He was so mad, his voice had dropped to barely a whisper.

"Praying over your dead body, for one breathe. Just one. I'm a Reaper for god's sake! And I'm praying for you to breathe, just one more breath. I deal in death. But, you dying? Brings me to my knees. Every fucking time."

Elle brushed the tear away, she was sure he would deny. "I love you too, Victor."

Her words pulled him up short and he jerked like she had slapped him and he just stared at her for a moment. Then he was kissing her, and she didn't care about breathing didn't care about anything but the man holding her. Elle speared her hands into his hair, anchoring her to him. Then pressed against him.

Victor took a couple of steps and she was pressed against the wall, which was fine with Elle. She wrapped her legs around him Elle knew she would never be able to get close enough to him. Even when he was buried deep inside of her she wasn't close enough.

She clawed at his clothes needing to feel his skin, Victor pulled away only long enough to pull his shirt off and then he was back. He ripped her bra off and shredded her panties. Elle didn't know how he got out of his pants but then he was sliding into her so fast and hard Elle couldn't do anything but hold on.

"Mine," Victor growled, as he placed open mouth kisses on her throat. Elle could do nothing but agree. She was his. There would be no other man. Elle felt her world unraveling as he pushed her to the limits of ecstasy. "Never letting you go." He moaned and drove into her over and over. He leaned back and stared into her eyes. "Elle, do you understand me?"

Elle nodded. "Mine," she moaned and he groaned so low his chest vibrated and her entire body ignited. It was all she could do to just hold on to him.

Her orgasm was so powerful, it felt like her entire body was going to explode. Still, Victor never stopped moving. He rode it out with her, prolonging her pleasure, until she was almost in tears.

Only then, did he take his pleasure. His head buried against her neck, the muscles in his back tense, as he found completion. His entire body shuddering over and over again.

After several minutes, Victor carried her over to the bed and they collapsed there. Neither spoke for a long time. He cradled her close as if he was going to lose her if she moved and she let him, knowing he needed this right now. She knew it would be hard for him to say the words she had given so freely.

She was surprised she had given them; it wasn't something she had planned. But she knew he felt the same way. Or he wouldn't have said or done half the thing he did. It didn't matter he hadn't said the words back. Now she just had to convince her heart that she didn't need the words.

Elle was surprised when she felt him relax and his breathing evened out. She peeked up and he was indeed asleep. She nudged him. "I thought we had to go?"

"In a minute." He pulled her close and adjusted so they were more comfortable on the bed. Tomorrow was soon enough, she guessed. Elle pulled the covers over them and held him close. He thought she was the one that needed protection and saving. Maybe, just maybe, Victor needed someone to save his heart and hold it close. She would help the Reaper find out love was a good thing, after all.

Chapter 12

"This is stupid." Elle was not going to stay in the van. "I did not come all this way to sit here and watch what was going on. Besides I'm a sitting duck out here in the van. Have any of you thought about that?"

"She has a point," Skylar said.

"Shut up," Tabitha snapped at the Tracker. "Let's use him as bait."

Everyone ignored Tabitha's outburst. "I'll take her with me," Celeste offered.

"No." Victor immediately vetoed that suggestion.

Elle was getting irritated; he had been odd since their last night at the Daughters complex. One minute he was all protective and the next he was the distant Reaper, during those times his brothers and Celeste would step in like avenging angels. Elle was getting whiplash from his treatment.

"We can't leave her here unprotected," Tabitha argued.

"Yeah fuck you," Bowen said holding up the semi-auto weapon he had and kicking the bag of backup weapons he kept at his feet.

Tabitha rolled her eyes. "Your attention is going to be on the op, not on Elle. So get over it."

"Are we doing this or are we going on a Sunday fucking drive?" Falcon shouted into the earpiece making everyone who was wearing one cringe. Falcon, was in another vehicle as was Ryder and Kyra and Nathaniel. Lykar, Marlee and Hunter were coming in from another position as well.

"I'm with Falcon. Let's set this bitch on fire." Ryder said. A little too excited.

"My girls are ready," Tabitha said climbing from the van.

Victor glared at Elle, who smiled back at him. "I'm not staying in this van. Why else did you bring me?"

"Because you wouldn't have stayed away," Victor snapped, making Elle smile. "And tranquilizing you wasn't an option."

"Just give me a weapon, and I'll protect your back. I've been practicing." Elle held out her hand.

"God's help us all." Sky shook his head and climbed from the van.

Victor handed her a gun and they both climbed from the van, Elle was practically bouncing on the balls of her feet. "Who's been teaching you?" he demanded.

"Tabitha was teaching me," she admitted not telling him Tabitha had been teaching her knife fighting. And she didn't really know anything about guns. She tucked the weapon into the back of her pants.

Victor grabbed her and kissed her. "Stay behind me." Elle nodded. Victor moved forward and didn't notice when Tabitha pulled Elle aside and gave her a knife.

"What's the heat signature like?" Victor asked when they reached the compound in the deserts of Nevada. It was just past sundown but it was still hot as hell and they had moved in slow and steady. A forty minute hike had done nothing for his mood.

"He picked this place for a reason man." Bowen's voice crackled over the earpiece. They were spread out over a ten mile radius of hills and valleys. Victor was pretty sure most mortals thought this is what hell felt like. When full dark hit they wouldn't be able to see their hands in front of their faces. "Thermal is shit here."

"I need to send out a drone. But the moment I let something fly over, the bastard is going to know we're here." Bowen swore, and Victor could hear the Tracker pounding away on a keyboard. "Satellite images says he has underground levels. Victor, your team is hitting the heaviest side. Falcon's team has the lightest..."

"What the fuck dude?" Falcon snapped obviously mad he got the lightest hits.

"Shut up, Falcon. I need you to go in and hit the tower. Get me into any surveillance the place has. Otherwise, none of the other teams have shit of a chance. Everyone else, cool your heels." Bowen pounded away. Victor laid in the desert dirt, itching to end this fight.

Celeste crawled up to sit next to Victor. "You okay?"

Victor nodded.

"Because you've been a little weird," Celeste added.

"You do realize, everyone can hear you right?" Victor asked not wanting to have this conversation with his sister. Not just because everyone could hear, either. He wanted to beat his head against the hard dirt for the way he was treating Elle. After she had told him she loved him, his entire world had re-focused. It was like with the words out in the world everything had changed.

He felt the same, and he needed to say the words. Elle deserved the words but it wasn't the right time. And every time he opened his mouth he felt like a bastard for not telling her he loved her back when she had told him.

Now he was microphoned in, and they were headed into a fight.

"Shit's just happening… So fast and not fast enough." Victor had to admit.

"Oh my god, is this and episode of Dr. Phil, or a fucking mission?" Skylar asked with a snort of laugher.

Celeste raised an eyebrow and shook her head. Letting him know she totally understood. "By the way, have you ever seen Elle use a gun?"

It was exactly what he needed to hear, because his brain refocused. Victor swore and turned to take the gun away from Elle when gunshots rang out from the compound. "What the hell?" Victor shouted. "Falcon?"

Bowen was shouting as well, but the gunshots continued. And Falcon was screaming. "Freaks are everywhere, element of surprise totally gone."

More gun shots.

"I'm going in." This was from Lykar.

"Wait wait wait!" Bowen was screaming but then Victor could hear gun shots to the south where Ryder's team was stationed.

"Bowen, we are all moving in," Victor shouted.

"Of course you are, because why the fuck would we want to stick to a god damn plan." Victor ignored Bowen, motioned to Tabitha who nodded and made some hand signals to the Daughters and they all blended into the darkness, Celeste and Marcus Flashed out, leaving Skylar and Victor. "Ready?"

Skylar smiled. "Shit, man. I'm always ready." He took off at a lope.

Victor turned to Elle. "Stay at my back. Do you understand?"

She nodded and smiled. Christian and Garrett Flashed in. Both taking a defensive stand on either side of Elle, they all took off.

Elle had to admit, she kinda felt like GI Jane in her desert camo. Tucked between three Reapers though, she was pretty sure she wasn't going to see any action.

But the closer they got to the compound, the worse the fighting got. First, it was just Freaks. The kind they had already had contact with. But, as they entered the impressive walls of the compound, the Freaks changed, too. These Freaks were different, some were larger. Most were mutilated in some way. Elle stumbled along in disbelief at what they came across, Freaks with missing limbs, or deformed limbs, malformed skulls, hunched backs. Slavering beasts with crazed eyes that barely resembled a mortal form.

"Victor!" Elle grabbed onto him, stalling his "I know, Elle. We need to keep moving." Elle stumbled on behind him, Tabitha met up with them.

"This place is unholy," she spat out. Elle had to agree. She actually wished she had stayed back in the van. Whatever Aldon was doing here, was sick and unholy. If she had any illusions before she was sure now, she wanted nothing whatsoever to do with Aldon and his crazed creations.

They all staggered to a halt when an explosion rocked them all. Victor grabbed Elle, protecting her as rubble rained down around them.

"Gods. Find out what the hell that was." Victor shouted to Garrett and Christian, both men nodded and took off.

Tabitha ran off in a different direction as another explosion shook them nearly off their feet. Victor took Elle's hand and they raced toward the nearest building he pressed her against the wall for protection. The building swayed, and they both looked up as something streaked across the sky.

"Oh, my god!" Elle watched in morbid fascination. Thank god, Victor reacted, as the missile aimed for the building they were leaned against, rocketed for them. He grabbed her and dove out of the way.

"What the hell?" Victor shouted. "Bowen where the hell did the missiles come from?"

"Good fucking question!" Bowen screamed over the earpiece. "We have incoming!"

Elle looked up as another missile hurtled through the early night. "Victor!" she screamed, crawling toward Victor.

But in the midst of the chaos Aldon appeared.

"VICTOR!" Elle screamed. "Bowen, we need to get the hell out of here." She back peddled on all fours away from Aldon and the missiles, trying to put as much distance between them as possible.

But he stalked through the smoke and fire like he was untouchable, more missiles flew in through the dark night but he didn't even flinch. Rubble sliced into the palms of Elle's hands but she didn't care. The only thing on her mind was putting as much distance between herself and Aldon.

"You aren't getting away from me, this time, Elle. " Aldon leapt, landing on top of her. Elle grunted as the air was pushed from her. Still she fought to push him off of her.

Then he was pulled off of her, and tossed aside. Victor looked down at her "Are you okay?" Elle nodded and waved him off. "Get out of here," he snarled and then went after Aldon.

"Like hell." Elle sucked in air and pulled herself to her feet she stumbled to where Victor and Aldon had disappeared into the dust and rubble. Missiles whistled overhead, and the ground shook. She wasn't going anywhere, until she knew Victor was okay. And Aldon, the bastard, was gone for good. Elle climbed over rubble as she screamed for Victor, she reached out with her senses he had to be close, she thought, as she tried to pinpoint just where but couldn't. Cursing she rubbed dirt from her face as another bomb went off sending her back to her hands and knees.

Bowen was screaming for his brothers to check in. Trackers, Daughters of Eve and other voices were talking so rapidly in her ear she couldn't concentrate. Clawing the device from her ear, she flung it into the recesses of the ruined building.

"God dammit Victor! Where the hell are you?" She ground out, as she squeezed herself under a beam she assumed had held up part of the roof at one point. When she found Victor she was going to kill him herself. How dare he run off and leave her alone, what the hell had he been thinking?

She stopped when a hand reached out from underneath a beam. It scared her so bad Elle wasn't even able to scream. In shock she stared at the hand for a moment not moving.

"Elle." Her name was whispered.

"Lykar?" Elle flattened herself on the floor. Lykar looked to be pinned under a beam.

"My brothers?" the Tracker asked. Elle shook her head.

"I don't know about them." She looked around, swearing a blue streak, for taking off her earpiece. "Lykar do you have your earpiece?" she asked, leaning down so she could look at the Tracker again?

She could tell he was in pain, it was written plain in his blue eyes and he lay in a pool of blood. "No." She didn't know how much time he had.

"I'm going to get help," she said, but he didn't release her hand.

"Marlee." He moaned the Lycan's name Elle had met only a hand full of times.

Elle panicked a little. "Where is she?"

Lykar looked like he would pass out any second. "She was ahead of me when the missile came in, don't know now." Elle sat up and looked around, and didn't see anything. But didn't know if she had the heart to tell Lykar that. She flattened herself back on the floor and patted his hand, "I'm going to find her, and get help Lykar."

The Tracker nodded and closed his eyes. "Brothers." He coughed and blood splattered out. Elle knew she didn't have a lot of time.

"Oh. My. God. Oh my god. Ohmygod!"

Elle chanted as she climbed back over the beam and headed back the way she came. She spent a fruitless ten minutes searching for the ear piece she had tossed into the rubble and cursed herself for throwing it away.

When she reached the courtyard she looked around but it was eerily quiet. The bombings had stopped and nothing moved but the fires and smoke.

Elle ran in the shadows, whispering for Tabitha or the other Trackers. She really didn't need to because she took a corner and came face to face with the barrel of a very very large gun. She skidded to a halt.

"Shit, shit, shit." Large hands grabbed her by her upper arms and drug her forward. Elle squeaked and tried to jerk away.

Victor was suddenly there, pulling her toward him. "Touch her and die."

"Victor." Elle threw her arms around him.

"Why do you never listen to me?" he snarled into her hair.

She thought about that for a moment. Then shook it off and looked around. They were in the middle of the compound, and everyone was there, the Reapers and Trackers. They were surrounded by what looked like an army of men, the Trackers were all kneeling in the middle with their arms on their heads. The Reapers were at the side of the group, the Daughters looked as if they were holding court with the men at the side.

Elle looked around. "What the hell is going on?" she asked.

"Looks like the Sons of Adam have intervened?" Victor snarled.

Elle got her first good look at Victor. And he didn't look happy at all. She wanted to clean him up, but was stopped when a group of armed men brought in a large group of Freaks about thirty of them.

Elle stepped back, a man separated from Tabitha and went to the group that held the Freaks, conversed with the leader holding the Freaks.

When he was done the leader of the Freaks and his men turned and led the group away. Elle wondered what they were going to do with them. And knew it couldn't be good.

Then she remembered Lykar, Elle started to run over to the Trackers but had a gun shoved in her face again.

"I have to talk to the Trackers." She tried to get past the man again.

"I don't think so, sweetheart." The gun toting thug said shoving her back.

Victor pushed the idiot back. "Don't talk to her like that. Does she actually look like she is going to do any harm?"

Elle didn't like the sound of that, but she was going to let that one go for now because Lykar needed help.

"I don't give a shit, Reaper. She doesn't go anywhere near them until we decide what to do with them," the thug said.

"You don't understand, their brother needs medical attention," Elle explained loud enough for the Trackers to hear.

The Trackers had, to this point, been quiet calm. Threaten one of their own and they would go bat shit crazy. Something Elle knew, just not on what level.

"Where is he?" Falcon asked.

"The large building to the east. He's stuck under the main beam. Marilee is there as well, but I couldn't find her," Elle said.

Elle was surprised they didn't move except for Falcon's question. However, Victor looked at the Reapers and then stepped back holding Elle.

The thug narrowed his eyes at the group. And Victor shook his head. "We want Aldon," Victor told him.

The leader stepped forward. "We don't condone what he is doing nor do we want a seat on the Tribunal," he said.

"Good to know." Victor nodded. "A Tracker is trapped," Victor said. "And one of ours is still missing in the rubble."

The leader looked from the Trackers back to the Reapers. "I'm sorry, but we still have not located Aldon. We cannot allow people to wander through the complex until it has been swept clean. You triggered his missiles, I need the complex intact. You and your team almost destroyed it. So until I say so, nobody moves."

"No you don't understand, Lykar is trapped. You can't just leave him there." Elle argued.

"Not my problem darl'n." The man said to Elle. Who bristled at his words.

"I'm not your darl'n." Elle muttered. "And you can't just leave one of our men out there.

"That is unfortunate," Victor said. "My enemy's enemy and all."

"What is that supposed to mean?" The leader asked.

Elle wondered the same thing herself.

Then the Trackers and Reapers were moving, and all her questions were answered.

The three Trackers moved so quickly they were a blur, but it was Ryder who moved so fast he was practically invisible. Kyra became several Kyra's disarming men so quickly they really didn't know what hit them. At the same time the Reapers struck, in seconds the Sons of Adam stood or lay unconscious and unarmed.

Victor had moved only to pull Elle next to him and disarm the man in front of him. "We cannot leave one of our own injured and another missing, and possible injured. We will collect them and be on our way. Bowen, bring in the van."

The leader crossed his arms and smiled at Victor. "How did we get the upper hand in the first place?"

"Surprise does a lot of things, plus we did want to know who else was interested in Aldon," Victor said conversationally.

The leader held out his hand. "Well played Reaper, if you ever get tired of your gig with Dante you can come and train with the brotherhood. By the way the name is Devon."

Victor took his hand and Elle wanted to slap them both, instead she pinched Victor's shoulder. "Are we really playing nice with this jackass?" she whispered.

Devon looked around Victor at Elle. "You must be the demi-god causing all the problems."

Well she definitely didn't like the sound of that. "Umm, if I understand it correctly. Aldon is the asshat causing all the problems. Not me."

Devon threw his head back and laughed. "Asshat?" he asked.

Victor narrowed his eyes and laughed. "Aldon is many things. And asshat seems like a good moniker for him."

"Yeah. So glad you approve," she said and turned to Victor. "What happened to said asshat?"

Victor shrugged. "One minute he was there and the next he was gone."

"We believe he has an underground fortress." They both turned back to Devon. "I have my men searching for the entrance. He is probably watching us right now. That is why I can't allow anyone to wander around the compound. Aldon has set the place with various booby traps. As you have found out with his missiles. Which are his failsafe; if his compound is taken, the missiles would destroy the compound. Luckily my men were capable of disabling the majority of them before the entire compound was destroyed. If we're lucky we'll be able to find the entrance."

It made Elle's skin crawl.

"Let's burn the place to the ground," the thug from earlier said. "Smoke the bastard out."

Elle rolled her eyes. "Not all that original. And how do we know it will even work?"

Tabitha walked over. "How long can he stay down there?"

Devon shook his head. "We have no idea. Probably a life time."

"What does that mean? A life time?" Elle asked. The skin crawl had changed to a sick feeling and she felt like she wanted to empty her stomach all over the dirt.

"Ahh." Devon gave her a sad smile. "Aldon hasn't shared his dirty little secret with you has he." Devon looked around the clearing and raised his voice. "I would have thought you would tell her Aldon. You should have shared this information with the woman you wanted to carry your soulless bastards."

Elle reached out and Victor took her hand. Elle gripped it hoping it was enough to keep her on her feet.

Devon turned back to her, but didn't drop his voice. "I'm giving you the chance to come clean Aldon," he screamed as he spoke. "Don't you think it appropriate to come from your lips; don't you think you should follow even a few of the codes of the brotherhood?"

Devon finally broke eye contract with Elle and looked around again. "Law 3: Let the words of truth always be spoken. As a Son of Adam I shall hold the chalice of truth and bear the weight of god's great wrath when lies sprout and take root in my soul and choke out the light."

Devon ended his words as any great sermon would on a high note with a fist raised to the heavens. Several of his soldiers nodded and pounded on their chests in agreement. Even the Daughters of Eve seemed to agree. By raising their own weapons.

"Let the honesty start now, let the light come back into the darkness," Devon shouted. When he stopped talking the silence was deafening.

Devon shook his head, and he turned to Elle. "It would seem Aldon has truly given up on the beliefs of the Sons of Adam."

"I am the only one who truly believes in the Sons of Adam. It is you who have strayed." Aldon's voice boomed from the darkness.

"How am I a prevaricator?" Devon asked smiling as if he thought being called so was amusing to him.

"We are the fathers of mortals. We should rule them. As a Son of Adam you shall hold sacred the brotherhood and the sons produced of the brotherhood," Aldon screamed making the speakers crackly and buzz. "You are burning my sons in mass graves, should I go to your estate's Devon and burn your sons?"

"Aldon what you are creating in test tubes are not sons, they are things. When you bend the laws of god you break the laws of the Brotherhood," Devon announced. "Now present yourself so you can be judged."

"Wait." Victor held up his hand. "He belongs to me."

Devon shook his head. "He is a Son of Adam and therefore he will be held to judgment by the Sons."

Victor shook his head. "The hell you say. Dante wants him, and Dante will not be swayed on this.

Devon gave him a smile. "Dante will have his soul I will promise you this. But he will be judged and punished by the Brotherhood."

Victor threw his hands in the air and turned to his brothers, Elle still clung to his back. "We will return to the Infernos and see what Dante has to say about this," Christian offered "We will be back."

Victor didn't really have a choice and the bastard was still squirreled away in the ground somewhere. Victor nodded and his brothers all Flashed away, he turned to

Elle and cupped her face. "And what exactly am I supposed to do with you?" Gods he just wanted to put her someplace safe. But he had tried to get her to go someplace safe but no matter what he did she seemed to follow him into danger.

She leaned forward, pressed herself into him and kissed him. "I'll be happy and safest with you, I think."

He agreed with her there. "Just don't move from my side." She nodded and linked her arm with him. "Like glue."

"What say you Aldon?" Devon asked.

They waited but after ten minutes there still wasn't an answer. Victor snorted. "Now what?"

"We continue to search for a way in. Nothing changes." Devon shrugged. "Now where were we..." he tapped his chin. "Oh yes Aldon's lies." He chuckled. "Aldon has been on the outskirts of the brotherhood for some time now. But it wasn't until the Tribunal made the..." he trailed off thoughtfully and then tried again. "Shall we call it an offer to the non-Tribunal Others? We are a scattered, lawless and hunted sect of Others. There are the Sons of Adam, the Daughters of Eve, the demi-gods, the last of the world benders, I know of four Sandman's they are siblings three sisters and a brother they would love to be represented on the Tribunal but not at the cost that is being asked. And a hundred or so other Others, that truly deserve to be represented but that really isn't a Reaper problem is it?"

"Anyway, Aldon decided he was going to do what none of us wanted to do. And he was going to represent those who couldn't represent themselves. And it sounded too good to be true." Devon shook his head sadly. "So we looked into Aldon, and what we found was so sad it broke the heart of those who believed in him."

"Aldon had given up everything to make his dreams for his people come true," Devon explained.

"Not anything new," Victor said.

Devon reached forward and patted Victor on the shoulder. "It is when that something means it takes your soul and leaves you unable to die."

"Wait what?" Elle felt her mouth fall open. "Is he immortal?"

Devon sighed. "Oh, he dies, Elle. I've killed him myself with a bullet to the head. But Aldon does this freaky thing by coming back."

Chapter 13

"Did I faint?" Elle asked when she opened her eyes. "I have never, in all my life fainted."

Victor wasn't sure if he was going to shake her or kiss her. "You scared the hell out of me."

"Sorry." She wrapped her arms around him and he let her because he needed to feel her close to him right then. If the news they had just gotten about Aldon had affected her as much as it had affected him he had wanted to faint too. "I had the strangest dream," she whispered into his ear. And he was pretty sure it wasn't a dream.

Gods he wished he could just Flash her to the Infernos where he could keep her safe. "Why can't I Flash you? I just want to keep you safe, you know that, right?"

She smiled at him. "It wasn't a dream, was it? Aldon has the same curse as I do?"

Victor nodded. "I think so, yes."

"How is it even possible?" Elle asked. "I mean the Druid who cursed me died. Aldon isn't that old..." she had a horrible thought and rushed to get to her feet, Devon was standing with Tabitha as Victor pulled her close. "Tell me he isn't that old?"

Devon shook his head. "As best as he can guess he has only prolonged his life by twenty-five or thirty extra years. Just long enough to build his little army and find out about you via Chaos, by the way what happened to your lovely brother?"

"I took care of him and Helena," Victor said, as much as Victor had said to her about the two and she hadn't wanted to know more but she knew she would have to get more information about them eventually. She just wanted to take it one issue at a time. And her sister and brother were not an issue she was ready to deal with.

Devon nodded. "Chaos was a spoil of Aldon's conquests from some Lord overseas in the 70's. It was what led us to figure out what had happened to Aldon," Devon went on to explain what they knew. Which wasn't a lot. Most of it was conjecture, up to the point where Devon had captured Aldon. He was tried, sentenced, and pronounced guilty of his crimes. Devon carried out the sentencing.

Once they had carried out the sentence, woman came to prepare the body. And shockingly, Aldon woken up. And acted as if it was a miracle. Devon and the Brotherhood hadn't known know what to think.

Thankfully, the Brothers have several criteria, before something is considered a miracle. And Aldon did not meet any of them besides rising from the dead. So they sentenced him to die again. Apparently Aldon did not appreciate it, and had barely escaped. He had been on the run ever since.

"During this time, he started creating the Freaks." Devon looked around at the group. "To this day, I don't know how he was able to escape. And we haven't seen him, until now."

Something had been bothering Victor all evening. "Are you working with the Daughters? Why are you here?" He didn't believe in coincident. The Daughters of Eve seemed awful chummy with the Sons. The fight he was going to have with the Bitch was working up to an all-out brawl.

Devon shrugged. "I won't lie to you, we bugged the Daughters. When information was sent to us that they had information about Aldon and that he had created Freaks. We mobilized. The Freaks held our hands, but as far as I was concerned, the kill order should never have been lifted. He and his creations need to be destroyed. I know that Tabitha and her warriors have been sent to deal with Aldon. But I've killed him once; I'm here to make sure he stays dead this time. Personally, I think you're wasting your time. Aldon has no soul, you have nothing here to reap."

"What makes you think he is soulless?" Elle asked Devon.

Devon gave Elle a sad laugh. "Of course he is soulless how can something like him have a soul?"

Victor was about to come to her aid, but she stepped around him with her arms crossed over her chest. "What the hell does that mean?"

Devon didn't back down. "I didn't mean to offend you Elle, and I am not sure how you ended up the way you are. And it is commendable you haven't given into darkness without a soul. But that doesn't change what has happened."

Victor tried to grab Elle but she stomped over to Devon and slapped him upside the head. "Were you dropped on your head as a child?"

Several of his men jumped forward but Victor shook his head at them and they immediately backed away. Elle was holding her own, but he'd be damned if the Sons raised a hand against his woman.

Devon rubbed at his head. "You take your life in your hands, lady."

"You're an idiot." Elle turned back to Victor. "Victor do I have a soul?"

"One of the brightest I've ever seen," Victor said with all honestly.

Elle turned back to Devon. "Why do you think Aldon wants me? He wants me to add a soul to his creations. If he got a Druid to curse him the same way I was he still has a soul. His might be black as oil pitch but he still has a soul."

There was a popping noise and suddenly Aldon appeared holding a dagger to Elle's throat. "I knew I still possessed my soul," he whispered against her cheek. "I just need the light of yours to complete my work."

"I knew I killed you in that damn car!" Elle said back. Just as all hell broke loose.

****

Guns were grabbed, and actions were cocked. Elle stilled her breathing. Aldon didn't have a problem killing her and she wanted very much to stay alive for this show. The last thing she needed was to die right now.

Victor held up a hand. "Don't anyone move."

Making Aldon smile. "Ah I see you recognize the Dagger."

Victor could barely breathe, as Aldon held the Blood Rite Dagger to Elle's throat. If that Dagger killed her, he would lose not only her, but her soul as well.

"If you spill one drop of her blood you will live to regret it Aldon," Victor snarled.

Aldon laughed. "But I will live Reaper, and she won't. Do you want to risk it? I wanted to save my people, save those who didn't have a voice." Aldon said to Devon as he backed up dragging Elle with him.

"You aren't going anywhere, Aldon," Devon said.

Aldon laughed again. "That's what you think. See, I've been working on this little spell…"

Victor lunged but it was too late, the popping noise was the only warning they had and Aldon and Elle disappeared. Guns exploded around him as he landed in the dirt where Aldon and Elle had been milliseconds before.

He rolled to his feet. "What part of don't anyone move didn't anyone understand?" Victor shouted at the group. He felt like his head was going to explode.

"You would have rather he get away with her?" Devon snarled.

Victor grabbed the man and shook him. "He got away with her anyway," he snarled. Victor threw Devon aside and stalked away, shoving his hand through his hair. Feeling like his world was spinning out of control.

"He can't go far, he had to have taken her into the ground," Tabitha said taking Victor by the arm.

Victor swung around to her. "What?" he snarled he would rather kill the woman then take her advice.

She stepped back fear in her eyes and rightly so. "I care about her too, Victor."

Victor took a breath. "Tell me what you know."

"Our ability to perform Magik is limited and he said he had just learned the spell. It would be limited. Something he wouldn't have been able to have a great deal of power over. Therefore he was taking a great deal of chance to include Elle in the transportation spell. He didn't go far. He is close, still in the compound." Tabitha motioned to her sisters and they spread out. "We need to find a way into his underground stronghold."

Christian returned with Hunter "What happened?" Christian asked looking around.

"He took her," Victor snapped.

"Dante wants Aldon. If you take him whole or he just gets his soul, he cares not." Christian explained.

Victor growled. "Good because Dante is going to get him in pieces."

****

Elle thought her head was going to explode. She moaned as she rolled to her hands and knees. Dizziness assaulting her. She emptied her stomach in a trashcan, collapsing, barely holding onto consciousness. She was going to kill Aldon herself slowly. Again and again. The bastard.

"What the hell did you do to me?" she moaned trying to keep herself in the here and now.

"You will recover in a moment," Aldon promised from somewhere close.

"Go to hell," Elle said, between her teeth. Not believing him, as the room kept spinning slowly. She pressed her face against the cool marble floor. The room slowly stopped spinning and she was finally able to breathe without wanting to vomit.

Elle peeked her eyes open. Aldon was sitting in an overstuffed chair, several feet in front of her. A fire burned in a huge fire place behind him. The Dagger he had been holding at her throat, balanced on one knee. A gun balanced on the other.

"How are you feeling now?" He asked his voice so calm it gave her chills.

Elle pulled herself into a sitting position and pushed herself back against the wall. "Well I don't want to throw up." But she still wanted to kill him. "You realize you will never get away with any of this right?"

"Actually I have gotten away with it." He said. "The strange part? I've been desperately trying to get you to my home? And you brought yourself to me? How wonderful is that?" he asked with a wicked grin.

Setting both the gun and Dagger down, he poured a glass of water from a pitcher. And walked over to her, offering it to her. She only glared at it, he shook his head and took a long drink of the water and then handed it back to her.

Elle took the water and drank until it was empty. "Would you like more?"

Elle shook her head. "But, if you are granting requests, I would like to be let go."

Aldon returned to his seat. "I would like for us to be partners, Elle. I think if things had gone differently we could have had a love match."

She felt her mouth sag open. It was probable the wrong reaction. By the look of stark pain he gave her she knew it was the wrong response and she snapped her mouth closed.

"I would think you would find comfort in the arms of someone who shares your condition." His voice was cold and hard.

"Condition?" Elle asked. "I was cursed, I don't have a condition Aldon. I am cursed as you are."

"See that is the problem Elle and something I can help you with. I can help you understand it isn't a curse. It is a blessing," Aldon said with such feeling Elle knew he truly believed it.

"How did you get cursed?" she asked.

"It's not a curse!" he roared. Making Elle jump, but he quickly covered by smiling and continuing. "I sought out a Druid to give me the blessing."

"What?" Elle almost didn't believe what she had heard so she asked again. "I'm sorry, I think I might have misunderstood you." She had the strangest urge to get up and shake him.

"It's a blessing Elle, after a time you will understand," Aldon promised. "We will be the parents of a new beginning. An entire new species, which will rule the mortal plane, like the gods of old." His eyes shown with glee and madness.

"I don't want to be the parent of a new beginning," she said honestly. Just the thought of what kind of offspring he wanted to create, made her shutter.

Aldon laughed, but the sound gave Elle chills. "You're only saying so because you don't understand what it means."

Elle just stared at him, he was totally insane, and she knew reasoning with him was useless. She only needed to wait for Victor to get her or get her hands on the Dagger to kill him.

"I bet losing Helena and Chaos sure put a kink in your plans," she offered.

Aldon's head tilted in thought then he shrugged. "Ah yes, those two were bumbling idiots at best. I was going to save their deaths for you, did you enjoy seeing their downfall? How did it all play out, Elle?"

He shot out of the chair, The Dagger and the gun, skidding forgotten across the floor. Aldon boxed her in with a hand on each side of her head. "Did you kill them?"

"They're immortal, Aldon. They can't be killed," Elle said. Pressing against the cold wall, she tried in vain to get as far away from him as possible.

"So what happened to them Elle? What did you do to them?" Aldon asked quietly, his body relaxed against her.

"Victor took them to the Infernos where they belong. They are suffering for their betrayal." She thought she would feel pain for them but she didn't. In fact she didn't feel anything.

"Would you like them to die, Elle?" Aldon whispered into her ear, it could have been a lover's caress. But it turned Elle's stomach. "Because I have the ability to kill them Elle, kill them dead. And I will help you do it."

Elle shook her head, more to get the feel of him off her than anything else. "They are being punished." And that was enough for her.

Aldon traced a finger over her cheek and Elle slapped it away. "I will do anything for you. What do you want? Just name it and I will make it happen for you that is what lovers do."

"All I want from you is for you to let me go." Elle said more to herself then to him. "They are going to come for me."

"They can try. But I buried the entrance years ago. There is no way to get in or out." He laughed and she pushed him away.

"I will not submit." He laughed at her words.

"I wouldn't expect you too." Aldon leered at her. "And I really could care less if you do." He reached out to her and Elle slapped his hands away.

"Touch me and you will regret it." Elle snarled.

Aldon shook his head. "It's worthless to fight me Elle."

Elle shook her head wildly. "No, it isn't. I will not submit!"

Aldon slapped the floor. The sound seemed to echo through the room. "He is not coming for you!"

There was such finality to Aldon's tone, Elle knew she was in a fight for her life, until Victor found his way to her. When he reached for her again, she glared at Aldon. "I will never submit. I would rather die than submit to you"

"So be it." Aldon came at her with that uncanny speed. Elle rolled away, kicking out to avoid Aldon's hands as he scrambled to grab her. He latched onto one of her legs and tried to drag her back to him. Elle kicked him in the face, causing him to howl in pain. He released her to grab his now bleeding face.

"You bitch!"

Elle scrambled to her feet and pulled out the gun Victor had given to her. She pointed it at Aldon. "Tell me how to get out of here!" She was breathing heavy and shaking. She knew she could kill him and wasn't afraid to do it.

Aldon rolled to his back and glared at her. "I told you there is no way out." He lay there, his nose bleeding. "And I'm too weak to use the spell again."

"Too bad for you," Elle said pulling the trigger, she was off just a little and the bullet entered just left of the center of his forehead. But it didn't change the look of shock on his face.

Elle turned and ran from the room glad she had already emptied her stomach otherwise she would have thrown up again. But she wasn't sure how much time she had. She threw open ever door she could trying to find a way out. There were bedrooms, and offices and a kitchen, a bathroom. A bedroom with clothes in the closet, and nursery with bedding, toys and a mobile over the crib. A rocking chair by the fake window.

Everything a person could need or want to live. The thought made her lightheaded. Aldon had planned on living here. There were windows with scenes painted of sunny days, making Elle scream and pound on the cement until her fists ached.

There were doors leading nowhere. It was the perfect prison, and Elle was weak with fear and terror. Tears rolled down her face as she threw open another door leading nowhere.

She pounded on the brick and screamed, "Are you freaking kidding me?" her hands were bleeding now but she didn't care and she turned and ran to the next door. She wasn't going to give up. She was going to go down fighting; he would have to kill her because she would not go to him without a fight.

"ELLE!"

Elle stopped dead, how long had she been searching through this underground make-believe home? She tried to slow her rapid breathing. She was totally freaked out and wasn't sure how Aldon couldn't hear it. Along with every other sound she was making. It thundered in her ears as she ran down yet another hallway, she skidded around a corner praying this would finally be the way out.

She slammed into a set of locked double doors. She yanked on them but they wouldn't open, and they were the first set of locked doors she had come across. And if they were locked then she definitely wanted to get into them.

Pointing the gun at the lock she pulled the trigger.

It's not like in the movies and she had to shoot the door several more times before she was able to get the door open. The racket made Aldon start bellowing and screaming like a mad man. Which meant, she was headed in the right direction. She heard footsteps when she finally shouldered her way through the door.

"Elle don't..." but it was too late. Elle could feel her freedom as she pushed through the doors.

Some things you can never un-see, you think if you close your eyes fast enough you might be able to erase it from your memory. And sometimes, it's so horrible, your brain stutters. Your eyeballs freeze and you can't blink. No matter how bad you want to. It is in that moment your brain is holding onto the image and forever solidifying it in your memory forever. Time slows down, and everything stops, your breathing, your heart, everything. Nothing moves and therefore it is forever frozen in time. A broken moment that can never be taken away.

Elle pushed herself forward to the first basinet knowing she didn't want to really see what was in the blood soaked thing but she couldn't stop herself. It was empty and she thanked the gods for it, she slipped on the blood soaked floor and caught herself on another blood soaked basinet. Only too stumbled to the next basinet, and the next. Knocking them out of her way as she went, ignoring the glass jars lining the walls filled with tiny broken bodies. Her brain had already frozen the images in her brain forever.

The huge fluid containers that housed what looked like juvenile sized bodies, the two grown bodies suspended in water. Elle couldn't stop herself from looking into them. Elle slipped again. Falling hard onto the bloody floor.

"Elle, you shouldn't have come in here," Aldon said from behind her. Elle looked over her shoulder. He stood just in the doorway. His eyes wild. The whites stark against the rest of his face. He looked wildly around the room.

"What have you done?" Elle croaked. She wiped the tears from her face with the back of her hand. This was a room of horror. The kind you only saw in scary movies, with a mad scientist. This was not something you stumbled on in an underground bunker.

"I couldn't expect you to raise my other children," Aldon said. His black eyes wide, as he looked around the room. "I had to get rid of them. They were unclean."

"Oh, my god." Elle swallowed the vomit clawing at the back of her throat. "These were your children?" she gasped.

Aldon walked in and ran a hand lovingly over one basinet. "Yes but they were mortal, they were flawed." He turned back to Elle. "I could not afford to have flawed children. I believed them soulless." One shoulder shrugged as if that could explain it.

Elle tried to back pedal but she slipped in the pools of blood. She looked down and looked around, it was the wrong thing to do. Because that was when she saw the pile of bodies. "Oh, my god." She couldn't get away fast enough, couldn't move away from the horror of it. Elle screamed and skidded and slipped in the blood. Tiny bodies holding each other.

Aldon grabbed her and pulled her away. "I tried to tell you Elle, you didn't want to see this. The children you bear, will not be forced to endure this fate." Elle was shaking and she pushed at him.

"They..." She pointed a bloody finger at the small bodies in the corner. "They are just children, your children." Her voice was growing hysterical.

"You are a monster." She shoved at him. "Who does this to their own flesh and blood?" her hand pointing at the horror started to shake. "How many were there?" she cried.

Aldon shrugged, as if it didn't really matter, making Elle crazed with remorse. "Eighteen. Why do you care? They weren't your children, and until this afternoon I didn't even believe they had souls," Aldon said casually.

Elle grabbed him and shook him. Leaving bloody hand prints on his shirt. "They were children, your children," she screamed. Unable to understand what type of man could kill his own children.

"But they were mortal, they died," he sneered. "What good were they?" he shouted back. "I have no use for them if they cannot further my power."

"I hope you suffer. You deserve to suffer the worst type of hell possible," Elle cried, she collapsed to her knees unable to even stand, it hurt so badly. The pain she felt for those souls that had died what she wouldn't give to redeem them?

Aldon grabbed her and tried to pull her to her feet. "Don't cry for them they were worthless."

Elle yanked her arm free. "No. They were not worthless. They were souls, they deserved a life. And you took that from them. You, who should have protected them above all else!" Her body was racked with sobs. She felt it from so deep in her chest; she was surprised she could breathe much less talk.

Aldon tried to grab her when she saw the Blood Rite Dagger strapped to his side. She pushed Aldon away as she pulled the Dagger free holding it out.

Aldon looked at her and then at the Dagger. "Elle don't be stupid."

Elle shook her head the sobs nearly taking her off her feet, she stumbled back and Aldon attacked. She slashed at him and she knew she must have hit him with the Dagger because he backed away bellowing.

Elle held the Dagger and shook her head. "What you have done is wrong, Aldon." She held the Dagger out, not sure of its power. She had to do something about the loss here, Aldon lunged for her again. Somehow, she managed to avoid him. Still sobbing, Elle looked down at the blood soaked floor. So much lost innocence. It was wrong and unholy! She sliced the Dagger over her wrist. Aldon screamed as light exploded around her.

"I give my life for those he took," Elle called to the light. "Please," she begged into the void. "They deserve to live."

****

"That's not the way it's used daughter." A slight man said taking the Dagger from Elle.

Elle gladly let it go, "Umm, excuse me?"

"Typically the Blood Rite Dagger is used to take a soul into oblivion. However, you have found the one loop hole. I believe my child you have lived several life times of loop holes." He laughed gently.

"If I've heard it once." She said rolling her eyes.

"This Dagger, when used against on an individual steels a life and its soul and they are gone." He said, folding his arms behind his back. "But you turned the knife on yourself. You cannot be killed. You are a God."

"No, no, no, no. Demi-god." She corrected.

He smiled and shook his head. And leaned forward so his lips were just inches from her ear, "From where I am it looks like you're a God to me." And then he leaned back.

Elle looked around, they were surrounded by light. "Who exactly are you?" she asked.

"Dante." He offered with a lift of his chin.

"I don't want to be a God, Dante." Elle said.

Dante gave her a sad smile, "Do you think there is a choice in the matter, daughter."

"What of the souls of those children?" she asked.

"What of them?" he asked. "If you were a God, what would you have made of them?" He asked his voice booming in the vastness.

Elle thought for a moment. If she really was a God, then she wanted those children to live. They deserved to have a life, it wasn't their fault their father was Aldon. No, they deserved to have a life.

"They deserve to have a life." Elle said with more strength in her voice.

Dante shook his head. "Then that is what is going to happen."

"Now what?" Elle asked.

"I think someone is looking for you." Dante explained. "And frankly I've had enough of the Disney happy ever after bullshit." He reached forward and placed a hand on her chest. Elle felt a pull and it took everything she had to stay on her feet.

When he pulled his hand away, he held a dark shadow. Elle was sure he had just taken her soul, "I think you are done with this."

"Um…" Elle was afraid to ask.

"Your curse?" Dante asked.

Elle breathed out, "Really?" Tears filled her eyes.

Dante nodded, "Yes, really."

He turned, but Elle stopped him by throwing her arms around him. "Thank you, Dante."

He froze, she laughed. "This is where you say 'you're welcome.'"

"Actually, this is where you pull yourself off of me woman." He growled.

She released him but stopped him, "Dante?"

He turned back to him, "One more thing."

He sighed heavily, "Yes?"

She placed her hands on her hips, "Am I really a God?"

"I really believe that is up to you?" he said honestly. "If you choose to be a demi-god then that is what you will be."

Elle nodded, "I don't think the world needs another god. Demi-god is good enough."

He nodded, "Demi-god is fine."

"Oh and one more thing. You really shouldn't whip you children anymore." Elle said.

Dante burst out laughing, "I shall punish my children, anyway I see fit child." And then he was gone.

****

Victor was about to lose his mind when Dante showed up on the mortal plane. Victor was so shocked he ended up ass down in the dirt looking up at his father.

"What the fuck?" Victor muttered.

"Interesting," Dante said looking down at Victor.

Within seconds all the Reapers appeared circling Victor. Dante picked up one foot and tapped it against the dirt, it opened a sink hole big enough for a van to get through. The Reapers all stepped back.

"That will get you into the underground complex. Aldon is down there. He is now trapped in his underground complex. Too weak to use his own Magik. Give him to Devon, but his soul is mine." This he said to Hunter. "There is a woman and children prisoners down there." Hunter nodded and jumped into the hole, Victor went to join them but Dante stopped him.

Christian and Garret held back as well.

"She's not down there," Dante said. "And neither is the Blood Rite Dagger."

Victor didn't want to hear this, didn't want to know she was gone. He heard blood pounding through his ears and a rage so deep he wasn't sure he could contain it, but Dante was suddenly standing in front of him.

"She attempted to trade her soul for those of eighteen innocent souls Aldon had killed in order to keep her," Dante explained. "She used the Dagger on herself Victor."

Dante placed the Dagger in Victor's hands. "And the eighteen?" Victor gritted between his teeth?

"They had not been reaped, they will live," Dante explained. "By the grace of your demi-goddess."

"Where is she?" Victor demanded. "Where is her soul?" he glared at the Dagger in his hands wondering if she had suffered in the end. Praying to the gods she hadn't, and he wondered how much longer he had to stand here listening to his father ramble on about it before he could walk away and join her in oblivion.

"I'm right here." He'd finally lost his mind but he didn't care he turned and she was just standing there. In those stupid fatigues. Her golden brown hair shining actually glowing, her eyes glowing gold. "Shit. You're a demi-god again." He said breathlessly.

Elle threw herself into Victor's arms, crystal like tears streaming down her face. "I thought I had lost you forever," she cried.

They fell into the dirt, but Victor didn't care. He pressed her to him and kissed every inch of her he could reach with his mouth. "Gods Dante said... gods I thought I lost you." Then he pulled away and looked at her. "Don't you ever do that to me again," he growled.

Victor looked up at Dante. "What the fuck? You scared me to death."

Dante shrugged. "Just gave you the facts. Melodramatic much?" Dante asked

Dante then stepped forward and extended a hand to Elle. "You are a very unique female."

Victor pulled Elle to her feet and Elle took Dante's hand. "As you are Dante," she said. Dante dipped his head. "You will not whip Victor again for loving me," she demanded.

Dante tipped his head back and laughed. Making Victor and the other Reapers hold their breath in shock. When Dante had regained his composure he nodded to Elle. "I shall do as I please because I am Dante. And we will not discuss it again, girl."

Victor squeezed Elle and she looked at him her golden amber eyes so beautiful it took his breath away. "Well that makes sense."

Dante turned to his other sons. "The Tribunal will not like this outcome." He looked again at Elle. "She is no longer cursed, but she will always carry the extra protein in her system. God or demi-god, she is special. And she is now part of our family, how will the Tribunal feel about that?"

Victor started swearing a blue streak, making Elle giggle and she covered his mouth with her hand. "Hush." She laughed.

"One more thing," Dante said. And turned to Christian "Return the stone to your brother. And make sure Hunter brings me my soul."

Christian nodded and then Dante was gone.

Christian snorted and Garret burst out laughing. "Does Dante truly have a sense of humor?"

"Hell no," Christian said. "But would Elle please tell us what actually happened down in that hole? Then you can have your way with her."

Victor would have preferred to have his way with her then she could explain but the look his brothers were giving him said otherwise. So he pulled himself to his feet and pulled Elle to a standing position to allow her to stand next to him.

****

Elle looked at Victor and then wrapped her arms around him and kissed him on the lips. She really had thought she had lost this fight and would never see him again. But she was standing here in his arms and she was never going to let him go again.

"You better answer their questions. Then I am going to take you home and never let you go," Victor said and pulled away but not before giving her a kiss on the tip of her nose.

Elle smiled and turned back to the other two. She explained about Aldon telling her about there not being an entrance and how she killed him and tried to find a way out and then finding the nursery.

They were not happy about that. She shuddered, and Victor pulled her closer, nuzzling her neck, whispering into her ear that everything had turned out okay in the end. She reassured herself that yes it had, but what she had seen down there had burned a place in her soul and she would never forget it.

"So we fought again. And I got ahold of the Dagger," Elle told them. "I was sobbing. Drained and destroyed by what I had seen. I cut myself with the Dagger and begged to trade my soul for those Aldon had killed. For the innocents he had taken."

Victor snarled something, but Elle was remembering what had happened. "It was so strange. I was surrounded by this light..." Elle looked around at the Reapers. "You know that feeling like when you take a step off something and its farther then you think it should be?"

They gave her a look like she had lost her mind. "Anyway that is what it felt like, and then your father was there. And we talked about those poor souls. That it was up to me whether those poor children got to live or not. And we talked about me being a God vs a demi-god. Oh and we talked about him punishing you. I told him not to."

Victor shook his head, "Really?"

"I didn't really have anything to lose." She said with a radiant smile.

Victor kissed her, and then turned to his brothers. "Are you happy with those answers?" Victor asked them.

The brothers looked at each other and smiled, making Victor growl low.

Christian smiled. "Not really I've got several others."

Victor shook his head. "Too bad." He turned, grabbing Elle.

Elle tried to pull away but Victor tucked her into his arm and held her close. "They can ask next time they see you."

"And when will that be?" Garret asked.

"Month maybe two," Victor said over his shoulder.

The two Reapers just laughed. Elle didn't think it was funny. "Wait what about everyone else? The Trackers? Tabitha? The other Sons of Adam? The Tribunal?"

Victor pulled Elle into his arms. "You saved Lykar's life, he was gravely wounded burned badly but he will live. The Trackers have taken him back to Illinois. Marlee wounded, but not badly. The Bitch and her sisters are fine no wounded. Devon and the Sons have wounded, but will survive. And of course, The Tribunal will live to terrorize another day. We will get them, eventually. Now may we go home?" She looked into his dark blue eyes and was lost.

"I should talk to Tabitha." Elle said.

"I'll tell her you'll call." Garrett offered.

"Thanks Garrett." Victor

"Where exactly is home, Victor?" Elle asked wrapping her arms around his middle and holding on. She put everything else aside, this is what she needed. Quite time with Victor. No beasts breathing down their necks, know bad guys waiting in the wings.

"Wherever you are. But for me, the Infernos. But I will take you anywhere you want to go," he said.

Elle had never felt so loved in all her life. "I would love to see the Infernos."

"Then hold on."

"Wait?" Elle said stopping everyone in their tracks. Elle turned to Christian "What was Dante talking about, what stone?"

Christian nodded and Flashed away only to return a moment later holding the gravestone from the first night, it was still covered in her blood. The Blood Call scribed into it. He handed it to Victor.

"Dante didn't want you to do something you shouldn't, or something you would regret. But it looks like..." Christian smiled he and Garrett turned and disappeared down into the hole.

Victor looked at the gravestone. "I just need to add my blood and your soul belongs to me."

Elle bent down and clutched it to her chest. "Aren't we headed home?"

Victor felt his heart warm and he wrapped his arms around her and Flashed them both to the Infernos. To his fortress, his bedroom... where no woman had ever been.

Elle looked around, it was so beautiful it took her breath away. She wanted nothing more than to explore but she had something more important to do right then.

Victor led her out onto the balcony, the colors of the sky were so beautiful and everything Victor had ever said they were. Elle turned to him. "I love you Victor."

Victor pulled the gravestone from her and placed it on the stone table and held his hand over it. But Elle stopped him. "You know my soul already belongs to you right?"

Victor looked up, his heart in his eyes. "Does it?"

Tears sprang to her eyes. "Yes and so much more."

Victor held his hand out, and pulled a knife out slicing his palm open. He took ahold of Elle's hand "Will you Blood Bound with me? Let me give you my soul," he said with tears in his eyes. "Let me show you the depths of my love."

Elle gave him her palm and he cut her gently wincing when blood welled in her palm, they clasped their hands together.

"Hold on tight," Victor whispered.

Elle smiled. "I'll never let go."
"Forever?" Victor asked.
"And ever." Elle whispered.

—The End—

www.ingramcontent.com/pod-product-compliance
Lightning Source LLC
Chambersburg PA
CBHW060520180626
46817CB00002B/432